What people a

Jenny Gardiner's books:

"A fun, sassy read! A cross between Erma Bombeck and Candace Bushnell, reading Jenny Gardiner is like sinking your teeth into a chocolate cupcake...you just want more."

— **Meg Cabot**, NY Times bestselling author **of *Princess Diaries, Queen of Babble*** and more, on ***Sleeping with Ward Cleaver***

"With a strong yet delightfully vulnerable voice, food critic Abbie Jennings embarks on a soulful journey where her love for banana cream pie and disdain for ill-fitting Spanx clash in hilarious and heartbreaking ways. As her body balloons and her personal life crumbles, Abbie must face the pain and secret fears she's held inside for far too long. I cheered for her the entire way."

— **Beth Hoffman**, NY Times bestselling author of ***Saving CeeCee Honeycutt*** on ***Slim to None***

"Jenny Gardiner has done it again — this fun, fast-paced book is a great summer read."

— **Sarah Pekkanen**, NY Times bestselling author of ***The Opposite of Me***, on ***Slim to None***

"As Sweet as a song and sharp as a beak, ***Winging It*** really soars as a memoir about family — children and husbands, feathers and fur — and our capacity to keep loving though life may occasionally bite."

— **Wade Rouse**, bestselling author of ***At Least in the City Someone Would Hear Me Scream***

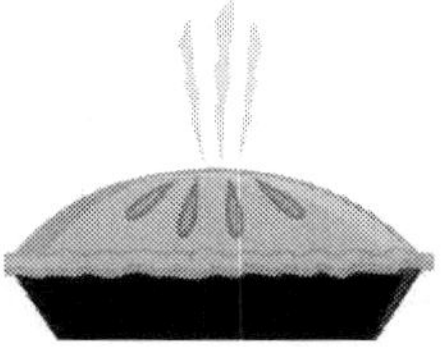

SLIM TO NONE

by
Jenny Gardiner

PUBLISHED BY
Jenny Gardiner
SLIM TO NONE

ISBN-13: 978-1518611223
ISBN-10: 1518611222

For more information, email jenny@jennygardiner.net.

When we lose twenty pounds we may be losing the twenty best pounds we have. We may be losing the pounds that contain our genius, our humanity, our love and honesty.

–Woody Allen

A Teaspoon of Sugar

I am not a glutton. I am an explorer of food.
–Erma Bombeck

I miss my Spanx. I outgrew them about fifty pounds ago. Somewhere between the decadent foie gras at La Grenouille and the joyfully simple pigs-in-a-blanket at Payard Patisserie. It was like a seasonal transition: it happened so gradually I didn't even notice it, until one day my control-top-pantyline-avoiding-God-Bless-America-for-inventing-these-things Spanx refused to oblige me by fitting comfortably.

No longer gently hugging my curves, respectfully holding all of me in, they'd become a boa constrictor and I their victim. Evidently Spanx are made for far thinner women than me. And so I graduated up to Flexees. But now, as I ready myself for yet another meal out by attempting to contain my expanding girth in my latest girdle of choice, it's become abundantly clear that I've fallen into Flexee disfavor as well. I heave a sigh of resignation. What's a girl to do when her life revolves around having to eat for a living?

"Jesus, this is a mess," my best friend Jess says as she trails small heaps of greasy lupini beans across her plate with a fork, forming them into a smiley face with what appears to be tears streaming down its cheeks but is probably just excess oil. Jessie mocks the bean face with her own broad smile. Her blond hair, the color of farm-churned butter, softly frames her face in the flickering light of our table's blazing torch. Jess' truffle-brown eyes twinkle with mischief: my tasting assistant caught playing with her food.

I nod in agreement. So far what we've seen at Puka, the new pan Italian-Hawaiian-Greek restaurant in midtown Manhattan, doesn't look too promising. I'd held out hope, what with the luau décor, tiki lamps aglow, and the bouzouki player plinking out a half-decent version of That's Amore. How often can you get a taste of Hawaii, Greece and Italy in one sitting? I dip my pita bread into the complementary poi served in a dugout coconut bowl in the center of the table, hoping for a miracle. Instead, I choke on the soupy gray paste and reach for my water glass, which is still empty.

"Jess, gimme a swig of that!" I point to her glass of water, my hand around my throat for emphasis. I can't wait for a reply and instead grab the water and throw it back, like Zorba tossing down a flaming shot glass of ouzo.

"Appetizers suck, they can't even keep our water glasses filled, the signature tiki drinks haven't materialized despite waiting over half an hour, and the freebie poi appears to be the key ingredient in the fixative that holds up the wallpaper," I mumble as I jot down notes surreptitiously in my iPhone, mindful to be sure that no one is paying attention to my musings.

"Sure, it's not exactly Le Bernadin, but seriously, Abbie, it's all relative," Jess says. "At least it's better than the doner kebab I'd have been eating had you not called me at the last minute to come along tonight. But for you, yeah, I'd imagine this pretty much bites the big one."

"At this place, I'm afraid to bite anything, big or small. But seriously, I'm just looking at the silver lining in this stormy cloud. At least here I have no desire to eat even the smallest of portions. So it's a little diet in disguise."

Jess laughs but just barely, and instead squirms in her seat, clearly hating my fat reference. She's lodge pine-thin and could probably go on a week-long eating bender and still lose weight. That is if food really even mattered to her that much, which it doesn't. I, on the other hand, seem to have assumed the uncanny silhouette of a beluga whale, while cursed with the sluggish metabolism of a three-toed sloth and blessed with the culinary palate of a Michelin reviewer. Not always a good combination if you savor your size-tens. Oh, wait, I'm in Manhattan. Make that size-twos. And I am most definitely not a size two. Maybe size twenty-two, perhaps, but I've lost count, so who knows?

"You can't help it, Abs," she says. "It's not like you go around stuffing your face with donuts."

"Yeah. Instead I ingest a steady diet of the world's richest food." I shrug. "Ah, well, occupational hazard, I suppose. As are restaurants like this. People are expecting me to rate this place, so I'll review it. Sure, I always hope for good things from a restaurant, but I'm totally prepared to call them on it if it's lousy."

Our waiter arrives, his vision evidently obscured by the pile of leis stacked along his neck, and sloshes two martini glasses filled with something resembling transmission fluid before us. They're on fire. How adventuresome. Jessie dips her napkin in what's left of her water and blots the splash of alcoholic neon that has landed uninvited across the front of her white silk shirt. It looks like someone smashed a firefly on her boob. Lei-Boy returns moments later with our entrees: cold, congealed grouper for me and seared mahi-mahi for Jess that looks as if the chef used a blow-torch on it. A hardened heap of Minute Rice accompanies the entrees, with beans that in an ideal world would be green, but are instead a sickly shade of cadaverous ash.

"Bon appétit, I suppose," I say, not at all looking forward to that first bite. I hate to be disingenuous, but at thirty bucks a plate, the kitchen could've at least tried.

Jess scoops a bite of fish with her fork and pops it in her mouth, just as Lei-Boy rushes over and wordlessly grabs her plate away. Fast on his heels is an angry-looking bald man in clogs, checkered pants, and a chef's toque, hurling what must be obscenities in Greek, maybe Italian, but definitely nothing gently Polynesian sounding. He smacks Lei-Boy up the back of his head, dislodging a few leis onto my grouper.

An A+ for presentation, I jot down in my phone.

"What is up with them?" Jessie asks.

"Hell if I know." I reach for my transmission fluid to quell the drought in my mouth. As it reluctantly washes down my throat I can't help but elicit a hairball noise.

A swarm of hula dancers closes in on our table as the

bouzouki music gives way to a pulsing luau thunk. If I am seeing properly beyond the blur of grass skirts—my God, how do they do that?—there appears to be an extra from South Pacific pounding a drum back there.

"Aloha, wahini," the Greek chef intones through a volcanic crater-sized smile. His accent is deceptively French-sounding. "E komo mai. Welcome. Buona sera. Good evening."

I expect him to throw in a Phi Beta Kappa just to incorporate all of the restaurant's themes. "Ladies, zere has been a slight mistake in zee kitchen." No thanks to Lei-boy, I'm thinking. "Pleeze, allow me to present you vees more better food." Our Greek chef sounds like he must've apprenticed for a hell of a long time in Paris.

With this, our drinks are rounded up, and in their stead are placed two smoldering cocktails that appear to contain dry ice. I peer into the void of my thermally-reinforced cup (artfully disguised as a small volcano) and see through the rising steam something somewhat thick and orange-ish red. I look at the chef—the spitting image of Telly Savalas without the lollypop—for the go-ahead from him, wondering if one can actually ingest dry ice. I always thought it was toxic.

He motions with his hands to drink up. "Ladeees, ees gud. Ees a Lava Flow. Really, really good. You drink, no?" He rolls his "r" with such authority I feel this is an order, and I comply, placing the drink to my lips with apprehension and taking a tiny no-thank you sip, trying not to make a face, in case it's disgusting.

I taste a slight dribble, licking my lips to catch the overflow. Not bad, actually. Sort of cool and warm at the same time, like Ben Gay on the rocks. I'll give them credit: it's certainly different.

Telly is on to the next order of business already, seeing that our new entrees are properly plated. Lei-Boy and his assistant Hula-Girl bring out two heaping dishes of food, much of it unidentifiable but at least it's piping hot. Telly Savalas leans forward, so close to me I can smell the garlic on his breath, and wipes a smudge of sauce from the edge of my dish with his towel. He adjusts the plate a quarter-turn and bows while wishing us buon appetito (why he didn't say this in Greek is Greek to me).

"Whoa!" Jess stares at me as if she'd just witnessed the shocking conclusion to a weird movie. She takes a bite of something in front of her. "I don't know what that was all about, but bring it on, baby. If we've gotta go through that to get some of this, I'll volunteer to be the sacrificial lamb."

I don't know where to begin on my plate. Everything looks so unfamiliar, yet appetizing. I decide to aim for the starch first, and settle my fork into a generous portion of what turns out to be risotto with bite-sized pieces of suckling pig. I'll take creamy risotto over that vile poi any day. The pork, so tender and juicy, has me humming Mele Kalikimaka, cause it feels like a Hawaiian Merry Christmas gift.

I next try the entrée, a tender, flaky and surprisingly un-oily mackerel sprinkled with feta cheese and olives and cloaked in taro leaves. I have to give Telly some credit, I didn't know how this place could pull off merging three such divergent flavors, but somehow it works despite itself.

"I can't believe how fantastic this food is," Jess mumbles through a bite of her pineapple-balsamic glazed wild boar spare ribs with tzatziki sauce. "Who'd have thought you could actually assemble a menu with Italian, Hawaiian and Greek food? I honestly thought it was a joke."

"Joke's on us, cause this stuff is amazing."

After dinner ends, Telly returns with a selection of desserts (including a baklava made with mascarpone cheese, coconut and pine nuts), a tray with sample shots of grappa, ouzo and okolehao, and a somewhat excessive appreciation for his customers.

"You like, no?" Telly asks me as he hands me a leftovers bag with more in it than we had on our plates, I'm sure, then straightens out my napkin in my lap. I really don't like people fondling my linens in restaurants.

"It was wonderful," I tell him, shooing his hands from my lap (after all, I don't need old Telly to get an up-close look at my too-tight Flexee-induced bulges.) Despite the culinary false start. I might even have to give the place three stars.

"Meesees Jennings, on behalf of zee entire staff of Puka, I sank you for dining vees us zees evening," Telly says as he bows repeatedly while backing away from me and disappearing into the kitchen. "Zee meal is on zee house, vees my undying gratitude."

I look at Jessie and blanch. Meessees Jennings, he called me. Missus fucking Jennings. How stupid could I have been? I should've known! There was no mistake. The only mistake is that my look has become unmistakable. For the third time this month, I've been recognized in a restaurant.

"Son of a bitch," I groan under my breath. "Mortie's gonna kill me. He's going to absolutely kill me."

Shaken by the revelation that my food critic cover has been effectively blown, I leave Jessie to pay the bill and slip out a side door to hail a cab, handing my bag of leftovers to a homeless man on a nearby grate. Well, slip might be a gross understatement, considering at my size, I'm probably beyond the point of slipping out of anyplace with much facility.

I tip the cab driver too much, just grateful to be away from there and able to go home to ponder this most unfortunate turn of events. I plod up the flight of steps up to our brownstone and unlock the door, flicking on the hall light as I regain my breath from that exertion. Tartare, my beefy tomcat, weaves a few figure eights around my ankles before meowing as he always does to go outside, even though I don't dare let him out on the mean streets.

"William?" I call out for my husband, who I'm sure was planning to be home tonight. I'd invited him along to Puka but he declined, saying he was going to catch up on some things. I'm beginning to suspect that being married to the food critic of the *New York Sentinel* holds very little charm to William at this point. It was never something he'd wanted for us, but he was willing to put up with it, if it made me happy.

If it was up to William, we'd leave Manhattan in a New York minute (excuse the pun). He cashed out years ago after the teeny little start-up company he worked for hit it big during the tech boom, and now only dabbles at his day job for fun, waiting for me to pull the plug on living in the city. He'd like nothing more than to escape the traffic, the noise, the excessive demands on his wife's time. Maybe start a family. Oh, jeeze, the thought of me getting pregnant at this weight is one I simply can't contemplate. Not without a fat finger of bourbon to help tamp down the hysterics that accompany such thoughts.

My Harvey Nichols pumps—optimistically purchased when I could lay claim to that size-ten physique—click with groaning desperation across my polished hardwoods. I think if they could talk they would beg for mercy. Please, give us a freaking break and don't wedge your bloated feet into us, they'd say. We weren't meant to haul so much weight; we're not tractor-trailers, you know!

No, they're not, but I feel like I am. A tractor-trailer loaded with cargo but out of gas on a desolate highway. I switch on the living room lights, peel off my unforgiving shoes and sink into the butterscotch leather sofa, which gasps like a dying man beneath my girth.

"What to do, what to do," I ask Tartare, who is clearly unconcerned with my dilemma as he strains to escape my grip. I stroke him with one fingernail in his sweet spot at the curve of his chin and he relents, frozen with feline desire. I wish my problems could be solved by a little chin scratching.

I lay my head back and take in the living room. William and I argued for weeks on the color we'd paint this room. He wanted cranberry. I finally won the argument and chose a distinct chestnut shade. I actually brought a wedge of my favorite chocolate—from this amazing French chocolatier in the East Village—to the paint store because the color was precisely what I was looking for. I knew I could readily relax in a room that reminded me of Guillaume's to-die for ganache.

"William?" I call again but get no response, so I hoist myself up and pad to the kitchen. The varnished concrete floor is cold on my feet, so I slide them into my banana split slippers, which I always keep nearby. Comfortable shoes are so important for cooking. I'm feeling very agitated by what happened at the restaurant, and decide that the only thing to take my mind off it will be to whip up something tasty. As I reach for the cabinet that houses my cookbooks I notice a note on the counter.

Abbie,

The house was kind of quiet so Cognac and I decided to get away. We hopped on the bike and headed down to the Jersey shore for a couple of days. Call if you need me. Or better yet, come join us. Maybe we can prowl the backstreets in search of a new restaurant. We'd sure love the company.

Love,

William

p.s. Don't worry, Cognac is secured into the sidecar with his doggie seatbelt.

William keeps insisting Jersey is retro, thinking that will lure me down there with him. I had enough of Jersey growing up, thanks. I'm not ready to revisit my past, even under the guise of campy fun. I ball up the note and toss it in the trash, then send him a quick text message. I think I'll keep mum for now about what happened this evening. No need to bother him with details, especially when I'm sure I can clear this all right up in the morning.

Hi sweetie. Sorry u weren't home when I got back. Have fun with poochie @ the beach. I'm off 2 bed soon so don't worry about calling. Luv, me

I rifle through the cabinet and pull out grandma Gigi's recipe box. For me, job stress—or any kind of stress, really—means concocting an old favorite from her collection. I leaf through the worn pages of Gigi's recipes until I find precisely what I'm looking for. I pull out the card gingerly, as the corners are dog-eared and yellow with age. Albumen stains speckle it, as well as grease marks from her lard-smeared fingers. Grandma's impeccable cursive sweeps across the card, even and angled, precise. Like baking: methodical and exact.

I pull out the flour, salt, butter, and shortening and begin to blend together the ingredients, putting a little muscle into it as I mix, adding ice water to consistency. Five simple ingredients that combine to sooth my nerves and please my palate.

Next I mix the pudding, then slice bananas. Crack eggs,

separating yolk from white. Pull out the Kitchen-Aid mixer, whip the whites on high with a pinch of salt. Adding the sugar, one tablespoon at a time, a splash of vanilla for good measure.

I dust the granite countertop with flour and roll out two crusts: I think a pie might be just the thing to turn around Mortie's mood when I break the news to him. Who can't get happy over a banana cream pie? It's the mother of all comfort foods, the comfort food of all mothers. At least for my grandmother it was.

As I slide the pies into the oven, I glance at the clock and realize it's past midnight. I've been cooking for almost three hours. Just about long enough to forget that tomorrow I have to face my boss.

BANANA CREAM PIE

This is a single recipe, but you might as well double it if you're going to go to all the effort.

FOR THE PIE CRUST

Preheat oven to 375°.

With pastry blender mix 2-1/2 c. Wondra Flour (it's the only flour for this pastry) with one stick softened butter (8 tbl.) and 1/2 tsp. salt.

Then add 6 rounded tbls. Crisco shortening (do not under any circumstances use the butter flavored, and by all means don't even consider using any other brand of shortening). You can use the Crisco shortening sticks, just cutting at the appropriate line.

Blend till mealy.

Add 5-6 tbl. ice water, mix with pastry mixer until dough pulls together but is not gluey. If needed, add a little bit more water. If too damp, a small bit more flour.

Gently pound into a ball, and roll out on floured countertop or pastry sheet until 1/8" thick.

Roll gently onto pastry roller and ease into pie pan. Snugly roll crust up. Poke holes along bottom of pie crust with fork to allow crust to breath.

Place baking parchment on top of crust, pour rice or pie weights on top of parchment, to weigh crust down as it bakes.

Bake for ten minutes, then paint inside of crust with a mixture of one egg white and 1 tsp. Water. Replace the parchment pie weights and bake for another 5 minutes. Remove parchment with pie weights and bake another 5 minutes. Allow to cool completely.

FOR THE FILLING

Use two packages of Jell-O brand banana cream pudding mix (not the instant). Hard to find but worth the effort. You may have to track it down on the Internet. Cook as directed on package, using slightly less milk. As the pudding thickens, separate out three egg whites and yolks. Just before pudding comes to a boil, add about 1/2 cup of the pudding into the egg yolks, stir well, then pour in to the pudding that is just coming to a boil. Remove from stove and let cool. (By the way, don't even bother making homemade banana pudding. It's not nearly as good).

FOR THE MERINGUE (a vital ingredient to this pie's success)

Using the 3 egg whites, whip with mixer on high with a pinch of salt. Add, one at a time, 9 tbl. of sugar (take that South Beach!), then 1 tsp. vanilla.

TO FINISH PIE

Preheat oven to 350°. Once crust and pie filling are cooled, line bottom of pie crust with banana slices. Add filling. Spread meringue on top. Bake for 15 minutes, till meringue is a light golden brown on top.

A Generous Splash of Vinegar

Does my fat ass make my ass look fat?

– refrigerator magnet

A famous Chinese-American chef once told me that she always incorporates a touch of bitter into anything sweet she is preparing—because life balances out in much the same way.

Maybe it'd have been better to open that little ditty in a fortune cookie back in high school—perhaps then I'd have had ample warning before my dreaded prom fiasco, the jarring pinnacle of my emotionally-pimpled teen years.

High school was in no way a high point of my life; I spent much of my time comfortably cloaked in anonymity. I excelled at flying under the radar as much as possible, in fact. I was plainest of plain Janes, the highlight of whose looks was a dull splash of freckles across my nose and stick-straight hair reminiscent of squid-ink linguine. It's not that I avoided being part of the action; rather I just sort of blended into it, like butter and chocolate whisked together over a double boiler. I was the girl everyone was perfectly happy to ask to help out with the student council car wash but wouldn't usually think to invite along for pizza at Greasy Vinny's on a Friday night. The same girl who toiled away in relative obscurity, seldom asked out on a date, spending mostly empty Saturday nights baking crème puffs and quiche Lorraine while the rest of the kids made out in dark alleyways or drank Pabst Blue Ribbon beer at keggers in the woods behind the park. I don't want you to think I was a complete loser or anything, but I never quite got past B-level status in high school. I was to Thomas Edison High School what Kathy Griffin is to Hollywood: I had a purpose but no one quite knew what it was.

But then I invited Chip Schnoebel to the prom. Don't ask me why. It was completely out of character. But my grandmother was determined to construct a social life for me, and she wouldn't stop haranguing me to invite someone if no one asked me. She said if I wasn't going to step out of my comfort zone, then she was going to give me strong encouragement. I hesitated to guess what that would entail, but I figured it might be like an unexpected push off the edge of the Grand Canyon. Finally I relented, because it was less humiliating for me to embarrass myself than for her do it for me: I couldn't imagine having my grandmother finding a blind date for me for the prom, of all things. And I figured if I was going to take the plunge, I might as well step into the abyss on my own free will.

So I drummed up the courage and invited Chip, with whom I had already been thrust into a default relationship as lab partners. You could say that Chip and I had chemistry. Well, I had chemistry skills, and he had the need for chemistry answers. So our symbiotic relationship was the basis for me asking him. He was one of few guys I spoke with on a regular basis, so I knew I'd be able to choke out the words without vomiting on his feet.

Chip teetered on the fringe of the popular crowd. He played on the basketball team and occasionally even started in games. At the very least, I guess the cheerleaders noticed him. I knew nothing about his social life, though. For all I knew he could've been dating someone. So I was definitely expanding my horizons by asking him. And when he said yes, well, I mean, who wouldn't have been thrilled?

I guess in hindsight I should have known something was up, since I was definitely out of his league. He'd called me one night in search of answers to a take-home chemistry test. As I walked him through alcohols, thiols and disulfides for the umpteenth time I somehow drummed up the wherewithal to squeak out the proposal in a fit of daring-do.

"You wanna go to the prom with me?" I sounded like a hamster-wheel in need of a good oiling.

Chip was silent for a moment, perhaps taken aback with my

forward ways. Or maybe I rendered him speechless. Finally he spoke. "Um, er, uh. Yeah. I guess so."

That was the extent of the conversation about the prom, and we returned to the world of acids and alkalines, a far more comfortable arena in which to converse for me.

My friends—all B-listers, all pretty smart and disinclined to engage in too much social discourse—were stunned at my ballsy maneuver. No one would have pegged me for a prom-goer, first off, and certainly not a date-asker!

For the weeks leading up to prom, Chip was noticeably quiet in my presence. Almost as if he was mustering up the courage to speak but unable to. Which was okay. I was busy preparing for exams and didn't mind focusing on my work. I mean sure, a little part of me was excited that one of the almost-cool guys at school was willing to go to the prom as my date. But I didn't get too terribly worked up over. Eventually we mapped out timing for the prom, and when the big night came, things seemed to be fine. Until he disappeared immediately after the sit-down dinner somewhere in the vast ballroom of the Sheraton. In a sea of prom gowns, tuxedos and boa feathers, he wasn't easy to spot.

I thought he'd gone to refill our punch glasses. I took advantage of his absence to run to the bathroom. When I returned he was nowhere to be found, so I sat down to wait, knowing he must've gone to the rest room as well and he'd be back soon. It was like one of those time-lapse scenes you see in a movie, where you can tell the change of light and the shift in bodies and yet it all seems static. But you know it's not. You know that Amanda Coggins is slow-dancing with Matthew Frenecky and you'd give about anything to be Amanda Coggins at that very moment that Matthew's hands are sliding perilously close to her perfect little heart-shaped bottom. And then you know that Phil Deruto is dancing awfully close to Emily Hutchinson even though it's a very fast song by the Gap band and you wonder if the teacher chaperones are going to say something about too much fraternizing. And later you know that everyone is on the floor, laying on their backs, shaking their legs in convulsions to "Rock Lobster," and that you're the only one not on the dance floor. And that almost two hours have passed.

At about ten thirty, Jackie Rankin wriggled by in a skin-tight dress as red as my face was about to turn when she said to me, "Isn't Chip back yet?"

I looked at her, perplexed, my eyebrows making a furrow so deep you could plant a row of corn in them. "Back?"

"From Central's prom, over at the Holiday Inn."

I squinted my eyes at her, perfectly symbolic of how in-the-dark I obviously was about my date's intentions for the evening. Central's prom? Why would Chip be there? He was my date to our school's prom. And then Jackie realized I didn't know that Chip had pulled an Elvis and left the building.

Jackie covered her mouth in exclamation. "Oh, gosh, I must be wrong about that. I don't know where I got that from but seriously, I'm sure he's not there. I think that's just Jason who went."

"Jason?" I asked. Jason was Chip's best friend. Who'd sat with his girlfriend at this very table during dinner a few hours back.

"Yeah, Jason's girlfriend goes there and so they split up prom night at both hotels. And Chip used to go out with her friend Vicky," she said. "But I'm sure they broke up."

I felt a rush of molten heat sprint up my neck and dash across my face. And red was never my color, dammit. Everything was beginning to make sense, and I felt like such a fool.

Jackie reached out and looped her arm through mine. "Why don't you join us until we can figure out where Chip's wandered off to. He's probably just found a football game on TV somewhere." Except that football season had been over for months.

As much of an introvert as I was, I decided I couldn't suffer the humiliation of being ditched by my date and left sitting alone at an eight-top with an endless succession of ginger ale and orange sherbet punches, so I agreed. Jackie and her friends were dancing to "Get Off My Cloud" and using somebody's shoe as a microphone. At some point a flask of Southern Comfort found its way into my hands. I'd never once had alcohol, in all my years. I'd cooked with it plenty, deglazing the pan for bananas foster or chicken piccata. But never ingesting even a sip. It seemed as good a time as any to drown my sorrows in it, so I took a swig. And then a gulp. And then a guzzle.

By the time Chip returned, all that was missing on me was a lampshade. I was in the middle of belting out "Like a Virgin" into Jennifer Rigo's black satin pump when Chip reached around me and whispered "Boo!" into my ear, acting as if he'd just slipped out for a moment for some fresh air.

Not realizing what was happening, my heel slipped and my arms swung up reflexively, smacking Chip Schnoebel hard across his until-then aquiline nose, bashing it enough to set off a real gusher and maybe set it off-kilter just the teensiest bit. It was hard to tell in the dark with the sparkly disco ball scattering diamonds of light around us, really only illuminating the harsh crimson of his profuse bleeding.

As soon as I realized what I'd done, I just froze in absolutely humiliation. But Chip was just getting started. "My nose! My nose! She punched me in my nose!" He kept pointing at me like I was a thief, making off with the jewels, glaring over the rapidly-reddening white polyester blend napkin someone had stuffed beneath his nostrils. "My tuxedo! My white shirt! They're never going to give me back my deposit!"

Soon people were gathering around, and the buzz of conversation became a swarm of gossip. "He left her for Vicky Sangrinella. Abbie got mad at him so when he came back she punched his lights out."

I looked at the boy who said that and I tried to tell him that wasn't the case. But then I heard someone else say, "She's been dating Chip and she's got a really hot temper." Dating him? I couldn't even have considered going to prom with the guy a date, he was gone for so much of it. And about the hottest thing in my life was our electric oven when I was searing a piece of meat or browning the top of a casserole.

"He was using her for the chemistry exam." That came from a skinny girl with bucked teeth and her hair plastered into an updo with what must have been industrial-strength spackle.

Well, that was the final blow.

As the tittering swelled to a fever pitch, I wove in between the elegantly-attired lynch-mob, past the scenic backdrop for memorable prom portraits, pausing just outside the ballroom door long enough to dry heave into a grove of decorative plastic potted palms. I finally found my way outside to the turnaround, where taxicabs awaited. I knew I could get my grandmother to pony up for the tab, under the circumstances.

"Where to?" the cabbie asked.

"Anywhere but here," I muttered, then told him my address. Only then could I allow my tears to surface.

So much for the sweet side of life.

I'm sitting outside my favorite Italian coffee shop, running a little late for work, but I can't start the day without a double decaf ristretto cappuccino, bone dry, whole milk. As I enjoy my drink and an almond-fennel biscotti at a sidewalk table, I'm momentarily transported to a cliff-side coffee bar along the Amalfi Coast, overlooking the sapphire waters of the Mediterranean. The chatter of Italian, the language of amore, drifts in and out while schoolchildren play football on a nearby pitch, nothing but a high mesh fence protecting them from the churning blue ocean, one mile below. The smell, the taste, the place all become one to me.

When William and I traveled through Italy, we spent a couple of months along the Amalfi coast. No better place to be in June than in Praiano. Sitting at a cliffside café, sipping prosecco with a raspberry at the bottom of the glass, dipping spongy peasant bread in local olive oil, and relishing the briny olives as we watched the fishermen bring in their catch. I can still see the adoration in William's eyes as we toasted our good fortune for having found one another.

I take a deep breath and exhale. Life is good: the birds are singing over the roar of Manhattan rush hour, fruit trees in the park are in full flower, my husband still adores me, and I have the best job in the entire world.

Things couldn't get much better. Well, maybe if I were to

suddenly wake up tomorrow quite a bit thinner... Without having to starve myself. Now that indeed would be a perfect day. But the truth is, I love food. And it loves me, judging by the way it doesn't seem to want to subsequently let go of me once I've finished with it. Like some bunny-boiling stalker, dammit. Yeah, that is the sordid downside of decadent food: once it joins the party, it never wants to leave. It's the drunken guest with the lampshade over its head, the one you have to take the car keys from but really don't want it rearing its ugly head in the morning and would just as soon shove out the back door.

Don't get the wrong idea: I don't love to eat volumes of food. I'd probably sooner not eat than opt for fast food, for example. But asking me to forego tonight's sumptuous six-course meal prepared by Michelin-starred chef Etienne Lordeaux simply to be a calorie-miser would be like asking a mother to throw her child from a moving train. Absolutely no can do.

So I suppose when it comes to weight issues, I have just yielded to the reality of my life. I am a food critic, after all. The premier food critic for the New York Sentinel. It's my job to love food. And to eat it, often. I have no choice but to be fat, I suppose.

I divert myself to a park bench en route to work to deposit an egg sandwich and a half dozen cookies to George, a homeless man I walk by each day to and from my job. George may well be one of the best-fed street people in Manhattan, as I usually bring my leftovers straight to him whenever I try out a restaurant. Since I didn't have it in me to run them by him last night, I had to provide him with some sort of consolation meal this morning.

"What's this, no entrecôte, today?" he asks, grinning.

"Sorry, George. Mission aborted last night. But I didn't want to leave you hanging, so I brought some of my specialty oatmeal cookies instead. Hope that'll tide you over."

"You didn't have to do that on my account!"

"I know that. But I also knew how hungry you'd be by now. It's not filet mignon, but it beats nothin'." I give him a shrug.

"That's why I call you Saint Abbie." George tips his hat at me as if we'd just finished a lovely dance together. Poor fellow. I don't know why he's without a home, but it doesn't mean we should pretend he doesn't exist.

"What'dya think about the mayoral race?" he asks.

I wave my hand dismissively. "Honestly, I haven't given it much thought. I've been so busy with work that I don't even seem to get around to paying attention to my own life, let alone worrying about things like politics."

"You should read the piece in last Sunday's *Sentinel*," he says. "It'll tell you all you need to know."

"Yeah, well, if I don't get my butt into the *Sentinel* pronto, I'll have a lot of free time on my hands to read every little article plus the want-ads in there, thanks." I give a little wave.

"Have a good one." He waves back at me as he bites into his egg sandwich, giving me a thumbs up.

"You bet!" I scurry off so I'm not late. Don't want to draw any more attention to myself than I've already done.

I arrive at my mid-town office to the overly enthusiastic greeting of Julio, the security detail at the front desk.

"Good morning, Mrs. Jennings," he says with a nervous insinuation of something vaguely disconcerting—I can't quite put my finger on it. Odd, as normally we just smile and wave. Don't think I've ever heard him mention my name, for that matter. I return a quick hello and mount the elevator like a lamb headed to slaughter. Marinated with some rosemary and thyme. Maybe some balsamic vinegar. Grilled medium rare on rosemary skewers. Served over fresh pita with a simple yogurt sauce. Now that sounds divine …

I can't help but notice people staring at me. I must have lipstick smeared above my lip or something. I avert each gaze and feign the need for something urgent in my purse. Far easier to rifle than drum up elevator chat.

Normally when I arrive at work, I join a few colleagues for a cup of coffee and a daily diet of gossip—delicious and calorie-free. Invariably someone's read the other papers on the subway, and there's always something to dish about in Manhattan. But today I get off at the forty-second floor and divert immediately to my desk, as I know I have guilt written all over my newly-recognized face.

I'm concentrating intently on finishing up my extensive notes on Puka when my intercom buzzes and I jump like a trigger-happy soldier to answer it.

"Abbie, I need you in here, now," Mortie growls, his gruff voice the end-result of an out-of-control-nicotine dependency.

I hope this doesn't take long. I'm planning to check out Cheery-O, a new teahouse in mid-town, in forty-five minutes. I heard the place serves real clotted cream. I have been loyal to the same teahouse for five years, but the truth is, while good service and customer allegiance are all fine and good, I'll readily switch favorites for true clotted cream. Especially if served with house-made jams.

I pry myself out of my seat (when did this chair get to be so tight?), grab my purse and pull the pie from my mini-fridge. Scurrying through the office I bump into Barry Newman. Barry's been working in the food section for years. I've heard he coveted the position that I landed, but he's been absolutely gracious toward me nevertheless.

In fact, sometimes he can be so thoughtful, bringing me lovely pastries from an Austrian bakery across the street from his Queens apartment. At six foot three, Barry towers over my diminutive five foot four frame. His thick brown hair fluffs up like a chocolate soufflé atop his head, adding even more height. His pale blue eyes are tinged with red, something that I've noticed on him more and more lately. I hope everything's all right with his personal life.

"Just the woman I want to see," Barry says with an incriminating smile as he drums his fingertips together in mid-air. "I've got a little treat for you."

He passes me a bag with something warm inside.

I open it, feel the rush of steam leaving the bag and smell the unmistakable aroma of Corfu.

Loukoumades. Drizzled with honey and dusted with a flourish of cinnamon. Sugared perfection in the form of golf-ball sized fried dough. Brings me back to the days of William and me scootering up those long and winding roads past Corfu. When we discovered that perfect little mom and pop restaurant, where we went in the back and the stooped, gray-haired, watery-eyed yia-yia opened the lid on each of the pots of simmering stews so that we could choose our dinner. Life sure was simple and pleasurable back then, before the days of hiding behind my persona, and working crazy long hours in the name of my craft.

I extract a sticky chunk and taste, closing my eyes to savor the bite.

"Oh, Barry, you shouldn't have," I say between mouthfuls, moaning just a little. "I knew this was my lucky day!"

"There's a festival at Saint Sophia's Greek Orthodox church on Fifty Second Street," he says. "I knew you'd enjoy them."

"You're a doll to think of me." I beam at him and remember I've been summoned to Mortie's office. "I wish I could stay and chat but I've gotta run—have to answer to the man."

Barry gives me a knowing wink. "Better not keep the boss man waiting."

I dash into Mortie's office and immediately hand him the pie. Too late I realize I have loukoumades crumbs on my face and discreetly brush them off.

"I brought you your favorite pi-ie," I sing, hoping to butter him up. That reminds me, I need to check out that new bodega two blocks from my place; they're selling fresh butter three times a week, direct from a Mennonite farmer in Pennsylvania. And I can pick up a loaf of that yeasted jalapeno corn bread from the bakery. Maybe barbecue some ribs for with it, in honor of spring. William loves those harbingers of summer-to-come, that sense of getting away from it all that comes with warm weather and fresh, local foods. He'd far rather flee the city for the quieter confines of the countryside or, better yet, the ocean. Just the two of us, walking hand-in-hand along the shoreline, Cognac ten steps ahead of us investigating the beached jellyfish and horseshoe crabs. But if I can't give him that, at least I can offer it to him in the form of an escapist meal.

Mortie, who's sporting a scowl, looks at the pie with tepid enthusiasm.

"Aw, Abbie, I wish you'd stop trying to fatten me up," he says. "My stomach might love this stuff but my arteries are going on strike." Nevertheless he grabs a spoon from a drawer and scoops it into the pie. After all, who can resist banana cream pie? Mission accomplished, I think confidently. Even if he did know about last night, he'll have forgotten it with the pie.

"So what's up?" I ask.

Mortie spears his spoon back into the pie and stands up.

"Abbie—we've got a real problem on our hands," he says. He picks up a copy of today's *New York Post* and holds it up to my face. I blanch.

Staring back at me from the tabloid is a picture of me. A grainy picture of me looking like someone I don't know. Someone fat and lumpy. Someone clearly in the throes of Flexee failure. Stuffing her face from the dessert sampler at Puka.

Oh, God, even worse than the truth-serum of a picture of my corpulent twin (it is, isn't it? It simply can't be me. I don't look that bad, do I?) is the banner headline, which has obviously been screaming out from newsstands across Gotham this morning, up until now to my merciful oblivion:

STUFFED TO THE GILLS: Sentinel Food Critic Exposed!

"Well?" Mortie fixes his gaze on me, expecting a response.

"I can't believe my girdle is that incompetent!" Maybe if I make a joke of this it'll soften the blow.

"Abbie, you've been outed!" he snarls. With that he slaps the back of his hand across my grotesque photograph. "What the hell do you think we should do about it?"

"Wellllll..." I'm tap-dancing for time, trying to come up with a brilliant response. "Uh, I know when you hired me I said I wasn't a big fan of disguises." And I'm not. They're sticky and uncomfortable and my head itches with those wigs and I'd really rather go out to eat as me. I'm a food critic, not an actress. "How about we give that a try?"

I bat my eyes at Mortie in a lame attempt to charm him, but he's shaking his head. "It's too late for that, Abbie. It's one thing to disguise a woman who's a size twelve. But it's another thing to try to hide someone whose appearance is, uh, how to put this delicately? Whose appearance is a foregone conclusion?"

"Maybe you can just spell it out for me, Mortie. You think I'm fat, don't you? You think your top food critic has eaten her way out of being able to eat for a living."

This time Mortie locks his eyes on mine and nods almost imperceptibly, like he's trying hard not to nod, his pursed lips set in a grimace, as if he's disappointed in me. "I'm afraid so, Abbie. I can't have my premier food critic being known all over town by dint of her girth. And right now, with this picture of you being blanketed across Manhattan, you have become the elephant in the corner of the room, forgive the insensitive cliché. You'll never get an honest depiction of a restaurant's food and service when everyone knows exactly what you look like."

My face must look dejected, because he tries to assuage my humiliation a bit.

"Think of it like this. Take the Queen. You think she could get a true idea of what it's like to be served at some of the most exclusive restaurants in London? No, because everyone knows what the Queen looks like."

"Not to mention her entourage would give it away." I roll my eyes at him. I hardly think there's much comparison between me and a stuffy old goat who looks and dresses like an aged governess and carries outmoded handbags. Though I bet her Flexees work better than mine. Hers are probably hand-woven of royal gossamer, and even if she got too fat for them, the damned things would fit by royal decree or something. No, wait, she'd have little puffy-sleeved minions sewing faux sizes in the waistband of the things, just to placate her regal sensibilities. Oh, if only I were a queen. Then my Flexees would gladly fit me, too. Instead, I'm only queen-sized. Actually, at this point, I'm probably more like empress-sized.

"Well, this is sort of like that. Only you can't even disguise yourself. You've just gotten too, er, expansive."

"That's not true, I don't talk very openly," I say, but my joke falls flat because we both know exactly what he meant when he said that word.

Mortie perches both hands on his desk and leans forward,

staring directly at me. "Abbie, it's like this: I am responsible to this paper and to its readership. I can no longer continue to send you out to review restaurants right now, because everyone knows who you are and what you look like. No one will be able to trust a Sentinel restaurant review under the circumstances."

Whoa. He didn't just say he was firing me, did he? Me? Is he honestly chucking me to the curb?

"You're firing me? Giving me the old heave-ho? You're booting me, like sending an old horse to the glue factory? After all I've done for you? Boosting your restaurant advertising revenue. Ensuring that the Sentinel is the go-to source for restaurant reviews. And the thanks I get is a swift kick in my—oversized—ass? Don't you think that's a pretty cheap—not to mention easy—target?"

"Calm down, Abbie, I'm not firing you. You're our champion reviewer. I'd be crazy to get rid of you. Trust me, this whole thing will die down. In six months time there will be enough turnover at city restaurants that this will be a moot point. But until then, you are stepping away from the restaurant review duties—you'll get a food column instead."

He couldn't do this to me.

"How can you demote me like this?"

"Abbie, it's not a demotion. It's a lateral move."

"Lateral schmateral. Lateral moves are fine in a game of checkers, maybe, but not when one is happily ensconced in her dream job."

"Plus it's only for a set period of time." As if that'll sell me on the idea.

"Yeah, just long enough for you to realize you don't need me. And for me to lose my reviewer's edge. You know how bad that is? My palate will lose its touch. I'll be barren. Barren-tongued. This is probably a known condition listed in the pages of *Gray's Anatomy*, you know."

I pick up a dictionary, pretending it's the medical compendium, and leaf to the middle of the book, as if I'm looking it up, and with flourish jam my finger on a page.

"See? 'Barren tongue: An affliction particular to demoted

food critics.'"

Mortie just waves both hands away from me, like he's trying to get rid of an odor that's lingering nearby. "Look at it this way: with this column, it will free up time for you. No more working dinners. Spend some time with William. Maybe you can join a gym. Research a book."

"Or why don't I use the time to invent the cure to cancer? At least make good use of myself."

My face burns with shame. In one fell swoop I have gone from the pinnacle of my professional career to a fatso posting in food critic Siberia. Lateral move my ass. Make that fat ass. A column. Yeah, maybe I can write a column about being humiliated by being exposed in a major daily and then having my boss tell me I'm too fat to do my job.

My gaze drifts to the banana cream pie in front of Mortie. I want so badly to just take the pie back. Or at least grab that damned spoon, Mortie-germs and all, and just go to town eating it in one sitting, right here, in front of my lard-averse artery-clogged boss. Show him what a real fat girl can do. He thinks I'm a Tubby McTubbster? Fine, lemme at him. He can see how us chicks with the feedbags do it. Although truthfully, I certainly would relish smashing it in his face, but could never waste such good food, what with the effort that went into preparing the thing. Let's not forget the high quality ingredients. Thank goodness I made a second one, waiting patiently for me in the Sub-Zero at home.

"Effective immediately, for the next six months, Barry will take over the restaurant critic posting. You can come and go as you please, but I expect one column a week from you, and you've got complete latitude on your subject matter."

Whoop-tee-doo. I've been impeached. Well, that's just peachy. Yummm, like those heirloom Elberta peaches from the farmer's market on Block Island last summer. Juice that dripped down my arm with each bite I took. I made a fantastic peach tart, with black raspberry puree on a crispy bed of buttery phyllo dough. Served with a dollop of crème anglaise. Oh, if only I could transform myself back to that day. Then I wouldn't be standing here out of a job. Well, out of my job, anyhow.

"So that's it, then?" I ask, my shoulders slumped in dejection. "I have no recourse?"

Mortie shakes his head. "Not if you want to come back after your hiatus."

I turn and slink toward the door, all too many pounds of me, feeling about as small as a woman who's pretty much outgrown the women's department can feel. Only right now, feeling small couldn't feel worse.

As I leave, Mortie softly calls my name. "Abbie?"

Tears threaten to spring from my eyes, but I refuse to blink, denying them access. No way will I let Mortie see how hurt I am. I'm too choked up to speak, so I just look at him and cock my eyebrow.

"Abbie, this is nothing personal. You know that? I'm doing my job—what's best for the paper."

Nothing personal. Yeah, right. When you're pretty much fired for being fat, that's personal, no matter what anyone says. "Gotcha." I say, even though I'd like to say something harsher.

I return home, having gathered up my laptop and not much else and hastening myself out of the building; I couldn't bear to deal with my colleagues and their questions. Thank God Mortie told me to take a week off to collect myself before starting the column. Now if only if I could actually collect myself, no doubt I'd be too heavy to carry off wherever it was I was supposed to take me.

The house is quiet; William is still finding himself in Jersey, apparently. I'm sure he'll be gone all weekend, which leaves me on my own to wallow in my new reality for at least three whole days. God, being alone in this brownstone is not what I need right now. Instead of distractions, I'm left to fester in my shame. The shame of knowing that ghastly picture of me gorging my corpulent face is blanketing Manhattan. Meanwhile, I sit here thinking how much I'd love to eat something warm and comforting just to shut it all out. Something that would simply cancel out the events of the past twenty-four hours. Except I know deep down that what's done is done: the fat cat is out of the bag.

I know, I know, it's not like I didn't realize I'd physically expanded beyond acceptable societal standards. I'm the first to admit nothing I own fits me without a serious amount of physical exertion to tug it onto my body. Which then leaves me huffing and puffing, I'm so out of shape. But it's always been my private thing. Even William has never faulted me for it. Sure, other people have probably noticed it. I see their looks when I pass them on the street. The handsome men whose gazes catch my eye for a split second, before they turn away, repulsed at what they see. Or when someone bounces off of me on a busy Manhattan sidewalk because even though they turn sideways, they can't help but ricochet off of my generous flesh. Human pinballs, they are, and yours truly is the rubber bouncer. Step right up, folks! A hundred points if you boing off the Lard-o Lady! Don't think for a minute I don't notice their glares.

I guess I always just figured I was more than my sum parts. Sure, I'm overweight. But I'm so much more than a bunch of blubber. I'm a smart woman with skills and intelligence and I'm friendly and nice and—I have really good qualities. Can someone tell me why all of these characteristics seem to be cancelled out just because I'm fat? Fat equals invisible at best, repugnant at worst. And in reality, I could be thin and beautiful and be a hateful person—maybe a supermodel who throws phones at people and beats staffers who covet her jeans—yet that seems to be more valued than all that I have to offer. Simply because of my physical appearance.

I heave a sigh of resignation. To quote an old sage, Popeye, "I yam what I yam." Although maybe if I'd have laid off the hollandaise sauce in favor of the steamed spinach, I'd be a little less of me.

With little else to do for the indefinite future, I retreat to my kitchen and do what comes naturally when I'm feeling blue—I cook my favorite comfort food: lasagna. I bypass three recipes in favor of the quick-version, because I just cannot wait to sink my teeth into something that will help me to forget how miserable I'm feeling.

LASAGNE

FOR THE SAUCE:

1 clove garlic
1/2 minced onion
olive oil (couple of tbls.)
1-1/2 lb. ground beef
2 tbl. parmesan cheese
2 small cans tomato sauce
2 small cans tomato paste
1 tsp. each: oregano, salt, pepper, basil

Lightly brown onions, adding garlic (be sure not to burn garlic, allow to turn golden), add beef, brown, drain. Put back in stock pot with tomato sauce, paste, spices. Fill sauce cans with water and add to sauce. Stir well, bring to boil, reduce heat to simmer for one hour.

FOR THE FILLING:

1/2 lb. grated mozzarella cheese
1 small container cottage cheese
1 small container ricotta cheese
1 egg
dash nutmeg
1 tbl. parsley, chopped
salt and pepper to taste
1 package lasagna noodles, cooked, drained

Grease 13" x 9" baking dish. Put layer of sauce, 4 overlapping noodles, layer 1/2 the cheese mixture, layer 1/2 the sauce, then layer of noodles, cheese, sauce. Sprinkle with parmesan cheese. Cover with aluminum foil for all but last 10 minutes of cooking time.

Bake at 350° for 30 minutes.

One Half-Cup Sour Grapes

Self-delusion is pulling in your stomach when you step on the scales.

–Paul Sweeney

I gaze into the mirror, stripped down to my sensible bra and flab-trapping panties, and all I see are waves. Undulating waves. Something that can be so calming under the right circumstances. Like nice, invisible sound waves conveying your favorite song. Or gentle ocean waves, viewed while sitting on the rooftop deck at the beach house, absorbing a sunset, Mai Tai in hand. Indulging in your favorite goat cheese and artichoke dip with some freshly-made crostini. And of course steamed shrimp, the tang of beer in which it was steamed, the gentle marriage of Old Bay and horseradish and ketchup (grandma's recipe) feeling so decadent in its simplicity.

But I'm not feeling calm, because these waves I'm beholding are composed of something far more permanent than that which courses across the dark ocean's surface with the regularity of a heartbeat. They're waves of flesh, veritable breakers. Make that a tsunami. And as I tug and pull and coax my Flexee girdle over the mountainous terrain of my Paul Bunyan thighs, my generous behind, my stomach that overlaps like a layer cake on steroids, I can't help but wonder: how the hell did I turn into such an ocean of a woman?

After donning all the necessary accoutrements of figure camouflage, including a jacket to cover my Jell-O arms and large, chunky jewelry to distract from everything below my neck, I take one more glance at myself in the mirror. Only to be drawn immediately to my telltale chinny chin chin. I still remember the first time I detected a hint of a double chin. Until that point, I didn't think I looked all that bad. I mean, granted, I'm definitely lugging around enough of me to constitute at least another small person, which is a depressing thought. But it's always seemed to be spread out in an agreeable enough manner across my body, like a nice homemade huckleberry jam slathered generously on a piece of rustic bread, rather than a harsh glob of shortening thwacked into a mixing bowl. So nothing stood out as grotesque.

But the shadow of a double chin did leave me feeling unsettled. I mean, who has a double chin but fat folks? Well, also people whose jaw lines are conducive to chin repetition, I guess. One look at my family photo album will tell you that no one carries the double chin gene, however. And I admit, while I noticed that little excess lumpage sort of flapping there like a wet nurse's overused breast, I didn't heed the signs. Like that little pea-sized growth one wants to pretend isn't there, the one that can be a harbinger of much worse. Ignore it and it doesn't exist, right?

You might expect someone who eats rich for a living to have at least a double chin (and perhaps double wide hips as well). But for a long time, that wasn't the case. I was able to manage to eat out most of my meals and eat well without getting too fat. I suppose after I hit thirty, that became harder to do. That was the bellwether that ushered in not only a double chin, but obviously, now, it's more lethal sister, the triple chin.

Oh, the triple chin. A secondary heart-shaped bracket of flesh at the base of the chin, the point of which functions like a giant arrow at a roadside strip joint advertising Girls! Girls! Girls!, pointing in lurid corporeal neon to the wobbling flap of facial flesh hanging like a slab of meat in a butcher shop. Three Chins. Sounds like a dish at Wing Chow's, my favorite little dim sum spot in Chinatown. Even my vast levels of self-denial can't spin this one into a positive attribute. Nothing good can come of one's countenance taking on the appearance of Howdy Doody's hinged mouth, the cruel after-effect of multiple-chin syndrome.

As I stare into the full-length mirror, the harsh light of my bathroom illuminates me as if I'm a suspect in some sort of interrogation. Where were you on the night of your gluttonous binge? It mocks me. Did you really think you could live on pate and crème fraiche forever without suffering the consequences?

Honestly? Yes. I did. I never thought I'd see the day I'd become what I've become. It seemed impossible to fathom. And it's so unbecoming. I'm a gourmand, not the fat girl.

Okay, to be fair. I'm not exactly the Creature from the Black Lagoon. I have beautiful, straight shoulder-length hair, with the shine and coloring of black lacquer. And my eyes are, oh, I've never thought to describe my eyes. I'd say they're honest. Yep, I have honest eyes, the color of brandied mushroom sauce. Who wouldn't want to have eyes like that? Though I know in our society, those attributes are vastly outweighed (there's that word again) by my size.

So now what? Here I am, thirty-eight years old, the doyenne of dining in Manhattan, a woman whose entire being centers around food. And yet if I continue to eat, I won't be able to have an entire being that centers around food. I'll be that dog dropped off on the side of the highway, left to wander with no destination, no purpose, no kibble. Huh. No kibble. How ironic is that? I end up losing weight because I'm kibble-free, having consumed too much of the stuff throughout my eating career.

Weary of this assessment, I drag my feet into the bedroom. There, in the corner is what William and I jokingly call my fainting chair: an overstuffed crushed-velvet lounge chair, whose welcoming deep brown coloring reminds me of a beef reduction stock I make and freeze every autumn when the weather turns chilly. I could go for a hearty beef stew made with the stock right about now. It might fill up this sense of despair I'm feeling.

I ease my girth into the lounge chair, propping myself up on the egg yolk-yellow satin pillow (I fear if I actually fainted into the chair, I might well break off a leg or two of it in the process). I toy with a tassel as I weigh my options. Weigh my options. Good one. I'd laugh at my little play on words, if it weren't so completely not funny.

I realize my choices are this: lose weight, keep my job. Not lose weight? Lose my job. Either way there's dramatic loss. Okay, fine, and losing weight has an upside to it besides not giving up my beloved profession. I'd also be able to wear my

Spanx. Maybe delve into the collection of smaller outfits gathering dust in my closet, arranged in an arpeggio of sizes from a relatively diminutive eight all the way up to a double-digited none-of-your-business.

And not losing weight? All I can see are downsides. Downsides to being up on the scale. Marvelous. But aside from the "me factor" in this equation, is the bigger picture. I have aspired to being a premier food critic since back during the lean days, when we lived in Europe, when I realized how very much food is an integral part of the human condition. Here I always thought it was just me who was all about food. But it was there that I realized in many countries, food is life. And life is food.

To celebrate when I finally landed my fantasy job, William surprised me by preparing—all by himself— a feast of my favorite French foods: escargots with garlic butter and a splash of cognac; langoustines (flown-in overnight from Brittany), sautéed in their shells with butter and garlic and a hint of malagache curry; potatoes daphinoise (a little overpowering with the langoustines, I know, but I was going after my favorites); and haricots verts sautéed in shallots, all paired with a vintage Dom Perignon. The meal couldn't have been more perfect: conceived in love (sounds like a baby, doesn't it?), dining by candlelight, Edith Piaf on the stereo. Cognac even got his own china plate to dine alongside of us.

This is what I know: food is the common thread of all humans. The quest to improve upon any existing type of food, to create something so beyond merely satisfying—this is a universal mission. I feel complete when I can be a part of this greater good. When my efforts poke and prod chefs to do better, when I can be the conduit to the public, to say "Hey, wait'll you try this!" Conversely, to save them money and tell them, "Don't bother. You'd be better off staying at home than eating the swill" if a restaurant falls grossly short. To have a hand in someone's celebratory moment—that silver wedding anniversary dinner, a fortieth birthday celebration, well, you just can't put a price tag on that privilege.

It's as if all I've worked toward my whole life was to attain this one goal: My years of cooking with my grandmother; dabbling in foods throughout Europe, working in those shoebox kitchens in the French countryside, so hot I'd lose three pounds a night from sweating; all of those tiny little reviewing gigs I had in local weekly papers; freelancing for every magazine imaginable. And then: the Mount Everest of the food critic's world. Mine to appreciate for the treasure it was.

Until now.

I suppose there are those who fall in the eat-to-live camp. Those sad souls who don't even notice the taste of their meal; rather they view it as a linear progression to get from point A—hungry, to point B—fed. I'm probably proudest when I can lure one of that ilk over to the live-to-eat side: to convert someone who had been so preoccupied with the mundanities of life that they're unable to relish in the simple joy of a meal, the conviviality involved in gathering family and friends and food and wine, really, the recipe for a happy life, if you ask me. When I've succeeded with this, I've accomplished my goal.

So, then, I've answered my own question. The choice is I have no choice. I must lose weight. And fast. Six Months to Slim. Ha! Take that for a headline, you smarmy New York Post. Six Months to Less-Than-Morbidly Obese is more like it. I always pictured "morbidly obese" as someone who needs a crane to get them out of their apartment, because they're too large to fit through the doorway. I fit through my doorway quite well, thank you. But with the less-than-generous actuarial scales (scales! Those miserable bastard devices), if I'm really honest, I think it's probably true that I would be considered morbidly obese.

Now it's a question of how to diet. I know, I know, this is something about which there are vast reams of information. I've just never paid attention to any of it before. Someone in my position just doesn't do that. Or doesn't think she needs to, despite mounting evidence to the contrary. Like Flexee failure and such. Dieters view food as the enemy. But guess what? There have been times in which food has been my very best friend. Food has been there for me when my life has been at its worst. How can I abandon it now, then? crutch for me, it's a damned wheelchair. replacement limb. And I don't exactly know h it, frankly. Even if it's become cumbersome and

I get up out of the chair, knowing what I ha alk to the kitchen desk as if headed to the gallows. I o my laptop and pull up the email from Jess with the phone number she sent to me after hearing about my meeting with Mortie yesterday. And with one brief phone call, I make my date with destiny.

Two hours later I find myself precisely where I'd totally not like to be.

"Mrs. Jennings! So glad the doctor was willing to squeeze you in this afternoon. It seemed…urgent," the receptionist greets me. "I'll just have you fill out this paperwork before the doctor sees you."

She hands me a clipboard with a stack of forms on it, and I get to work. All of these medical questions are making me feel sick: numbness, fatigue, seizures, heart disease, kidney problems, trouble breathing. Sheesh, all of these serious conditions they're asking about. Mine pales in comparison. So much so that maybe I should just go ahead and leave. Good ol' Doc Crenshaw doesn't need to be bothered with little ol' me. Or not so little ol' me.

Just as I ponder slipping out discreetly, a perky middle-aged nurse calls out, "Abigail Jennings?" and since I'm the only poor slob in the waiting room, she stares straight at me, curling her finger to beckon me to follow her. Which I do obligingly. A sheep being led to the slaughter.

I know what's next. We both know it. Only I suspect she secretly relishes this, while I dread it with the same sort of anticipation one would if sending their only child off to war.

"Now, if you'll just hop up on the scale." She points to the torture device and actually smiles as she says this. What I'm hearing, however, is this: "Now, if you'll open wide and just let me carve out your tongue, we'll be done!" And I don't think hopping is an option, frankly. I picture the springs blowing on the thing, setting off alarms and all sorts of mayhem ensuing.

I feel like a dog about to be beaten with a newspaper for pooping on the carpet. My frowning eyebrows implore the nurse to change her mind. I swear I'm tempted to whimper.

"Is everything all right, Mrs. Jennings?" she asks.

Surely she jests. Is everything all right? Sweet God in Heaven, nothing could be more wrong at this moment in time, short of imminent mutual destruction by the world's super powers.

I point to my shoes. "Can I take these off?" I choke out.

I wonder how much added weight my combined skirt, sweater, traveler's jacket and Flexees will contribute to the overall poundage, and debate if it's worth the humiliation of standing stark naked in the inner sanctum of the doctor's office just to shave a few grams off the grande totale. I wipe my sweaty palms across my skirt as I debate my options.

"Mrs. Jennings?" The nurse stands there, authoritative, with chart in hand. I notice her pen is red. This seems deliberate, her wanting to mark in bold, scarring color my Mount Kilimanjaro-of-a-scale-total.

I draw a deep breath, exhale as much air as possible, and take a baby step onto the scale. So much for that exhalation, because suddenly I'm breathing so fast I fear I'll hyperventilate. Which wouldn't be so bad, because at least then I wouldn't have to be awake for this moment of deep shame.

I squeeze my eyes shut and hear the clanging of those metal squares as the nurse adjusts and re-adjusts the balance, which will certainly not be in my favor. No scales of justice here.

The nurse starts to announce my weight in a voice as loud as a squad of cheerleaders belting out support for the home team: Two, four, six, eight, Abbie's weight is really great!

"Shhhhh!" I hiss. "If you don't button your lip, I'm warning you, I actually own a set of Ginsu knives and I'm not afraid to use them! Keep that number to yourself!" She doesn't know I mean I'd use the knives only to menacingly cut through aluminum cans, like they do on the infomercial; they're really useless for cutting meat, anyhow. But that's okay, because my veiled threat seems to shut her up. She goes through the nursing motions with me, taking my blood pressure (did she actually whistle when she saw how high it was?), pulse and drawing blood. Vampire nurse.

"Go ahead and put on this gown and the doctor will be in to see you in a minute," Nurse Perky says, now looking a little intimidated. She exits the room, leaving me to my hospital gown. Which is mighty snug, I find, and leaves a gaping uncovered section of my back end, which would be somewhat tolerable if the exam table was up against the wall or something. But poised as it is, smack in the center of the room, leaving its occupant to lay in wait in mortified splendor, I have no choice but to look the fool. It's one thing to be overweight, dressed head-to-toe in slimming black like a trendy Manhattan mortician. It's downright humbling to be stripped down to this threadbare excuse for a baby diaper and left to shiver and await a virtual stranger's gaze upon all that I've become.

I hear a knock on the door. For a minute I think if I remain silent and still, he'll go away. He knocks a second time, and then a third. Finally he cracks the door and peers in.

"Oh, gosh, come on in!" I feign ignorance and play the hayseed, as if I simply hadn't noticed his knocking. Golly, gee willikers!

"Mrs. Jennings?" a hand reaches out to me and I divert my thoughts from my meandering mind to see before me this magnificent specimen of man-dom. Deep, saturated midnight blue eyes, thick, inky-black hair that gently waves across his head. Note to self: remember to kill Jess for recommending her hottie doctor to me. His smile is so dazzling, I expect to see a few asterisks pop up before my very eyes to emphasize the glean of his snow-capped teeth. And he has dimples. Which I think tend to make a man look more sincere, don't you? No man with dimples would lie to a girl, is my supposition. Except that his stunning good looks merely serve to remind me of all of those men who treat fat chicks like me with disdain. Or who simply see right through us. I hate that.

"Doc" Crenshaw doesn't look so much Doc-like as he does god-like. Like some sort of Grecian God of Pulchritude or something. A quick memory-jog of high school mythology doesn't stir up a recollection of any such god, but if there was, this man is certainly descended from him. I look at his name, inscribed against his crisp, white doctor's jacket, and see the name Dexter embroidered in blue. Dexter Crenshaw. Dex. I heave a sigh.

"So, Mrs. Jennings, to what do I owe the pleasure?"

I look at him, bedazzling man that he is, then glance down at me, overweight and busting out of a dingy hospital gown, and my spirits fall faster than an erection in a cold shower. Not that I'd be pursuing Dex-baby, anyhow. No! I'm happily married. Except I haven't heard a thing from my husband since he disappeared on me at the zenith of my despair, so maybe I'm only half-happily married. My half. Haffily married, maybe. Although to be fair, William doesn't even know about all that's gone down in my life. I didn't want to ruin his weekend with the details. So it's not as if he's deliberately avoiding me. Besides, I've got a man-god in front of me, and can't a girl fantasize a little? Except when that moment of truth dope-slaps me into reality, like it or not. Abbie Jennings is not Dex Crenshaw material. I just wanted some old fellow named Doc Crenshaw, someone who wouldn't snicker at my weight and embarrass me to no end.

"Ms. Jennings?" he looks up at me over the chart, his eyebrow cocked up in inquisition. Which is what this feels like. The Inquisition. What's it his business what I'm here for?

I hem and haw over my words, not quite sure how to 'fess up to the studly doc that I'm here to discuss, er, um, uh, (diets! Shhhhhh!).

"Says on your chart you wanted to discuss ways to 'perhaps be less zaftig'," he reads in broken words verbatim from what I wrote on the registration forms. Right to the core of it, that's me. Less zaftig. Who am I fooling?

I squeak out a one-word reply. "Yeah."

The doctor chuckles, shaking his head back and forth. "Less zaftig. Okay, then. First let's talk about you."

I don't talk about me. I talk about food. It's what I am

known for. Me? Not so much. No one even knows about me. Well, they know about me, but they never knew who I was. Until now. Which reminds me of why I'm here.

"I'm looking at your vital statistics," he says, leafing through some notes on my chart. Notes probably written in red. "To tell you the truth, Mrs. Jennings—"

"Please, if I'm going to sit her in a state of virtual undress, we might as well be on familiar terms. I'm Abbie." I then finally reach out my hand to shake it. I notice he doesn't offer up his first name back.

"Anyhow, Abbie, your blood pressure is quite high. We'll be testing your blood sugars. If you're not careful you're looking at a case of Type II diabetes, or even a heart attack. I'm glad you're here to, uh, make yourself less zaftig. This is a good plan of action. You're still so young, and you have such a pretty face."

Such a pretty face. Such a pretty face. If I weren't a lady and if I weren't in a state of disrobement and feeling vulnerable I think I'd like to wind up and punch this guy in the nose. I hate that phrase. Such a pretty face. Pretty face, my ass. As if how one looks is more important than what one is like. Who gives a care about faces or not? Why can't I be special, looks be damned?

I smile a grimace of a smile. "I'm not sure whether I should be flattered or insulted. I'll give you the benefit of the doubt and pick the former."

Doctor Crenshaw only looks confused and continues his stream of thought. "Have you given any thoughts to a plan of action? I'm happy to sit down with you and discuss suggestions for how to get this going. Perhaps you'd like to see a nutritionist. Do you watch your intake of calories? Do you exercise? Are you mindful of your cholesterol?"

I am being machine gun-pelted with questions for which I have no answer, so I shake my head no to each one as he looks quasi-dismayed at me for my lack of restraint and self-maintenance or excess of gluttony, take your pick.

"The bottom line, Abbie, is this mathematical equation: calories in, calories out. You eat 'em, you gotta burn 'em, it's as simple as that."

Simple schmimple. If it were that simple, we wouldn't be the fattest nation in the world. Though I don't think it's particularly fair that I got fat in this country, because it's not like I'm eating fast food, which is how everyone else has apparently porked up.

"I'm looking on your chart here and it says Jess Jamison referred you to me?" I notice his eyes light up significantly at the mention of her name.

"Yes, Jess. She's a good friend of mine."

"Oh. I see. Well, she's a patient of mine and all."

For a minute I think I see him blush. Nah, can't be.

"She's a great gal," I say.

"And then some," he says under his breath. Whatever that means.

I perk my eyebrow up, waiting for him to elaborate, but instead he takes my folder with my chart and bangs the bottom edge of it against the surface of the desk, as if he's straightening out a deck of cards. Okay, then.

He and I talk for a while, he recommends that I join a gym, start out slowly, start cutting back portions, and it will be healthy for me to lose a pound a week, tops. So to calculate the loss, that would be a pound a week for six months, four pounds a month that would be, four times six is twenty-four. Uh, twenty-four pounds? That's not gonna get me my job back, that's for sure. Maybe if I reverse those numbers I'd start inching toward the ballpark figure. Ballpark. Makes me think of Sabrett's. After this appointment, I could stop and get a Sabrett's hot dog from Joey Fabrizio, a vendor I love to visit when I'm near Times Square. That would make all of this stress go away, at least for a little while.

"And I think you might want to start giving some real thought to what's at the root of your overeating," the doctor is saying to me now.

"I don't overeat!" I insist, all evidence to the contrary.

"Clearly you have some need to feed, Mrs. Jennings. The sooner you figure out why, the better."

"I'm a food critic, Doctor Crenshaw. I eat for a living. I

have no choice in the matter!" I'm feeling a tad bit hysterical. Can't he see that I'm not some sort of overeater or whatever he thinks I am (that I'm obviously not)?

"Oh, sure!" He says, snapping his fingers in recollection and then pointing at me. "That's where I recognize you!" He rifles around in his trash bin and pulls out the now infamous headline. It's at least reassuring that yesterday's news becomes today's trash, so maybe hardly anybody even noticed it. "That's you, isn't it?" He smacks the picture, just like Mortie did yesterday. As if I needed a damned reminder.

There I am, in living, grainy color: my lips, half-wrapped around a cigar-shaped piece of baklava, looking as if I'm making love to my pastry. A veritable baklava blow-job, I realize now. Jesus, thank god the headline didn't read: THERE SHE BLOWS. I should be grateful for small favors. Besides which, that pastry was good, but it certainly wasn't orgasmic. If I could remember what that feeling even is at this point, it's been so long since William and I, er, since I had a baklava-like experience, I'll say.

"I think I'd better go now," I say. "Thanks for your great suggestions. I'll be sure to do them. All. Every last one of them." I flick my hand at him as if shooing away a particularly annoying insect. Thank goodness for high medical costs, insurance issues and malpractice, because no doctor can afford to stick around for longer than a few minutes anyhow, so the doctor, handsome or not, gets up, shakes my hand yet again, and skedaddles out of the room.

And I am left to shovel myself back into my Flexees and the rest of my ensemble and go forth and figure out how to diet, now that I have official confirmation of the need for such dramatic measures. And maybe I'll not get that Sabrett, after all.

Add Salt Water and Whip into a Frenzy

My wife is a light eater. As soon as it's light, she starts to eat.

–Henny Youngman

"YOU'RE back?"

I'm startled to see that William has arrived home without advance notice. Cognac barrels over to me and jumps up against my chest. It's probably a testament to my size that I can withstand a full-fledged pounce by a 100-pound Bernese mountain dog. But I also like to see this as an advantage to being a little bit larger: I've got staying power—nothing knocks me down easily. Cognac's tongue swipes a trail of beef-scented slobber across my cheek.

I'm loaded with grocery bags, a sure sign that something is up with me.

"Yeah. Weather was bad, so we decided to come back early," he says. "You stressed out about something?" He points at my bags, knowing as he does that this means cooking is on the horizon and that stress and cooking go hand-in-hand for me. He leans over and gives me a cursory peck on the saliva-free cheek. Not that I'd notice the cursory part of that, but I'd like to think that after being gone for a couple of days there might be an elevated level of enthusiasm with one's spouse. And I'd also like to think that the absentee spouse would be the one inclined to offer up said zeal. Just like Cognac has done. At least my pooch missed me. But I guess I'll need to be satisfied with a mere peck from my husband.

Hmmm…Maybe I'm feeling a little vulnerable, what with this huge life-rejection I've just suffered? Surely William is nothing but my ally. Right?

"What's new, babe?" He grabs a carrot from the fridge and

rinses it before taking a large chomp out of it.

I study his face for a minute to see if it betrays any knowledge of what is new with this babe (not to be confused with the squiggly-tailed Babe of pig fame). But it's a blank slate, as far as I can tell. It appears that William is ignorant to my news. I wonder if I can just pretend nothing's new. I mean, after all, it's not like he follows me around and knows what I do all day, right? And heck, that newspaper article? Lining bird cages and wrapping dead fish all over the city by now. Yesterday's news, my friend!

I begin to unpack my groceries, putting the heavy cream in the refrigerator, the whole chicken onto the cutting board, the basil in some water, and set aside the sun-dried tomatoes and thyme. I reach into the fridge for the eggs, and pull the flour out of the food pantry.

I rinse the bird, dry her off well, season the skin with my special blend of secret herbs and spices, wedge several large dollops of butter beneath her tender flesh, and pop her into a dutch oven pan then into the convection oven to roast.

"What's new?" I ponder, drumming my fingers across the cutting board. "Well? Let me see. I've become a cover model, it seems. An unwilling one, in fact. And I've learned that everyone is replaceable in their job, even if you're really, really good at it."

Then I set about making the pasta: mounding the flour, forming a small well, adding the eggs and massaging the ingredients with my fingers, gently marrying the two together bit by bit, eventually kneading the mass into one. As I press the heel of my hand into the ball of dough, I put a little extra oomph into each thrust: Take that! Mortie. Take that! Dr. Crenshaw. Take that! Crappy metabolism. Take that, Abbie, for letting yourself get so out of control and now having no damneding clue about how to get it together. Take that, stupid Abbie.

"I've met a new and extremely handsome doctor, like it or not, and amazingly enough, I've learned that I have a pretty face. Which apparently conflicts radically with the rest of me."

With that the waterworks are switched on, and a stream of tears descends from my eyes directly onto my ball of pasta dough, which can't be a good thing. I don't want to run the risk of imparting a bitter flavor into my fresh tagliatelle, so I tilt my head up and back, avoiding the food, but then the tears well up into my eyes, so instead I stand upright with firm posture, and they flow down either cheek and meet in a confluence at my chin(s), then trickle down my neck.

William looks a little confused, but nevertheless he walks over and puts his arms around me, collecting flour and tears on his pressed white button-down as he pulls my head against his chest.

"Why don't you take it from the top and tell me what this is all about, Abs, okay?" He strokes my hair gingerly with his fingers, which feels divine.

"I'm going to die—" I begin.

"You're dying?" he interrupts, shock in his voice.

"Oh, God no. I mean not now. Some day. But hopefully not till I'm old. No, I'm going to diet." And I begin to bawl again.

And then I deluge him in a hurricane of details: the restaurant and the food and the pies and the job and the no job and the doctor and the diets and by the way, how does roast chicken and fresh pasta with sun-dried tomatoes and basil in a cream sauce sound for an early dinner?

At which point he sort of pushes me back off of his chest, then, extending his arms, he presses his hands on either of my shoulders and looks me straight in the eyes. He repeatedly dabs away the tears with his thumb, which he keeps wiping across my apron. I sob a few times, interspersed with great heaving gasps for good measure.

"Honey, I thought you just said you were going to diet?"

"Well, yeah," I say.

"Homemade pasta? Heavy cream sauce? That sounds like a diet for a starving refugee who needs to beef up suddenly in order to be able to swim the Olympic 100-meter butterfly time trials in the morning."

I peer up at him like a student might look at a professor after having been caught cheating on an exam. My lower lip trembles, the floodgates poised to re-open.

"Well," I say, with no other ammunition in my artillery.

"Well?"

"Well, I was planning on having a smaller portion. And no seconds."

"No seconds. No doubt," he says as his face breaks out into a grin. He grabs the tip of my nose between his pointer and middle finger and tweaks with his thumb. "Silly Abbie, are you sure you want to do this diet? I think you're looking at this all wrong, honey. Let's flip this 'death sentence' on its head. This is a fabulous chance for you to re-think your life a little bit! Maybe now is the time for you to take a step back, enjoy a little down time. You and I could even take some time off to travel. Or make that baby we've talked about…"

He's bringing up the baby thing at a time like this? We haven't talked about that baby! He's talked about that baby. While I've busied myself with food prep or scrubbing the toilet or something equally escapist. It's not that I don't want a baby, but my God, I'm a busy woman! Although at the moment, nothing could be further from the truth. I'm practically a retiree. If I didn't yearn to keep my job so badly, and if I was a manageable size, now would be about the primest of times to pursue that biological mandate. Although what on earth would I do with a baby? That seems like quite an undertaking, if you ask me. And I don't mean undertaking like committing to making risotto, and trust me, once you get going with that, you're stuck with it—you can't leave the stove till it's done. No! A baby means you're tied up for the next, oh, eternity! How could I do my job that way? You think I'm recognizable now, showing up to a restaurant to review it in all of my fluffified glory? Well picture that, plus the baby weight I'd never shed, plus the baby! It stretches my imagination past the realm of possibility.

"William, I thought we'd agreed to not talk about any babies," I whisper, thinking my solemnity will lend an air of hush to the conversation. As in hush up!!!

"We're not getting any younger," he says. He's now got my head clasped between his hands and it's like his eureka moment, only there are no gold nuggets involved. I can't help but notice how well William has aged. He only has a slight sprinkling of salt in his hair, the color of which reminds me of fried rice. His face is wrinkle-free, but for laugh lines that only enhance his visage. And his physique, well, what can I say but that he's a hell of a lot better at keeping up with himself than I am, that's for sure. "Think about it! We don't need your income. Our savings will keep us living comfortably forever, sweetie. You know that! What are we doing here anyhow? In this crazy city, with too many people and too much traffic and too many things to keep us away from, from, from us. Maybe we go off and live in Italy, just like we used to dream about." He scruffs my head in that friendly I-got-your-back kind of way.

If this were a sitcom or TV drama, right now I'd be cuing the harp music, throwing us back to umpteen earlier conversations in the same vein. The ones where William wants to blow this Popsicle stand and I just can't seem to commit. I know it's not necessarily fair of me to avoid this topic forever but this is my career, and you only get one shot at the big leagues.

I remember when William started grumbling about city life. It took me by surprise, because we both loved living in Manhattan. It's the city that doesn't sleep—how could you not love it here?

"Abbie, I have to tell you, my days are numbered with this type of living," he'd said. "I'm tired of the grind. I'm tired of having to navigate through hordes of people just to get from point A to point B. I'm tired of having to walk five blocks before being able to successfully hail a cab. I'm tired of going to a restaurant and being charged the price of tenderloin for a pimped-up hamburger."

"But sweetie, I have to be here. This is the food capital of the entire nation. New York is the chicken part of the turducken. Smack dab in the center of it all. Without the chicken, you wouldn't have turducken. Without New York, you wouldn't have food!" Okay, so that might be a little histrionic. Of course there is food with or without New York. But maybe mere peasant food. Nothing trendy, experimental, downright heady in nature.

"What happened to that family we were going to have? What happened to 'Oh, William, I was so lonely as a child, I hated being stuck in the middle of my warring parents. I want to have lots of kids, a loud, happy household!' What happened to that?"

I hated to have my words thrown back in my face. But those words were spoken long before I had gained such traction as a professional foodie. Back then, William and I both loved food for food's sake. It was about simple goals. Simplistic goals. Goals that got surpassed by bigger goals. I can't understand why William didn't get that. Kids? That can wait. But the pinnacle of my career only comes around once. How could he begrudge me that?

"Earth to Abbie, come in Abbie," William has his hand over his mouth and is making crackling noises with his mouth to sound like the Space Shuttle commander talking to mission control.

I look over at him and realize that this isn't a sitcom or a Lifetime movie or even an HBO special. This is really stressful is what this is.

"What?" I'm not even sure what tack my argument has to take at this point so I'm hoping for a refresher on whatever my husband last said to me.

"This is the cosmos, calling out to you. Giving you a wake-up call, Abbie Jennings. Wake up and smell the husband. I am over this all—" he spreads his arms out to encompass everything here that must represent his life. "I want something more. Something more than materialism. Something more than sitting home alone yet again while you go off to sample the abundance. Something more than lonely weekends with my dog and not my wife. It's what I need, Abbie. And I hope you can find it in your heart to figure out how to share this with me."

With that William turns around, practically clicking his heels in his haste, and leaves the room. The medicine ball's been thrown back at me, right in my gut. And I've got to decide what one does with a nine-pound medicine ball, anyhow. In the meantime, I've lost my appetite for my yummy treat. I think I'll go curl up with a good cookbook instead.

ROASTED CHICKEN AND FRESH PASTA WITH SUN-DRIED TOMATOES AND BASIL IN A HEAVY CREAM SAUCE

You'll have to forgive me if I'm guesstimating on this recipe but I have found that throwing things all together without a lot of direction makes for a more satisfying outcome.

FOR ROAST CHICKEN:

1 3-4 pound chicken (I buy mine freshly-butchered from the farmer's market)

variety of seasonings: kosher salt, pepper, garlic powder, perhaps a little onion powder, a dash of cumin, a pinch of saffron—use your imagination

1 stick butter, sliced into 1-tbl. increments

1/3 c. white wine (for deglazing)

Preheat oven to 400°. Rinse bird under cold water, dry well with paper towels. Place bird on small rack in roasting pan. Blend together seasonings in a bowl and sprinkle generously over skin. Carefully lift skin and distribute pats of butter throughout between the skin and the meat.

Throw in the oven and cook till done, about 75 minutes (generally 20 minutes per pound). The legs will loosen on the chicken when it's done and the skin will be a glossy golden color.

When done, remove from oven, use tongs to place chicken on a plate or cutting board. Then put roasting pan on stove, with heat on high just to get pan hot, then splash about 1/3 c. white wine into the pan, turning heat down to medium, allowing the liquid to pull the delicious brown drippings. Turn off heat. You can save this and freeze it to use for gravy some time, or add to a chicken stock base, or even splash some of it into your cream sauce for flavoring.

FOR PASTA:

3-1/2 c. bread flour

pinch of salt

4 duck eggs at room temperature (from farmer's market)

3 yolks (from large chicken eggs, again fresh from farmer's market)
1 tbl. olive oil (optional)

I'm going to give you the food processor version to prepare this as it's quickest.

1. Put flour and salt in food processor, pulse to combine.
2. Whisk eggs, yolks and olive oil lightly and pour into machine while it is running.
3. Dough will begin to come together but not in a neat ball. If the moisture is correct, there will be a few dry bits on the bottom.
4. Test dough—add liquid or flour, if needed
5. Remove from machine and knead 5-7 minutes until silky smooth. It should be a bit tough to knead. When it gets harder to get the seam side of the dough to come together, then it is usually ready. The dough will be glossy. Wrap in plastic and rest at least 30 minutes.

When ready to roll flour, dust clean countertop with a couple of tablespoons of semolina flour. A wood surface works best for rolling pasta. Roll out the dough with a roller into palm-sized sections. Feed into pasta machine, starting on #1 and repeating all the way up till it's at the finest level. At that point, place pasta back onto floured counter, and slice with knife to tagliatelle-sized pieces. The pasta can be boiled immediately in lightly-salted water for about 4 minutes, or can be spread on cookie sheets and frozen, one layer at a time.

FOR SAUCE:

1 cup heavy cream
1/2 c. sun-dried tomatoes, packed in oil, drained, rinsed, patted dry, and sliced into thin strips
1/2 c. fresh basil, rinsed, and finely chopped
1 tsp. finely minced shallots
1 tbl. butter
splash of reduction sauce from drippings (optional)
kosher salt and pepper to taste

Melt butter on medium heat and sauté shallots until soft. Add sun-dried tomatoes, cooking for about 2 minutes. Add cream and bring to simmer, adding basil, seasonings and reduction sauce to taste. Serve over fresh pasta with sliced chicken.

Serves 4

Separate Fat from Meat with Tongs

Probably nothing in the world arouses more false hopes than the first four hours of a diet.

–Dan Bennett

THE thing about gyms is they really should be manned by overly-large ugly people. You know, the mainstream populace. I think it's an enormous disincentive to have God's chosen few, the beautiful people, working at health clubs. It's merely rubbing salt in the wound to the rest of us. To go to a gym and have to hold yourself up to the standards of physical perfection that work these places—especially in Manhattan, where every other woman is a supermodel—is really beyond the pale.

Only reason I'm even here is because, well, I went on the Internet last night and there just seemed to be an overwhelming amount of evidence pointing at exercise being an important component of weight loss. I'm thinking if I combine exercise and dieting I'll double my poundage down. Maybe then I can write my own weight loss journal: *Six Months to Thin—Diet and Exercise Your Way Into a New Body.*

Actually, I'm just joking. I know this is what you're supposed to do. But up until this very moment in time, me going to the gym would have be like Arnold Schwarzenegger tasting things in the kitchen at Jean Georges. Highly improbable at best.

For motivation, I downloaded Arnold's exercise tape from iTunes last night, and it was so bad it motivated me to go straight to the gym today instead of having to listen to him again. Only now that I'm here, I wish I were back home, just me, Arnold and the kitchen, where I could escape his drill sergeant commands and whip up something yummy and un-Schwarzeneggerish.

Right now, before me, is a man with biceps carved as ruggedly as the Grand Canyon, and bands of massive thigh muscles that course like rivulets down his legs. With a powerful barrel of a chest that I can assure you contains a healthily-beating heart void of blood pressure issues or fat-clogged arteries. And an instrument in his hand for which I could probably find about ten far better uses in the kitchen than its original intent. Its pincer-like tips look like they'd be great for grabbing something. Just not me. This man is actually trying to calibrate my percentage of body fat with the things. I'd so rather be grabbing a steamed lobster from the pot with them. A bowl of melted butter awaiting me, fresh corn on the cob, grilled to perfection. Maybe a simple baked potato on the side.

"If you'll just raise your shirt, I can fasten the calipers on here," he's saying, pointing at my waist. I've got news for this dude. I don't raise my shirt for just anybody. In fact, I don't raise my shirt for anybody, period. What's beneath my skillfully camouflaging outerwear is something no one should ever see. Hell, I don't even look at it.

"Mrs. Jennings?" Thor, the personal trainer (I think his real name is Mark, but he looks more Thor-ish to me) asks again. "Can you lift your shirt? Don't worry, it won't hurt at all."

Ha! It won't hurt, my ass! Of course it's going to hurt: my morale, my psyche, my appetite, my pride. Pain extends far beyond the physical, young man, I want to tell him. But of course I don't because I'm too ashamed to express my shame, quite frankly.

"Can't we just bypass this little step altogether? You can make a rough guesstimate, just jot it down on there and no one will be the wiser? Just between friends?"

I'm hoping that friends comment will tip the scales, so to speak, in my favor. But instead Thor calls over Jana, she of the quarter-bouncing abs, to do the honors. Jana grabs my shirt, lifts it up, clamps that puppy down on the largest layer of overlapping flesh, then on another and another, and jots down numbers on her chart.

"There, quick and painless," she says, slapping the calipers back into Thor's hand, who then gets to work on the rest of me: my biceps, triceps (which I didn't even know I had), thighs, calves. Even my back fat. Jesus Christ in a handbasket, must they see my back fat?

After a brief five-minute consultation between Thor and Jana in which eyebrows are knit enough to produce a sweater, I am beckoned forth by Thor, who has a plan of action. The man of action with the plan of action.

"You're going to need to start out slowly, Abbie," he says as I take a swig of my water bottle. I haven't even worked out yet and I'm thirsty. And hungry. A fresh croissant from Patisserie Paris would do my heart good right about now. Better yet, pain au chocolat. I wonder if they make that with Splenda somewhere. Splenda and carob. Pain au caroba, we'd call it. Oh, God, how can I ever diet? This is all just so unnatural!

"Your body isn't used to exercising, so you don't want to overdo it, which will leave you unable—or unwilling—to stick to your regimen. I'll work up a plan for you to allow you to alternate cardio machines and weights. Before you know it, you'll be running five miles a day."

I know this might be a little childish, but that last line elicits a spit-take out of me, and I spatter water on us both. Thor pretends it's nothing and continues.

"Have you thought about dieting at all?" Maybe this question is his revenge for that saliva/water shower.

Uh, no, but for the fact that I'm in such a hurry to lose weight that I feel like a *Supermarket Sweep* contestant. I've got six fleeting months, so I'd better maximize my efforts (and I haven't the slightest idea how!).

I shrug my shoulders and wince. I think that gets my message across.

"So here's the deal, dudette," Thor says, evidently having just dismounted a surfboard, what with the lingo.

Dudette. Reminds me of Creamettes—sponsors of *Let's Make a Deal.* Remember those contestants who would choose door number three, and instead of winning a wheelbarrow full of cash (sorry, that was door number one), they'd be stuck with a lifetime supply of Creamettes macaroni noodles? Even I would tire of homemade macaroni and cheese after a while. Although maybe instead of cheddar, throw in truffles and some gruyere, blend it with cream from that fabulous dairy in the Hudson River Valley that William and I detour to every so often, now there you have a real meal.

Thor taps me on my shoulder. I must have drifted off.

"For quicker weight loss? You're gonna want to ditch the carbs. Everything white. If it's white, it's blight, I like to say. Definitely go for the two-week flush of all carbs from your system. Then slowly reintroduce only complex carbohydrates: fruits, whole grains and legumes. Brown rice and such. Stick to tiny meals, five times a day. Avoid fats. But the bigger picture is figuring out why you eat the way you do, and retraining your brain. "

Jana, who's happening by and evidently eavesdropping in, gangs up on me next. "Think of it this way: you know how the snowmelt runs down a mountain, creating pathways for the water to follow? This is the same in your brain: your brain has been conditioned by the same information, the same feedback, for so many years, that it is the only path it knows: this 'need to eat and to eat hearty fattening foods.' So it's your choice: you can have neuro-pathways to the brain that speak to food and hunger and are conditioned to expect fattening foods, or those pathways can be reprogrammed to follow a different course. Does this make sense?"

Does this make sense? Well, sure. I'm a veritable mountain range of fat-dom. I've got a chocolate soufflé pathway slogging through my brain, evidently. Another brownie pathway, no doubt. Brownies on my brain, brownies on my hips, brownies in my gut. So much so that you could probably press my center to test for doneness (I'd rather you do that than stick a cake tester in me!).

"So what you need to do, Abbie," Thor interjects, "is figure out how these paths started, and then you can start working on changing their course. It's up to you to figure this out. I obviously can't be with you twenty four/seven to be sure you're following my instructions. So like it or not, you're on the self-guided tour. I'm here if you need advice, I'll even be here if you need to be talked out of sneaking donuts. And of course I'll make sure that your workouts when you're here maximize your weight loss goals. You with me then?"

Am I with him? Oy. With him in spirit but not in reality, maybe? But I have to be, dammit. I nod, just like I'd acquiesce if someone were about to feed me castor oil because it was good for me. Oh, and p.s.: I don't even eat donuts. Too plebian. Now if you said beignets, well, that's a whole different matter.

"Let's do it, Abster!" He high-fives me to seal the deal.

Over the next hour, Thor works me through the circuit of machines. His goal is to find things that I like to do, but that's pushing it for me. This isn't about like; it's about need. If I liked exercising, I'd have done that instead of loading up on desserts, obviously.

As I leave the gym—oh, wait, I'm told to call it a fitness center—I begin to ponder these "feed-me" paths in my brain. It doesn't take long for me to find the source of this snowmelt. It all goes back to my parents. My parents and Grandma Gigi.

My Grandma Gigi was larger than life. Large, physically, a veritable bear of a woman, Gigi provided great comfort to a girl trapped between battling parents. My mother was so obsessed with being thin—and ensuring that her daughter, too, remained thin—that she'd spank me if she caught me eating junk food. Three Chips Ahoy cookies would earn me a hairbrush spanking plus being locked in my bedroom for the night. Coupled with a shrill lecture about how I'd grow up to be as fat as my father's family if I didn't watch myself. Already she was calling me the Crisco Kid: fat in the can. This before I even had a fat can. Hell, if she were still alive now, she'd be calling me the damned Crisco factory.

You'd think after a while I would learn to shun junk food to avoid the punishment, but I was conflicted in a few ways. For one thing, I wanted to reject her cruelty, and so in some ways it forced me to dig my heels in and eat it just to spite her. And then there was the fact that I was getting seriously mixed messages.

Food was comfort and love when it came from my grandmother. It was discomfort and rage when associated with my mother. Throw in an absentee father who was—we found out later—too busy dispensing his love and concern to his other family to even bother interceding much with my mother, and you got one very confused girl who sought out love and rebellion with the very same weapon. Food as weapon sounds horrible, though, doesn't it?

But my father's stepmother, my Grandma Gigi, on the other hand, loved me enough for two parents. She lived in the other half of the brick duplex right next door to us and I often retreated to the comfort of her home immediately after school. There she introduced me to the joy of cooking, her kitchen enveloping me in its warmth as pies and roasts baked in the oven. It was in that room as a small child she would read me stories while we waited for treats to come out of the oven, and as I got older, I learned all that I could about baking and roasting and sauces and marinades by her side. I was probably the only six-year old on the block who not only knew what a velouté was, but could spell it. And make it.

Of course Gigi and I got to eat everything we made, which was like finally unwrapping that present that had been sitting beneath the Christmas tree for a week. I can't recall a meal that wasn't superlative, and I credit my grandma with imbuing in me a rich appreciation for food and for its gift of salvation. Because food did save me: it gave me an identity, kept me from being nothing more than that lonely girl who fell asleep with rolled tube socks secured against her ears to avoid hearing the arguments that invariably ended in the gasping sobs of my mother and the slamming of the front door as my father left, presumably to seek the solace of his better family.

Food was my happiness when I was growing up. How can food now betray me in such a grandiose manner?

GIGI'S APPLE CRISP

20 apples (preferably crisp, tart heirloom apples, like an Arkansas Black)

1-1/2 c. sugar

1 c. flour

1 c. old-fashioned oats

3 tsp. cinnamon

1 c. butter, softened

Preheat oven to 375°. Butter 13" X 9" baking pan.

Peel and quarter apples, keep from browning by setting aside in ice water till ready.

Blend together all other ingredients. Layer apples, crumble mixture, apples and top with thick layer of the crumbled mixture, patting it down. Bake for 40 minutes or until bubbly and golden.

Blend Wafer Well with Liquid

Me want cookie!

–Cookie Monster

WHITE is blight. White is blight. White is blight. My new mantra.

Do you know how much of what I eat is white? I think I've been on the monochrome diet for half my life, it's so white, white, white, white, white!!!! No, I'll be clever and call it the Nanook Diet. Because of the blizzard white-out conditions. All I can see to crave is white food, everywhere. South Beach Diet? No way, baby, I've been living the South Pole Diet. And loving it all the way. Bring on those Eskimo pies! Oh, but I can't. Because white is blight. White is blight. White is blight.

Thus my current dilemma. I'm at Saint Patrick's for Sunday services, listening to the sermon. Father Kerrigan is talking about sacrifice, about what we as humans must do to sacrifice for our God. And I can only focus on the food I'm sacrificing. It's been eight days now and all I can think about, morning, noon and night is my lack of white food. I need carbs. And in about seven minutes I have to decide if I'm supposed to give up the symbolic Christ because that communion wafer is calling my name. And I'm hungry. And dammit, I want my communion wafer! I love those things. It's always been one of the high points of church, the melty, bland but salty, slightly tangy but not, goodness of the things. Am I supposed to sacrifice my communion wafer for the greater good of all diets, simply because it's the wrong color? Or is the Higher Power picture more important. I'm not sure if I want to take my chances. Forty years from now (God-willing) I'm at the pearly gates and Saint Peter gives me a thumbs-down because I refused the sacrament because it contained carbohydrates?

"But it was my sacrifice," I'll insist to his menacing scowl. "Just like Jesus gave up all of those things for us men and for our salvation, remember that line? We say it every week at church, remember? So I figured since Father Kerrigan was talking about sacrifice, it was code, some secret message from God that I had to give up the communion wafer!"

And then I would tumble in a dizzying spiral, Hell-bound, all for not taking communion. I can't risk it.

The truth is, not only do I want my communion wafer (and I'm gonna have it, I'll show you, low carb!), but I want mine with a dollop of goat cheese topped with this fabulous homemade balsamic black pepper strawberry jam I put up last spring during strawberry season. That would be the best way to eat it, now that I think about it.

And since I'm on a roll, and it is Sunday, and Sunday is a day of rest, doesn't that mean I'm entitled to rest and relaxation? And rest and relaxation to me means fixing up a lovely Sunday supper. And I just thought of two things that are white that I can eat! Crabmeat and chicken. And I've got just the recipe.

I make a couple of stops on the way home from church to collect up the vital ingredients. When I get back William is downstairs in our unfinished basement tinkering with one of his motorcycles. My eyes scan the dimly-lit room with the battleship-gray floors and cinderblock walls. The room is so contrary to the type of space with which I like to surround myself, with no windows, feeling imprisoned all day. But to William this is his haven. He's working on his favorite bike, a 1968 baby blue Lambretta Lui, which he's nursed back to health after previous owner-abuse. He loves this motor scooter so much that I'm not sure which is William's top priority, his Lammy, me or Cognac. Or me on top of the Lammy with William. Nah, that would definitely not work well, at least not these days.

Judging by the way he's caressing the manifold, well, honestly, I wouldn't even know if the thing has a manifold. It just sounds like the right thing for him to be caressing. Far better than a womanfold, at any rate. God, he wouldn't caress some woman's manifold, would he? William looks up at me from over his goggles. I guess he was tinkering with something blinding, and felt the need for protective eye gear. Sometimes I feel badly that I don't share William's interest in hogs (and maybe it's presumptuous to call a scooter a hog). I know to him it's just as pleasurable as food is to me. Call me crazy, but give me a roasted pig in a spit any day over a hog in a Harley shop. Although actually, I've asked William to stay out of the Harley business, because I can't abide the noise of the things.

But his scooters are sort of fun. I prefer the hot pink Vespa he's got tucked away in the corner of his workshop. He bought it for me last year. But I never had the heart to tell him it's too small for me. So I've made every excuse in the book to avoid mounting the thing, unless I can rest some of my weight against the wall or something equally supportive while balanced atop it. I'm afraid the tires will pop on me. Now that would be embarrassing.

I know, I know. Isn't this all the more reason to lose weight? You avoid doing things with your husband because your weight gets in the way (better than it getting in the weigh). I'll tell you a little secret: I'd love to hop on that little pink Vespa and take off. Somewhere. Anywhere. I'd feel like Vespa Barbie, all sexy and blond (although I'm not blond, but maybe I'd dye my hair for the occasion). Of course I can't tell William that, because I'd then have to tell him the bigger truth: that the Vespa and I are inherently incompatible.

I was just thinking about something. How funny it would be for William and me to tool down the streets together in our baby blue and hot pink scooters! We'd look like a movable baby shower where you didn't know the sex of the baby-to-be! Of course this only serves to remind me of that gigantic diaper-clad hundred pound Baby Huey in the middle of my household. We've had no further discussions about our prior discussion. The one I refused to discuss.

"Whatcha doing?" I ask William, questioning the obvious.

"I'm having problems with this piston."

"Is it pistoning you off? Get it?"

William rolls his eyes—even though he's got goggles on, I can see it. But that's okay, because he often rolls his eyes at me. Usually in an affectionate way. But now, I'm not so sure.

"How was church?"

"Very church-like. The incense and candles smelled good. Shame they don't have a high-protein communion wafer yet. I bet they do in LA."

"Okay, then," he changes the subject, ignoring my wit. What've you got going for the rest of the day?"

"I thought about going to the gym but it is a day of rest and I thought I'd tinker around in the kitchen for awhile, see what I come up with." Cognac comes over and I scratch his ears and give him a big kiss on the forehead.

"Nothing white on the menu, right?" "Nope, nothing white. Wait, I lied. The chicken is white meat, and the crab is, of course white."

"Great. Let me know if you need me for anything."

"Toodle-oo!"

I wander off toward the kitchen, wondering about the dispassionate tone to that offer.

I set to work on my Sunday dinner masterpiece. First, rinsing the chicken breasts, patting them dry, and cubing into bite-sized pieces. I pick through the jumbo lump crabmeat, knowing that there will be plenty of crab shells despite the fact that I paid top dollar to avoid them.

Next I grate the cheeses with my food processor. What an invention! Saves me hours of work.

I heat up a couple of tablespoons of peanut oil in the wok, quickly stir-frying the chicken on high, then stir in chicken broth and a few other flavorings, then set them aside to assemble the ingredients in a baking dish.

Now comes the time-consuming work of building my phyllo feast. Phyllo dough, the gossamer of the food world, requires deft handling. Can't be too cold or too warm. Can't be exposed to air or it flakes to bits. And so I peel off one sheet at a time and spread it out on the counter, covering the roll with a damp towel, quickly brushing melted butter across it. I build layer upon layer and then pop it into the oven.

I light some romantic candles on the table and put Michael Bublé on the stereo for a little mood music. I've pulled out the fancy Villeroy and Boch china and the Baccarat crystal—seldom used relics acquired during our traveling days of yore. Because I am avoiding all things white, I use the burgundy tablecloth instead of the usual ecru linen one. And I've instead opened a bottle of a one of our favorite Brunellos. A little food critic rebellion of sorts. I hope it doesn't overpower a dish for which white wine would seem a natural, but I think with the strength of the gruyere cheese, we'll be okay. Plus, William prefers reds, and my goal really is to please him with this lovely dinner.

I ring the dinner bell, and William comes up from the basement and washes the grease off of his hands with pumice soap we keep in the task sink. He peels off his coveralls to reveal his blue jeans and a black t-shirt. He looks like a high-end grease monkey, with that contrasting banker/biker boy charm. I love that about him.

"Dinner smells great!" He smiles at me and I know all will be right with us.

We sit down and I cut into my "casserole" and I serve William a large portion. I dish out a helping of the token salad I threw in at the last minute, thinking a salad isn't such a bad idea for a dieter. The creamy poppy seed dressing and the caramelized walnuts probably offer a lot of protein as well.

He takes a bit of the entrée and his eyes grow wider with each chew.

"Honey, I thought you said you were avoiding everything white?"

I nod my head and take a bite, savoring the heavenly blending of ingredients that is melting on my tongue. "I am."

He takes his fork and begins to dissect his meal on the good china. "Let's see here…Chicken. White. Crabmeat. White. I know you said those were okay to be white. But what about all this gooey cheese?"

"Cheese is allowed in high-protein diets," I say, feeling a bit defensive, after all the effort that went into this meal.

"Isn't it awfully high in fat?"

"According to my sources, fat is fine as long as you're avoiding those carbs." I beam at him, assuring him—and me—that all is right.

"But I'm afraid your sources are Escoffier and Julia Child. Neither of whom met a pound of fat they couldn't put to good use somewhere."

I scrunch my face up and clench my fists, my food-related defensive reflexes suddenly on high alert.

He picks about with his fork some more. "And isn't this phyllo pastry white? And slathered with white butter? If I'm not mistaken, the main ingredient of phyllo is flour. White flour, to be exact."

I have to defend my honor! "Butter is yellow! And so is phyllo! Totally legal and in the books!"

William shakes his head. "Nice try. I'm not a chef, but I play one on TV." He smirks at me. He actually smirks at me! "I've seen you cook with this enough to know that phyllo dough starts out white. Virgin white. Pure as the driven snow white. It changes to a golden color once it's baked—thanks to the fattening butter slathered on it."

My face falls. My feast of salvation is rapidly devolving into a feast of an epiphany—I guess the epiphany is that my meal is an imposter! What sort of inquisition is this?

"Urgghhhh!" I shriek. "Why are you trying to ruin my perfect Sunday dinner by telling me how to eat? You're being just like Mortie. I've already got one boss in my life telling me I'm too fat. Are you joining in the Greek chorus of my detractors? I thought I could count on you, William. I never thought you'd be like my mother and choose to drag me down!"

I no sooner say that than know I've gone too far. Accusing William of being like my mother is like saying that Santa Claus steals toys from boys and girls. We both know that William is the least controlling, least critical spouse imaginable. He's perfectly happy with me as long as I'm perfectly happy with me. Which I am. Well, which I thought I was. Until I was called out on it. And it was pointed out by none other than my boss that I'm too fat to succeed in my job. I know I'm shooting the messenger here, but somehow I can't seem to help myself.

"Look, Abbie. I'll pretend you didn't just say that. Because we both know nothing could be further from the truth. I love you just the way you are, baby. I'm just trying to keep you on task. You say you want to keep your job?"

I shake my head yes.

"What, pray tell, do you have to do in order to keep your job?"

I mumble under my breath.

"I'm sorry, I couldn't hear you."

I mumble again.

"A little louder please."

"Okay fine," I holler. "Lose weight. And lots of it. Are you happy, William?" I start to cry.

"No, in fact, I'm not happy, Abbie. Not at all. First and foremost, I'm happy when you're happy. So if you're not happy, then neither am I. And aside from that, well, you know how I'd vote on this whole thing, anyhow. Yet you're not interested in that. So instead I'm going to try to protect what is in your best interest. You want to be Gotham's high-powered food critic? It comes with a quid pro quo."

"Fine! You want me to not eat? I'll not eat. I'll not eat so much that you won't be able to find me when I turn sideways. Is that good enough for you?" Perhaps I'm overreacting, but hunger does this to me. I'm beginning to realize why I fail at diets. They make me really surly. Poor William. And here he probably thinks it's hormones talking. If only.

"Look, I just need to clear my head. I'll be back later." With that I gather my plate and wine glass and begin to bus dishes into the kitchen. I continue this in silence till all the dishes are cleared. I pull out my disposable plastic storage containers and package up the entrée and the salad, throw in a couple of plastic plates and some utensils, then put them in an environmentally-friendly Whole Foods shopping bag. I whistle for Cognac, grab his leash, and we head out the door, leftovers in tow.

CHICKEN AND CRAB WITH CHEESE IN PHYLLO

1/2 lb. grated cheese (equal parts gruyere, mozzarella and fontina)

2-3 boneless chicken breasts, cubed

1/4 lb. lump crabmeat, picked thoroughly to remove extra shells

Stir fry chicken on high in 2 tbl. peanut oil. Drain chicken well, using liquid from stir frying chicken, mix with 2 chicken bouillon cubes, 3/4 c. water, and 3/4 c. half and half. Bring to boil and thicken slightly.

Blend chicken and crabmeat together.

Prepare phyllo: butter 3 sheets, one on top of the other (keeping the remaining phyllo covered with a damp towel so that it does not dry out), then fold in half.

Place layer of cheese in center of phyllo sheet. Add chicken and crab mixture.

Drizzle 1 tbl. chicken broth sauce over it, and fold at 90-degree angles into triangle.

Bake in 400° oven for about 20 minutes. Serve with remaining sauce.

Serves 4

Mix Two Parts Despair, One Part Rage, Serve with a Splash of Regret

What is food to one, is to others bitter poison.

–Lucretius

GEORGE is bent over a book, deeply engrossed, when I find him. It appears to be a library book, with the crinkly cellophane cover over the top of the thick tome.

"Anything interesting?" I ask him, disturbing his solitude.

He startles, looks up at me, and claps his hands with glee.

"I haven't seen you in days!" he says. "My stomach's been rumbling." He rubs his belly for emphasis. He jiggles his shopping cart out of the way to make room for me on the bench.

I place the bag in front of him and begin to take out the containers, handing him a plate and a napkin and utensils. He tucks a napkin into his shirt, which strikes me as funny, considering his clothes aren't exactly dry cleaner-fresh to begin with. Although come to think of it his clothes look far cleaner than most homeless guys I see wandering the streets—they're not exactly soiled. I wonder how he keeps himself so clean without benefit of a washer/dryer.

"Whatcha reading?" I ask him. I know that George has unexpectedly refined taste in literature and I'm often surprised at his book choices. Two weeks ago he was reading War and Peace. He holds up the book and I see the title.

"*The Passionate Marriage: Keeping Love and Intimacy Alive in Committed Relationships*," I read aloud. I smack my lips aloud, pondering the title. "Interesting light reading for a Sunday evening. Any reason in particular you chose that?"

"Our therapist assigned it to us," he says as he dips into the dinner.

"Your therapist?" I ask, incredulous. "Yours and whose?"

"My wife's. Has me going to some new guy now. He thinks this book will help."

As I watch George greedily delve into my pastry-crusted supper, I'm taken aback that a man who takes freebie meals off of virtual strangers on the streets of Manhattan actually has a wife and a therapist.

"You see a therapist?" I ask. "You're married?"

He nods his head. "Yep. Thirty-five years this year."

"If you're married, does this mean you have children, too?"

Again he nods. "Four of 'em. Jenna's married, 'sgot two kids. Tamara's separated from her husband—we hope they can work things out. Josh is working down on Wall Street, and Tobin just finished up at Harvard Business School."

My eyes are so bug-eyed open I have to squint them back into normal shape. "You have family? Nearby?"

"Oh, sure. Everybody's in the area now that T's back here working with Morgan Stanley. Sally, my wife, she's up in Pound Ridge."

"Pound Ridge? New York?" I cannot believe this homeless man before me, the man I deliver gourmet leftovers to, hails from one of the most elite communities in the tri-state area. Pound Ridge is practically Martha Stewart territory.

"Yeah, sure, you've heard of it?"

"Of course, my husband loves to ride his motorcycles up that way. It's where we pick apples each fall. It's so gorgeous up there, especially when the leaves change."

"Indeed." George takes a bite of the chicken and crab and smiles a satisfied smile. "Mind if I ask what restaurant you got this from? Damned good stuff."

I blush. "Chez Abbie," I joke.

"Oh yeah? New place? I haven't heard anything about it."

Until a few minutes ago that would not have surprised me. But now that I know he hails from the upper crust, all bets are off.

"I made it, George. It's just a little something I whipped up at home. Wasn't exactly what my husband wanted tonight, so I figured you might enjoy it instead."

"Abbie, you've missed your calling. This is top-notch cuisine."

"It's nothing, really. But thank you for the compliment."

It's silent for a few minutes.

"It's none of my business, but do you mind telling me why you're here—" I spread my arms out everywhere, "And not there? I mean, Manhattan's lovely and all, but really. I wouldn't kick Pound Ridge outta bed for eating crackers."

George laughs, then shakes his head. "It's complicated."

I look at my watch. "Hey, I've got time. All the time in the world, in fact." Tomorrow's the first day in my new job, and I'm in no rush to get going on that. Plus I'm not too jazzed about returning home to William, what with my starvation-induced spat and all. Maybe I should pull up my own copy of the Sunday Sentinel and sleep here tonight, in fact. Though it might get chilly, even with a blanket of newsprint.

"I had it all," he says, taking a bite of salad then closing his eyes as a sublime look spreads across his face.

"You like the dressing? My own recipe," I tell him.

He nods his head. "It's got something different in it, can't quite put my finger on it."

"Orange juice. Tiniest pinch of saffron."

"Clever. Nice touch. That's what I like about you, Abbie. You march to the beat of your own drummer."

Wonder if William would agree with that. Maybe that's true, I'm listening to the beat of my drummer, not ours. If one can extrapolate from salad dressing to bigger picture situations like career choices and child-spawning options. And dieting.

"We lived the life everyone aspires to. The kids, the dogs, the girls had horses. Country club memberships. A household staff. Vacation spot on Mustique."

He has a domestic staff? He's eating my food as if he's desperate for nourishment. Which would've made sense but for this revelation that is spilling out before me.

"Mustique? Where Princess Margaret used to go?"

"Yep," he says between mouthfuls. "Mick Jagger, too."

"Mick? Scrawny in swim trunks?" Inquiring minds want to know.

"Scrawnier still in none."

I burst out laughing. Somehow can't quite imagine Mick Jagger naked in the surf. Or perhaps I choose not to.

"Sounds like a perfect life. What happened?" "I don't know if something went wrong or if I saw the light," he says. "It started with the tennis pro on the island. Javier."

"With your wife?"

He looks at me, surprised. "No, no, no. Not that! Not at all. It was my daughter, Tamara."

"Forgive me for my confusion but how did you go from a tennis pro hooking up with your daughter to living on a park bench?"

He sighs. "It's hard to say, really. I think it made me take stock."

I offer him my bottle of water I'd tucked into my purse. He takes a swig.

"It made it all seem wrong. It no longer made sense. I just realized I'd been working my ass off for what? So that my children could live this indulged life and my wife never bothered to talk to me and I realized one day when I came home from work that the only creature in the house that gave a shit about me was the dog. And then only because it was her dinnertime and she was waiting for me to feed her. So I called everyone together. Handed a file this thick with all the necessary paperwork to Sally—" he holds his hands about six inches apart to demonstrate. "It had information on bank accounts and insurance and accountants and lawyers, the usual stuff. And I said I was taking a hiatus from our lives. I needed to re-think things a bit."

Jesus, what is with this re-thinking stuff? If this is what re-thinking looks like, I'm perfectly happy with my life and in absolutely no mood to re-think a thing.

"So how long have you been here?"

"Oh, two years, give or take."

"Do you mind me asking why you didn't choose somewhere more user-friendly to be homeless, like, say, Hawaii? I mean Hawaii would be much warmer. And it seems like such a friendly place. New York? Sure, we're all as nice as can be, but really. Enough is enough. Then again, Paris would be lovely, too. I bet you'd get some wonderful leftovers there. But all the merde would be enough to keep me from choosing there."

"Yeah, I thought about going someplace warmer. But my wife persuaded me to stick a little closer to home. And don't go saying I'm like a kid who runs away down the block."

"I wouldn't dream of it." It's like he was dipping his toe in the ocean of escape, but not quite ready to swim too far off-shore. "So are you planning on staying here forever?" "It's hard to say. Sally's been forcing me to meet with a shrink uptown. Says she's gonna leave me if I don't."

"You show up there with your cart?"

He nods. "Took a while to convince the doorman to let me in. Now he greets me with an open door."

"What's it going to take for you to go back to your old life? Will you have a job to return to?"

"I'm lucky. I never have to work another day in my life. I made buckets of cash, and invested well. Sally will never have to worry for a day in her life either."

"But don't you think she's had to worry a lot—about you?"

He looks at me, almost mystified.

"Huh. She's got her life. Her friends, the grandkids. She golfs every Thursday and plays Mahjong with the ladies in the neighborhood. She doesn't need me."

"I don't know about that. Don't you think she'd like to share her life with you?"

"You got any dessert?" he interrupts me.

I shake my head no. "Sorry. I'm dieting."

"And this is your diet food?"

What is this—a conspiracy? Did Mortie get a hold of him?

"I only had a small portion." Oh, God. Who am I kidding? Small portion my ass. I think the only one getting small portions is my husband—small portions of me, that is.

I look at my watch. "I'd better get going, George. My husband'll be wondering where I am. Let me know how the book goes."

"Good luck on the diet, Abbie."

"Thanks. I need all the help I can get."

ABBIE'S ANAL RETENTIVE SALAD

I actually love salads, but somehow once I've gone to all the trouble to make them, I've lost interest in eating them. I'm very exacting in pursuit of the perfect salad, so I can assure you that you'll love my salad, even if I don't:

Ideally the ingredients used in a fresh salad should be local and in-season. Obviously this is not always possible, so in that case, go for organic high quality produce when possible.

Mixed greens, including arugula, butter lettuce, maybe some baby romaine and other tender baby lettuces

3-4 radishes, finely grated on a culinary microplane

Fresh baby carrots, thinly sliced in rounds (I especially love maroon carrots because their gorgeous crimson color offset by the carrot's orange insides is so beautiful when sliced)

Fresh bell peppers, in a medley of colors, depending upon what's available in-season (I love purple ones in the early summer), diced. Slice three rings (in mix of colors) and set aside for garnish

Cucumber

Tomatoes—I'm sure you know that summer heirlooms are my preference, however if not available, I'd suggest going for a handful of grape tomatoes

Broccoli, in tiny florettes

Cauliflower, in tiny florettes

Toss all of the above together, and then add any of the following:

Broken bits of crostini, for fabulous taste/texture

Smoked chicken—I often throw a couple of chicken breasts into a smoker—and you can find stovetop ones that work wonderfully—for an hour, and then use the chicken for add-ons

in salads, or in chicken salad)
Caramelized walnuts
Marcona almonds
Dried sour cherries
Dried cranberries
Fresh blueberries
Crumbled goat cheese
Breaded sautéed goat cheese
Shaved slices of parmigiano reggiano

DRESSING:

There are many variations you can choose for this, I'll include options. I'm a guesstimator with amounts, so will give you rough ideas of them:

About 1/2 c. canola oil (can use olive oil)
1/4 c. red wine vinegar (can also use sherry vinegar, raspberry vinegar)
1/2 clove crushed garlic
splash of white wine
1 tsp. Dijon mustard
pinch sugar
1/4 tsp. each of basil, oregano and marjoram
dash each of herb pepper blend and seasoned sea salt from Sunny Caribbee spice company (www.sunnycaribbee.com)
pinch of salt
two twists of pepper mill

Mix together, shake well. Now do you see why this is an anal retentive salad?

Stir in Abstinence, Reduce Calories by Half

A waist is a terrible thing to mind.

–Tom Wilson

WILLIAM'S sound asleep by the time I return home. In the morning he's gone before I get up.

Today I shun my coffee shop routine, opting instead for an early morning workout before I have to show up at the office for the first time since the Great Debacle. This should be rich. So rich that I'll gladly divert to the gym just to avoid it that much longer.

Thor is there, waiting to put me through my assigned chores. I haven't felt this much dread since I took trigonometry in high school—it's like I haven't done the homework, don't understand the questions and won't be able to answer a thing when the teacher calls on me.

"How goes the diet, Abster?" It appears he's hung this moniker on me that I can't seem to shake. Though I'm getting used to it. Abster. Sounds like something they'd sell on a late-night infomercial to help strengthen your core. I need something better than that. Like say, the Resolvster, to help strengthen my resolve. Otherwise what am I gonna do??? I haven't got one iota of willpower in me.

"Diet? Somebody say something about a diet?" I crack a smile, and Thor smiles back at me.

"Not so good, huh?"

I roll my eyes. "That's being generous. If it's any consolation, I'm really good at eating. I mean really good at eating. If there were an Olympic category for that, I'd be a gold medal contender. But the not eating? It goes against my grain. Against my very core—the core that's not exactly strengthening, by the way. I hate it."

Thor comes closer, puts his hand on my shoulder, drawing me into his confidence. "I think it's time you stepped back and decided why you're doing this, Abbie. Are you doing this for you, or are you doing it for someone else? Because quite frankly, unless you want to do something about your situation, nothing's going to change. It's all up here." He taps my head with his pointer finger. "Until you're reconciled in your mind about all of this, it's not worth your efforts. You call the shots, Abster. And you need to do this for you. Your body is a temple, so treat it with respect."

Christ, if my body is a temple, it must be in honor of Bacchus, god of wine (and debauchery, but I wouldn't necessarily put myself out on that limb). Or perhaps the Fallen Temple of the White Goddess—yes, that's it! That's me! White is blight. White is blight.

I sigh. I think I've sighed more in the past week than I have in my entire adult life. "I know you're right, Th—, er, Mark. Intellectually, I understand this completely. Emotionally? That's another thing altogether. I'm tied up with food so badly it's as if I'm married to it."

"In that case, d'ya ever think maybe it's a toxic relationship? Maybe you two need a divorce? Or at least some serious couples counseling?"

I can't help but laugh at him. I picture a cartoon image of me at a shrink's office with a plate of pâté en croûte, a good old-fashioned rump roast, and a large serving of tarte tatin (à la mode) on the couch next to me, all of us turning a cold shoulder, our body language conveying our mistrust of one another.

Thor's not such a bad guy after all. Despite those calipers. I know he's looking out for my best interest. Which means I'd better get working. We set about with my routine, and I hit a roadblock after about ten minutes the treadmill. You see, one of the benefits I can see to working out is I get to wear sweats. Sweats are good, because they hide a lot of flaws. They don't look particularly attractive, but function over form or whatever that saying is. The only problem is, once I start to sweat, then my sweats are cruel captors, trapping me in a terrarium of heat and humidity. I think I could actually measure the heat index inside these puppies. But I don't dare disrobe down to something lighter (and shorter) because no one, but no one, should be subjected to the sight of the likes of my enormous white legs and wobbly arms in the flesh. So I suffer through in overheated silence, gushing sweat into my eyeballs, ready to faint. Remind me again why people do this to themselves voluntarily?

After my workout I shower and dress, feeling quite obese next to the host of slender, fit, naked women getting ready for work alongside me. The club-issue towels actually wrap around their bodies and then some. For me it's as if I'm trying wrapping myself in a handkerchief.

I just can't see how I could ever look like these women—so why try? Why try? I'll tell you why. Because you won't keep the best job of your career if you don't, that's why. I swear I feel like I'm in a Bugs Bunny cartoon, with the angel bunny on one shoulder exhorting exemplary behavior while the devil bunny on the other shoulder is encouraging me to get my wild on. I finally decide to tell them both to shut up and leave me alone, then flick them each off my shoulders as if there's a bit of dandruff there. Time for my day of reckoning to begin.

I choose to walk the seven blocks to work: a sure sign that I'm in no hurry to get there. Normally the idea of trudging that far when there are taxis that can get me there quicker just doesn't even cross my mind. But the sooner I get there, the soon I'm going to have to face the firing squad: colleagues who will be snickering behind my back, with my demotion front and center for me to contemplate. And that conniving double-crosser Barry Newman who will gloat himself into a coma, no doubt, at my very presence. We can only hope, because at least in a coma they'd be forced to replace him with another—better—food critic. Me.

The walk turns out to be downright pleasant. I love springtime in Manhattan—everything seems especially alive and vital. People are practically smiling. There's a sense of promise in the air.

But then the promise of things to come is squeezed out by the reality of the present: the motion of my ample hips as I walk is shoving my belt right on up beneath my boobs. I don't know why I even wear a belt—it's not as if I have loose pants to hold up. It's only there as a trompe l'oeil of sorts—anything that tricks the eye away from my misshapen self. I've become quite skillful at this over the years. I wonder if I'd devoted such time to ensuring that I not have to hide my figure, maybe it would have been time better spent. But it's such hard time spent. I don't know that I've got it in me.

Today Julio is back to his usual wave and go, no great big greeting. That's okay. I'm not in the mood for small talk, anyway. As people climb into the elevator I feign a search for some elusive necessity in my purse; the only necessity really is to avoid eye contact. The longer I wait till this dies down, the less I'll have to confront it.

The elevator door pings on my floor and I look both ways before getting off, hoping to avoid people. Too late.

"Abbie! We've missed you! Where've you been?" Barry, the dirty dog, accosts me with a disingenuous hug. "Look here, I brought a surprise for you, just in case you showed up this morning!" He holds out the telltale bakery bag. Even the damned bag is white!

A half dozen zucchini-chocolate chip muffins, each one the size of a boxer's fist, from the Muffin Top. My hands-down favorite muffin shop. For a minute I forget myself and start to reach into the bag to eat one of the things. I've got the paper peeled and the muffin so close to my lips I can taste it through the aroma alone. It's still warm. But then I toss it back into the bag. How could I bite on the bait that easily? Am I that predictable? I'm almost ashamed of myself. Although zucchini muffins aren't white, and they do have vegetables in them…

I brandish a weak smile, the kind of smile that might arise when you find out your boyfriend just got engaged, to another woman. "Gee, thanks. So thoughtful of you Barry. I think I'll wait till later."

I spin on my heels the other direction and head toward my office, marching in and turning to close the door. Until I realize that my office is not my office. It's been commandeered by none other than Barry of the betraying muffins. He has a poster of Corks from Around the World on one wall, and autographed photographs of Kylie Minogue, an Abba tribute band, and the Phantom of the Opera on another wall. Is this guy for real?

I storm into Mortie's office unannounced. "I lose my prestigious job and I lose my office? All in one fell swoop?" I ask him. "Maybe I should just don a hairshirt and self-flagellate while I'm at it. You got a whip handy?"

Mortie holds his hands up in self-defense. "It wasn't my idea, Abbie."

"Then whose was it?"

"Barry's," he says.

"He can just strip my office bare because he deems it appropriate?"

"Well, you had vital things in there that he needed."

"Vital things? I'll show him what I can do with his vital things. Name one thing he needed from my office."

"The refrigerator, for starters."

"Why didn't you just put one in his cubicle? Or take it out of mine and put it in his?"

"You know his cubicle was too small for that. Plus you had the view. Barry said he did his best writing looking out the window. I figured you weren't going to need that so much, only being in part-time. At least for the time being."

"I just wish someone had warned me when I took the job that I was being employed by Pontius Pilate. At least now I know who I can trust around here." I storm out of his office, a tempest in stretch nylon I am. I navigate my way through a cluster of colleagues, all exchanging niceties with one another, discussing their exciting weekends. A couple of people say hello to me but I dodge them for the most part, wend my way to the far corner of the office and find my new office: a cubicle between the gal who writes movie reviews and one who writes obituaries.

I sit down to my new (old) desk, and sift through the stack of mail that has gathered since last week. There is a noticeable absence of invitations, announcements of restaurant openings, and any other hint of my former stature. Obviously Barry has pillaged my inbox along with every other aspect of my professional life. All this time he fed me like a fatted calf. While I stood there with mouth wide opened. Why I oughtta…

My gaze is drawn to an envelope with familiar looking handwriting on it. The scrawl looks like something they teach you in med school, it's that illegible. But I do recognize the name on the front: Abigail Louise Cartwright Jennings. Jennings in parentheses, oddly.

I open the letter to find this:

Dear Abbie,

Get it? Dear Abbie. Like the famous newspaper column?

I know, you're not laughing right now. I know you're not, because even after all these years, I know my Muffin. You probably don't believe it, but I do. After everything that's come between us, even.

Muffin. I flinch at that reference.

I saw you in the Post the other day. Usually I go straight to the sports, then Page Six. But when I saw that face smack on the cover, hot damn, I knew it was you. It was a no-brainer. I didn't even know your last name—you got married?—but I could tell. I saw your mother and me in your face.

I guess life's gotten ahead of us, hasn't it? I had a stroke a few years back and can't move like I could. Now they tell me my ticker's ticking down. Nothing much for me to do each day other than read the obituaries in the local paper and maybe watch a few ball games on TV. I know it's too late to make amends. I don't even want your forgiveness—I don't deserve it. But I do owe you some explanations. I've got some things to say that I think you should hear. I beg of you, please indulge an old man his dying request.

He proceeds to give me a phone number at the nursing home he's at in Jersey. As if I'm going to go visit him. Give a dying man a chance to alleviate his guilt. As if. My father, the commodian. He should be flushed. I forgot that he had a really corny sense of humor at times. He didn't know I was married? So what. Would he have even cared? Historically his track record would prove that not to be the case. He says we haven't seen each other in too many years to even recall? Well, I can recall, to the precise hour.

I was eleven years old. It was 9:31 p.m. My chocolate pound cake, which I was baking from scratch, was due to come out of the oven in eleven minutes. The perfume of warm chocolate was at that point wafting throughout the kitchen, where I sat at the pink speckled formica tabletop working on my history homework. I got up to start fixing the penuche frosting, had the butter melting on the stove in one pan, the milk heating up in another. I added the brown sugar to the butter, stirring till it boiled, then let it thicken for a minute.

Upstairs the arguing had commenced. Tonight was worse than previous nights—I could tell that things were being thrown. The sound of heavy objects hitting the walls reverberated downstairs to the kitchen. I began to hum to myself. When that didn't work, I started to read aloud my recipe, over and over again, louder and louder to block out the sounds from above.

Something shattered, I don't know what. I heard heavy footsteps on the staircase. My father pushed open the kitchen door—it was the type of door that swung open on a hinge and closed behind itself, like at a wild west saloon. Which was probably fitting, because this sounded like the gunfight at the O.K. Corral. My father didn't say a word, but he was breathing heavily, as if he'd just run a couple of miles. His hand was bleeding in about five different places. He walked over to the kitchen sink, turned on the water, and ran it over his the wounds. I could see the overhead light refracting in the shards of glass sticking out of his palm.

"You making a cake, Muffin?"

My dad called me this affectionate nickname, Muffin, just like that really sweet dad on Father Knows Best used to call his daughter Kitten. It always made me feel special. About the only thing that did, though.

The irony does not escape me that his nickname for me was food-related. Christ, my parents should've just named me Betty Crocker, or Little Debby, and cemented my fate early on.

I couldn't bring myself to say anything, so I just nodded my head up and down. A mute bobble-head doll.

"Smells great. Mind if I try a swipe of this?"

With that he scooped his finger, blood dripping from his hand, into the mixture I had on the stove, his blood blending with the caramelizing brown sugar.

"You sure can cook, Muffin. Just like your Gigi."

He leaned over me from behind and planted a short kiss on the top of my head. He grabbed the dishtowel out of my hands, pressing it up against his bleeding palm.

"Look, Muffin—" he started to say. But then he didn't say anything more. He just turned me around and stared at me for a long couple of seconds.

"I've gotta go. You'll be okay, won't ya?"

I didn't have a chance to answer. He was gone, lickety split.

I took the cake out of the oven and let it cool to the backdrop of my mother's loud sobs upstairs. When she finally came down I was spreading the penuche frosting across the top of the cake in delicate swirls. I could tell by the disapproving look on her puffy face that my cake would not last long intact in her kitchen. So I took the heavy glass lid of the cake pedestal and covered the cake with it. Then I walked out the front door and took my masterpiece to my grandma.

She came to the door in her housecoat and curlers, her short gray hair barely wrapping around the rods.

"That's a beautiful cake you made there, Abbie. You should be proud of it."

I set the cake down, hugged my grandmother, and finally allowed myself to cry.

To this day, I've never made another chocolate pound cake, so I haven't got a recipe to share with you. I do, however, have a yummy dessert that I think you'll enjoy just as much.

ÉCLAIR DESSERT

Line 13" X 9" pan with graham crackers.

FOR FILLING:

3 c. milk (whole, of course, no skim here, thank you)

2 boxes of French vanilla instant pudding

Beat those together, let set for 5 minutes, then fold in one 9-oz. container Cool Whip

Pour mix on top of crackers. Top with another layer of graham crackers.

FOR TOPPING:

Melt together:

3 squares (3 oz.) of semi-sweet chocolate

1-1/2 c. powdered sugar

3 tbl. milk

3 tbl. butter

Pour on top of graham cracker crust and chill.

Sear Ego in Reality, Simmer till Tender

I've been on a diet for two weeks and all I've lost is two weeks.

–Totie Fields

GOD, I need to get off the maudlin-mobile here and get cracking on my column or I'll never get out of this place, and right now, I need to get away from all reminders of my life upheaval.

I've been wrestling with how to handle this "food" column. I mean, I already wrote about food in my first incarnation at the Sentinel. Maybe I should take readers along on my current journey since they followed me on my food journey as well. Do people want to read about my chubetto woes? Will this merely reinforce my standing as now a fat person rather than a highly-respected food writer? Do I want to put my raw emotions out there for public consumption? And why can they consume yet now I'm not allowed to consume (unless I want to stay underemployed).

The more I think about it, the more I think my readers deserve to understand not only me, fat or not, but anyone like me. To know that we're far more than the superficial exterior they see and then stop at. Surprisingly, the words flow like marinara from a gravy boat once I start typing.

Are You An "Eat to Live", or a "Live to Eat"?

Or:

Can You Just Be an "Eat to Eat"?

To many people food is just a functional part of daily living. Something they need, but don't give much credit to. Like toilet paper. Although I guess technically you don't need toilet paper, but you know what I mean. These people are known as ectomorphs: by definition, tall with long lean limbs. My slender friend Jess is an ectomorph.

But then to others—me included—food is Food, with a capital "F." It's so much more than sustenance; it's a lifestyle. It's indulgence. It's soul-nurturing. It's gratifying. It's life.

We're called endomorphs. I can remember that because the prefix "end," reminds me that endomorphs tend to have big rear-ends.

Do you know the official definition of an endomorph? Somebody whose body has a stocky build and a prominent abdomen. God, that sucks.

I started a diet recently, and so food has weighed heavily (excuse the pun) on my mind lately. I've been pondering how different people view food and how that affects how they look.

Not long ago, I offered to send some pumpkin muffins home with a co-worker. Cindy, his beautiful and slender ectomorph-of-a-wife hadn't been feeling well, so I thought maybe the treat would cheer her up.

"Are you kidding me?" he asked, eyes wide with incredulity.

"Do you know what Cindy sees when she sees a pumpkin muffin?" he pointed accusingly at the perpetrators, the warm umber-colored delectable little breakfast treats sitting innocently on the plate under a light dusting of powdered sugar.

"She sees four hundred and forty calories, fifty carbs, fifteen grams of fat, arteries hardening, a bloated stomach, and basic all-around misery," he joked.

Whoa. All that wretched desolation in a sweet little innocent food offering?

Now I will grant you this: Cindy looks damn good in clothes. She's got a body fat index of about minus fifty. She's probably never in her life wrestled with what to wear before going out, searching for the outfit that will best hide her figure and that she can successfully zipper up. But then again, maybe Cindy's missing out when it comes to the joys of food.

When I look at a pumpkin muffin, I see the brilliant orange

glow of a sugar maple in its full autumnal glory. I see the crisp blue sky of October, so clear and restorative and reassuring. I see hayrides, and I feel Halloween just around the corner, kids dressed up in homemade costumes, bobbing for apples and awaiting trick or treat. I think of children dressed as Pilgrims in a pre-school parade, or a Thanksgiving feast, the bounty of harvest foods burdening a table with its goodness. I picture pumpkins at a farmer's market, piled happy and high, awaiting a new home where children will carve them into scary faces or mothers will bake them into a pie or stew.

Yeah, somewhere in my guilt-ridden soul, I know that the pumpkin muffin is The Enemy, that for a grown-up it's off-limits to see joy in it. But it saddens me that I even have to view it that way.

Perhaps this is how we view food in a society that has too much. Food becomes wretched excess. Because in another society—say, in sub-Saharan Africa, where food is often a luxury—a pumpkin muffin would be treasured. Maybe we are a society of spoiled, overindulged, overfed hedonists-gone-awry. And isn't that just a little bit sad?

Now that I have started this diet, I suppose I, too, will have to view those pumpkin muffins with a level of hostility. For now, they are Enemy Number One. But I will miss the sensory pleasure of such calorie-laden luxuries, and will be counting the minutes until I can again contemplate indulging in these simple joys without remorse.

I sit back at my desk and read over my words. Wow. A week ago I'd not have imagined what I could write about in this column that would do justice to my readers, but now it all comes pouring out of me in a pique of fat-girl angst. I read and re-read the thing, wondering if I am bold—or crazy—enough to splay myself out there on the slaughtering block of public opinion when it comes to food. I mean, girls like me aren't so inclined to publicize much about ourselves that relates to body size and caloric consumption. True as it is that while I might only eat the same amount of food that Jess does, I retain it while she burns it, and there's just no sense in making this argument public.

Plus, I won't deny that I'm dueling with a tricky carving knife, one side of whose blade is a lack of willpower, and the other an overwhelming appreciation of food. That combined with poor metabolism and a possible connection with abandonment issues and food filling a void in my life have helped me to land in this swamp of excess in which I'm mired.

Normally I find—at least on a face-to-face basis—that I instinctually try to deflect any potential fatso insults by being too upfront about it voluntarily. I tend to readily offer up the notion that I'm oversized to most anyone willing to listen. Mind you, I'm not fishing for a complement, not looking for someone to say, "Oh, no, Abbie, you're not fat." Instead, I am trying to head off the potential insult before it can be used as a tool against me. I mean, if I come right out and say, "Hey, I know I'm fat," it certainly defuses the artillery of cruel words before they're launched at me.

But saying this to an intimate audience of a few is one thing. Admitting this to a potential readership of tens of thousands is another. I won't be merely admitting I'm in need of a serious diet; I'll be officially branding myself as fat. Making myself the poster child of chubby. Dangerous territory, I will say.

I ponder whether to just hit the send button and forward this onto my editor, or instead hit delete, and start anew, maybe write about something universal like the seasonal quest for the finest asparagus. But then, with the timing of divine intervention, my eyeglasses fall off my face, landing hard enough on the return key to jettison my column and its inherent acknowledgment of my own shortcomings through cyberspace, before I have a chance to make up my own mind.

ABBIE'S FAVORITE (Low-diet!) PUMPKIN BREAD

4 c. flour
2/3 tsp. baking powder
2-1/4 tsp. baking soda
1-1/2 tsp. salt
1 tsp. cinnamon
1 tsp. cloves
1/2 tsp. ginger
1/2 tsp. allspice
3/4 c. cold water
5 eggs
3-1/2 c. sugar
3 c. pumpkin
1-1/3 c. oil

Grease three loaf pans with plain Crisco shortening.

Sift dry ingredients together.

In separate bowl, beat eggs well. Add sugar, beat well. Add pumpkin, oil, water, beat well on low speed to incorporate. Add dry ingredients, mix well.

Fill pans 2/3 full.

Bake at 325° for 1 hour, until golden brown and toothpick inserted into cake comes out clean.

Freezes well.

Dredge the Past, Marinate with Memories and Sprinkle with Regret

Please God, if you can't make me thin…make my friends fat."

–Confucius (just joking!)

"YOUR father contacted you? Your deadbeat dad?" Jess is incredulous as I describe the letter my dad sent to me. "He's got some damned nerve!"

God, I hate to dredge up my childhood. It is really just unpleasant. And it makes me crave some sort of comfort food, maybe a roasted porc et choucroute, something warm and filling and loaded with fat. I ask the waitress if the chef can fix up something like that and she looks at me like I'm mad.

"I'm sorry, ma'am. La Lettuce only serves salads. But you can add shrimp or chicken to the salad if that helps." The restaurant choice was Jess' idea of helping out.

Lucky me. This promises to be a memorable meal. Jess and I order our respective rabbit food, and continue on.

"I don't know. He's dying or something. Wants to explain things."

"So like his type. Goes off and does whatever he damn well pleases and then comes gallivanting back into your life just in time to keel over, expecting you to absolve him of his behavior? That way you get to cry all over again because now you've found him and he's leaving you yet again? What does he think—he's directing a Lifetime movie? Bastard."

Jess is one of my staunchest defenders, an ally you want to have when you go into battle. My father is assuredly not going to have Jess on his side on this one, and may want to consider donning chain mail as protective gear. Jess can be a human lawn mower when she wants to be.

"Meh. I don't see what good it'll do to go see him. I'm over him. He was over me long ago. He showed me that by walking out that door. What do I owe him? A big fat nothing. Speaking of big and fat and me, I saw your doctor fellow the other day."

I reach for a sugar packet, reconsider, and instead open a packet of Sweet 'N Low, stirring it into my iced tea. I take a sip and spit it back into the glass. Gah! People use this stuff on a regular basis?

"You saw Dex?" Jess' eyes light up. "What'd ya think—he's pretty hot, isn't he?"

The eye-lighting thing gives me pause and I set my drink down.

Jess backpedals a little bit. "I meant Dr. Crenshaw." She's positively glowing, like a pregnant woman.

"Yes, Dr. Crenshaw is heavenly," I say. "Not that it made the event any easier. Packed like a sausage into that hospital gown and having all of those embarrassing things forced upon me."

"Embarrassing? Like what?"

"Like having to get on the scale," I say. "You can't fathom the degradation that entails. A scale has never been your mortal enemy."

Jess laughs. "Oh, Abbie. You're right, I'm not afraid of a scale. But I'm also not a fabulous cook and one of the top food critics in the country, either. It all balances out. Never mind about that. Tell me, what did you think of Dex? Did he say anything about me?"

I'm thinking back to the appointment and it jogs my memory. "Now that you mention it, he suddenly paid attention to me once I invoked your name."

The waitress brings our salads and Jess digs in with relish. I fish around in the salad with my fork, in search of anything that might be something I might otherwise anxiously await at mealtime. Aside from a couple of wayward shriveled-up shrimp that were probably cooked two days ago and dumped into the prep station, nada. Not even a crouton.

I look over at Jess who looks a bit too zealous about her

meal. As if she's avoiding eye contact with me.

"Is something going on that I should know about?"

"This salad is delicious, isn't it?" Jess stares directly into her arugula as if divining tea leaves.

"You're having an affair with him, aren't you?"

Jess gasps quietly and pops her head up to stare at me. "No. No. Of course not," she stammers.

But it's too late. I recognize all of the signs. This isn't the first time that Jess has strayed from her husband, only the latest.

"You're sleeping with Dex Crenshaw! And you sent me to see the man you're sleeping with, and now I have to keep this quiet and never say anything to your husband when every time I see him I'm going to be thinking about Dr. Crenshaw and scales and calipers and all of the horrid things I've been subjected to at his behest. Oh, Jess, how could you?"

Jess is putting her pointer finger to her lips to shush me now. "It's not what you think it is, Abbie. Calm down! I'm not sleeping with Dex. Yet. Since you needed to see a doctor anyway… I thought I'd maybe get you to vet him out for me, just a sort of second opinion."

"Jess! People get second opinions on doctors when they have to have hysterectomies! Not to decide whether they should screw them!"

The thing about Jess is that she and her husband aren't exactly faithful to one another. At all. I've lost count of the number of times Jess has caught her husband, Charlie, in a lie about a woman. We're at least up to the second hand's worth of fingers, and counting.

At first Jess had wanted to leave Charlie. But then she considered how much harder life would be. She'd gotten used to the private clubs, the lovely restaurants, the weekly masseuse and mani/pedi, the bi-weekly hair coloring touch-up. It's hard to maintain that in Manhattan without some sort of cash cow. Yet his repeated betrayals were wearing on her psyche. Sure, she didn't want to live alone in a 500-square foot efficiency in Yonkers, having to work cleaning jobs to pay the rent. But she also didn't want to be disrespected by a philandering dickwad of a husband. Did I just say dickwad? That is so not in my vocabulary. I think this diet is toying with the inner-workings of my brain.

So Jess decided to even up the score, and has since had dalliances with a few men whose judgment I'd question simply because they knew they were fooling around with a married woman. Is there any integrity left around here, people? I do understand where Jess is coming from, and I don't necessarily fault her. I mean, were I to be in her situation, who's to say I wouldn't do the same thing. I do, as I say, wonder about the men who choose to partake, however. And absolutely, I resent the hell out of Charlie for leaving my friend to fend for herself in this way. Bizarrely, though, they seem content with the way their cockeyed relationship works.

"So Abbie, I thought maybe we could somehow work it so I could go with you to see Dex and maybe I could get to talking to him and—"

"So I'd be your beard? Thanks, I've got enough facial hair without turning into an actual beard. Besides which, how cliché, picking me to be your fat chick wingman. Or would that be wingwoman? Surely you can be more imaginative than that."

"Ha ha. Come on, Abbie, he's really cute and really sweet and I like him. I was going to ask him to come along on one of our restaurant outings, but—"

"Don't remind me. There are no more restaurant outings."

"Of course there will be. This is just a little temporary setback. You'll lose some weight, you'll be back there before you know it!" I rub my finger along the rim of my water glass, creating a humming sound that is soothing. "It's more complicated than that. First of all, I don't know if someone hijacked my willpower or what, but it is gone. I've looked everywhere, even under the bed. No willpower to be had. Without willpower, I'm not going to succeed. But on top of that, I'm just starting to wonder what I should be wanting or needing in my life. William is nipping at my heels, haranguing about babies again."

Jess makes the sign of the cross, an apparent show of

solidarity. "Not again?"

I nod with a solemn face. "Only this time it feels like the Battle of the Bulge. No, wait. That's the diet part. How about the bridge over the River Kwai? Battle of the Midway? Whatever. What I mean is it feels like there will be a victor and a loser this time. And I have a feeling if he wins, I lose, and if I win, I lose. Jess, I don't know what to do about everything."

I stab about ten pieces of limp, brown-edged lettuce onto my fork and stuff the wad in my mouth. There's no tasting involved, no pleasure involved, no sensory anything. Just the cursory act of eating. Like sex with a hooker. Or what I presume that would be like.

"I'm hardly the advice-giver. You know that. But I think you should just let your conscience be your guide."

I blurt out a laugh on that one. "Thanks Jiminy Cricket. I'll keep that in mind."

"I'm serious. Let me explain. One time, Charlie was golfing in Thailand."

"Charlie went to Thailand?"

"Yes. Probably because of the number of inexpensive prostitutes."

"Ugh."

"Uh-huh. So Charlie was golfing at this gorgeous golf course when he came up to a green and saw a sign. Play the ball where the monkey drops it."

"And this has what to do with my little life crisis?"
"Everything. Absolutely everything Abbie. The monkeys sneak up on the golf course and steal golf balls, run around with them, and drop them somewhere else. It became a huge problem and all the golfers were pitching tantrums and throwing their clubs. So the rules were changed around to accommodate the monkey business, so to speak. 'Play the ball where the monkey drops it.' Just take it as it comes. It is what it is. You do what you have to in order to get by. Don't go getting your panties in a wad. Stop trying to orchestrate your life. Let life happen to you, Abbie. It'll all work out."

"I'm glad you feel so certain about that. Because I sure

don't. But I kind of like the philosophy, because it takes it out of my hands and leaves it up to fate."

"Crazier things are done than leaving things up to fate."

"But I'm not going to be your beard. Just remember that."

"Okay. Fine. How 'bout a moustache?" She laughs.

"No, no type of facial hair and that's final."

"Back hair count?"

"I have to get back to work Jess. I have to pretend I have value in my place of labor."

"Think about that, okay? The back hair?"

"Shut up, Jess."

"So, how was your day?" I ask William, trying to keep things light and fluffy. Like me. Only I'm more like heavy and fluffy. On the menu? Skewered vegetables and marinated Greek chicken. Not so bad, is it? Except for the accompanying cucumber sauce I couldn't help but make that has whole milk plain yogurt—the kind with the layer of cream atop it—and the good kind of sour cream. I'm sorry, I just can't shun the whole, natural goodness of things. My experience is every time I have something with reduced X, Y, or Z, it tastes as if the most important thing in the food has been expunged. Case in point, Oreos minus trans fats. Agreed?

"Fine," William is quiet while working on a mouthful of food.

"Anything exciting on the horizon?" I ask.

"Not a thing."

Clearly I'm not going to get any elaboration without some cajoling. Guess he's still brooding on the baby thing.

"So, I got an interesting letter in the mail today."

"Fan mail?"

I used to get fan mail—and hate mail—on a regular basis when I did restaurant reviews. I always suspected the hate mail came directly from relatives of the restaurant owner—or investors. But the fan mail was always lovely. I think people appreciated my candor, my honesty, and my approach to food.

I grimace. "Fan mail is a thing of the past for me. I don't even have an office anymore."

William stops chewing. "Mortie stole your office?"

"Not for himself. He gave it to my replacement."

William groans. "Oh, ho, ho. I bet ol' Barry is one happy pig in shit now that he's got the window office. Honey, you'd better hang up your cleats because he's digging in for the long haul."

I've decided I really don't want to talk about work anymore. My job has gone from the zenith of happiness for me to the raw source of my misery.

"Don't you want to know about my letter?"

He cocks his eyebrow and angles his head up out of curiosity.

"My father. Wants to talk to me about things."

"Things?"

"Yep. Seems he's been feeling his mortality and he wants to tie up loose ends. Me being one of them."

"You planning to see him?"

I shake my head. "What's the point? He did what he did. I paid the price for it. I don't see a need to resurrect dead issues."

"Unless…"

William gets that look on his face like what Thomas Edison must've looked like just when he deduced that the carbon filament was the answer to his prayers. His light bulb moment, if you will.

"Unless what?"

"Hell, I don't know, Abbie. But maybe you need to tie up loose ends with him. Did you ever think of it that way?"

"Ha!"

"Yeah, you laugh now. Go right ahead. But then he dies and you'll never have the chance again to ask him why. Don't you have the slightest bit of curiosity about that? Why did he walk out on you? Sure, it's obvious why he walked out on your mother. But you?"

With that I dollop about half a cup of sauce on top of my up-til-then-modestly-healthful dinner. Thank goodness there's that healthy cucumber in it to balance out the fat content.

"Abbie?"

I stare at my plate and practically will a huge forkful of food into my mouth. Filling the void.

"What if he says something I don't want to hear?"

With that William gets up and comes over to me, pulling me up out of my seat, and into his arms. "Sweetie, what your father did wasn't aimed at you. He loved you, in his own stupid, selfish way. You know that, don't you?"

"I don't know! Why would someone do that to his kid? Why do you think I'm so afraid of committing to owning a child? I'm afraid I won't be able to tough it out, just like him."

With that, I admit my own folly. Something I hadn't even admitted to myself.

William looks at me with new eyes. New and confused eyes, maybe from hurt at this revelation, I don't know. Yet also with understanding, as a parent would while listening to a child speak gibberish. Instead of saying anything, he just holds me tight. His body trembles slightly. It makes me wonder if somewhere deep down inside, he's crying. Whether for me or for us, I'm not exactly sure.

GREEK CHICKEN SHISH KEBABS

2 lbs. boneless chicken breasts, cut into 2-inch cubes

1 basket cherry tomatoes

1 each orange and yellow bell pepper, cut into 1-inch cubes to skewer

1 zucchini, sliced

1/2 pound white button mushrooms, rinsed, ends sliced off

FOR THE MARINADE:

4 tbl. olive oil

2 tbl. balsamic vinegar

3 cloves minced garlic

1 tsp. oregano

1/2 tsp. cumin seeds (or powder)

1/2 tsp. ground pepper

Serve with Sour Cream Sauce and Grilled Pita Bread (recipes to follow), and brown basmati rice.

Combine ingredients in Ziploc bag, add chicken. Marinade for at least one hour, or up to overnight.

Prepare vegetables. Rub oil on metal skewers so that ingredients do not stick. I skewer chicken separately, then skewer vegetables, drizzling veggies with olive oil.

Grill on medium high grill, for 5 minutes. Turn skewers, grill 5 more minutes. Transfer skewers to platter.

Have ready 1 package of pita bread, brushed on each side with olive oil. Place pita bread on grill, one minute per side. Transfer to platter.

SOUR CREAM SAUCE:

3/4 c. sour cream

3/4 c. plain yogurt

1/4 c. finely chopped onion

1/2 c. coarsely chopped fresh parsley

1/2 tsp. salt

1/4 tsp. freshly ground pepper

1/2 tsp. oregano

Combine all ingredients and refrigerate until 1/2 hour before serving, at which point bring to room temperature to serve.

Simmer Discontent on Low till Just Before Boiling Point

I've decided that perhaps I'm bulimic and just keep forgetting to purge.

–Comedian Paula Poundstone

"FAN mail!" Mortie calls out to me as I step off the elevator for work this morning. "You, my dear, have a fan base!"

He taps me on my head with a small stack of emails some intern no doubt printed out on his behalf. Wow. Fan mail. I mean sure, I've had comments before on my reviews, but I somehow have viewed myself as a third party to that. For this, they're writing in response to my feelings, my emotions. That's something entirely foreign to me.

I pull out one and begin to read.

> *Dear Ms. Jennings,*
>
> *Finally, finally, finally someone gets it. Someone gets me! Never in my life have I seen put into words exactly how I feel about food. I read your column and stuck it right underneath my husband's nose after re-reading it, just to show him I'm not a freak. This is what it's all about to me, too. Thank you for understanding me and letting me know I'm not alone.*
>
> *Yours,*
>
> *Stef Jancowitz*
> *Queens*

So I took a chance and someone loved it! It made sense to another human being! I just knew that someone out there would feel the way I do!

I proceed to read through the rest of the stack of emails, emboldened by each one to resolve to continue to write more on issues about which we tend to never speak, out of embarrassment or whatever. Maybe this really is a good thing after all, me launching this column.

But soon my joy is overshadowed by the black cloud that is Barry Newman. Barry's smile—or is it a smirk?—is about as wide as the George Washington Bridge span. I think a couple of 18-wheelers could easily careen across it.

"Abbie! How great to see you here this morning!" He's laying it on as thick as gumbo, which sounds so divine, now that I mention it. I once had a gumbo in Waterproof, Louisiana (population 834) that I swear would bring about world peace if only everyone got to taste a bite. Can't imagine I'll be getting back there any time soon to have another bowl of it myself. Maybe that's why my life is so lacking in peace these days…

"Hello, Newman," I growl at him. I think he gets my drift. Nevertheless, he feels compelled to talk about this wonderful new restaurant he ate at last night that I'd been dying to review: Black Tie Bali, which features Balinese cuisine served by tuxedo-clad waiters and waitresses wearing chiffon ball gowns and white gloves. Would I kid about this? The restaurant is the brainchild of master chef Alain DuFuss—just kidding!—Alain DuLongue, proprietor of several chi-chi Manhattan eateries. His ox tongue in sweet nutmeg sauce is rumored to die for. And to think I could've even eaten that guilt-free—I am certain that ox tongue contains no carbs. Plus it's not white. I even heard the boiled bananas were amazing—and fat free (though white, darn it!).

"It's so fun dining surreptitiously, isn't it, Abbie?" Barry digs in the knife a little deeper. "I mean, here I am, eating the most amazing meals, sampling everything, and no one knows why! It's like our little secret."

Our secret? That bastard. I wonder if it was our secret. Or if someone tipped off certain restaurant owners about a certain food critic who was going to be dining at certain restaurants in the near future…

"And the wine!" he's blathering on. "Do you know the

Sonoma Cab I had the other night retails at $800 a bottle?"

He's buying bottles of wine that cost three times an average monthly car payment? Is he off his rocker? Didn't Mortie tell him there's a budgetary limit to the madness, even by Manhattan standards? Huh, well, I'm sure not going to let on. Maybe I can just sit back and watch him crash and burn.

"Oh, and the power. The power! Imagine, I can single-handedly bring down a restaurant owned by ultra-rich investors. It's a heady feeling. Isn't it, Abbie?"

I wonder if he's noticed yet that I've plugged my ears.

"So I've given the restaurant review column a new name. I think it fits," he says, holding his hands up, his thumbs and forefingers forming "L's" as if showcasing a sign. "The Frenzied Foodie!"

Yes, indeedy, he is off his rocker. I roll my eyes at him and try to get back to my computer screen, but he's not done. "I want my readership to know that I'm whipped into a frenzy seeking out the best dining experiences for them."

I nod my head as if in complete agreement. "Barry, you've obviously mistaken me for someone who cares. Now if you'll leave me to my work?"

"Geeze, Abbie. No need to be a spoilsport about things. I can't help it you've gone over the tipping point. I'm just glad I was here to pick up the pieces."

I wad up a ball of paper and whip it at his face. "Tip this, Newman."

Finally he leaves and I count to ten. Then I count to ten again. And again. I think I get to about 988 before I can breathe without fear of a panic attack (or a need for a bite of something). I decide to channel my anger into my writing. I'm sure somewhere someone has said that writing can be therapy. And if food can't be my therapy, then something's gotta be.

Neurotic Obsessive or Quixotic Realist?

Or

You Can't Fight City Hall, Especially if You

Can't Fit Through the Doorway

Once again, I caved. I couldn't sustain my dieting nature for twelve measly waking hours. My food compulsion got the best of me, despite myself. So perhaps rather than fighting my nature, I should accept it. Sort of embrace my inner cow.

You know, I wrestle with this fat versus thin concept pretty much all day and all night. Not that I'm fixated or anything, but it is a bit of an obsession. I mean, how can it not be? If you're one of those thin-by-nature people, well, you'll never understand. But if you're like me—and I know there are lots of us out there–then you know with practically every commercial on TV (except maybe for the cell phone ads), every magazine at the grocery store with a scrumptious dessert on its cover, even songs like that one by Train where they're talking about fried chicken—food is everywhere.

And for me, merely thinking about food practically makes me gain weight, so at some point I just have to give up sweating about it and give in to the siren call. Ride the horse in the direction it's going. Play the ball where the monkey drops it, as my friend Jess likes to say.

So I decided to make a list, to bolster my psyche about this embracing-you-inner-cow movement. After all, there must be legitimate pluses to being a bit overweight. So just to get off on the right foot, here are some advantages to toting around some excess poundage:

A FEW GOOD REASONS FOR BEING A LITTLE BIT FAT

1) Your outie becomes an innie with that extra pooch of fat on your stomach

2) Blubber provides greater ease in floating (any whale or polar bear will tell you that!)

3) Extra weight keeps your fat clothes from collecting dust

4) Leaves you better prepared for famine

5) Keeps you warm during those cold winter months
6) Makes you better-appreciate being thin
7) Much easier to pierce your navel with a bit of gut to grab onto
8) Fatter face means you look younger (those hollow gaunt faces betray ones age)
9) You learn the limitations to elastic's ability to hold things in
10) Greater cushioning for a fall
11) Bigger bod = bigger boobs
12) More padding for riding bicycles
13) Gives you a good excuse to avoid the pool during peak crowded hours
14) Built for comfort, not speed
15) Eliminates having to debate whether to say that bogus obligatory phrase "oh, no, I couldn't, I'm too full" when the waitress asks if you want dessert
16) Fluffy is an affectionate term of endearment
17) You have a blues song named after you (Fat Legged Woman)
18) Your stomach makes a comfy pillow for your child
19) Polar bears are cute, and polar bears are fat, therefore fat is cute
20) In Africa, your voluminous size would indicate wealth and stature in society, so somewhere out there it's good to be fat
21) Living fat=living large, literally

Of course, because of the continual weight-related ying-yang with which I wrestle, I had to torture myself with these following truths as well.

SURE SIGNS THAT YOU HAVE OVERRIDING WEIGHT ISSUES

1) You view food poisoning as a positive thing because of the accompanying (though inevitably brief) weight loss

2) Your first reaction when you find out that you have to have any sort of –ectomy (appendectomy, hysterectomy, kidney-ectomy) is one of good cheer—the loss of an organ at least

means a few pounds down on the scale
3) A little part of you secretly hates your best friend for losing two dress sizes
4) You start to strategize how to approach stepping on the scale in order to soften the psychological blow of seeing the registered poundage
5) You figure that eating ice cream out of the carton means the calories don't count
6) You enviously view liposuction as a Hollywood trade secret
7) You catch sight of your reflection and assume it's someone else, because you couldn't be that big
8) You look longingly at pictures of a younger you, wishing you were that thin (even though at that time you'd looked longingly at pictures of a still younger you, wishing you were that thin (even though at that time you'd looked longingly at pictures of a still even younger you, wishing you were that thin (you get my drift; it's kind of like seeing yourself in a mirrored room—you become increasingly distant and smaller in the infinite reflections)
9) The idea of wearing horizontal stripes is as foreign to you as the notion of sticking to a diet
10) You spy a picture of Kate Hudson in a pair of Levi's and either a) tape it to your refrigerator as incentive not to eat, or b) say a little prayer that she gets really, really fat with her next pregnancy and stays fat afterward
11) You welcome the idea of travel in a third-world country, knowing that you'll at least lose weight because you aren't keen on eating cat or dog, and as an added bonus might even contract a parasite which would mean dramatic weight loss
12) You cling desperately to the theory that your extra pounds are merely "muscle weight" from all that exercising you've been doing
13) You map out your strategy before arriving at your doctor's appointment to avoid having to step on the scale for the nurse
14) The saccharine strains of Barbra Streisand singing "The Way We Were" drift through your mind as you drive past Baskin-Robbins whenever you're on a diet

15) Most milestones of your life are accompanied by the thought, "Oh, I was thin then," or "Yeah, that's when I was really fat."
16) Your definition of brave is tucking in your shirt
17) Your wardrobe is limited to varying shades of black (after all, black is slimming)
18) You've given up on control top, because after a while, why bother?
19) You're starting to look like Bea Arthur during her Maude days, wearing long duster jackets that conceal your fat ass
20) Strangers in the grocery store pat your burgeoning tummy and ask you when your baby is due
21) You refuse to consider purchasing new underwear, even if the elastic is disintegrated in yours, because the indignity of seeing your dimpled flesh strain through those delicate fabrics in a dressing room mirror is too damned demoralizing
22) Upon seeing home movies you silently reflect wistfully at how beautiful and slender you looked just hours before delivering your last child.
23) The phrase "such a pretty face" makes you want to slug someone
24) You've lost significant amounts of weight for two or more of the following life events: high school graduation, college graduation, family reunions, new boyfriend, your wedding, wedding of anyone at which people who haven't seen you in a while may be in attendance, high school reunion, college reunion
25) Your family photographs are starting to have a lot of you with your hand blocking the camera lens when it's pointed in your direction
26) You envy those Indian women who get to wear saris…Nothing clinging about those outfits

I am of two minds when it comes to weight and dieting. The stubborn part of me wants to reject our cultural obsession with thin, which requires a complete denial of all things indulgent. I want to say—and truly believe—that life's too short to worry about size and shape. That the pleasurable sensory quest of food is worth the downside that accompanies it.

But then the other side of me knows that I'm far happier if I'm thinner and look good in my clothes. I even take better care of myself when I'm thinner—I wear make-up every day, even paint my nails, I don't schlep around in oversized sweatshirts and sneakers.

But still I wonder if Dr. Atkins had any regrets about spending his entire adult life passing on the banana splits. On his deathbed, was he satisfied that life was over and he had deprived himself of a lifetime of yummy food?

I'll end the chapter with this freakish thought I had last week, after not splurging all day: "Hey, I did good today. All I had for breakfast was two small bites of a low-carb bar." That was the extent of my gustatory pleasure while enduring my last low-carb diet. Life truly is too short for that, isn't it?

William has been awfully quiet since my gut-spilling episode, and his silence makes everything seem a bit off. Like when you pour the shampoo into your left hand instead of your right hand and begin to lather up, and it just feels wrong. In fact he's been spending an awful lot of time at work, I suspect being a typical man, off in his cave mulling things over. And perhaps the lack of him contrasted by my near omni-presence at home draws particular attention to the situation. The silence is downright distracting. It's enough to make me lose my appetite. Well, not quite. I fear it would take an act of Biblical proportion for that to occur.

Since I've got so much more time on my hands, I've decided to start taking over some of the dog walking duties. This is something that has always been William's job, since Cognac is so powerful and easily distracted into making a break for it the minute he sees something interesting ahead. Up until now I've assumed my rotator cuff wasn't up to the task. I guess we'll soon see. I might as well walk the dog, now that I only write one measly column a week, which I can knock out in about ten minutes flat. Thank goodness, because then I don't have to hang out at the office and feel inferior. A girl can only take so much of watching Barry jaunt off to his three-martini lunches on the expense account. The one I so closely guarded (and coveted).

I figure while I take Cognac for his constitutional, I'll divert by way of George and bring him something to eat. I throw together a box lunch with curried chicken salad, couscous and red lentils from the fridge.

I call for the dog, who comes running the minute he sees the leash being taken out of the coat closet. He sits patiently, his enthusiastic tail sweeping the floor, his loving brown gaze fixed on mine, a cuddly teddy bear of a dog, not expecting a thing from me. It's so refreshing. Someone—make that something—that doesn't want me to lose weight or have babies or pretend I give a shit about this, that or the other. I suppose this is what they call unconditional love. Or maybe he just wants a doggy biscuit. Which is fine, because if nothing else, I'm all about satisfying hunger.

"Come on, boy, let's start this walk off on the right foot, with a yummy treat." I toss him a slice of organic dehydrated yam, which isn't exactly the pig's hoof he'd probably choose, but it's way better on his breath.

We head up the street at a brisk pace and after about ten minutes I realize that this effort somehow approximates exercise. I'm actually sweating. Who knew taking the dog to go potty was like walking on a treadmill. Minus the swarm of beautiful people around whom I feel inferior to the extreme.

I'd completely forgotten that William and I used to walk Cognac together all the time, when he was a puppy. It was our quiet time, really. After being gone all day at our respective jobs, we'd come home, walk the dog, return back and fix dinner. It was lovely, really. I wonder what happened to those days. Why did we stop with our daily ritual?

Because I got too busy with work. And I had openings to attend. Restaurants to review. Long, belabored dinners that William found to be tedious and bled one into the other. That's why. Because of me.

Things were so much easier when we were young and traveling around Europe, picking up odd jobs wherever possible. Working as dishwashers at Michelin-starred restaurants in the French countryside, watching, learning, absorbing. And if we were lucky, dining on the scraps of others' indulgences. Geeze. That sounds a lot like George. Dining on the scraps of others' indulgences...Not so different, really. By choice, in fact. Exactly like George.

Ahhh, those were the days. Nothing but us and that crazy Italian scooter that carried us across the continent and back. Back when I could fit on an Italian scooter without blowing the shock absorbers or busting the tires. I think we had a total of four outfits between us that we stowed in a tiny knapsack along with our toothbrushes. Simple. Keep It Simple, Stupid.

I start to think about the phrase, less is more. Less is more. It's so true, on so many levels. Less is more. More simply complicates things, causes misunderstandings, resentment, bitterness. I mean, look at us. When we had next to nothing was when we were happiest. Once we added in high-powered jobs, crazy schedules, a fancy home, all of that, then it got crazy. In a bad way. How does one strike a balance between nothing and too much?

And if less is more in life, would the same hold true that less is more with food? Could I be totally satisfied with eating far less? Have I simply lost my perspective? Less means not filled. Can I be happy not being full? Is this different than being unfulfilled? Is that what it is—that I somehow have created a situation whereby I need to be fulfilled? And if so, then why?

Lost in thought, I barely notice that Cognac has begun to tug hard on the leash and he's got me up to a trot. I am so not trotting material. He recognizes George before I do, apparently. Only George is sitting with someone at the bench. I squint to get a better look. I'll be darned. It's a woman. A very attractive older woman.

I try to lay low and observe, in case George needs his space, but Cognac won't grant me that courtesy and instead tugs me along till I'm front and center before George and a lovely, very classy-looking woman with a shoulder-length silver bob and inviting blue eyes. She's got on a pair of black suede Tod's driving shoes and crisply-pressed khakis. Her white button-down is tucked neatly into her waist, which is concealed with a smart belt (which she probably needs, unlike me). A scarf is wrapped snugly around her neck the way the French know how to do so well. I swear I've seen this woman before on a Dove soap commercial.

"Abbie!" George greets me like a long-lost friend.

The woman's eyes track me head to toe and I can't help but feel a little bit interrogated just with her mistrusting gaze.

I reach out with my little care package. "I brought you a little something. It's not much."

George takes the food and then elaborates. "Abbie, this is my wife, Sally. Sally, Abbie keeps me dining like a king."

Sally arches her eyebrow with suspicion. I reach out my hand to shake it. She hesitates before extending her own. The diamond on her hand could be Plymouth Rock, it's so enormous. "Pleased to meet you. I was so happy to learn that George has such a lovely family."

She glares at George for a long, cool minute, clearly in a mental wrestling match about whether to discuss their lives with me present.

"Hmph. George was never one to go for your run-of-the-mill cliché midlife crisis. He couldn't have just gotten a sports car—"

"I already had the sports car," he interjects. "Two, in fact. You're just lucky I didn't go for the mistress."

Crossing her arms tightly to her chest, she rolls her eyes at him so hard I think she might cause ocular damage.

"As if one would want you."

It's George's turn to glare now. I feel like I should've brought along a missile interceptor or something, what with the bombs being lobbed left and right near me.

"Besides, Dr. Saravio said you need to self-actualize more."

"What do you call this? I'm self-actualizing as we speak. I've just not self-actualized myself back to Pound Ridge."

"I guess you aren't quite done punishing me."

"If I can interrupt for just a second, I'll be going now," I poke my hand up to interject. "I just wanted to drop off this meal. Buon appetito!" I wave with cupped hand and turn to leave.

"Aww, Abbie. I'm sorry! I guess you can see why me and the missus are in therapy."

Sally looks embarrassed. Because they're fighting in public? Or that I officially know they're in therapy.

"No, no, really, it's fine," I insist.

"It most definitely is not fine," Sally says. She has a look on her face like she's scheming—like a teenager who's figured out how to sneak out even though he's been grounded. She drums her fingers atop her still-crossed arms. "Wherever are our manners, George? I think we ought to invite your lovely friend to our home for dinner to make up for our rudeness."

"She's the food critic for the New York Sentinel," he says. "I don't think that Gretl's cooking is enough of a lure to bring her all the way up to Pound Ridge, frankly."

Gretl? They've got the little girl from the Sound of Music cooking meals for them? They really must be rich.

"Correction—was the food critic for the New York Sentinel," I say, holding my hands up in surrender. "On indefinite hiatus."

Sally taps her fingernail to her mouth on her tooth in thought, then holds up her pointer finger in her light bulb moment (which seem to be contagious lately). "So that's how I recognize you. The New York Post!" Now she's pointing straight at me, interrogation-style.

I shrink back, humiliated.

"What's wrong with them? You're the best darned critic they've had in years. Makes a hell of a trout amandine, too." He winks at me.

"It's complicated," I say. I can't get into this whole thing with the two of them.

"Honey, I think you've got the idea. We'll have to get her up to Pound Ridge, introduce her to the kids."

"Poor Gretl will be beside herself, worrying about serving such a discerning palate," Sally says. "Maybe we won't tell her."

"No, honestly, you don't need to have me up to your home, really, that's not necessary." I can't think of anything much more bizarre than joining this happy family I don't even know for a formal sit-down dinner. Cooked by Hansel's sister. Maybe I could wear a black and white striped shirt (vertical, of course, since horizontals are contraindicated for my size) and bring a whistle as a hostess gift.

"But I love to entertain. And I haven't had anyone over since George skipped out on me."

"I didn't skip out, Sally. I like Abbie's term. Let's just say I'm on hiatus."

"From life."

"Yep. From life."

I start to wave my hand up high again. "Well, I really must get back with the dog. I'll look forward to the invitation. Maybe I can escort George back there."

"I'll be in touch," Sally says. Which is sort of weird, considering her husband has no fixed address, and she lives an hour away from here and she hasn't the slightest idea how to get in touch with me. I think I'll chalk this up to George's wife thinking of any ruse to get him back to home base. All I know is I've got enough turmoil in my life without having to add on someone else's, thank you anyhow.

CURRIED CHICKEN SALAD

Four chicken breasts, bone-in
4 scallions
1/2 bell pepper, diced finely
small can mandarin oranges
1/4 crisp, tart apple, diced finely
1/4 pear, diced finely
1/2 c. raisins or other dried fruit (cranberry, cherry, currant, golden raisin)
1/4 c. pine nuts, toasted (can substitute almonds)
1/4 mango, cubed
1/3 c. papaya, cubed
1 banana, sliced
1 small jar mango chutney
1 tbl. curry
1/2 tsp. cinnamon
1/8 tsp. ground ginger (or grate 1 tsp. fresh ginger on microplane)
pinch nutmeg
pinch ground clove
pinch turmeric
1/3 c. sour cream
1/3 c. plain yogurt
1/3 c. mayonnaise
coconut flakes, optional (desiccated unsweetened preferable)

Cook breasts on cookie sheet in oven at 350° for about 35 minutes, until done. Let cool, then shred meat and set aside.

Blend all ingredients together, serve on croissants.

Discard Zest and Skewer All Naysayers

I bought a talking refrigerator that said "Oink" every time I opened the door.
It made me hungry for pork chops.

–Marie Mot

I drop Cognac back home and decide to go out to the bookstore. Newly resolved to make something of my sad self, I'm going in search of diet books. I'm sure there are a few on the shelves—it's practically an industry unto itself, isn't it?

I mount the elevator one floor, two floors, all the way to the nosebleed section on the third floor in search of sage advice from some sort of dieting guru. And what I find are shelves. Shelves giving birth to more shelves, all buckling under the weight of the diet books (excuse the pun). Who'd have known? The heck with my foodie career—I should've been writing diet books all of these years. Clearly there must be a market for them.

I simply cannot believe the various types of diets out there! Who knew there were diets for every mood, nationality, and place of residence? There's the Skinny Bitch Diet, the French Women Don't Get Fat diet, the South Beach, Beverly Hills, Hollywood, Scarsdale. Damn, if only I were a French woman living in a warm clime (or Scarsdale) I'd have nothing to fear.

The thing that seems inherently unfair is that I'm obviously living in the wrong time: there was a day when skinny implied poverty, and fat suggested wealth and prestige. I've always felt myself to be wealthy in appetite. But unlucky for me, that sort of wealth is not valued. Whatever happened to those Rubenesque beauties with a wealth of flesh? They used to be all the rage. That would be just my luck that my body type will come back into vogue after I die, dammit.

I decide to set my sights on the most obscure diets out there, figuring the tried and true isn't really for me. I like to buck the trend. What I should buy is the Wheels of Wisdom Dial-a-Diet I see over there—I could pick my diet du jour that way. I pull it off the endcap display and give it a whirl. Wheee! It's like a spin the bottle game, only instead of having to kiss the pimply boy sitting across from me at Janie Jacobs' seventh grade birthday party, I leave it up to the spin of the wheel to decide a diet that will no doubt be the answer to all of my prayers.

I pile up a stack of diet books and my Dial-a-Diet wheel and head to the check-out counter, my basket laden with healthful goodwill. At the counter I notice the latest *People* magazine issue is featuring a svelte woman holding up a pair pants that you'd be able to fit a Panzer division into with ease. "Half My Size!" The headline proclaims. An inset photo reveals a corpulent version of this cover vixen and I can't help but throw the issue in with my purchases—I must find out her secrets to lifelong thinness and apply them to my life. I also toss in a Godiva chocolate bar because sometimes at about midnight, the only thing that satiates those late-night cravings is chocolate. And I made William hide all of the chocolate last week so now I don't know where it is. Which is fitting since I don't know where he is either.

Three hours later I find myself absolutely exhausted over my dieting options, and craving a juicy corned beef and pastrami sandwich with Russian dressing on seedless rye from the deli around the corner. Only I really don't feel motivated to get up off the couch to pick it up, so I order it for delivery. I'm kicking myself the second I put down the phone. The ultimate lazy slob maneuver. At least I could've ventured out for the exercise. God, am I the queen of self-sabotage or what? Her Royal Highness, Abbie Scarf-It-Up. I can't understand what it is about me that simply cannot latch onto the overall messages I'm getting everywhere. I'M FAT. I HAVE TO LOSE WEIGHT. What is it about this that isn't able to sink in to my thick skull? Why am I not like everyone else who does this with such apparent ease? And how can I contemplate this still a half hour later as I sink my teeth into the best damned deli sandwich I've had in ages?

So far I have only served to further frustrate myself with my task. That chick from *People* magazine? Sure, she's half her size, but she's also given up living. Well, not exactly. But she's give up eating pretty much altogether.

She's now a size two—a size two!!!—and a fitness buff. When asked if she ever splurges, she bashfully admits, "Sure, once a month or so I'll order a skinny decaf latte." Uh, that's her splurge? A modest splash of fat-free milk in coffee? That would be my diet alternative and the splurge would be a Frappucchino mocha supreme with whipped cream and ice cream. Possibly served over pasta. But seriously, where is the sensual pleasure in a skinny decaf latte, will someone please tell me? A lifetime of broiled chicken, steamed broccoli and maybe some sautéed chard is what I have to look forward to in order to be tiny?

Whatever happened to an indulgence being a pint of Ben and Jerry's eaten standing up over the kitchen sink? Now that's a splurge. Plus calorie-free, since it's eaten out of the carton. Of course it's nothing like my kind of splurge, which would probably include a five-course meal at Le Cirque. I mean, if you're gonna go all out and blow the diet, you might as well do it memorably.

So obviously what worked for her is not going to do the trick for me. Besides, I'm not aiming for a size zero. I'll be happy staying in the double digits, just not in the stratospheric numbers to which I've become accustomed. Although I'm starting to wonder if the only diet that will work for me is the Tragedy Diet: you know, when something so horrible happens to you that you simply cannot eat at all. Obviously job-lessness doesn't fall under this category for me. But I've exhausted my brain cells on diet books tonight, and finally, with Tartare curled up at my feet, I fall into bed exhausted, thoughts of deprivation swirling through my head.

The week flies by quickly, oddly enough. I've taken to walking Cognac through the park for a good long time, until even he seems tired out. At least there we don't have the traffic hazards we encounter on the city streets. Yesterday I lost track of the time and before I realized it, we'd been strolling for over two hours. I feel like a retiree. Maybe I should look into Elderhostel programs to fill my days. Perhaps a cooking class or two. Except that I'd be inclined to teach the class, not take it. And then I'd probably feel compelled to sample—or at least review—the output of the class. Nothing good could come of that in Abbie's diet world.

I've set up a whole system to my days, just to fill them as much as possible. I walk the dog, go to the gym, piddle around on my computer trying to come up with great ideas for my column. I've even enlisted a spy or two in my quest to nail Barry's ass. So far I'm quietly fielding information, hoping I can find some damning evidence to return his favor. And then I walk Cognac yet again. The dog's going to have calloused paws soon at the rate we're going.

Cognac especially likes to explore the scene over by the Conservatory Water; it seems he just loves watching those model boats go zipping by. Although perhaps he loves them a little too much, as he keeps chasing after them, and on more than one occasion I've had my arm tugged nearly out of my shoulder holding him back. Maybe Thor will be impressed with the upper body strength I'm building. After all, between hog-wrassling the dog, my daily workouts, and of course these walks, well, something must be going on. I did notice that my stretchy black travelers pants didn't seem quite so stretched when I put them on yesterday. They'd started to seem almost gray, they were straining so much on my body. I'm pretty sure they looked more black.

The cherry blossoms rimming the area near the pond have erupted into glorious pink powder-puffed splendor. They look downright edible, like a fluffy meringue. I decide to sit down at a park bench just to absorb this most agreeable afternoon. It seems that half of the city is in the park today, soaking in a gorgeous spring Sunday. The dog is enjoying a steady stream of loving from children, one of whom accidentally granted him a large tongue-swipe of ice cream. Which turned into a charitable donation when the child's mother took the tainted cone away from the wailing child and handed it to Cognac, who gobbled it up in about two seconds. Which makes me wonder if I might be able to go up and just lick some kid's ice cream and get a freebie that way. Clever canine.

I've been trying to maintain discipline about food this week. Before going to crazy dietary lengths, I decided to try to channel those neuro-pathways that Jana and Thor had talked about. Instead of allowing those pathways to instant gratification to be gratified with food rewards, I've tried forge new pathways, healthier ones, by rewarding myself with other pleasurable things instead. For instance, each time I craved some form of dessert the past several days, I've instead bought songs on iTunes for myself. My credit card bill is going to start ratcheting up, however, what with the seventy-five new songs I've purchased this week alone. Only problem is I'm running out of music I really want to hear. I've started walking the dog with my iPod on just to justify the expenditure, though I hate to tune out the ambient sounds. I'd be lying if I said I didn't cave and eat some sweets anyhow. But a couple of times I decided to do sit-ups instead of reaching for the ingredients to make a peppermint chocolate soufflé or something, so I'm making modest progress.

I hear a familiar voice from a nearby bench, and glance over to catch Jess, of all people, out of the corner of my eye. I start to stand up to say something to her when I notice she's not alone. She's with Doctor Dex! Quickly I turn my back to remain incognito and try really hard to strain my left ear in their direction so I can overhear their conversation. Between snatches of "I loved when you did that to me, bear!", "that felt SO good" , "when's he going out of town again?", a couple of growls, a purr, and a few "pookies,"", "bunnies" and "babes" thrown in for good measure, I'm fairly certain I'm either at a petting zoo or else I've found myself wiping the steam off of the window of the intimate world of Jess does Dex. Or the other way around.

I can't believe Jess lied to me! She wasn't just thinking about launching into something with him, she'd already launched an all-out campaign! I loved when you did that to me! Please. I can't bear to think about what it was he did to her. For that matter, I can't seem to recall when something like that was last done to me. But that's beside the point. How could Jess have drawn me into her adulterous web? And after all of those fabulous freebie meals I've lavished upon her! I never thought she'd taint me with her sordid sordidness! I feel like I'm personally involved in this thing.

I ponder this for a minute. It's weird, but it never bothered me when I was so far removed from it. Her little liaisons were sort of long-distance, out of sight, out of mind. But up close and personal, with all the pillow talk, blech. I feel downright soiled, like I'm the used sheets at the cheap motel.

I hear him whisper something to her that rhymes with "wussy" and she giggles. I risk a backward glance and see them locked in a kiss. And his hands roving beneath her skirt. Oy. How can I bear witness to this? And this time I'm not even the intentional beard—I'm the unwitting beard. Well, more like sideburns. Those horrible mutton-chop types you don't know why anyone would ever deliberately groom onto their faces. I scan the horizon and see happiness surrounding me. Grown men locked in carefree play with remote-control boats, kids with sno-cones, couples running in tandem, two seedy fellows who look like one is scoring drugs from the other. There are children nearby singing happy birthday, a cake aglow with six candles and a rich, delectable-looking buttercream frosting. My favorite kind.

Icing. I need icing. There is no way I can get this Jess-Dex thing off of my mind unless I can retreat into something that will take this Jess-Dex thing off my mind. Wait a minute. What am I? Knee-jerk Nelly? The instant I feel stressed about anything, I seek the comfort of food? Yeah, dummy. You do seek the comfort of food. And you're still going to seek the comfort of food. Because that's what it's there for. Your comfort.

I feel as if I can just shout out "The devil made me do it!" the force is that intense, the need to feed that overwhelming. Part of me feels an intense gratitude that I need food, not smack. I mean sure, it's bad enough that I'm filling my voids with food. But imagine if the addiction took over my life even more than this, if I was some junkie in a dark alley, scrounging for a dirty needle just to get my fix. Lord, at least my addiction is cleaner, less vulgar. And cheaper. Usually.

Okay, where can I get my hands on ready-made buttercream frosting on a Sunday? Suddenly it comes to me: my salvation. Three blocks away, Takes the Cake (and Cupcakes Too), open seven days a week. They serve icing shooters for the icing-addicted. Like me. A little mainlining of double buttercream might shake the images of Jess and my doctor in pre- (or was it post-) flagrante delicto from my brain.

I'm trying to figure out how to slip off without them noticing me, when they do me the favor of getting up and wandering away, their hands furrowed together as if fused with one another.

Back home, sugar buzz in full gear, I hunker down to write my column. This column thing is pretty easy, I realize. Since it doesn't involve much in the way of research or even effort. It's become my soap box, from which to launch into some of those emotions that I know so many other women share. I feel good that I'm giving voice to women all over the country who are in the same (sinking) boat as me.

Maybe It'd Better If I Was a Vampire

My girlfriend and I were discussing photographs recently. Specifically how depressingly horrid we look in them. She was dressing up to attend a ritzy black-tie event at the British Consulate, at which she would be photographed alongside her husband and Prince Andrew. The Prince Andrew, of Fergie-with-the-foot-fetish fame.

Amy lamented the fact that her husband was going to look good, as usual, and that she would end up looking like a cow in the picture, forever preserved as the unidentified heifer in the photograph. I suggested that she take the celebrity approach to having her picture taken: tuck her head beneath one arm while extending her other arm out, quasi-blocking the photographer's lens with her hand spread wide. You achieve two effects this way: one, your little tromp l'oeil with the photograph makes it look as if you're so famous, you merely don't want your picture taken again— you're simply so weary of everyone wanting to snap your image; and two, you end up not being frozen in technicolor, front and center, as the blivet in the picture with British royalty.

Sometimes I wonder if it would be easier just being a vampire, because then at least your image doesn't appear in photographs. So you're not preserved for all of posterity looking too damned fat for the pictures.

Mercifully technology has come to the rescue of those of us unhappy with our Kodachrome images. Now we can photoshop our blubber away. My friend's son came home with a project he'd worked on in computer class a few weeks ago. In it, he downloaded an image of a dreary plain-Jane jowly-looking woman. Through the magic of photoshopping, he was able to put a sparkle in her eye, trim the turkey gobble from her neck, style her hair, rid her visage of wrinkles, and just generally make her look like someone she'd probably rather look like.

If you can do this for a complete stranger downloaded from the internet, then why can't we just doctor up our family photos for the viewing pleasure of all? Wouldn't you rather be remembered as slightly better-looking than you might currently be? After all, think about those dreadful turn-of-the-century tin-types in which young women of childbearing ages look like they already have one foot in the grave. Dark circles ringing their eyes, stony-faced gazes, no smiles. Surely in real life these people had humor, had spark to them, and were a little bit more pleasant than the dour image left in their stead. That's all I'm after: to be preserved as how I think I ought to look, rather than how I actually look. Is that asking for much?

Much like a photographic negative, we see our self-image in the negative, rather than the positive that is projected from a photographic enlarger. Perhaps we would do ourselves well to focus on the projection, rather than the image in reverse.

Grate One Set of Nerves till Jangled

To safeguard one's health at the cost of too strict a diet is a tiresome illness indeed.

–Francois de La Rochefoucauld

"HOW'S it hangin' Abster?"

I think you can guess where I am. Yep. Procrastinating about going into the office. So I've gone to the fitness center for my personal training session instead. Thor is straddled backward against a chair, whacking a set of calipers against the seat back like they're drumsticks.

"It's hanging, I guess."

"You ready for the moment of reckoning?"

"I reckon." I smile a pained smile, like you would at the dentist who you really like but is about to yank your tooth out with no Novocain.

I knew it was only a matter of time before I had to get on the scale again. Though I think this time it'll be a bit like what I've heard other women say about childbirth: once you've had your legs splayed open, naked as the day you were born, with a handful of people focused on your gaping maw of a crotch, most everything comes with a sense of resignation after that. Granted, I can't speak for the baby birthing, but it's pretty much the same goes with once someone like me has finally mounted the scale of doom, in public, no less.

"You're not using those things on me again, are you?" I point to his calipers.

"Only if you want me to. We save them for milestones."

"Milestones?"

"Yeah, like once people lose an obvious amount of weight.

Then we take measurements again."

"Oh." I feel a little disappointed. Like it's obvious to him that I haven't lost any weight of significance. Not that I've tried too much, mind you, but still.

In stealth mode I creep up onto the scale with delicate steps, knowing that a light touch will work in my favor. I squeeze my eyes closed, awaiting the verdict.

"I don't suppose you can read the weight in stones?"

"Huh?"

"You know, stones, the British measurement. I think it'll be a far more palatable figure that way."

Thor laughs but continues with the weight-sliding. The sound reminds me of the executioner sharpening his blade on a whetstone. I know a scale is all about equilibrium, but where I'm concerned, it's just imbalance, pure and simple.

"Well, would you look at that!" Thor says, sounding surprised.

I half-raise one eyelid, as if I might be blinded by too much exposure to whatever is visible before me. "What?"

"Abbie Jennings, you're down fifteen pounds!"

"That's impossible! How could that be? You must be wrong!"

Wait a minute. I'm trying to talk the guy out of my weight loss? What the hell is my problem?

I stare for a moment at the scale, the figure still being high enough that even though it's less, it's still more than I can look at without a sense of mortification. I turn my eyes away—I'm the Wicked Witch of the West: I'm melting…

"Can I get off this thing?" I think I might shrivel up like a slab of bacon over hot coals just being near a scale for too long, let alone on one.

"Sure, but Abs, this is great news!"

I'm still shocked. I mean, I haven't exactly lived on carrot sticks and lettuce over the past couple of weeks. Sure, I've cut back some. But I haven't taken up residence in the Hotel Denial or anything. The only big difference in my behavior is all of that walking I've done with Cognac. Who'd have known?

I go through the rounds of weights and cardio machines with Thor, this time feeling a smidgen less cynical and a heaping helping more optimistic. Maybe I can lose this weight and save my professional ass after all.

Emboldened by my weight loss I divert to my coffee shop to grab a cappuccino. With whole milk, mind you. I figure I need my calcium intake and surely there's more calcium in thick, rich whole milk than there is in that wimpy, watery skim alternative. Isn't there?

At work I slip into my cubicle and start writing immediately. I've been doing some research into what I think is at the root of my problem: I've got a damned heartless reptile at the helm of my brain. And so I thought I'd write about it, since it definitely ties into food. Clearly I am dominated by the lizard brain, that primitive section of our skull that responds instantly and emotionally to life events. The lizard brain does not ponder out solutions to complex problems. No. Instead it flicks its sensory tongue, seeking the immediate, that which will satiate it, regardless of negative ramifications. The lizard is obviously hard at work, eating its young deep within my gray matter, when it tells me to go ahead and eat that gorgeous, puffed-up buttery croissant (especially because it's made the real way that croissants used to be made, so how could I not eat it? In fact, I'd be crazy if I didn't eat a few of them because they're practically antiques, they're such relics of a day before you could buy such dreadful pre-processed things as tubs of prepared cookie dough at the grocery store).

My lizard brain is a devious, hulking Komodo dragon, urging me into indulgences that otherwise would make no sense, but under the terms of his persuasion seem as if they are a fait accompli.

The lizard brain is where our thinking is based on impulse—it's the land of the three S's: shelter, sustenance and sex. It's the brain that encourages the guy to screw his secretary, even while his lonely, overwrought housewife is home feeding the kiddies franks and beans for dinner. It's the brain that ensures that rival tribesmen murder each other so they can take over their village and move, unimpeded, into their neighbor's fancier dung-hut. It's the same brain that encourages me to leap at the chance to reach for food in my hour of need. Lizards are my enemy, I'm convinced.

I glance up just as Barry slithers by me, speaking of lizards that eat their young.

"Abbie, have I got a hot ticket for you!" He gushes.

"You got a pass to Hell?" I'm surprised this guy even needs a ticket to get into that place. I figured he had a standing invitation.

"Abbie Jennings, do I detect a sour note in your dulcet voice?"

I ponder whether the judge would throw the book at me if I choked the life out of the man right now.

"Sorry, Barr. Lizard got my tongue—"

"I have two front-row tickets to the big cook-off next month, between dueling uber-chefs Louis Garçonnes and Yves Champignon. Ancien français versus Nouveaux français. This event will put the Rumble in the Jungle to deep shame."

I stare at him with eyes agape. "The Rumble in the Jungle was a boxing match, Barry."

"Yes, and here we have two preeminent French chefs slugging it out, only over their Aga stoves."

"They're using Aga stoves?"

"Figuratively, Abbie. I'm just using loose terminology."

"So let me get this straight—you're inviting me along to this thing?"

"Sure! I think we ought to let bygones be bygones. I understand you might be feeling a little raw about my taking over your slot, but hey, it all comes out in the wash! Consider this a bury-the-hatchet gesture." Bury the hatchet, indeed! I'd like to bury that hatchet deep into that man's reptilian gray matter. Sorry, must be the lizard talking again.

"Thanks, but I'm not really in the mood for French carnage. I've got a dog to walk."

"Suit yourself," Barry sniffs, heading off in search of more gullible prey. Or maybe another baby lizard he can eat.

I'm finishing up my column an hour later when I notice a cell phone on the floor near my desk. I haven't the slightest idea how it got there. I pick it up to see if there's a name on it, but nothing. Hmmm. It feels like such an invasion of privacy to snoop on someone's phone. But how else can I figure out whose it is? I open it up and start diddling around to see if it contains some sort of identifiable information.

Whoa. The wallpaper is a picture of me. The very picture of me that appeared in the *New York Post.* How weird is that? I start pressing buttons, desperate now to figure out what this is all about. I open up the picture gallery and what do I find but about ten pictures of yours truly. Up-close head shots. Full-figured shots (damn whosever phone this is!). All obviously taken on the sly, when I didn't realize I was modeling for anyone. All pictures of me, me, me, me and me. What is this about? I push more buttons and go into the call history. I find a succession of email addresses to which my picture was evidently sent: Albert LeDuc at Le Mistral, the trendy new French restaurant at which powerful fans force a chill wind on the customers, giving them the sense they are in Provence in the off-season. All that was missing from that dining experience were the fourteen elderly Frenchmen drunk on pastis. Nguyen Bok Choi, proprietor of recently opened Korea Gate Restaurant, which features props from the 0's and life-size wax figures of Richard Nixon, Tongsun Park and Sun Myung Moon; and of course that damned little Telly Savalas look-alike chef from Puka.

I am normally quite bad with math, but right now everything is adding up, and the new math smells rotten to the core. Two plus two means Barry is a slimy, sneaky bastard, passing my picture around to sabotage me.

I'm not sure exactly how I should handle this, so immediately I take the phone to the Xerox machine and copy the list of emails, and the various images of me. And then I decide to storm into Mortie's office with proof.

"You see this? The cat's out of the bag, Mortie. I had help in being outed—thanks to your cronie. Proof is here." I flip open the phone and it goes black.

Nothing.

NOTHING.

"It was right here! I found Barry's cell phone and I couldn't tell whose it was so I started looking at it and he had me—me!—on the wallpaper screen. The big ugly picture of me from the Post article! And then I found a slew of photographs he'd taken of me on the sly. And then I found that he'd emailed them to owners of restaurants I was reviewing. He was trying to blow my cover, Mortie!"

"Look, Abbie, I know you're still upset about what's happened, but this is taking it a little too far. Barry wouldn't stoop to something so low." He takes the phone and tries to see what I'm talking about. "See, there's nothing here—the thing doesn't even turn on!"

"Aha, don't you worry. I've got this!" I show him my Xeroxed pages, which I realize now don't look too damning, though with a magnifying glass and some detective tools you might vaguely make out some data. Though you certainly can't pin it on Barry with this evidence.

"I can't believe you're not going to believe me!"

"You know, Abbie, even if this crazy tale was halfway true, the fact is, we can't use you right now. Everybody knows you! And guess what? Everybody loves Barry's reviews. He's a huge hit. I hate to tell you, but you'd better be watching your hide—literally—or you'll be out of this job permanently."

I storm back out of Mortie's office, slamming the door behind me.

"Where the hell is he?" I am a human hurricane, and my eye wall is blasting through the newsroom in search of that dirty rotten bastard.

"Barry!" I scream, sounding like a fishmonger in London's Billingsgate fish market. Once when William and I wandered London's fish market we picked up the most delectable, mouthwatering sea bass. If I had that fish in my hands right now I'd club Barry over the head with it.

Barry skulks out of his office, looking every bit as sleazy as I now know for a fact he is.

"Abbie, babe. Calm down. No need to make a public scene. We can figure out a solution to your problem. Fire away." He pretends to whip out pistols from each hip and engages the triggers with his thumbs.

"You double-crossing below-the-belt lying lizard of a dog. I know what you did, you bastard." I'm breathing hard now. I hope that heart attack Dr. Dex warned me about isn't going to rear up now. "You are so low, I couldn't even scrape the dog poop off my shoes with a poop scraper like you."

Barry pulls me into his office and shuts the door. He smiles a hey, I didn't just stick a dagger in your gut sort of smile.

"Calm down, Abbie old girl. Now, what's going on?" Abbie old girl. As if I'm a dog or something.

I hold his phone up to me. "This. This is what's going on."

He snatches it from me before I think to secure my grip on it. "Gee, thanks. I wondered what happened to this. It's been missing for weeks!"

I try to grab it back. "Gimme that thing. Weeks my ass. I saw what you did. I know you took my picture and sent it to restaurants I was scheduled to review. You set me up!"

"Why Abigail Jennings, whatever do you mean?" He cocks his head and flutters his fingers against his face like a fan, as if he's Scarlett O'Hara.

I grit my teeth and snarl. "You know damn well what I mean. My pictures are all over your cell phone!"

He tries to turn on his phone but it still won't boot up. He bangs it twice against his desk, then tries again, and it works. "Battery's been acting up."

"Ahhhh!" He holds his hand, fingers pressed tightly together, to his mouth, as if he's aghast. "That's you!"

"Don't play stupid with me, Barry."

"Me? Stupid? Why did you put your picture all over my cell phone? Why were you playing with my phone? I think that's rather unethical, don't you?"

I stare at him, my eyes as wide as silver dollars pancakes. Which sound pretty damned satisfying right about now. Buckwheat pancakes with homemade maple syrup. Like the ones we relished at a B&B in New Hampshire last winter. Warm and cozy by the crackling fire.

"You know I didn't do that. You did it."

"Shucks, Abbie. I haven't the faintest idea of what you're talking about. But if you don't drop it now, I'll be happy to tell everyone that you obviously cannot face the fact that I was chosen as the better critic to take over the reviewing post and were so distraught about it you planted a series of freakishly ugly pictures of yourself on my phone to try to frame me."

"Frame you? Freakishly ugly? You, you, you—"

Just then his phone rings. "Yves? Oh, absolutely! Yes. Yes. Yes. Uh-huh. Uh-huh. Certainly. You can count on me, Yves. In a blank envelope. I'll get it from you that night. Uh-huh, afterward. Great."

He snaps his phone shut. "Gee, Abbie, love to talk but gotta run!"

He pushes me out the office and shuts the door behind me before I can stop him.

Left to stew in my juices, I decide I have to plot my revenge. I know he's got something up his sleeve. Something involving Yves Champignons. Something that has a stench about it, no doubt.

THE BEST PASTA SALAD EVER

1 lb. pasta—I like to combine things like orecchiette, rotini, farfalle, campanelle, and conchiglie

1/2 red pepper, sliced lengthwise into thin strips

1/2 orange pepper, sliced lengthwise into thin strips

1/2 red onion, sliced lengthwise into thin strips

2 tbl. olive oil (more as needed)

1/3 lb. button mushrooms, sliced thin

3/4 c. broccoli florets

1 large zucchini, cut into thirds and sliced lengthwise into smaller strips

1/2 lb. fresh asparagus (or can use tips)

1/2 lb. sugar snap peas or snow peas

1 basket cherry or grape tomatoes, halved (ideally use orange heirloom cherry tomatoes in season)
1 6-oz. jar marinated artichoke hearts, not drained
salt & pepper to taste
(see remaining ingredients for dressing, etc, below)

To prepare (add oil as necessary while cooking vegetables):

Sauté peppers and onions in olive oil till beginning to soften, add mushrooms, when softened set aside in large bowl.

Stir fry broccoli till bright green on medium high (couple of minutes), adding zucchini after a couple of minutes, cook till tender but still crisp. Add to other veggies in bowl.

Stir fry asparagus till bright green, add to bowl. Add tomatoes and artichokes to bowl. Season with salt and pepper.

FOR DRESSING:

Combine in food processor:
1/2 c. fresh parsley
1 c. fresh basil (or 2 tbl. dried)
2 cloves garlic
2 tbl. oil

Pulse till blended

Then stream in:
1/2 c. olive or canola oil
1/2 c. red wine vinegar or balsamic vinegar
1 tsp. each salt and pepper

Next sauté 1/2 c. pine nuts or almond slivers in butter till lightly browned, drain on paper towel.

Toss together: pasta, veggies, pine nuts, 1/2 c. parmiggiano reggiano, grated, and dressing, taking caution to use only as much dressing as needed to marry ingredients.

Serve immediately.

Take One Fat Critic, Stir in Sneaky Replacement, Let Stew in Juices

A balanced diet is a cookie in each hand.

–Anonymous

AFTER the fiasco of yesterday, I've decided to start the day anew with a different diet. Nothing like a clean slate to get things going in the right direction. In fact perhaps each day should be a different diet. Variety is the spice of life. And I do love spices. Usually, though, the spices are mixed in with fattening sauces and calorie-packed carbs.

Today I am trying the Letter M diet. Last night I was reading about the Alphabet Diet and technically they tell you to start with the Letter A but I wanted to be a little experimental so started in the middle instead. So far today I've had macaroni, macadamia nuts (protein—which puts me in the passing lane of the superhighway to weight loss, they say), mulberry muffins (two M's in one), a modest serving of mahi mahi with glazed mandarin oranges, and malted milk balls (which I couldn't help, really, because these days it seems that whenever I eat something salty I just have to follow it up with something sweet. Since I already ate my Godiva chocolate bar while reading my diet books, the only sweet thing lying around was a carton of malted milk balls that William must have bought at the movies and not finished). I feel fairly proud that I haven't had any M&Ms.

I could get used to this alphabet diet.

I'm a little bit bored today and can't figure out what to do. I don't want to call Jess, because we have bigger fish to fry than to chit-chat about my issues. I'm so upset with her right now that fried fish doesn't even sound good to me. Although once in Calabria, William and I had the most perfect fried sardines, silvery melt-in-your-mouth crisp and not at all fishy. God, what I would do to have a platter of them, along with a helping of 'nduja, the region's famously spicy pepperoncini salami spread, smeared across a fresh loaf of crusty bread. And an earthen pitcher of vino rosso, made by the contadini locali.

I'm lost in thought when the doorbell rings. Cognac barks several deep, bellowing barks to alert me, in case I've suddenly gone deaf and can't hear the bell on my own. Sometimes I don't quite get why dogs have to overreact to doorbells like they do.

I peer through the peephole to see Sally, George's wife, standing on the stoop, tapping her toe. She's wearing a pair of pink Pappagallo flats and has on bright fuchsia and neon green Lily Pulitzer pants in a bold print, paired with a solid lime green top. Her smart hairdo is pulled back with a headband. She looks as if she just won her singles match, six love, six love, and is now about to head out to play nine. I open the door, not a little surprised.

"Sally? How'd you find my home?"

She strolls into my foyer without a formal invitation. Very un-Westchester of her—I'd have thought someone of her breeding would simply have had her footman leave a calling card.

"I knew you worked at the Sentinel so I tried to find you there. A very charming man named Barry—he said he was good friends of yours—told me I should just pop by your home instead."

Yeah, charming as in snake charming. Just pop on by. What a snake. "Barry gave you my home address?"

"He assured me it was fine."

Jesus, what did I do to deserve this vendetta from the man?

"Okay then. Mind if I ask why you're here?"

"Look, Ms. Jennings, I won't beat around the bush. I want you to stop your shenanigans with my husband." Her face is heating up like a toaster oven all of a sudden. She looks downright menopausal with what can only be seen as ire. So much for her Westchester cool demeanor. "I don't know what you're up to, but I think you're trying to tempt George into staying here with that food of yours. I'm trying my best to bring him back to Pound Ridge and I don't need some, some, some food whore to be luring him away from me."

Food whore! Me? Food whore? Why—

I stand in my foyer, thinking I should sic my dog on this woman who is accosting the very heart of who I am. Food whore! I'm a food lover, sure. But not a whore! Big difference between the two. But I decide to remain calm. After all, I'm sure Sally's been under plenty of stress, what with her husband going AWOL and all.

"Look, Sally, I'm going to give you the benefit of the doubt and presume you aren't as rude as you've just led me to believe. First of all, I knew nothing about you and your family. I just happened upon your husband one night after I left a restaurant. I had all of these leftovers and I thought a hungry man living on the street on a bitterly cold night would be happier with my still-warm food than I would be. Call it the latent nurturer in me, I don't know. I haven't got kids, so maybe I need someone to fuss over."

Maybe I should have some kids like William wants and then I would have someone to fuss over.

"All I know is since you've worked your magic on George, he's perfectly happy to remain here. I can't see what else would keep him living this lifestyle, sleeping on park benches, scrounging for food and pushing around a shopping cart." To emphasize her comment she's randomly pointing around my first floor. As if my home is decorated with park benches or something!

"My magic? I haven't got any magic! My intentions were all completely honorable. I'm sure that nothing I have said or done has either lured or kept George sleeping on the streets. Have you ever thought that maybe he doesn't see a huge need to go home?"

"How could he not? We have everything at home. And here, he's got absolutely nothing."

I look at her in that "no duh" way, my head tipped down as I look up at her. I'm tempted to ask her if she's daft, but I just won't stoop to her level of attack.

"Haven't you figured out that he doesn't want anything? Isn't that what this is all about? He said as much last week! He had everything, but it didn't seem to do it for him. Maybe you need to figure out what it was that was lacking in his life."

"Such as?" "Such as relationships? Look, Sally, I don't know you. And I barely know your husband for that matter. I just feed the man occasionally. But certainly in the conversations I've been privy to, he's made it abundantly clear that he didn't feel wanted or needed back home. He figured he was just as well living on the streets as living in the lap of luxury. Seems to me that if someone feels so disconnected from his family that he's willing to run away from them, well, then, maybe that's a big fat red flag that you ought to figure out how to bring him back into the fold."

As I'm saying this something is stirring deep within my primitive brain. I'm pretty sure it's not the lizard, though, since I'm not exactly hungry or looking to kill anyone. Something about this message hits home a little too closely.

Sally simply looks miffed at the suggestion. "I can't even begin to figure out what you expect me to do about that. That's George's problem."

But I'm starting to hatch an idea. Speaking of hatching, I need to meet up with my farmer friend tomorrow—I schedule clandestine meetings with him in town where I score my stash of farm-fresh eggs for the week. I like to do this in ironic locales, like Washington Square, where other people are scoring products for their addictions as well. Just me, my dealer and a discreet exchange of cash for merchandise.

"What if…" I start to say, tapping my finger against my lip while I think out loud, "When we met you mentioned dinner. At your place. What if you set up a big family dinner? George mentioned your anniversary's coming up, right?"

Sally nods her head but grimaces. "For what it's worth."

"Stop. We're going to think positive thoughts here. What if

I can bring George back to Pound Ridge for a family anniversary dinner?"

Sally puts her hands together in a steeple as she drums her fingertips together. "I think you're brilliant! I can assemble the kids, we can all be together. It'll remind George of what he's been missing. And Gretl can prepare one of her famous feasts—"

"Even for me?"

She pooches her lips together, lost in thought. "Maybe I just won't tell her. It'll be our little secret. But what makes you think you can get him back there?"

Hell if I know. But I can't tell her that.

Cognac and I are just returning from a long walk when the phone rings. I run to grab it hoping it's William.

"What up beyatch? How's Operation: Crash Diet going?"

It's Jess, obviously wanting to joke around, but I'm in no mood to elbow anyone in the ribs right now. At least not any adulterous women who tried to get me involved in their extramarital flings. Instead of laughing, I'm silent.

"That bad, huh? What's the matter, Abs? Cat got your tongue?"

"Huh. Certainly not in the same way Dex had your tongue."

"Uh-oh."

"Uh-oh is what you say to the toddler who spills a cup of milk. I'd say you're way past the spilt milk stage, Jess."

"Whaddya know? Who told you?"

"You told me, you imbecile! In plain sight of half of Manhattan, no less. Nothing like a shameless exhibition of PDA in Central Park to tell the world you're engaged in yet another extramarital affair. Did you really think nobody would spot you? So is he married too, or are you the only betraying spouse in the equation?"

"Sheesh! If I'd have known this was going to be the Inquisition, I'd have called someone else instead. Maybe dial-a-friend or something."

"Look Jess. Of course I'm your friend. But it really doesn't sit well with me what you're up to. I know this isn't the first time. But it's the first time I feel embroiled in it, and I don't like it."

Broiled. Asparagus. Sprinkled with a little lemon juice and dusted with just a hint of white pepper. Topped with lemony Hollandaise sauce, made orange with the sunny yolks in the eggs of a free-range hen. Well, crap. I'd better dream of the diet version of this: topped with syrupy, tangy-sweet balsamic vinegar. Not that soupy excuse for vinegar mass-produced and pawned off as authentic in the grocery stores. I mean the real stuff: aceto balsamico. Tapped from a cask in some elderly nonna's attic off of a cobbled street in a small village in Emilia-Romagna. Aged longer than me, my husband and my dog combined. That's the only kind of balsamic vinegar worth ingesting.

Although today is the Letter M day, so perhaps it would have to be topped with mustard, which just won't be the same.

"God, Abbie. Talk about an about-face. You've known all along about my husband and what he's put me through. I thought you were sympathetic to the cause."

"I understand about that. And I have been empathetic. But it just feels really wrong: you, your doctor. My doctor. Isn't this against that vow thingy they make with the hippos—what's it called, the hippopatic oath?"

"That's Hippocratic. And there are no hippos involved."

"Uh, Except me. I'm the big hippo who he weighed on the scale, remember? And you know exactly what I mean. Isn't it illegal or immoral or unethical for him to do the clientele? Besides which, what if he's married, too? What about his wife? What about his kids? Did you ever think about that? What might he now be putting his family through, thanks to you?"

"His marriage is on the skids. He told me so."

I laugh minus even a hint of humor. "Oh, ho, ho. Of course he's going to tell you that. What do you think he'd tell you—that he loves his wife and that things are just hunky dory between them? That's not how these things work, in case you were too busy with your heavy petting to notice."

"Heavy petting?"

"Yeah. Heavy petting. I should've directed the two of you over to the Tisch Zoo where petting is encouraged."

"Oh, aren't you the punster. So funny I forgot to laugh."

"Affairs don't happen in a happy marriage, Jess."

"And you're the foremost expert on this? Perhaps because your own husband is so displeased with your anti-baby stance that he's practically missing in action? Maybe you think he's out doing it with some tramp like me?"

"I didn't call you a tramp. And way off base to bring William into the conversation. I just don't feel good about this. Any of it."

"Look, I really don't want to talk about this anymore. Call me once you get off your high horse, or when you take a happy pill, whichever comes first."

Truss Feelings with Butcher's Twine, Steep in Juices

Food is the most primitive form of comfort.

–Sheila Graham

WELL, that didn't go too terrifically, did it? Get off your high horse? I'm not on any high horse. In fact I'd hardly fit on a horse. It would be like a horse hauling a cow. Unwieldy, that's for sure. I'd never force that sort of torture on any animal. Hell, I won't even do that to my hot pink Vespa.

Besides which, I'm perfectly happy, thank you very much. Sure, I might be feeling a little uptight, but who wouldn't be under the circumstances? I mean, in one of those Glamour Magazine stress test, I'd be off the charts right about now. First I lose my coveted job, then my absentee father shows up out of the blue—in the midst of dying, no less. Then my husband decides to tighten the screws by forcing the breeding issue. My former colleague—with whom I thought I was on good terms—is waging an all-out campaign against me and I know not why. I have an argument with my best friend, who is having a very public affair with my doctor, and if nothing else I could never double-date with them! I mean, my God! He knows my weight! He's seen me in a hospital gown! If anyone knows my Achilles' heel, it's that man. Seems the only really uplifting thing in my life right now is my dog. And I can only walk him so much before he'll start refusing to cross the threshold of the door, his legs will be so tired out.

Right now I'm still reeling from that phone call with Jess. The more I think about Jess and her marriage-busting behavior, the more I think about my father and his marriage-busting. And maybe that's why I can't seem to let go of my anger toward her right now.

It was hard enough that my father left us the way he did. But then when I found out he'd had another family—his good family—all along, well, that was more than I could bear.

I don't like to talk about that day. I've never even told William about it, it's so raw to me, even still. My father had been gone a few months at that point. My mother whiled away her days submerged in gloom beneath her down comforter in the shade-blackened living room. Grandma Gigi tried to keep me from the house as much as possible, so she'd decided to take me to the shopping mall. We'd gone there because her rubbers had sprung a leak. No, not those sorts of rubbers. The kind little old ladies and dentist-types used to wear, the ones you'd pull over your shoes to protect them in wet weather. Her rubbers were letting in water and the forecast was for continued rain, so when I got home from school that day, Grandma Gigi and I hopped the 22B bus and rode it to the mall.

We'd just come from Sears Roebuck, the store's usual odor of new tools, lubricants and hard work still lingering on my nose. I was carrying Grandma's bag with the new rubbers. We were talking about my schoolwork, and Grandma Gigi was asking if I had any new friends at school. I hated that it even mattered to anyone whether I had any friends. At that age, I just wasn't the kind of kid that the other kids really wanted to be friends with. I wore thick glasses back then, and I wasn't very pretty. I never seemed to wear the right style of clothes and I don't think I really cared that much, to tell the truth. But it mattered to others that I was a loner. I guess that comes of being alone in a family like I was.

I heard a commotion up ahead and saw a man who was pushing a stroller with a bitty baby inside swoop down and scoop up a girl of about five from his side who had been crying. Next to him was a tall, thin woman with elegant legs and smiling eyes. She could've been a model. He leaned over and kissed her, then turned his face so I could see more clearly. It was my father.

And in that instant I knew. I just knew. It was too obvious to pretend anything other than that he'd had another family long before he'd left us forever.

I watched, my eyes unblinking, as my father sat down on a bench with his good family, and interacted with them like a father should do. He bounced the baby on his knee. He reached over to an older girl who had been helping to push the stroller and started playing slapsies with her. She looked so much like me, who mostly favored my dad's looks, that I thought for a second someone was playing a trick on me. Then he took a playful lick of the middle girl's ice cream and they both giggled. This man was everything a girl would want in a dad in a shopping mall.

My grandmother looked over when I stopped walking and saw where I was staring. All of a sudden she pointed in the opposite direction of my father.

"Lookie there, baby. There's an Orange Julius! Your favorite! Why don't we go take a look over there and see if we can get you an Orange Julius for helping your dear old Grandma today? Okay, honey?"

She grabbed my hand and tried to pull me away, but my feet remained planted in place. I watched as once again he leaned over and kissed the pretty long-haired woman, the woman who looked so in love. The woman who let her daughter eat ice cream without spanking her. And I tried to imagine that was me playing slapsies with my father instead of my anonymous twin. But I knew I didn't get to play slapsies ever with my dad. He must've been too busy playing it with his favorite family all along to bother with me.

I wish I could say I was too strong to cry. I wish I could say I went with Gigi and drank an extra-large Orange Julius and we smiled and laughed about it, and she reassured me that I was imagining things, that it wasn't my father at all, and then I helped Grandma Gigi pull on her new rubbers for the trip home in the rain.

But I'd be lying if I said that. Because instead, I ran to my father and tried to jump into his arms. The pretty woman, the one who smiled and laughed and looked so in love, stared, aghast, at me. And my father, instead of reaching out for me, pushed me off with an extended arm, like a policeman stopping traffic, and then reached for the middle girl, the ice cream girl, who'd started crying again. He picked her up and stroked her hair and soothed her with his calm voice. And the woman looked at him and asked him what was going on. While I stood there, my eyes pooling up with tears so full I felt like my eyeballs would float away. And I gasped and cried out "Daddy!" again and again and my grandmother tugged on my arm while she reprimanded my father, saying "Richard, how could you?" and the pretty woman kept yelling "What is going on?" and my father was silent while he fathered his three girls, his three happy girls who didn't know what was happening but were secure with their soothing father who loved them so.

After a while I was so tired from crying and tugging away from my grandmother and shrieking at my father that I just about went limp, and then my grandmother, my strong oxen of a grandmother, was able to scoop me up and carry me away and I watched over her shoulder as my father and his good family grew smaller and smaller and smaller right before my very eyes.

That night, we went home and made chicken and dumplings and she fixed me a large chocolate marshmallow milkshake and she taught me how to make homemade fudge. And for a little while I felt full again.

Cognac loves to chase bicyclists. Which can be a real hazard on the streets of Manhattan. Take today. I was walking down Fifth Avenue when a delivery biker came screaming past us, and Cognac took off in the opposite direction, his powerful body motoring me along enough that I am sure I burned off that grande mocha (it's still "M" day) I'd just about finished before spilling the remains while in hot pursuit of the biker. I managed to get Cognac under control just before a taxi nearly careened into him. The episode left me shaken, which is why I'm now in search of a large bag of peanut M&Ms because, honestly, what stress-ridden woman wouldn't seek solace in them after everything that's gone on? If it was a "B" day I'd have a Baby

Ruth. Even though I'd far rather have European chocolate but it's definitely not "E" day.

I tuck into a lovely little park on East 53rd, one of those hidden gems in Manhattan, complete with a waterfall, where you don't even have to buy anything to sit down. I pull up a chair, securing the leg over the handle of Cognac's leash handle, and plunk down to catch my breath. At least the dog won't be going anywhere for a while, anchored as he is by my ample weight. The soothing waterfall drowns out all the city noises. It's a lovely place to contemplate everything, and nothing. I close my eyes and try to tune out all of the stresses of my life and be one with the water. I know, it sounds a little Zen, but what can I say? I'm nearly asleep when I hear a familiar voice behind me.

"'Scuse me, miss—that seat taken?" I look around to see George, of all people, pointing at a nearby chair. "You look lost in thought."

I extend an arm out for him to sit down. Cognac gets up and gives him a lick. "Actually I'm trying not to think at all. Thinking is too much work."

"Something wrong?"

"Better question would be 'is anything right?' If so, I'd love for someone to tell me."

"I got nowhere to go and I'm all ears," George says.

"Gee, George, that's awfully sweet of you to offer, but you've got your own troubles."

"Troubles? What troubles? I'm a free man. I do as I want, when I want. Don't pity me. I've made my choices and I'm happy with them. Can you say the same thing?"

I pause, not really knowing if I have the correct answer for him. For that matter, whether there is there a correct answer.

"I don't know, George. I just don't know any more. A few weeks ago if someone asked me if I was happy I'd have said 'the happiest!' But today, it seems like everything has tumbled over pell-mell on top of me. Like I'm having a life-earthquake or something and a huge fissure has opened up on me. I'm not sure what I want or even what I should want."

I reach into my half-pound bag of M&Ms and grab a

handful. I offer them to George.

"Nah, that stuff'll kill ya," he says as he reaches into his breast pocket and pulls out a pack of smokes.

"Oh, and that'll add years onto your life?" I laugh at him.

He shrugs. "Filthy habit. You wanna know a secret?"

I nod my head vigorously. I love secrets.

"I figured one of the side benefits of moving to the city like I did was that I'd give up smoking. It's the damndest thing, though. Everyone's always willing to share a smoke around here. And the great outdoors," he gestures around him, "it's the last bastion of free-smoking that exists."

He extracts a cigarette and taps it against the table, packing in the tobacco, then lights it. He takes a long drag on the cigarette, and holds in the smoke. I don't dare tell him now how much I detest second-hand smoke.

"Yep, one of the simple joys of life to me." The smoke snakes out of his nostrils. "But it got to the point I could never smoke anywhere. Sally banned it from the houses and the cars. My kids banned it from their places. My secretary wouldn't even let me sneak them in my own private office, for cripes sake. Smoke-free building, she'd say. After a while you just give up. I figured living on the streets, the last thing I'd even think about was smoking. But I've found that some days there's not much else to do but smoke."

"Food's too important to me to ruin it with nicotine."

"What are you talking about? The perfect way to end a good meal. Better yet, kicking back with a Cohiba."

"Says you. But all that smoking kills your taste buds, George. I know plenty of women who smoke so they don't eat. I could never sacrifice the joy of eating just to be thin."

I don't know if he feels guilty or what, but he stubs out his cigarette after the next drag.

"So what's weighing so heavily on your mind that you had to escape the city to ponder it all?"

"Everything. Just about everything has gone wrong. And I don't know what to do. I'm starting to wonder if my priorities have been screwed up all along." And then I just let go in a torrent of pent-up angst. I tell him about William and about my father contacting me and Jess and Barry and my dieting. I don't mention Sally's visit, figuring that's an ace in the hole I need to save for another time.

"That's a lot on your plate."

"Excuse the pun." He laughs at my comment. "Of course everything I really want on my plate, I can't have."

"You mean like the really decadent, fattening stuff?"

I nod my head. "Exactly."

"But can't you have it? Just maybe not as much?"

"Not if I want my job back. Which I might not get anyhow, since it seems that Barry has become the toast of the town. And all I seem to be is toast. Burnt toast."

"Are you sure you even want to be the toast of the town? Have you thought about why you want the job so badly? Especially if they're going to put you through such misery to get it back?"

I don't have an answer to that. I mean, I love my job, but why? Because I love food. Because I love to write about food. I love to bring people into the fold, into my figurative home and feed them, nurture them, give them a little bit of what Grandma Gigi gave me. I love the experience of food. I love that food can take the place of things.

"I love that food can take the place of things," I repeat quietly, not realizing that this time I actually say aloud what I'm thinking.

"What things?"

"Huh?"

"You just said 'I love that food can take the place of things.' What things does it replace?"

I shrug my shoulders while I try to come up with an answer. "Maybe what I mean is food can fill in for other things that aren't there. Like food can take away sadness and replace it with happiness. It's sorta like that pothole over there." I point to the nearby curb. "Obviously something's missing in that road. Cars drive over that the wrong way, they lose their hubcaps. But then finally the city comes along, they fill it with asphalt, and it makes it better."

"But does it make it better for good? Or until the asphalt comes out and the hole returns?"

"Does it matter? It fixes what's broken."

"I don't know about that, Abbie. What you're talking about only patches it up. It doesn't exactly fix it. And probably creates other problems along the way. It's like when I got tennis elbow. I kept playing tennis—I was in the club championships and I wasn't about to screw over my doubles partner because of a little injury. But I tweaked my swing because it hurt so damned much. And tweaked it enough that the next thing I know, my shoulder was injured too. You do one thing, it screws up something else is all I'm saying."

"What if it can't be fixed?"

"Everything can be fixed. You're talking to a captain of industry. It was my job to fix anything and everything."

"Maybe where you come from things can be fixed. But in my world, it's not so simple."

"Perhaps you're just not looking at things the right way. Or maybe you're trying to take the easy way out. Instead of repaving the road, you're just filling up the pothole with—"

"—With homemade ravioli in a sage butter sauce," I say, actually thinking out loud again. "Or maybe freshly-ground pork sausage with fennel, grilled and served with Italian gravy over Tuscan pici."

"Did you ever think that food isn't fixing your problems in life, Abbie, and maybe just contributing to them?" I look over at him. "What are you, basking in advice from that fancy Park Avenue therapist of yours?"

George clasps his hands together as if in prayer. "Forgive me for overstepping. Maybe it's easier to see how to fix someone else's problems than one's own. Or maybe I am being an armchair shrink. But I'm looking at your issues and I think you need to just think long and hard about what's important to you. And maybe while you're at it, figure out if you can get to the root of what it is you're filling. And why."

He gets up to leave.

"Say, George, I was thinking," I say, hoping to catch him before he leaves. "Maybe I should take you and Sally up on that offer for dinner at your place. It might do me good to get out of the city for a night. What do you think?"

Caught off guard, he doesn't have a chance to ponder it too much. "If you think that'll help you out, I'm willing to consider it. Anything for you, Abbie."

I end the day with an alphabetical transition. In other words, I've unilaterally decided that the letter "M" diet has turned into the Letter "O" diet. This is because the only thing that will get my mind off of everything are the Oreo cookies I bought at the bodega up the block from my home. Someone told me about Weight Watchers point system and while I don't have the actual point schedule—I mean, that would mean having to go weigh myself publicly to join, right?—I'm guesstimating. I figure I could have an orange ("O" food), or maybe four Oreos. That would be about the same volume of food, wouldn't it? Perhaps my Oreo math isn't quite kosher, but I can't seem to stop this self-sabotage train on which I'm riding.

I'm so furious with myself for having snarfed down those cookies, I scurry up to the bathroom to brush away the evidence. Lady MacBeth, I am. Only trying to dispel with Oreo evidence, not blood. As I spit out my toothpaste, the telltale Oreo cookie effluent seems to mock me: You're only cheating yourself, Abbie Jennings. You're only cheating yourself. As penance I write my column before going to bed, even though I can't wait for my head to hit the pillow.

IF IT DON'T FIT, DON'T FORCE IT

by Abbie Jennings

My husband rushed into the room to check on me when I was getting dressed recently.

"Sweetheart—is everything okay?"

"I'm fine! Why do you ask?"

"I was worried because you were talking normally and all of

a sudden I heard a sharp intake of breath—I thought you'd hurt yourself."

A sharp intake of breath...Betrayed by the dreaded gut-sucking inhale, a trick I have mastered in order to wedge myself into my ill-fitting clothes. And now my dogged determination to pretend all is hunky dory in my weight-world has been thwarted.

With the dawn of each day, I confidently step out of bed embracing my newly-commenced diet with the zeal of a missionary. Yet as the day progresses, and my determination wanes, the notion of starting the diet tomorrow becomes more and more appealing. I've grown used to this pseudo-diet rhythm, the think-I-can ultimately yielding to the don't-really-wanna. Alas, my clothes are now beyond snug, and much as I'd hoped that just cutting back on what I ate would melt the pounds away, I know deep down in my ample gut that the only way to thin-dom is by abandoning my jaded ways.

I've always had a yin yang-ish relationship with food. Intensely connected to food, glorious food. An indulgence of the senses: the texture, the taste, the feel, the sound. Not just nourishment, but so much more. The intangible lure of the nirvana-esque experience of biting into something so transforming that you want to name your first-born child after it. Yet there's that dark side: food, so determined to make me lumpy, fat and frumpy. So easy to add on layer upon layer of food byproduct (i.e. fat) onto my body. The price for a moment of sheer gastronomic pleasure equals a lifetime of hard work paying penance for my dining sins.

That's where I find myself in my complicated relationship with food—not caught with my pants down so much as unable to get them up in the first place. In this no-carb, no fat, no flavor, no pleasure world in which we live, I now must weigh—that most unforgiving of verbs—my options. Is it worth the momentary pleasure of a bite of this or that, for the enduring suffering that ultimately accompanies it? Ah, ah, ah, a moment on the lips, a lifetime on the hips. I'm living proof of that old chestnut (there I go, always thinking food).

I lament the damage done from my intimate relationship

with edibles. The closet full of clothes that once looked great on me, now relegated to decorating my hangers. The realization that my sagging willpower—or lack thereof—has left me in a state of excess.

I'm ready to admit that the Momily warnings were true: my metabolism is rapidly slowing down with age, just as every mother warns you. In fact, I fear I may have to forego sustenance entirely lest I'm resigned to wearing duvets, tents or tablecloths for lack of better fitting clothes.

I've long wrestled with dueling intent when it comes to body weight. On the one hand, I was raised by my mother to worry about it, taught that how much someone weighs is very important. On the other hand, I also learned early on from my grandmother to love and appreciate food. Conflicting wants and needs irrevocably ingrained and entwined in my psyche. And stubbornly, I want to fight our national predisposition for feminine thinness, for continual denial of food in exchange for having the boyish figure of a teenager. I want to live in a world in which size is irrelevant, that who we are far outweighs how we look.

But overriding that, alas, I also wouldn't mind fitting into my clothes again.

Okay, so maybe once I re-lose the weight I've gained and lost a dozen times in the past fifteen years, I'll be able to moderate my intake. Occasionally indulge in a celebratory apple or something. But then again, maybe life's too short to worry so much about it.

Maybe my destiny is to enjoy the here and now, and just get bigger clothes.

Chop Six Nuts, Eat Till Full

I hate when I read "Try that Jennifer Aniston Diet." There was no diet!

–Jennifer Aniston

IT'S breakfast time, yet again. Time to figure out what in the hell I can actually eat that might inspire dieting success. Before me on a doll-sized rose-patterned china plate (really a demitasse saucer from Grandma Gigi's china service) are the following items: two cubes of cheese, one inch by one inch in proportion, a half strip of bacon, and six peanuts, split into halves to go further psychologically. In the accompanying demitasse teacup is exactly one half-cup of homemade chicken stock.

Once William is seated, I too sit down at the table. I lift my fork and knife to my plate in preparation for cutting.

"What the heck is that on your plate? And why is it Lilliputian?"

"It's my breakfast," I say as I begin to cut my peanuts with a knife. The first nut shoots off my plate, pings William in the eye, then ricochets back up to the end of the table.

"Ouch!"

"Oh, honey, I'm so sorry!"

Who'd have known that a small breakfast could be so treacherous? After checking his eyeball for damage, I reach across the table to salvage my marauding nut; I can't afford to lose one fifth of my entire breakfast so randomly.

William looks down at the dog, shaking his head. "What do you say, Cognac? I'm betting this diet lasts till oh, about 10:21. A.M."

"Ha. Ha. Very funny," I say, trying again to carve my

peanuts into smaller pieces, thinking I can extend the duration of this meal just a little bit this way.

"Abbie, don't torture yourself like this. I love you just the way you are."

I smile, feeling somewhat gratified. I know I'm lucky to have married a guy who likes a little meat on his woman's bones. "I appreciate your moral support. But really, I'm going to do it this time. This time I'm going to love this diet and stick to it, come hell or high water."

William, whose patience with me is wearing quite thin, I know, rolls his eyes as he wolfs down the pancakes I fixed for him. I'm personally very impressed with my willpower—I didn't even nibble the dribbled pancake dots that fell onto the griddle as I cooked his breakfast. Normally I could make an entire meal on those alone (drenched in a puddle of warm Vermont maple syrup of course). Well, especially because I rationalize that the pancake drippings that just happen to cook alongside the actual pancakes don't have calories, since they're not really pancakes. Right?

But no pancakes for me, since today, I'm trying the South Beach plan. I mean if it worked for Jennifer Aniston, surely it can work for me. Only thing is I'm not exactly following the proscribed South Beach recipe plan. I just can't bring myself to settle for some of the vile recipes the author passes off as food. I mean, throughout that entire diet, the highlight of it is a "treat" known as Cinnamon Surprise. Would you like to know what Cinnamon Surprise consists of? A piece of whole-wheat toast with a dollop of low-fat cottage cheese, topped with a generous sprinkling of cinnamon. Broiled. Oh, my God, I truly think if I have to resort to spending my days looking forward to my Cinnamon Surprise, that life as I know it is over. Just take me out back and put me out of my misery.

So instead, I'm flying by the seat of my amply-sized pants, and hoping for the best.

William kisses me on the head as he gets up to leave for work. "Well, I hope you have better luck with this than the Alphabet Diet."

I choose to ignore that comment, knowing as I do that the Alphabet Diet wasn't exactly a home-run for me as far as diets go, and wave goodbye to him as he leaves.

On my way out the door a few minutes later I notice that William left his mobile phone on the kitchen counter. I grab it, figuring I'll swing it by his office since I'm headed to the gym, which is only a couple of blocks away from there.

The usual morning rush hour chaos is dizzying. I feel quite removed from it, now that I'm not going to my own office on a regular basis. It makes me feel as if I'm playing at being a city girl. It's almost as if I don't belong.

I'm about to cross the street from his building when I see none other than William buzzing by on his motorcycle. Only he's not alone. He's got a helmeted woman with long dark hair and a short red skirt riding behind him. Not riding behind him on a separate motorcycle, mind you; she's actually on the back seat of his motorcycle. Who is this person? And why does she have her hands around William's waist and her legs snuggled up behind his? Before I can notice anything more, they zip around a corner and disappear into a parking garage about a block away, leaving me to stand on the street corner in my black (it's slimming) velour sweatsuit, blinking back tears. Could there be a more public venue to discover your husband with another woman, first thing in the morning, but for smack dab in mid-town Manhattan as a bazillion cars, trucks and taxis crawl by?

I simply cannot believe it's possible that William could be off cavorting with another woman. That's just not in his nature. It would be like Cognac taking up with a new owner. I don't even think a big, fat, juicy, raw steak could lure him away. And trust me, that woman, from what I saw, was serious slab of rare Kobe beef tenderloin, complete with a sauce Béarnaise. And garlic mashed potatoes, with heaping gobs of whipping cream and cream cheese, lightly browned in the oven with pats of butter.

How can I think about food at a time like this!

Worse yet, what am I supposed to do about this?

First things first. I can't assume the worst. There must be a perfectly reasonable explanation. I think I'll just go home, get gussied up, and come back to surprise William at lunchtime. That's what I'll do. We'll go have lunch at Angus Amongus, a very manly steak house that has gargantuan bullheads mounted along the walls (it appeals to all those Wall Street types). And we'll talk over a hearty meal. That will make things better.

As I wander toward a taxi stand, my head lost in despair over what I've just witnessed, I smack headlong into a bulldog of a man, someone who looks like he won't take kindly to strange women wandering into him.

"Watch where you're going," he growls at me, before I've even had a chance to pardon myself.

"Huh?"

"I said watch it, you fat bitch!" I get a good look at his face and he looks like a particularly ugly member of ZZ Top: long tangled beard, eyes covered by a thicket of greasy hair. Dressed like he's been wearing the same woodsman outfit since rescuing Peter from the wolf in those menacing Russian woods lo, those many years ago.

He looks me up and down and no doubt can tell that I'm in shock that someone would be so ugly to another human being, right here on the streets of Manhattan. For a minute I try to speak but nothing wants to come out. But I'm not about to be intimidated by an oversized ogre of a person, one whose narrow-mindedness is so blatant he has no other conversational launch point.

"Excuse me?" I say, mustering up just a hint of you talking to me? into my voice, for authority's sake.

What I really should say now is "sticks and stones may break my bones but names will never hurt me" while sticking out my tongue. But I'm too fired up, and I can't pass up a chance to shove it back to this idiot. But not before he further insults me.

"Hey, I know you—aren't you—" he's pointing at me, snapping his fingers to jog his memory, and dammit, now I know what he's going to say. "*New York Post*! Fat food critic! That was hilarious!"

He starts to laugh, a deep-down belly laugh that would

almost sound funny if his aim wasn't to humiliate. "And now you're the one writing about how great it is to be fat. Clearly you know what you're talking about, Suzie Q."

"My name is not Suzie Q. And let me tell you something, you odious creature," I say to him, ready to poke him in that icky man-boobed chest of his if I must to make my point. "As you stand before me with a pot belly hanging over your soiled blue jeans, a beard that looks a bit too much like the pubic hair on the Jolly Green Giant, a florid whiskey nose that betrays your favorite pastime, and enough teeth missing that they should be pictured on the backs of milk cartons, you're in no position to be commenting on my physical appearance."

The guy looks at me sort of dopey-like. I figure he has no idea what some of those words I used mean.

"Look here, you fat bitch," he repeats himself. I'm mad enough at this man that I'm ready to slug him if need be.

I'm on the verge of tears—I mean who wouldn't be with a creepy stranger insulting you based purely upon your weight?—when some lovely young man intercedes on my behalf.

"Look, buddy, leave the lady alone," my knight-in-shining-trenchcoat says.

As the creepy man starts to raise his voice above than his simple ugly name-calling, we both realize the offender is as drunk as a skunk. At nine in the morning. Charming. We both turn away from the rancid aroma of stale liquor emanating from his filthy mouth. Finally my savior manages to convince ZZ to leave me alone, I thank him profusely, then flee the confines of that imbroglio and race home.

I arrive home, a little shaken by the incident. I don't get why insults about a woman's body size are considered socially acceptable. Especially coming from someone so skuzzy. As repugnant as his appearance was, I'd never have commented to him about it out of the blue like that. I shake it off and walk over to my desk.

I glance down at my computer and notice I have a bunch more e-mails, forwarded by Mortie. More fan mail! Who'd have thought? It's like receiving a love letter. Just what I need after what I just experienced. A quick perusal and I see that solidarity for us bigger girls is a cause that's needed a celeb. Sure, there was Camryn Manheim. Rosie O'Donnell. Oh, even that other Rosie, from that sitcom. But then she had all that fat sucked out of her, the cheater. Well, if I become the default spokesperson for the chubettos of the world, so be it. I'm up to the task. But now, I've got more pressing matters to attend to.

I rip apart my closet searching for something flattering. I'm starting to realize flattering and flabby do not go hand in hand terribly readily. At least not in my case. All I've got available is camo: a closet full of chubby chick camo. Chic chubby chick camo. She sells seashells down by the seashore. I'm losing it. I'm freaking losing it.

I wedge into my Flexees, which don't quite seem to need a shoehorn as much as when I last donned them. This could be modest progress. Despite my stress-binging. Maybe I have something modest to celebrate! That is if my husband was just giving a damsel in distress a ride, and not zipping around with a surprise mistress.

Christ, Abbie. Listen to yourself. Obsessing about how you look. Come on, girl. Take pride in your accomplishments. To hell with superficiality such as physical dimensions. Yeah, right. That's all fine and good till the next caustic remark from some vulgar stranger picks open that scab of embarrassment.

As I paint the finishing touches on my make-up, the doorbell rings.

I run downstairs amidst the dog's barking frenzy, and open the door to find me. Well, more like a skinny me. Only it's not me. It's someone who looks damned similar though.

"Can I help you?" The woman reaches her hand out to me.

"Jane Greer. We've, er, met before, actually."I cock my head and squint at her like she's a little crazy and is babbling in tongues.

"We've met?"

"Yes, yes. Only not formally. And it's been years. Many years, in fact. I believe we share something very important to me. And I would hope somewhat important to you, as well."

I'm hesitant to ask this woman to come into my home, because she's spooking me. But she looks normal enough. That is, assuming I look normal enough on any given day. I hate to admit it, but "I" look much better in the thin version of me.

"I'm sorry, but I'm a bit confused about what you're getting at."

"I believe you're my half sister."

I freeze in place, trying to process what she's just said, and she keeps on speaking.

"My maiden name is Cartwright."

I feel as if space aliens have invaded my home. Like standing before me is a scary green Martian who is going to suck my brain out of my head. Damn, I wish Martians would suck the fat out of my body instead. That I wouldn't mind so much.

I am feeling a little faint, so without words, I motion for her to follow me into the living room, where I sprawl out on the sofa. Which, yes, gasps under my weight yet again. Where's my fainting chair when I need it? Jane Greer sits down on the edge of a cranberry red overstuffed chair across from me, teetering on the edge of the seat, her hands propped atop her legs, which are politely clasped together, her ankles touching. I notice that her chair doesn't even breathe a gentle sigh when she sits in it.

"How in the world did you find me?"

From her purse she extracts and unfolds a creased copy of the now-infamous *New York Post* picture, tapping across my gaping blow-job mouth with her Jersey-girl red French-tipped acrylic fingernail.

Is this ghost gonna haunt me the rest of my days? And what is up with those nails? Why don't they paint the bottom half of their fingernails as well?

"My father saw this. He told me you worked at the *Sentinel*. He's been bellyaching for ages about trying to talk to you, but now the doctors are extremely worried about his health, so I finally decided to just go down to the paper to find you before it was too late."

"But I wasn't there."

"Right. And a nice man named—"

"—Barry directed you to my home."

"How'd you know?"

"Just intuition, I guess."

"He told me you were really good friends."

"Yeah. Really good friends."

I am rendered speechless, and remain so, not knowing what I'm supposed to say. Christ, it's like I live at the missing person's bureau or something, I'm so sought after in my own humble brownstone. And I, evidently, am the missing person.

"So. Sis—" she begins, launching a tentative smile.

But I don't reciprocate, and instead stop her dead. "Oh, no. No sis anything. I don't have any sisters. I don't have any living relatives. I'm an only child. My mother died years ago. My grandmother, who mostly raised me, too. That man you're talking about? Not my father." I shake my head back and forth for emphasis, my lips pursed, and wag my finger.

"Look, Abbie, I know this is all quite awkward."

"Awkward? No. Awkward is having your fat face plastered across the New York Post and ruining your career. That's awkward. This? This is just plain wrong."

Silence prevails and all I can hear is Cognac snoring now at my feet. Amazing how that dog can go from mid-bark to sound asleep like a damned narcoleptic. Next to me on the table is my dial-a-diet and I pick it up and spin the wheel around and around. Round and round and round she goes, where she stops, nobody knows. The first diet it settles upon is Gastric Bypass. Is this thing trying to tell me something? I could so not ever do that surgery. I'd be guaranteed to die on the table, which wouldn't even allow me the pleasure of the promised weight loss. How cruel would that be? Besides, even if I did live, after that surgery, you are essentially forced into the mother of all diets: low carb, low fat, low sugar, low everything, or you're buckled over in gastric pain. Reminds me of those prescription diet pills that cause you to lose bowel control. Um, not exactly a reasonable trade off. Thanks but no thanks.

"Look, what do you want from me?" I ask.

"I want you to let a dying man make his peace with you."

I stare at her. I think she knows that what she's asking is pretty ballsy. Especially since she looks a little like a cowering dog that expects to be spanked for eating out of the garbage.

"Make peace with me? He wants me to absolve him of all guilt for him having thrown me under the bus the way he did? He wants me to give him some sort of special dispensation for his two-timing on my family with a whole 'nother better family? Tell me something: would you do that? If some stranger paraded into your living room unannounced, asking for such a favor, do you really think you'd agree to such a request?"

Jane Greer takes a deep breath and exhales loudly. She puts her spread fingers to her temples as if assuaging a migraine.

"I knew this wouldn't be easy—"

"Easy? You bet your sweet buppy this isn't going to be easy. Wait, actually, I'll make it really easy. Thanks so much for stopping by, but no thanks. I gave at the office." I wave bye-bye with my fingers.

"Look, Mrs. Jennings. I'm not asking you to like him. I'm not asking you to respect, or even accept what he did. What he did was wrong, plain and simple. But sometimes even those who have committed the worst offenses need to be given the chance to at least admit it, to extend their apologies, even at this late date."

"I'm not sure that I buy that argument. What's the use in me going to any trouble to allow him to feel better?"

She looks at me with a blank stare. The line "serious as a heart attack" comes to mind. "How about to enable you to feel better, then?" "For me?"

"Yes. For your own closure," she says, her eyes locked on mine. "Look, obviously we have two entirely different takes on the man. And sure, my interest in your approaching him was for his benefit. But what I hadn't really taken into account until now is that you deserve the truth. You're owed answers. How could you not want to know them? I would think if for no other reason than curiosity that you'd feel a need to learn at least that."

Would this be like seeking out dessert at different restaurant after having a particularly bad meal at another one? Like ending the night on a high note after feeling so disappointed with what preceded it?

Once, years ago, William and I celebrated our anniversary at one of the premier French restaurants in Manhattan (which shall remain nameless). I'd looked forward to this meal for weeks—the reviewer at the Sentinel back then had heaped praises upon the place.

Nothing seemed to go right at the restaurant. First we were seated at a miniscule two-top next to the kitchen, despite nearly half the place being empty, on a weeknight, no less. When we asked to be moved, preferably to a window seat (there were five free), the maître d' rolled his eyes and promptly seated us next to the hostess station. Which is fine if you're interested in listening to the phone ring and the hostess acting surly to reservationless walk-ins, but not when seeking a pleasurable dining experience and conversation with your partner.

William wanted white and I wanted red, so we ordered our wine by the glass. The waiter practically had a ruler dipped in the glass for the pour, so as not to dare give us a splash too much for our money.

When I asked the waiter to describe the lettuce sauce served atop the halibut, he looked at me as if I'd asked him what two plus two equals. "It's a sauce made from lettuce," he said without cracking a grin.

Our meals arrived cold, over-sauced and with fava beans frozen in a lake of congealed butter.

At that point William and I decided to cut our losses, paid the bill and left, stopping in at a neighborhood café on the way home, where we had warm chocolate cake and cheap champagne, happy that we salvaged our disastrous anniversary dinner.

So by going to visit my ex-father, might I end up with a fresh slice of cake instead of cold lettuce sauce?

The grandfather clock strikes the top of the hour and my uninvited houseguest glances at her watch. "Crap, Dad's got some more tests today and I have to take him over to the hospital. I really must run. Look, Abbie, please. Consider going to see him. Give a dying man his due."

Due schmue. How about the bill's overdue on the therapy I needed to get over his abandonment. Not that I ever did go to therapy, but maybe I should have. And then sent him the bill.

She takes out a notebook and pen and scribbles down some information. "Here's where you can reach me. And here's where you can find Dad. If there's any way you can find it in your heart, I think you'll be glad you did."

I don't even need to usher her to the door as she scurries out like an unwanted mouse who's been discovered by the pet cat.

ABBIE'S CHICKEN BROTH
(it's not just for breakfast anymore!)

2 lbs. chicken parts (can use all backs and necks, or can include a whole chicken, whatever you want. I prefer white meat so I use a whole chicken and add a few packages of backs and necks for flavoring).

(FYI, I often use turkey parts if available rather than chicken as I prefer the flavor. And if you're really adventuresome, I recommend you find a source for chicken feet and throw a few of them into the pot as well—the marrow is fabulous and good for you!)

1 handful basil leaves
2-3 sprigs fresh thyme
1 long sprig fresh rosemary
1 handful parsley
2 tbl. peppercorns
1 large onion, rough cut
2-3 leeks, ends trimmed, sliced lengthwise and rinsed thoroughly, then rough cut
6 stalks celery, rinsed and rough cut
3-4 carrots, rinsed, peeled (optional) and rough cut
salt, salt and more salt (Kosher), using 1 tbl. at time* at each phase of the cooking process
4-6 chicken feet (optional)

Preheat oven to 350°. Rinse and pat dry chicken, then place in roasting pan. Sprinkle with salt and pepper, brown in oven for 1-2 hours (it doesn't need to cook through, just want to get it to brown up a bit, bring some flavor out of the bones, and get those fabulous brown drippings at the bottom of the pan).

With tongs, transfer chicken to stock pot, being careful not to burn yourself.

In the meantime, drain the fat from roasting pan, while keeping the drippings in the pan. Once grease is drained, put pan on medium high. When hot, deglaze pan with 1/3 c. white wine, stirring up the brown drippings. Add this to the stockpot after it's been brought to a boil (then turn down).

In large stockpot, cover with water 2" above chicken and add 2 tbl. salt. Bring to boil on high heat on stove. Just as it starts to boil, skim scum off surface of water and turn temperature to medium low. Then add rest of ingredients, simmer for several hours (3-4-ish), until meat is falling from bones, stirring occasionally.

Cool pan in ice bath in sink to bring temperature down quickly. Strain ingredients, then strain stock through a finer sieve to remove impurities. Pick meat from chicken, place in separate container. Separate out carrots, cut into bite-sized pieces, place in separate container. Discard all other ingredients. Season stock with more salt and pepper at this point if necessary, to taste. Refrigerate stock etc immediately until use.

I like to layer the salt into the stock by first salting the chicken before putting in oven, then salting the water before brought to a boil, then adding maybe a tablespoon of salt when throwing all ingredients into stockpot. Then adding a tablespoon or so more after stock has been separated from ingredients and strained. At that point salt and pepper need to be gradually added to taste.

If you keep the stock refrigerated, it can last for a week. Just re-boil it every few days. You can also freeze leftover stock for use at a later date. Whatever you do, don't keep the stock on the counter at room temperature, since it's a protein and will foster bacteria growth quite readily.

Distill Intentions, Mix with Confusion

Sharing food with another human being is an intimate act that should not be indulged in lightly.

–M. F. K. Fisher

"HONEY! What are you doing here?" I catch William before he's disappeared for lunch.

"Oh, nothing," I lie. "Well, actually, here." I hand him his phone.

"My phone?"

I try to glean whether he sounds guilty when he says that. It's really hard to determine complicity in the tone of voice of a two-word sentence.

"You left it in the kitchen. This morning. The phone, that is."

"I hadn't even noticed it missing."

We look at each other, two sumo wrestlers sizing each other up. God, the sad thing is I can almost visualize me in a sumo diaper and it's not a pretty sight. Nor does it seem far off-base. At least those sumo wrestlers don't get booted for their weight—instead they're revered for it.

When William and I are around each other at home, we've been able to gloss over the underlining friction of late by doing our own thing. But here in public, where I can't busy myself with food in the kitchen nor William by diddling away in the basement, well, it's awkward. Fact is, we've had a hulking elephant in the corner of our figurative living room for weeks now, and it's awfully hard not to acknowledge the elephant's undeniable presence. Particularly when the elephant has company, in the form of a mysterious beautiful woman with long dark hair. Who may or may not be having an affair with my husband.

I rub my hands together and then wipe my sweaty palms on my skirt. "I thought you might want to go to lunch."

"Lunch? Sure. Just lemme make a quick call."

I wait in the reception area for William to make his call, cranking my neck around the corner searching for her, though don't see a soul.

Twenty minutes later we're enveloped in the clubby warmth of the dark restaurant, enormous bull's heads eyeing me with malice from above. Can't say that I blame them. If I was on the menu I'd be a little ornery, too.

"So," I start off, grabbing a breadstick as a prop, "Anything new going on?"

I take a bite without thinking. So much for that South Beach diet I was working on. I wonder if I can think of a diet in which breadsticks might be acceptable. Maybe I can slop on some low-fat cottage cheese, sprinkle cinnamon atop and pretend it's whole wheat bread?

William opens the mammoth menu and begins to scan, even though I know he'll order his favorite item on the menu—the gluttons special. I've never known him not to order The Stampede to the Shore: a 32-ounce T-bone steak and a lobster tail, served with baked potatoes and an iceberg salad. Yet he is studying the menu as if he'll be tested on it.

"Huh?" he asks, not looking up at me.

"New? Anything new to tell me about?"

He throws in a few cursory sentences about some deal he's negotiating, about his secretary expecting her second baby, and then signals to me he's got to focus on his extensive menu-cramming.

The waiter finally takes our order, and I surprise even myself by order the tuna steak and a side salad. Call me crazy, call me desperate to compete with the woman with long, dark hair, I don't know. But something small and light sounds perfect.

"What'd you do this morning?" he asks after closing up his menu.

"This morning?" Well, er, I saw you with some dark-haired femme fatale atop your Vespa but aside from that…"Oh, a little of this, a little of that. I started off going to the gym, and then I changed my mind—"

"Oh, yeah? Why?"

"Why?"

"Why'd you change your plans?"

"Just wasn't in the cards, I guess."

He shrugs.

"Back home I found your phone so I figured I'd shower and bring it down to you when I had an unexpected caller."

He takes a sip of his drink. "Who was it?"

For the next twenty minutes I proceed to tell him the whole sordid tale about my thin twin. The whole father salvation gig I'm so not into. I figure he'll be completely behind me in not wanting to bother with it.

"When are you going?"

"When? As if!"

"I'm telling you, honey, you're making a mistake if you don't go. Seriously. Soon he'll be dead then it'll be too late. Mystery never solved. Do you really want to be left dangling forever?"

The waiter serves our food and I can focus on my tuna steak instead of the stake in the heart this feels like with even William pushing me toward my non-dad. Can't we all just let that sleeping dog lie?

Before I know it lunch is over and I haven't drummed up the courage to ask about her. I haven't the faintest idea how to without stirring up problems. He'll think I was spying on him or something and I'll look pathetic and after all I've been through, the last thing I want to do is look pathetic.

Up until now I've managed to remain completely un-pathetic with William, in fact. No use in working my way down that path any more than I've gone since being demoted. Besides, surely he's not carrying on with that woman. That's so not like William.

He grabs my jacket and helps me into it and we leave the

restaurant hand-in-hand, which makes me feel better about things anyhow.

We window shop for a block or two, with William checking out a suit here, a pair of pants there that he'd like to try on. I can't help but notice outfit after outfit in the windows of women's clothing stores that will never grace my hangers, let alone my figure. It's a frustrating thing, knowing that I can't just pop into the Gap or Ann Taylor and buy an outfit. Sometimes I think I'd give my eyeteeth to be able to fit into a pair of pants from Banana Republic. But I'm a realist, and I know that even under the best of circumstances, chances are good that those clothes, made for vastly slimmer humans, are not ever going to be on this girl's clothing menu.

We stop outside of Victoria's Secret while William answers an email on his phone, and I wince at the window display. I think I'm even too fat for Vicky's perfume, if that's possible. God, I can't imagine the day that I could wedge myself into anything they sell at this store. I'd look like Hyacinth, the ballerina hippo in Fantasia. Though she did had a certain panache in her frilly-wear. Plus that amorous alligator sure loved her in lace, girth or no girth. The idea of me in lace—even reallllly stretchy industrial-strength lace—does not conjure up the concept of sexy. Ever. More like laughable. Humongous. Pathetic. And we're not going there, remember? Like it or not, me, Victoria and her secrets will never be BFFs.

William notices the sad look in my eyes.

"What's wrong, Abbie?"

I sigh. It's one of those sighs that, if measured in words, would be about as long as an article in National Geographic. And no one would want to hear my lament any more than they can usually take the time to read an article that long.

"I don't know," I start out. "I guess I'm feeling sort of left out." He throws me a quizzical look. "Left out of what? Your job?"

"Job, life, Manhattan, women's fashions, the human race, I don't know," I say. "Everything feels really wrong. I feel like I'm reinventing so much of what I knew about me, and it makes me feel uncomfortable. Anxious. Wondering where I'll end up after everything's said and done."

William reaches out his hand and links it with mine. "That might not be such a bad thing, you know. I've been wondering how to bring this up again, waiting to see if you've given it any more thought—"

Oh, Lord, here comes the baby speech. Why is it that men always find the most vulnerable moments to bring up vulnerable subject matter?

"William, I can't talk about that right now. Now's not the time for me to have a baby." I have this particular look every time William brings up the baby thing—one of those Mommy's-going-to-spank-you-if-you-won't-keep-your-voice-down-and-sit-still during church looks. Not surprisingly, it doesn't sit well with him, judging by the glare he shoots back at me and the way he releases my hand from mine as if he burned it on the coils of an electric stovetop.

"When will be, Abbie? Sometimes I think you're just putting it off until it's too late and the decision is made for you, and then you'll have one more thing to regret having missed out on."

I fixate on a pink demi bra in the window to avoid eye contact with my husband. A hot pink demi bra with black polka dots. Pink. I can only wear black (gargantuan) underwear; it's slimming, they say. My undies cover not only the essentials, but pretty much everything else you can cover up while still being able to breathe unrestricted. Sexy, they are not. The mannequin, a perfect reproduction of Barbie, circa 1964, has the sexiest pair of boy shorts undies on. If she wasn't made of some sort of synthetic material but rather flesh and blood, I'm certain she'd have a pierced navel and a Certs-with-retsin smile. Her friend, Skipper—no wait, I think she's Francie—has a low-cut pink and black cami tank top on, with low-riding tie-string bikini panties. The front says "Think" and I can assume, based on her fiberglass friend, Midge—who's bent over a beach ball so I can see the back end of her undies, which say "Pink"—that Francie's panties repeat that mantra on the back as well. Although maybe

Francie's getting a thong wedgie from her panties, with no room for words there. Ha ha, I'm thinking of an old jump rope rhyme: I see London, I see France, I see Francie's underpants! As little of them that exist.

"Did you know you can actually shop by swell for your Victoria's Secret bra?" I say to William. I learned this from Jess, who indeed, can shop by swell. Not that she's got much of a swell, being as thin as she is. But she's thin, which qualifies you for membership in that club. "God, if I shopped by swell at Victoria's Secret, I'd have to order the Tsunami."

William laughs, forgetting for a minute that he's angry with me. "Swell!"

"Ha, ha."

"Seriously, sweetie, you'd look gorgeous in one of those bras."

I blanch. Ohhh, blanched white asparagus with a Hollandaise sauce is springing to mind, the spargel I loved so much when I apprenticed in a boulangerie in Paris and traveled to Germany for the highly-anticipated spring asparagus harvest. "Don't make me laugh. I'd look about as good in something in that window as you'd look in a man thong."

Oh, God, do you think he's worn a man-thong for the black-haired lady? Who no doubt is at the same time wearing her Think Pink undies—if that—and probably one of those sexy-as-all-get-out cami tops that I couldn't fit over my bicep, let alone the core of my body. I begin to cry at the mere notion of it.

"Sweetheart, what's wrong now?" William appears exasperated with me.

"I want to wear sexy underwear like the lady with the black hair. I want to be able to walk into Victoria's Secret and not have to know that every sales clerk is snickering about my mere presence in the store because I'm too fat even to buy the perfume. I want to be like every normal woman—look at them," I point to ten different women who are walking down the street, no doubt full after having eating salad with fat-free dressing for lunch. They are all waif thin and walk on high, narrow heels in pencil skirts. Heels that would fold like origami under the burden of my weight. I'd need a pencil skirt for each thigh. Nothing about those women betrays even the slightest existence of an appetite or any hint that at some point in their lives they might have ingested actual food. "Is that so much for me to want? To be a normal, thin woman. One with a gratifying job. And I just want to feel happy in my own skin, like they are, dammit."

I lean against the window, Barbie mocking me with her perfect 36-22-36 proportions, cellulite-free and toned like any self-respecting Barbie-ish mannequin would be. I don't know who I'm kidding—my little piddling weight loss after barely attempting to cut back on food intake will never get me anywhere in this life. That's like dropping a quarter in the church collection box on Sunday morning. Token gesture and little else. At this rate I'll be able to wear Victoria's Secret panties oh, in my grave. If someone put them over my head, maybe.

Why can't we be happy with who we are? But then again, why should we be happy with ourselves when we know deep down that we can improve upon ourselves? And why should I be happy with myself when I'm sabotaging my own attempts at rectifying wrongs done?

"Abbie, Abbie, Abbie, honey, calm down! Everything will be okay. You need to stop being so hard on yourself, baby." William has wrapped his arms around me and is stroking my hair. "And who is this woman you mentioned with black hair?" I mentioned the woman in the black hair out loud? I thought I only thought that thought.

I can't even bring myself to look in his face. I'm blubbering (literally, with boogers streaming down my face, and figuratively, if you're talking about my figure) all over the side of my husband's well-groomed hair.

"I saw you with her," I sob. "On the motorcycle. This morning. After you left for work."

"Shelly Hunsinger?"

I stop sobbing for a minute. "Shelly from your office? The one whose husband left her for a 23-year old?" Sweet Jesus, I'm screwed if her husband left someone who looks that hot on a motorcycle for a younger version. Leaves no hope for the likes of me.

"You saw Shelly with me and didn't say anything?"

I nod my head in silence. "I thought you were having a fling with a mysterious woman."

"Abbie—you saw me not an hour beforehand. When would I have had time to 'fling' with anyone today, anyhow?"

I frown. "You'd figure out a way. Maybe a quickie in the parking garage, I don't know."

"Quickie in the parking garage? You ever spend much time in a parking garage in the city? Not exactly the most compelling environment for hot sex, you know."

"Well, I don't know. I just know that I saw her nestled up to you like a baby joey in a kangaroo pouch. It all looked awfully cozy."

"You sure do have a vivid imagination. You ever think about writing fiction? If you must know, Shelly was interested in buying the Vespa."

I look up at him suddenly, alert. Red-eyed, with boogers streaming down my nose. "My Vespa?"

He nods his head. "The thing's been sitting idle in the basement for too long. It's crazy for something as beautiful as that to go untouched."

Yes. Beauty should be touched. And fondled. And such.

"Isn't it mine to sell?"

"In a way, yes. But it's something you practically recoil at any time I've mentioned it. I figured you wouldn't even know it was gone. Plus it was premature to mention anything to you. Shelly hadn't even been on a motorcycle before—that's why I gave her a ride today. She wanted something that could navigate the traffic in Manhattan during rush hour. I figured she'd get a sense of it riding on the back of my bike. And if she liked it, then maybe I'd take her to see the Vespa."

Wow, talk about executive decision. Not only am I being phased out, but so is my ride. Not that I actually ride my ride, but still.

I thrust out my lower lip in a thinly-veiled attempt at pouting. William always sees through the petty pout maneuver.

"Look, Abbie. If you don't want to sell it, we won't sell it. It's just that you seem so set in your ways, I hate to waste the thing."

I stare at Barbie for a minute, and find it weird that they put nipples on mannequins now. Is there a need for such veracity? What next—packages on the Ken mannequins? Why not, what with the enormous Abercrombie and Fitch hard-ons that just so happen to be at eye-level when you walk by the store. Not much is left to the imagination anymore. Maybe that's why it's even harder to be fat nowadays, because thin women adorn their bodies with so little that anyone who disguises their body with fabric stands out all the more.

"Forget about it. Barbie—I mean Shelly—can't have my bike. It's my bike. And I'll get around to riding it when I'm good and ready." I don't dare mention to him that I might actually pop the tires when the time comes.

"Fine. It's your scooter. If you're so concerned about losing hold of more of your life, then keep the damned thing. I don't care. But why don't you think about riding it, rather than letting it fester, like you seem to want to do with other important things in your life, Abbie?"

With that, William crosses the street and disappears in the late lunch throng of pedestrians, leaving me alone with Barbie and Francie, the odd girl out, the only real swell amongst us that of emotions burning through my breast like a bad case of heartburn.

Bring Issues to Boil, Reduce for Several Days Until Concentrated

Never eat more than you can lift.

–Miss Piggy

I suppose it's a good sign that following my troubled exchange with William, I decided to spend some time at the gym, venting my stress on the treadmill and elliptical machines rather than opting to divert to a patisserie and delve into a pot de crème or an éclair or two. I have been known to do just that on more than one occasion. All things considered, so far today I haven't strayed too far from my carb-free intent, even if I'm not exactly following the South Beach Diet the way God had intended it to be followed. That is, if God had any hand in it, which of course we all know he didn't. So if it's not God's word, hey, who needs it? Follow the logic?

At home I take out the pot of chicken stock—yes, the same breakfast indulgence from a few short hours ago, if you'll recall—and heat up a mug in the microwave. Something gravely unsettling about choosing to snack on stock, but I'm willing to give it a go, at least temporarily. If need be.

I notice an envelope on the nearby counter and pick it up. In William's wobbly handwriting on it I see a large heart with what appears to be a drop of blood escaping from where an arrow pierces it. Above the arrow says Abbie and below it says William, and he's made a little plus sign out of the arrow, with the feather vane at the end intersected with the letters TLA. True Love Always. How sweet. Curious, I rip it open.

Abbie, Love—

I hope you'll understand I've decided that I need a little break from us for a while. I'm just trying to work through my feelings right now, trying to understand why our paths have diverged so greatly and wondering if and when we might be able to get things back on track again. I'm trying really hard to see things through your eyes, babe. But I'd be lying to you if I didn't admit that so far I'm falling short. So I need some time to clear my head. I think you'll agree that that time apart could well help to clarify a lot of things for us both. So please, respect my wishes that our time apart be just that: separate. No visits, no phone calls, no communications, barring emergencies. Okay? I'll be in touch when the time is right.

Love,

Me

I stand for a good long while digesting this, my mouth feeling suddenly exceedingly arid. Huh. He's really taking a break this time. Not just a Jersey getaway, but more like an Abbie getaway. As if I'm a really harsh winter in Boston and he feels compelled to seek a Caribbean panacea. The cure to Abbie-dom. Wow. So. Okay then. What does this mean in the big picture? I read and re-read the missive, mining his words for a gem of a clue. I think maybe William just needs to get away for a while and he'll see things differently. He'll realize that everything's fine with us, really it is. Isn't it? I mean, heck. That baby thing? It'll all happen some time. Just not yet. That's all. As for right now? It's just a little break in the action. Every marriage needs a spell sometimes. This is just halftime of the football game. A digestive respite before the dessert course. Yeah, that's what it is.I fold the letter in half, pressing the crease carefully with the side of my hand as if stroking the wrinkles out of my laundry. I fold it again, pressing firmly on the crease, fold in half again. Then again. Before I'm done folding it it's a small wad the size of my thumbnail. I tuck it in the back of a kitchen drawer, making certain to shut the drawer all the way. I then take the ripped envelope, the one with the pierced heart, and hang it with a magnet on the refrigerator. Abbie + William. TLA.Well, looks like no William to be home for dinner tonight. No sense in sticking around here and listening to my voice bounce off the walls. Maybe I should just slip into the office now. Most everyone will be gone soon, I can work in peace and not feel yet again the perpetual eyes of pity on me. I gather up my belongings, including my laptop, feed Cognac, and head outside, the finality of the door closing behind me lending a solemn air to the moment.

The elevators are belching out clots of people headed home to loved-ones as I arrive at the office. Who else but the loved-oneless (or would that be loved-one-on-holiday?) go to work at this point of the day? But that's okay, because this way I can get my work done in an environment unrelated to my home, to keep my mind off of things.

I keep my head down, going right to my cubicle, avoiding the low murmur of a few voices. I've got scales on the brain: many issues weighing heavily in my brain right now: fair versus unfair, balance or not. Jess and Dex. Jess and Abbie. William and Abbie. Abbie and that sneaky rat bastard who stole my job. Abbie and her ex-dad. Abbie and her not-really sister. Something about my life seems extremely imbalanced, and balance, or lack thereof, always reminds me of scales. Which are, of course, the mortal enemy of yours truly…

You Know That Line About the Scales of Justice?

Well, That's An Oxymoron, You Moron

Or:

There is No Justice When It Comes to Scales

I think at this point it goes without saying (well, if it goes without saying, you editors are asking, why then are you saying it?) that scales to me are Public Enemy #1.

I hate them, they only upset me (with the exception of the period immediately following a long bout with a stomach bug), and they only serve to create stress in an already stressful world. They should be banned.

One of the downsides to gaining weight is of course the cruel reality of the scale readout. I can't quite imagine why anyone would buy the type of scale that has a magnifier glass on it. It's bad enough when the numbers are small and barely discernable. But amplified by the thick glass and with people nearby who will then be able to share in your painful secret—it's just not something I'm willing to consider. In fact, if I was asked to design a scale, I think I'd create one that could whisper your weight into your ear—leaving no visible sign of the true weight.

But in the meantime, I've come up with some suggestions that might make your daily/weekly/monthly/annual scale ritual a little more palatable:

RULES TO MAKE SCALE-MOUNTING A LESS OBJECTIONABLE TASK

1) Respect the laws of physics: never cough, sneeze, or apply any other type of undue force while stepping onto a scale;
2) Never, under any circumstances, mount a scale with clothing on;
3) Never—and this is punishable by severe depression—step on a scale after eating or drinking anything. My rule is a full twelve hours must pass before attempting a scale mount after ingesting anything. It helps if sleep occurs somewhere in this time frame; something about sleep can occasionally be forgiving when it comes to added poundage from the previous day's food intake;
4) Take a deep, cleansing breath. Exhale completely and then step gingerly onto scale without inhaling;
5) When things start to look really bad, you may want to consider looking into a scale that converts to kilos—it's a far more user-friendly number;
6) Consider two scales: left foot on one, right foot on the other.

Maybe the weight will be divided that way, and you can average out the combined weight from both scales to no doubt come up with a far more appealing weight;

7) Perhaps go online and order a scale from England. Your weight in stones versus pounds might even bring a smile to your face.

To me, the ultimate public humiliation involving a device that calibrates body mass (aka a scale), is the mandatory scale mount when you go to see the doctor. In my rebellious dotage, I have decided that no doctor needs to know how much I weigh unless I'm about to undergo emergency surgery and the anesthesiologist needs to get it right so he doesn't dose me with enough anesthesia to knock out a horse (who may, alas, weigh less than me at this point). Then, and only then, is this information being released to anyone.

Here's what happened to me not long ago when I had to visit the doctor…

I sit in the waiting room, dread creeping into my mind as I watch the clock slowly advance. Chewing my ragged cuticles, I know it's only a matter of time before the usual confrontation will commence.

"Abigail Jennings," the nurse calls for me.

"How are you?" she flashes her Mona Lisa smile as she leads me into the bowels of the office; I think she relishes what comes next. "Now, come on over here, and if we can get you to just step up onto this scale—"

"No, thank you, I think I'll pass," I quickly interject, hoping the words will breeze by her as rapidly as I'd bypassed that scale.

"Oh, but you have to," she insists.

"I'm sorry, but I'm just here to have two stitches removed from my thumb," I assure her. "I don't think it's necessary for me to do that."

The nurse, now glaring at me with suspicion and dismay, weighs her options (after all, who refuses a nurse's orders?). She steps aside to confer with a few of her colleagues, then returns to me.

"Well, I suppose, if you insist," she hesitates, her brow

furrowed as she furiously scribbles information in red ink onto my top-secret medical chart. "Then just follow me into room number three."

I'm sure I hear her crossly muttering syllable by syllable as she writes in my folder, "pa-tient—re-fu-ses—to—be—weighed."

The remainder of my office visit is punctuated by curt questions on the part of both the nurse and then the doctor, my red-flagged chart singling me out as an uncooperative patient, merely because I refused to mount that dreaded scale.

I simply can't believe I'm the only one out there suffering from scale-phobia—that doctors' offices across America don't encounter reluctant scale-avoiders on a daily basis. Yet the reaction with which I've been met whenever I politely decline a nurse's generous offer to weigh me seems to indicate that I'm the only one bold enough to reject this ritual.

To me, a scale is nothing but the bearer of bad news, confirming my worst fears about my unconfirmed weight. It's bad enough to experience scale mortification in the privacy of one's own bathroom, but to have to stand on that platform while watching a stranger repeatedly flick-flick-flick those weighted metal squares further down the right side of the scale balance—eyes all the while growing larger with astonishment–is more than I can bear.

No one, but no one, gets to see those three magic numbers on my illuminated scale dial. That is if I even got on that scale, which has been hiding in a closet for a couple of years. There is probably no greater secret in the world today (other than how did Michael Jackson morph from a dark-skinned black man into a pasty-skinned white woman) than how much I weigh. And I intend to keep it that way. I wouldn't even let my cat in the room were I to gingerly step onto that reviled household torture implement, and I'm pretty sure she doesn't even understand our whole numeric system.

Scales are just loaded with dark and nefarious issues. One time I had to weigh a package I needed to ship.

"You need to get the postage right," my husband informed

me. "So get on the scale twice: once with the package, once on your own. Then subtract the difference. It's the most accurate way."

Spoken with the ease of someone experienced in package shipping, but sorely uninformed when it comes to scale protocol.

A scale, you see, is a mercurial thing, an object to be approached tentatively and reverently. Be kind to your scale, and it'll be a good day. Step too heavily, or at the wrong angle, and things can go terribly awry. A few pounds overage and your day will be psychologically shot to hell. I had to set my husband straight on this matter.

"Don't you know," I said, "Under no circumstances should one ever mount a scale but for first thing in the morning, after you've gone to the bathroom?

"Plus, this process has to be performed totally naked, preferably with the lights off or dimmed, so as to make the entire process as painless as possible."

My husband rolled his eyes, laughed, and turned back to his work. Women.

Ah, we may be the objects of confounding despair in our husbands' eyes, but face it: we're in The Know.

I've seen people who at the gym work out vigorously for an hour or two, chug a vat of water, and then step on the scale – weighted down with sneakers and jackets—on the way out the door. It stretches my imagination to fathom this risky maneuver. Every true scale aficionado knows that: a) outerwear on the scale is verboten; and b) a liter of water consumed = five pounds of excess weight on the scale immediately thereafter. If I spent an hour on a cardio machine schvitzing my behind off, only to find I've gained weight, I'd never return to the gym again!

I suppose I can think of a few scenarios in which I might be able to regard the scale as friend rather than foe. Upon completing forty days on Survivor, for instance. Or after suffering through a lengthy bout of food poisoning, perhaps. After all, every seasoned dieter knows that the silver lining to a gastrointestinal bug is rapid weight loss. And after laying in bed feeling miserable for days on end, what better way to brighten your day than to step onto your scale and discover you've lost weight?

I suppose that my fear and loathing of bathroom scales is indicative of a deep-seated need to lose at least a few extra pounds. And believe me, I'll be first in line when someone figures out how I can do that while still being able to consume food on a daily basis.

Until that day, I guess I'll just have to avoid getting sick, so that I can keep my doctor's visits to a minimum, and keep my secrets to myself.

COFFEE CAKE FOR THE SCALE-AVERSE

1 yellow cake mix (preferably Duncan Hines)
4 eggs
1/2 c. vegetable oil
1 c. sour cream
1 package instant vanilla pudding
1/2 c. sugar
1/2 c. chocolate chips
1/2 c. chopped pecans
1 tbl. cocoa
1 tbl. Cinnamon

Combine first five ingredients, then beat for five minutes at medium speed. In separate bowl, combine remaining five ingredients. Beginning with batter, alternate cocoa-cinnamon mixture in well-greased bundt pan (should get four layers of batter with three layers of cocoa mixture in between).. Bake about 55 minutes at 350°. Cool 10 minutes before removing from pan. You may have to adjust time and temperature if using a bundt pan with dark, non-stick interior.

I'm entirely lost in my thoughts when I notice Barry speaking sotto voce nearby. I strain to hear what he's saying. "Look Ling, fella. It's up to you," he nearly whispers.

Ling? As in Ling Chung? Whose highly-anticipated two-floor indoor/outdoor Asian tapas martini bar, Happy Chung, is set to open in two weeks and has been beset by construction problems and staff firings already?

"Your call. You know where to put the cash-ola, my friend, by end of business Friday. No cash? Well, I'd sure hate to see any cute little whiskered vermin as I walk by the kitchen when I'm in there reviewing the place. We speaking the same lingo, Ling?" He starts to laugh and reminds me of a villain in a Scooby Doo cartoon.

I'd have gotten away with it if it weren't for you meddling kids!

Only meddling now is me, who is at once appalled that he would taint the good name of the *Sentinel* food section with thuggish threats like that, yet also curiously thrilled that he's setting himself up for me to exact revenge upon him, that rat bastard. Have I mentioned that term before in reference to Barry?

But how do I follow-through on this? I'm not exactly MacGyver. I'm more like Angela Lansbury in *Murder, She Wrote.* Minus the proper British accent (but certainly sporting the dowdy exterior).

As his voice draws nearer, I carefully crawl beneath my desk, aimed away from the entrance to my cubicle, hoping that Barry doesn't notice my presence. All I need is for him to know that I know something's up. But not to worry. There's more than one way to skin a rat. Thank goodness I'm a smart woman. Because like Angela (who, by the way, was a hottie in her heyday), Abbie Jennings will get her man. Or in this case, her rodent. All it'll take is a little cheese…

After slipping out of the office unnoticed I realize I have nothing to do with myself. What a lonely feeling that is. Here I am in a city teeming with humanity, and yet I'm all by my lonesome. There was a time when I'd automatically pop into one of my favorite restaurants, but frankly, that holds little appeal. I just start to wander and pretty soon I find myself approaching my latest regular haunt. It must be a sign. Even though I've already been here once today, I figure nothing bad could happen to me if I worked out at the gym for a bit longer, just to burn off the stress a little.

In the locker room I put on my sweaty gym clothes from this morning and head out to the elliptical machine. It's not too hard to get in the zone, and before I know it an hour has passed. I am drenched in sweat, and admittedly start to get bored of watching Extra on the personal screen in front of me. You can only take so much of Jessica Simpson's weight issues before feeling the need to tune out. I feel sorry for the poor girl, being unable to enjoy eating enough that she steps up to a size four. Crazy country we live in when a size four is fat.

"Can you believe they're calling her fat?" I hear a familiar voice and look next to me to see Jane Greer, of all people, looking very neat and clean (and yes, thin) for being in the middle of sweating. I look at who she's talking about.

"Yeah, I mean granted, the girl's petite stature reveals every ounce of fat she gains, but please, leave her alone already!" I say, figuring conversation with Jane Greer won't hurt me too much.

"I don't know what's wrong with the media, making her out to be such a clown. Well, sure, maybe there are things about her that legitimately make her out to be one, but not because of a few extra pounds on her butt," she says. I nod in agreement. Weird that Jane and I have anything in common. Aside from DNA. I never thought I'd have commonality with the woman on anything.

"I liked your column the other day, by the way," she adds.

"Yeah? The willpower one?"

"Where your pants didn't fit and your husband heard you sucking in your breath trying to force the zipper up?" I slow down a little so I can talk more clearly.

"Can you believe I am crazy enough to let the whole world in on my weight problems?"

"I think it's great," she says. "I mean no one talks about

this. We are in this world in which grown women are expected to have the bodies of tweens. Whatever happened to the Jane Russells and the Marilyn Monroes of the world? Now those were real women's bodies. Those extra pounds on Jessica Simpson would have been revered back in the day."

"You got that right, sister." Um. By sister I didn't mean sister. I meant it in the figurative sense of the word. Awkward!

Jane looks at me, wondering if I am finally conceding something to her. She has a confused look in her eyes, almost as if she's not sure how to process that one little word that slipped erroneously from my lips.

She looks as if she's about to say something, to acknowledge the term of reference, but then she shakes her head and continues to run in place.

It's quiet for a few minutes, but for the usual gym background noise: whirring treadmills, clanging weights, grunting men with excessive testosterone on display with too-heavy weights.

I am not good with awkward silence and can't help but open my yap. "What brings you to my neck of the woods?"

"My gym gives me reciprocity with other places. I had some work in the city and figured I'd get in a workout while I waited for rush hour to clear out. Too much of a pain getting back to Jersey at this time of day."

We whir away for a few more minutes.

"You wanna grab some coffee or something?" She asks out of nowhere. Taken aback, I'm not sure how to respond. It's not as if I have anything to do with my time. "Uh, sure. I guess so."

"Great. I saw there's a cute little juice bar in the lobby—you game?" I nod my head, wiping the sweat from my brow with a towel. Wondering if the sweat is from a hard workout or from being nervous about this ongoing engagement with Jane Greer.

Over a putrid spirulina wheat grass smoothie that tastes like something that has been ruminated from the stomach of a cow munching on a not particularly flavorful patch of grass in the median strip of a polluted highway, Jane and I talk. Well, more like we dance around hard core matters and talk very superficially about things. Jobs. Work. Jobs. Turns out Jane is a buyer for several boutique clothing stores in Jersey and makes frequent trips to Seventh Avenue for work. She has a flair for fashion, and in fact is downright passionate about it. Funny how I'm so not passionate about it, but perhaps that's because fashion has never suited me, or suited my form, as it is. Fashion is a huge afterthought in my life, in fact. It's all about hiding, not emphasizing. From what I gather from Jane, who, by the way, looks fabulous in a jog bra and clingy Under Armour shorts (no t-shirt over everything to hide imperfections, either), emphasizing one's attributes can work, if you've got something attributable. I'm thinking that might happen for me in my next life.

Jane slurps down her smoothie so quickly she orders another one. I'd gladly offer mine but probably not a great idea to share germs outside of immediate family members. Oh, but we essentially would be pretty much that. Only not immediate; rather by default. But genetically, there you have it.

"Hey, you want to start meeting here to work out together?" she blurts out.

Yikes. That would be like a date. She seems like a nice enough person, though. But does that make me somehow complicit in being part of my father and his whole lie if I socialize with Jane? Maybe if we're just working out at the same time that's okay.

"Are you sure? I mean it's awfully far for you to go—"

She waves her hand at me, swatting at the notion. "No big deal. I'm in the city a lot, between work and I come to visit my sister—"

Sister. One of those girls I saw?

"I don't know—" I hem and haw.

"Really. It'll be good. Keep us both on task coming here if there's peer pressure to show up." I weigh the options in my head but know there's no way I can just reject her without being rude and hurtful, so I succumb to peer—or would it be sibling—pressure.

"Okay, then. Sure. Let's."

We make plans to get together and after she finishes drinking her second green smoothie, we part ways. Although I don't feel as if I know her well enough yet to point out the pieces of green stuck in her teeth.

Mix Regrets with Elation, Strain Carefully, Serve Over Ice

The second day of a diet is always easier than the first. By the second day you're off it.

–Jackie Gleason

ANOTHER day, another diet. This one actually seems to makes sense. It's called the Chew and Chew Diet and the idea is simple: rather than racing through a meal, you chew each bite exactly thirty-two times. The idea springs from the braintrust of the Great Masticator himself, Horace Fletcher. Think of him as the Richard Simmons of the late 0's.

"Nature will castigate those who don't masticate!" Was his time-honored mantra. I think we can all be grateful he didn't choose the word masturbate instead. The Victorian world might not have cozied up to that notion. Or was it the Edwardian? They're all the same to me.

He claimed his Fletcherizing would turn a "pitiable glutton into an intelligent epicurean." Hey, seems to be the perfect diet for a food critic—after all, a food critic relishes each bite of food, right? And no food critic worth his or her salt (or sugar) wants to be considered a glutton.

In reading about Mr. Fletcher, I realized that the man seemed to have had his head on straight when it came to this dieting business. After all, he advised against eating before being "good and hungry," or while angry or sad. I certainly could've used that advice over the past, oh, lifetime.

It seems that our man Fletch kicked some Yalie butt at the ripe old age of fifty-eight, going mano a mano against Yale's best athletes and whooping them, thanks to his mastication-induced stamina.

I don't know if this diet's going to increase my overall strength, as Fletcher insisted, but damn, I expect my jaw power to increase exponentially. If nothing else perhaps I can be hired on by a freak show to be the lady who suspends a two-ton truck from her mouth. Now that would keep me from eating for a while.

Interesting that Fletch was a low-pro man. He must have valued his communion wafers too much to give them up. Though he did die of a heart attack, so who knows? And interestingly, a little further research reveals a letter to the editor of a famed New York paper suggesting that Mr. Fletcher's physique was much the same prior to his becoming a powerhouse, so perhaps the diet had little to do with it after all. It all comes down to genetics, doesn't it? And from whence spring my genes? A psycho skinny mother who barely tipped a hundred pounds on the scale, and a father whose size I couldn't even begin to tell you, since I spent most of my life without him.

Speaking of New York papers, after preparing my mastication meal, I settle down with the Sentinel to catch up on the day's news. After all, now that my picture is certain not to be in there, I don't feel quite so threatened by the paper.

After leafing through the headlines, I happen upon a story about a woman who was carjacked and kidnapped from a shopping mall parking lot just after purchasing new clothes to fit her newly-thin frame. Seems she'd lost fifty glorious pounds and was reveling in buying smaller clothes finally. Except that in the ensuing police chase to capture her carjackers, the woman died in a fiery crash.

Wow. I chew on that for a while.

How unfair: this poor woman spent probably the final year of her life—unbeknownst to her—in a state of denial of gastronomic pleasure. Albeit in pursuit of an important goal. But nevertheless, not allowing herself what she probably had regularly indulged in before. If she had known her days were numbered, would she have instead lived in the moment and not worried about the future so much? Would she have maybe found happiness within, with how she was, regardless of her size?

Or would she have been more content to know she'd accomplished a daunting goal? Enjoying the attention she was all of a sudden—finally—garnering. Loving looking at herself in the mirror. Maybe donning some figure-hugging Victoria's Secret undies? Certainly spritzing on the perfume!

The woman's family said that she'd been such a happy person that she had no loose ends to resolve, and that everyone was at peace with their loss.

Again, wow. Not that I want to envy a dead person, because I'm sure she'd rather be alive. And I sure don't want to be her, even if she is thin. But what a gift she gave herself, being happy with whom she was, living each day to the fullest, leaving no loose ends…

No regrets. If I died tomorrow, what would my regrets be? Well, first off, I'd regret that things weren't resolved with William. Of course I'd regret that the most. I'd probably regret how I've handled my recent employment situation. Or lack thereof. And would I regret not having given my father—my ex-father, if you will—a chance to have his say? To give him the gift of leaving no loose ends, especially because he knows his days are numbered. It's within my power to grant him this simple favor. Am I a big enough person (and I don't mean that in the physical sense, this time) to give him that final gift?

With William, I'm afraid the time is not right for me to try to rectify things. He's not ready for me to come to him yet. He said as much. Yet where my father is concerned, I know, of course, that I can't leave things till it's too late. I'm carrying enough weight as it is without lugging around that additional burden.

Ah, Jersey. Who'd have known I'd be finding my way to the Garden State so soon after William's last foray over the river. And to be headed to see my father, of all people. There was a time when about the only thing that would get me to Jersey was to review an especially spectacular restaurant. These fast-paced days just get ahead of you if you don't watch yourself, I guess.

As we cross the George Washington Bridge I stare back at the skyline of the city trying so hard to remember something, anything, good about my father. Somewhere in my retaliatory mind I managed to void any positive memories. I'm my own little dictatorship, censoring all information before releasing it to the public. Or to myself, for that matter.

I start to recall one Christmas Eve, I think I was nine or ten years old. I'm dressed in red and white candy cane-striped flannel nightgowns, the kind with the fringed cotton eyelet lace around the collar and hem. I have red fuzzy slippers with sparkly white pompoms made from fat strands of yarn shot with silver thread. I'm sitting on my father's lap; he's reading *The Night Before Christmas* to my rapt attention.

"Merry Christmas to all and to all a goodnight," my father says, closing the book and lifting me off of his lap. "And now, you'd better get to bed, if you want Santa to come down the chimney and bring you Christmas gifts."

I stand next to my father, cocoa-warm with delight: after all, here I am in my special holiday nightie my grandma had made for me. I hold the flannel in my hands and spread my arms out to admire myself and I spin in a circle of pleasure.

"Daddy, can't I stay up a little bit longer, please," I beg.

He chuckles, swiping my bangs away from my eyes. "Sorry, Muffin, but you need to get to sleep right now. Santa's rules!"

"I have a present for you," I say to my father. I reach under the tree and pull out a small box wrapped in silver snowflake gift wrap, tied with a royal blue ribbon, and hand it to him, beaming.

My father rips the package open and pulls out a pendant of a half of a heart. The jagged center-line obviously bears a mate, which I have already secured around my own neck and tucked beneath my cozy nightgown.

"The key to your heart!" He gasps, as if he's thrilled to be the recipient of my gift.

I pull out my half of the necklace and smile. "Only yours and mine match to make it whole."

"Muffin, this is something I will treasure for the rest of my life," my father assures me, bending down to kiss me on my forehead. And I believe him.

How would I have known then that soon my father would forever take half of my heart away?

The nurse's crepe-soled shoes whisper along the polished linoleum floor as she leads me to my father's room. The wallpaper's birds and butterflies mock the inhabitants of this place: not like they're going to have a chance to be outside with real versions of such creatures much ever again. The hallway reminds me of one of those faux model homes you see in large housing developments that on the outside look like a cozy home, but on the inside it's all business and set up for the sales staff to sell the rest of the houses in the complex. Sort of a reverse bait-and-switch for the old folks in here: they had their real home, now they're in the one that's made to replicate home, minus the warmth and all the vital components of one. No amount of decorative wallpaper in the world would make someone think this place was anything other than a place where people go to die.

The smell of bland food wafts from the industrial kitchen and mingles with the aroma of antiseptics, industrial strength cleaners, and bodies slowing dying from the inside out.

God, this place gives me the heebie jeebies. I'm afraid I'm going to turn a corner and see a guy garbed in a hooded cloak lugging a large scythe, crooking his finger my way.

We pass a host of decrepit men and women in wheelchairs with blank looks in their eyes. They stare up at me as if they're mute panhandlers begging for sustenance. Only there's not much here that will sustain them for long, judging by my impression of the place. The background noise is a blended patter of dueling television programs coming from the community room—white wicker furniture with cheerful floral cushions and generic prints of mauve, baby blue and sage green irises hugging the walls—and the inmates' rooms. I think it's fair enough to call the residents herein inmates.

Is this where people go to die when no one in the family chooses to deal with them anymore? Is this where people like me who can never seem to find the time to expand my family end up, having no heirs to care for me? And is this just desserts for my father for his failures on my behalf?

Gah! I have to believe that no one deserves to be piled into elder-pogroms like this. Of course at some point what do you do with aged relatives in failing health? I was lucky, if you call it that, that my Gigi passed so suddenly in her sleep that I never had to face these dilemmas. I only had to provide for her the proper funeral and burial.

The day before Gigi passed away, I'd gone to her house so that we could make pies together, a tradition we'd established years ago to celebrate the harvest. She and I were big on rituals like that, honoring the passing of the seasons, celebrating quirky holidays and such. We even planted trees on Arbor Day.

By then Gigi's eyes were failing, clouded as they were with cataracts. But she could make a piecrust in the dark, her tactile skills as sharp as they were 20 years earlier. I never tired of watching my grandmother's by-then gnarled fingers working the pastry dough till it was ready, blending and rolling and pinching the crust just so. A day earlier I'd cooked down two Musque de Provence pumpkins, elegant French heirlooms with a brilliant flesh with the intense coloring of a papaya. I took on the laborious task of peeling and quartering apples for the other pies we were making: all for Gigi to share with the ladies with whom she played poker every Wednesday night. Beer and pies, we laughed. What a combination!

As the pies baked in her old gas oven that filled her kitchen with warmth, we sat down with a pot of tea at her authentic farm-style table.

"This sure does remind me of old times," Gigi said.

"I learned from the best." I smiled at her. "Thank you for that."

"No need to thank me. I wanted to be sure I filled in where your mother left off—" She paused mid-sentence and covered her mouth with her hand to ward off the gaff. "Oh, baby, I didn't mean it like that."

"Don't be silly. I know that. No worries," I said. "Besides, it was her fault she failed so miserably at being a mother."

"Well, she tried."

I barked out a jagged laugh. "Yeah, right." I began to pick at lint on my sweater. I hated talking about my parents.

"Maybe it's time you forgave your mother, Abbie," Gigi said, wrapping her hand around my lint-picking one. This was something we seldom discussed, and something I very much wanted to keep that way. Sort of like William and the baby thing.

I held my fingers up to my ears and plugged them. "I can't hear you!" I said really loudly.

My grandmother wagged her coral-painted pointer fingernail at me. "You can go on ignoring me about this all you want. But I'm just looking after what's best for you, honey. Always have, always will. And I think it would do your heart a world of good if you could forgive your mama for her failings." Funny we didn't even bother to discuss forgiving my father. She was still boiling mad him herself.

"And then what? It's all I know of her. Am I supposed to just forget it all?"

My grandmother sighed and paused a long minute before continuing. "I'd like for you to remember the good in your life and let go of the bad. And I know you've had your share of bad, baby. Life's not always been fair to you. But the truth of it is life's not fair. Never has been, never will be. You've gotta take what you can out of it and just throw out the rest. The rest is just garbage that you don't need to deal with."

"Garbage is right." I frown. "I don't know what would have come of me had you not saved me from them, Gigi."

"Oh, Lordy, let's not even worry about that. Fact is I did save you. I made sure my sweet Abbie had a home. That was the most important thing to me, you know."

I nod. Of course it was. Weird, in a way, since my grandma wasn't technically even a blood kin to me. But then again, two people who were genetically connected to me behaved as if they weren't. So much for that "blood is thicker than water" theory.

"And I know right down to the end your mother dropped the ball—"

"That's putting it mildly."

"You know what I mean. But with everything that she did wrong, she did wrong for reasons we'll never know. Though I betcha they actually had nothing to do with little Abbie and everything to do with her own set of demons."

"And you're defending her why?"

"I'm not defending her, honey. I'm trying to get you to see that holding onto all of that negative energy is holding you back. It's not letting you move forward and live your life the best that you can."

"I'm the nation's top food critic, you know? That's not exactly small potatoes. And if that's being held back, I wonder what I'm missing out on then."

"What you're missing out on is the ability to forgive. To forgive your mother for her failings. To forgive your father for his. And ultimately, to forgive yourself for taking the blame for them. If there's one thing I need to do before I die—"

"Don't say that!" I hold my hands up against the thought.

"I'm an old lady. I won't be around forever. I worry round the clock that you won't have anyone to straighten you out."

"I've got William." "Sure, you've got William. Wrapped around your finger, that is. You say jump and he asks how high. He's not going to tell you to let go of that because he doesn't want to stir up any old issues for you. That's why I'm stirring them up for you—I'll be the cook in your psychological kitchen. It's time to let go, Abbie. Give yourself that gift."

I guess I eventually paid my grandmother some lip service and a couple of yeah, yeahs and then the pies came out of the oven and we got distracted from the conversation, thank goodness.

The next evening I got a call from one of her poker friends. Everyone showed up to play but my grandmother didn't answer the door. By the time I got there someone had found a key she'd hidden in an old condom wrapper beneath a tree in her side yard. Only Gigi would be so creative. We found her sleeping peacefully on her back, her face looking up, hands clasped in what appeared to be prayer.

Thank God the poker ladies were there to help me. And

William, of course.

Unfortunately by then I seemed to have a knack for unexpected encounters with the death of a loved (or not-so-loved) one, having weathered the untimely demise of my dear old mom.

My mother and I seldom spoke. I'd long ago basically moved in with Gigi, only popping into the house occasionally for good measure. I'd gotten myself through college, and when I came back to visit Gigi, I'd poke my head in to see if my mother was taking visitors. That was about what it had come to: she was like a bad version of Gloria Swanson, hiding in her darkened house, aging, miserable and alone. So it was a surprise one day when I got a message from my mother.

"I need you now, Abbie," she'd said in a weak voice to my answering machine. "I want to talk to you."

God, how I hated those times when she wanted to talk. Invariably her version of talk involved her berating me for something, usually it had something to do with my appalling weight (which wasn't so bad back then), and also to bash my father, even though they'd been apart longer than they'd even been married by that time. I hadn't the desire to defend myself yet again, and certainly wasn't going to stand and be an advocate for my selfish father. So what was the point?

I was reluctant to oblige her, but as was often the case, guilt, always the engine that powered me, advanced me forward.

When I stepped inside the house that afternoon, the air seemed terribly still. It was approaching dinnertime, and the late-day sun peering through the transom windows—the only uncovered windows in the place—shone a spotlight on the dust motes snowing down from on high. It was the only movement I sensed in the place.

"Mother!" I shouted. I could never bring myself to settle on a more endearing term with which to address her. It almost felt like I should've added the word "dearest" after that.

Usually if I called out like that, my mother would reply in her weak-tea voice, that diluted attempt to speak that lets the listener know how long-suffering the speaker is. But that day, nothing.

I climbed the steps two at a time, wondering what was up. A slice of light drew me toward a cracked door at the end of the hall—it was the spare bathroom. The one I used to use, till I moved in with Gigi.

"Mother?"

I opened the door and was bowled over by the noxious aroma of bile and vomit. My mother's body was suspended over the toilet, her face touching the water's surface. Her hair was matted with sick, her skin a pallid gray. Everywhere was puke. Puke and pills. And empty bottles that once contained those pills: barbiturates, valium, codeine, you name it, she'd evidently swilled it all down with the nearby bottle of vodka to cement the deal. God, I'm surprised she didn't just eat a half dozen chocolate éclairs instead, as I always figured she'd die if she ever ingested such a radically fattening bakery product.

"MOTHER!" I screamed it that time. I pulled her back out of the toilet bowl by her vomit-clotted, damp hair, and—frozen in place—her body thudded backwards. I was torn between feeling as if I needed to touch her to see if she was indeed dead and the sheer repulsion of coming upon her in such a grotesque condition and being terrified to touch anything of her. The rank odor permeating the room caused my stomach to double over on itself and I began to dry heave, soon retching up the contents of my own stomach as well.

I panicked—I didn't know if I was supposed to deliver mouth-to-mouth or feel for a pulse or shake her to wake her up, but, God, there was little doubt she was dead. Her eyes were open and staring up at me. Nothing moved on her, no slight rise of the chest to indicate even a shallow breath. Already cadaverously thin, her threadbare cotton nightgown clung to her skeletal frame, the fabric stained with excrement. I raced down the stairs, over to my grandmother's place. Yet I didn't want her to have to witness this either. Grandma called the police, who confirmed what we already knew.

The thing about losing my mother wasn't that I lost her. I'd lost her already, long, long ago. But that she had to make her exit in so dramatic a fashion, in a way that would remain with me forever, well, it angered me. It angered me deeply. It was selfish of her, the last of a series of deeply selfish acts by a woman who gave me life, but was incapable of subsequently giving any of herself to me.

My grandmother took care of most everything to do with disposing of my mother's remains. She insisted on a simple service for her, but I refused to go. My mother ended up buried somewhere one notch above a potter's grave. I honestly never asked where and my grandmother never told me, a secret that went to the grave with her.

The only good that came of my mother, in the end, was that I used the money from the sale of her duplex when I met William and we decided to take off to Europe. So maybe in some small way she did allow me a re-birth.

Distill Intentions, Mix with Confusion

It took a lot of willpower, but I finally gave up dieting.

–Anonymous

THE smell of this place reminds me too much of the smell that day with my mother. I'm teetering on flashbacks when the nurse ushers me into my father's room.

"Here you are, Mrs. Jennings," she says, pointing to one of those complicated hospital beds with knobs and buttons and protective railings that just can't help but remind you of the precariousness of the situation.

My father is asleep with the bed propped halfway up, his head cocked at an angle toward his chest, his near-hairless scalp on display front and center. He's dressed in a pilled gray plaid sweater vest and a pair of mismatched brown Hagar slacks that seem to swallow him whole, as such pants tend to do on old men. He's got the television cranked up loud on ESPN Classic, a football game from about thirty years ago on the screen in faded glory. Maybe he's trying to relive a time when life was more agreeable to him than it's now become. Although thirty years ago would be right about when things were going to hell at home, so doubtful. Or maybe that faded film serves to de-emphasize the reality of what was?

I feel almost like a voyeur being in here right now, privy to his apparently peaceful sleep. Though how he could sleep peacefully ever again after doing what he did to me I'll never know. I think about that sad, scared, confused little girl I was, being dragged away from him upon finding him with his real family, and I firm my resolve to not yield to him, even if he tries to sweet talk me.

I stare at his face, trying to see me there. Yet all I see are the ravages of time, a face that bears witness to life struggles, as evidenced by the hard lines set across it. I watch as his old-man's sunken chest rises and falls rhythmically; it's almost hypnotizing in its regularity. I think back to my mother, stiff with rigor mortis, frozen in place on the cold bathroom tile, no motion from her lungs, nothing hypnotizing about her, and realize that soon this will be my father as well. Maybe not sprawled upon a bathroom floor, but soon all that he was won't matter anymore, at least to him. And all that he will leave behind is either finished or unfinished business. Some of it in the form of me.

I think about Jane Greer and that twinge of jealousy rears its ugly head at me. Jane who had the Daddy. I instead merely had the Donor. Well, dad-for-a-while turned-donor. I think about the way he left, as if he'd gone out to mail a letter or something. And never came back. Like sending out a message in a bottle that shows up thirty years later. I ponder all of those events in my life that were glaringly void of a father figure: bringing boyfriends home (not that I did that much, but still), the prom (and we know how that turned out), graduation, going off to college, my wedding.

God, I could use something to eat right now. I rifle through my purse in search of anything that could be construed as food. Amazingly I pull up a relatively intact power bar, something I optimistically threw in there in case I was trapped in an avalanche and food was not an option for the foreseeable future so I'd have to make do. I bite off the tiniest of bites and proceed to chew. And chew and chew and chew. I just know with this diet I'm going to end up biting my cheek or my lip, and then I'll be sorry. I help myself to another nibble, chewing and chewing and chewing some more. I'm like a cow chewing its cud.

My father makes snoring noises that remind me of Cognac when he sleeps. Only Cognac is frequently chasing remote control airplanes in his sleep, and I doubt this is the case with my father. He's probably either running from the grim reaper or running from his demons, including me.

I settle into the brown vinyl recliner next to his bed, trying to seek comfort in my position but only feeling as physically awkward as I do psychologically. I study the football game on the television: it's some championship game with the New York Jets, and Joe Namath is the quarterback. Those were the days, back when men were men and some left their daughters for better families…

All of a sudden I feel a set of eyes settling on me. I look over to see he's awake. Oh, God, I'm not ready for this. I stand up, stiff as a board.

"Janie?" he mumbles, rubbing his watery faint blue eyes. "Janie?"

I don't know what to say so I just sit there, frozen in fear/stress/performance anxiety.

"Janie-pie. You look like you've put on some pounds. You'd better start thinking about losing weight or Jason will leave you!" He snickers at his joke. I gather Jason is Janie's wife.

Is this why he left my mother? Because of her weight? Or is this why he left me? For that same reason?

Whoa. That's impossible. My mother was the one obsessed with weight, not my dad. The bastard. Damn him, dissing Jane—I mean me!—for a body size. What is with this man? The things he's done wrong could fill a book, yet he'd criticize someone for having put on a few pounds? Well, maybe more than a few pounds, if he's thinking Janie went from her to me, size-wise, since he saw her, oh, maybe yesterday.

I'm starting to contemplate just slipping out, figuring he'd never realize it was me who had come, anyhow. As far as he knows I'm just Jane-who's-been-porking-out, when I notice a familiar something winking up at me from beneath his mock ribbed turtleneck collar. Despite myself I reach out to touch it.

Half my heart. He's wearing half my heart around his neck.

I drop it quickly, as if my fingers are scorched by the heat of it. How do I reconcile this with the father that I know? Knew? A father who completely forgot about me the minute the door slammed behind him. Yet remembered about my heart, after all these years. I take another bite of the power bar and chew as if my life depended up on it.

"He wears it all the time, you know."

I look over to see Janie leaning against the doorway, her arms crossed, her right leg bent, foot pressed to the door jamb.

"No, I didn't know," I say through my incessant chewing. But did I want to know?

"When we packed up the house we went through all of Dad's effects. I came upon this necklace and almost pitched it. Only he about pitched me when I tried to. You can't do that! He yelled at me. That's my last connection with my Muffin. And then he started to cry."

I'm silent, not quite sure what to say, letting everything just unfold while I digest it.

"I know you think that he forgot about you, but I'm pretty certain you're wrong about that." She starts to move forward and leans over her father's head, stroking his thin hair away from his eyes. "Right, Daddy? Did you say hi to Abbie?"

My father's eyes grow large and damp. "Muffin?"

Okay, this is sort of like a hospital, right? A nursing home? There are medical terms that are common between the two, right? Because I need something stat! I need something, anything, that will work to assuage the anxiety that is burbling up inside of me. Chocolate pudding would do, and it's a nursing home, so surely there's some chocolate pudding nearby. I could even settle for rice pudding in a pinch. Jell-O? Not so much. But maybe even some saltines could help matters.

My father's hand trembles as he reaches out toward me; it's as if he wants to touch me to be sure I'm not a mirage. I wonder for a minute what happened to those strong hands of his—the ones I saw last peppered with shards of glass and speckled with blood. Now they're mere shadows of the strong tools of the past: tissue-paper skin—spotted with age and threaded with blue-green veins—barely covers the frail bones. Reminds me of the fragile frogs' legs we had to pin down in those sticky pans during dissection in eighth grade science class.

Well. Life ultimately becomes the great equalizer, doesn't it? Even the less-than-mighty fall, eventually. I try hard not to flinch as his fingers slide between mine. It's as alien a sensation to me as it would be to bite into a Big Mac.

His voice is a hard cheese rasping against a grater as he calls out to me again. "Muffin? My little Abbie girl?"

Little? Now there's a word seldom used in conjunction with my name. I'll give him props for that.

I haven't the slightest idea what I'm supposed to say to him. My fantasies from long ago of cracking my hand hard across that face, or at the very least letting him know in no uncertain terms what I thought of him, all seem to have dissolved away at the sight of this diluted version of my former father.

"Dad, didn't you have something you wanted to tell Abbie?"

He nods his head so slowly I barely notice it. Jane takes this as her cue to leave us alone and slips out of this claustrophobic room, closing the door behind her.

The crowd roars in the upper left corner of the room. I look up to see Joe Namath has just scored another touchdown. The camera shows a close-up of his face, long before he would become bloated with age and alcohol. Long before his nose was gnarled like a tree root. Damn, he was a good-looking man. And I remember that my father, too, was a handsome man, so full of life. But my days of being pushed on the swing set by my loving father are long gone now, and the reality of how life can chew you up and spit you out (now wouldn't that be a smart diet? Zero calories!) has instead eclipsed the romanticized notion of the days of yore.

"You should know," my father begins as I jerk my eyes away from the grainy film on the screen, "I never meant to hurt you."

I never meant to hurt you: this line ranks right up there with I'll respect you in the morning or I love you as one of the top one hundred lies men will tell you in order to get what they want out of you. Well, he's getting nothing out of me, that's for sure.

I purse my lips together, and instead of chewing my latest bite of food I let it just sit there, softening up beneath my tongue. I know if I open my mouth now, out will gush forth a tidal wave of unpleasantries and I'd just as soon take the high road. No need to beat up an old man, even if he is my former father and probably deserves it. Hell, I can beat him up with silent treatment and still prevail.

"Your mother, she was a tough broad, that one was. It was okay at first—she was young and spunky and when we went at it, we eventually got over it. But the older she got, the more she let everything get to her. She could only think about how she didn't want to be fat. All the time, 'I'm not eating that! I'll look like I'm pregnant again!'" He says this in a high-pitched voice, mimicking her.

"Enough already, I'd say. Fat, thin, who cares? Pretty soon she cut me off." He slices his hand slowly across his neck. "Nothing! No more. 'What'd I do to deserve that?' I'd ask her. 'I can't stand how I look and I know you can't either' she'd say back. What could I do? I told her I loved her no matter what she looked like, even though she looked fine anyhow. No matter. For a long time I put up with it. But then Marjorie came back into my life—"

I clear my throat. "Look, I don't need or want to hear this—" I don't even know what to call the man—should I call him Dad? Or Mr. Cartwright?

He holds his hand up to stop me from continuing. "You should know this. This is the story of what happened. You need to know it."

He closes his eyes, apparently the strain of this confession takes it out of him. For a minute I watch his shallow breathing and notice his silvery eyelids flickering closed, then opening. "Marjorie and I dated before I ended up with your mother. We had plans to be married one day. But her father didn't like me one bit. When he thought things were getting too serious, he sent her away to live with an aunt somewhere. It happened so suddenly, I had no way of ever finding her. One day she was there, the next day she was gone."

Ugh. As if I want to hear how my father hooked up with his better family? I stare up at the television and wish I had a Budweiser just like the guy in the commercial. At least it would fill the void in my gut that my soggy power bar is clearly not occupying successfully.

"Your mother and I had known each other for a long time—even while Marjorie and I were dating your mother was hanging around all the time. Soon as Marjorie was gone, she was at my doorstep. I was heartbroken, so I just went along with everything. Before I knew it, she was pregnant with you and we got married. It happened like that—" he weakly snaps his fingers. "Lickety split. At first things were okay. Well, better than okay—we had you! But things got gradually worse and your mother became very mean. And then when Marjorie came back to town with Jane—"

"Jane? She came before me?"

He nods his head, hanging it a little as if ashamed. "Jane was why Marjorie left town. Only I didn't know it then. She was pregnant and her father turned her out, sent her off to live with her aunt in Wyoming."

"So not only were they your good family, but they were your real family. Now it's starting to make sense," I mutter under my breath.

"What's that?" he asks.

I shake my head. "Nothing."

"I didn't even know she was back in town. I'd gone to the park one Saturday to escape for a couple of hours after your mother and I had had another huge fight. I was sitting alone on a swing, rocking back and forth, my feet planted on the ground. Then I heard her calling out Janie's name. I looked up and saw Marjorie standing there, hands on her hips, a little girl right before her. And then I knew."

God, if this wasn't to do with my twisted fate I'd almost shed a tear at how sad this is. It's like Prince Charles never getting to marry that butchy Camilla.

"We talked for hours that day. Hours. By the time I left there, I felt as if I had my life back. Something had been missing from me since Marjorie was taken away. But still I stayed with your mother because it was the right thing to do."

"And me," I barely choke out.

"And my Abbie muffin." I roll my eyes. This muffin thing

is about plucking my last nerve. I feel as if he gave up nicknaming rights when he ditched me.

"But there were children. That day. At the mall. More than just Janie."

He reaches for a sip of a drink by his nightstand and sucks on the straw till he chokes. Oh, God, can't have him keeling over now with me here—I'll be blamed for it for sure.

He nods again, hanging that head again, too. "Yes, there were. Are."

"You were a bigamist."

He pauses, the air thick with unspoken words and my unexpressed anger. I look up at Joe Namath, hoping for my own Hail Mary pass.

His sigh sounds like the air being let out of a tire: quiet, slow, drawn out. "Was I dishonest? Yes. To everyone. Completely dishonest. And I can't excuse it away, not at all. The only thing I can say is I loved Marjorie and then she was taken away from me. And I tried with your mother, God, did I try with her. But it became impossible. Life with her was unbearable. I was weak—I turned to Marjorie to find some love in my life. I know it was wrong. But I did it."

"And the other children?"

"Maggie came next. Then Megan. And even though I know it was wrong, I didn't regret it for a minute. It was what was meant to be. But what I did forever regret was you–"

"Me? You regretted me?"

I sag against the wall, a fallen soufflé.

"No, no, Muffin. I didn't regret you, not ever. I regretted what I did to you."

"So when did you decide that you wanted to leave me for them?"

Again, the deep breath, followed by a long silence. The announcers are talking about an interception that happened. I always laugh at the urgent immediacy of football, but looking back on it, what did it matter? One more insignificant blip in time. Same here, all of this stuff. We're all living in the past right now, it seems.

"That night. The night I left. Your mother had found out everything. Everything. She was out for blood. You heard her. How could you not? She wanted to tell you. I begged her not to. The last thing I wanted to do was drag you into the whole mess."

I puff out a sarcastic laugh. "Don't you think I was already in the middle of it?"

He flutters his hand as if to say let me continue.

"I wanted so much to do something, to bring you into this family to be part of something good. But your mother decided to use you as a tool against me. That night after she confronted me, she told me to get out immediately. If I didn't leave then and there, never to return, she vowed she'd drag you through the entire mess. She said she'd be sure that you were so publicly humiliated that you'd never speak to me again anyhow. She didn't care if neighbors found out, if people at your school learned about it. As far as she was concerned, the more the merrier. She decided if she was going to be unhappy, then so was everyone else. So I had to make a choice, on the spot. At that very moment, I chose to leave in order to keep you from having to live my mistake forever. It's something I've had to live with my whole life, something that has pained me every day of my being alive."

My legs feel as limp as overcooked spaghetti, so I plop down in the recliner again and lay back, taking this all in. My eyes fixed on an oily stain on the ceiling and I mumble, "And the shopping mall?"

"God, Abbie. I didn't know what to do. I had no idea you'd be there. I had no idea how to handle it. My family knew nothing about you. Even Marjorie—she knew I'd been married but she didn't know about you. I never had the heart to tell her. So then there you were, and I panicked. Not only did I know that I could never have contact with you without your being destroyed by it one way or the other, but I didn't dare risk screwing it up with my…new…family."

"So my mother held me hostage with the threat of humiliation and you were too cowardly to stand up to her, betrayal or no," I say through gritted teeth. This certainly explains so much to me. I don't know that I feel better about any of it, but at least now I can start to understand it.

"I so wanted a family. A real family, lots of kids, a house filled with laughter," my father continues. "Your mother refused to consider it. But even as she refused it, she squeezed the life out of the one we had, so that we could never survive intact. I knew you had your Gigi, I knew Gigi would take care of you. I knew you'd be okay."

"So you gave up a family so you could have a family? A better family?"

He shakes his head with effort. "It all sounds so shallow when you say it like that. I don't know if I can ever make right what I did. I only wanted you to know it had nothing to do with you."

"You know mother always talked about your other family with poisoned barbs on her tongue. 'The Others,' she'd spit. I knew about you for sure, after everything that happened how couldn't I? I wasn't a stupid child. I knew them as your 'better family.' That was the family you wanted. The one you couldn't—or wouldn't—discard."

"I tried one more time. A few years had passed. I hoped your mother would realize by then that you deserved to have your father in your life. When I showed up at the house, she told me if I didn't get off the property immediately she'd call the police. Then she threw some books and things at me as I turned to leave."

"What about Gigi?"

"I tried to set up meetings with Gigi. But she was so angry at me, and didn't want you to be hurt any more than you already were. She told me I'd caused enough trouble for one child's lifetime."

Now it's my turn to sigh. It all seems so upside down. Upside down cake. I once had a spectacular mango upside down cake while on vacation in Jamaica. Drenched in caramelized mangos and saturated with Jamaican rum. Yet that oddly doesn't even appeal to me right now. Come to think of it, the more I realize how my mother's obsession with food led not only to her downfall but my entire family's, the more I'm aware of the danger of that obsession. Here I am, practically reliving my mother's life: fixated over my weight, even though I'm actually fat, whereas she was only fearful of become fat. It's as if I need mental gastric bypass surgery in order to radically alter my thinking and clear my mental passageways. How could I ever let myself allow my size to regulate my life so much? And when phrased in that way, how vain and downright silly it sounds to do so.

"So I have half sisters…" What an alien concept. Me, the girl with no family.

He nods his frail head. "Three. All of whom want to get to know you. And they have kids now, too." I don't know if I'm ready for holidays with this 'family' yet. But is there any harm in meeting the girls who got my father? Maybe I could work on gaining family instead of gaining weight for once?

"I've got nieces and nephews?" I catch myself. "Sort of."

"I finally told everyone about you about ten years ago. They all wanted to try to find you, but by then I had no idea where to track you down. Your grandmother was gone, your mother too. You obviously were married, with a new name, a new identity. I'd given up hope of ever finding you again. Until the picture—"

Oh, no. Not the picture.

"—And I saw that face. That beautiful face I never thought I'd see again. It gave a man his dying wish, to try to make things right again. Oh, Abbie—"

His eyes are glistening and I can't bear to watch an old man cry. He called me beautiful. Beautiful? I never think of myself as beautiful. I just think of myself as Abbie.

I'm not sure what I'm supposed to do. I don't have much experience with pouring out my emotions like this, like a pitcher of syrup onto a plate of pancakes, especially with someone who I've resented for much of my life. How do I reconcile myself with these competing emotions? On the one hand I know that he deserves some sort of credit for trying to right his wrongs, albeit a little late in the game. But on the other hand, I'm not sure exactly how to feel for him. If I sit back and look at this from a completely impartial perspective, everything about it is awfully sad. Lost loves found, too late. Children abandoned in order to reclaim that love, leaving a void never to be filled for either of us.

"Do you think you can ever find it in your heart to forgive me for ruining your life, Abbie?"

Ruining my life? Gee, my life is hardly ruined. For that matter, even though things are a bit of a mess right now, my life is—was, until my husband walked out on me—just about perfect, I'm starting to realize.

I hold my hand up to him to stop. "Hey. Look. Nothing's ruined about my life. I have a great life. I have a loving husband, a great dog. My job was the best. Nothing's ruined for me. And honestly, I was too stubborn to let you ruin everything, back when having a father really mattered to me. So really, I'm fine."

He reaches out and touches his hand to my chin, directing my head toward him. "You're fine, but are you happy?"

I think about it for a minute. "Happy is relative. Sure, there are things in my life I could fix. But overall, I'm just fine."

"Fine?"

"Yeah, fine."

"Happy?"

I'm silent some more. "Let's just say I'm working on it." And I am working on it. After all, I came here, didn't I? Wasn't that a good start? And what about all the other changes I'm going to make? Starting with right now. Becoming a better me, overall. Trying to bury old hatchets (with the possible exception of Barry). If I really want to start over and turn over a new leaf—or should I say fold over the egg whites—then maybe I need to try to swallow this all. Try to see things from my father's perspective. Maybe not forget, but find it in me to forgive him. After all, what good does it do me to hold this against this old man in front of me. Will I ever feel warm and fuzzy about him? Probably not. Too much has happened for me to just out and out embrace him. But I suppose I need to give him some credit for at least trying, at this late date. And maybe it is this late simply because circumstances forbade it earlier.

I hoist myself out of the seat yet again. Man, recliners these days really swallow a girl up. Although this recliner is probably about as old as I am. And if I'm to be honest with myself a girl of my girth isn't exactly made to gracefully exit one of these things. Once I heft myself out of the thing, I step forward toward my father and his imploring eyes. The same eyes I remember staring into when he read me storybooks as a child. The same eyes that looked at me that night in the kitchen and then looked away as he walked out the door. God, Abbie, just stop it. Don't focus on what was. Focus on what is. What will be. Enough of the past.

"Look, Dad." I choke out the word 'dad,' so uncomfortable is it passing my lips, like a snake swallowing a large mammal. Dad. Wow, who'd have ever expected me to speak that word under any circumstances in a personal reference? Except maybe regarding William, who wants so much to be a daddy himself. God, what a mess I've made of things. "So I'll be honest here and tell you I don't exactly know what it is I should say. Is there a part of me who has hated you for all of these years for walking away from me? You bet. But is there a part of me that feels terribly sad about what you must've gone through? Sure. I hate that everything happened the way it did. And part of me will never quite understand how you could have given me up if you really loved me—"

"You have to know I did—" I hold my hands up to stop him. No need for him to beg.

"Okay, I can appreciate your feelings about this. But still, this is an awful lot to swallow, even for someone who has to swallow a lot on a daily basis for her job. But my gut tells me I have to just trust that this is how it was meant to be, that something set this all in motion, so I have to let it all play out now. I mean I don't know that I can see trimming the Christmas tree with your family quite yet but—"

I look over at him and tears are streaming down his crevassed face. It reminds me of snowmelt seeking a path down a mountainside. And then he starts to cry, loud gasping sobs that send Janie rushing in to see if I've dismembered him or something.

"Daddy? Everything okay?"

My father—our father—can't speak, so overcome is he with emotion. Even I'm fighting back tears, struggling to figure out what to say to my half-sister. Wow, how weird is that to consider her anything but the enemy. Not that she had anything more to do with this than I did.

"It's okay," I reach out to pat her hand, which is resting on top of my father's hand. "It's just a little much." Tears are pooling in my eyes. I feel really foolish crying in front of everyone. I am just not one to emote. Just when I think I can suppress my tears long enough till I can get out of here, Janie reaches out for me and folds me into a hug.

"I don't know how to thank you for being a big enough woman to do this for Daddy," she whispers to me. Um—big enough woman? I hope she didn't mean that the way it came out!

I hold my hands up to indicate it's nothing. Of course I know better. It's something. Something really big. A paradigm shift in how I'm thinking, how I'm feeling.

We all talk a little longer, but I realize I have to be heading back to the city. We make plans to get together again soon; maybe if and when William comes back I can bring him along. As I'm picking up my coat and purse to leave, my father grabs my hand.

"You've given me the greatest gift a man could get," he chokes out. "You'll never know how much this means to me. I love you, Muffin. Always have, always will."

I wish I could eek out the words 'I love you' but I'm not there yet, if ever. Instead I just envelope his hands with mine and squeeze. "Take care, Daddy." I figure calling him that is enough for now.

Blend Tragedy with Heartache, Simmer on Low

Uh—oh! Mommy's on a diet and we're all gonna die!

–refrigerator magnet

I admit, my husband once dubbed me "our lady of immediate gratification" for a good reason. After what I've just been through, though, you can hardly blame me for a little binge-eating. I couldn't resist the temptation. Call me spineless, it's okay. I've heard worse. And it wasn't anything too much–just a little cookie. Or two. Full of healthful things like nuts (proteins) and chocolate (some studies purport its health benefits, right?). I mean, why not. It's a teeny weeny (well, maybe not quite teeny weeny, but not as big as Mrs. Fields' or anything) cookie. Or two. How bad can it be?

Just for good measure I chewed each bite thirty-two (or is it thirty-six?) times. Which took away some of the charm of the cookie, since once it's been masticated to within an inch of its life like that, it's not exactly the little chunk of baked heaven it was when it first went into my mouth. What can I say? My willpower won't. I will admit I've noticed a disturbing food trend with me: what I eat never involves what I should eat, but rather what I want to eat. I have to figure out how to want to eat what I should eat. Good luck with that one. The fact that I struggle to stick with one simple diet is the theme of my column this week, so I suppose for the contraband cookie I should be thankful for the inspiration it provided me.

ADD DIETER

I've done a little research and I've finally hit upon the reason I cannot stick to a diet. And I realize that like any other physiological problem, I can't really help it. You see, I'm ADD when it comes to dieting. Attention Deficit Disorder. Dieting just simply cannot hold my attention for long.

Well, it's no wonder! And here I thought it was lack of self-control or something pathetic like that. I'm so relieved to know my hands are tied in this situation. But in truth it doesn't help when I'm surrounded by friends who must not be ADD in the diet department. In fact, now that I think about it, perhaps they're actually ADD eaters. They must lose interest in eating as readily as I lose interest in dieting! Of course that's starting to tick me off over the years as I've watched them transforming into sylph-like shadows of their former selves.

A colleague of mine has been counting carbs and now she's so skinny that when I saw her a few weeks ago in this cute little June Cleaver-type dress, I complemented her on how slender she looked. She blushed as she told me her dress was from her trousseau. Now at first I wondered, what does a former Canadian prime minister have to do with her dress? But then I realized that she didn't say Trudeau, but trousseau, which is a quaint antiquated term referring to things you wear on your honeymoon or something like that. So here's this woman, old enough to be referring to her dress as having come from a trousseau, and she's been able to whittle herself down to the cinched waist of a Barbie doll, the size she was when she was first married, long ago. And part of me hates her for that.

Why can she do it and I can't? And then I remember my own smug little self the last time I got thin. My friends were still toting around excess flubber while I glowed with the newfound willowy shape with which I'd found myself. While humble to others, I secretly gloated because I knew I looked good. Little did I know that my standing in the slender department was only to be temporary.

But life has been teaching me so large lessons lately. Some of these lessons have to do with accepting who you are, large, medium or small. And others have to do with letting go of the past, regardless of what happened. And I'm starting to realize that something about letting go of that past lends itself to no longer caring so much about what size you are, rather what begins to come into focus is what's really important: what kind of person you are, deep down inside.

I know these sound like obvious lessons, but I suppose some of us are a little more dense than are others. Sometimes lessons don't come as readily. Or perhaps until we're ready for them.

So as I let those new notions sink in, maybe it's time to reconsider the ADD angle to dieting and instead follow my friends' approach and become an ADD eater, see where it leads me. I'll keep you posted.

Well, sometimes a diet finds me whether I've planned it or not. Since I saw my father three days ago I've been laid out in bed, so sick I could barely get up to walk the dog. I've eaten nothing more than a few saltine cracks and several bottles of Lucozade I keep on hand for stomach bugs. It's a British version of Gatorade but I think it has unique curative properties so I make sure to have it in stock for just such occasions. If you can call a stomach bug an occasion.

Poor Cognac has been going absolutely stir-crazy. He's become so acclimated to our long walks that he's like a junkie needing a fix; he's been pacing by the front door all day long, his claws clicking so loudly I hear it in my bedroom. Today I'm so tired of being bedridden that I've decided to force myself out and into the real world, even if I do feel weak and woozy. Some fresh air should do me good. I take a quick shower to wash three days of sleep out of my hair, slip on a pair of sweat pants and an old Princeton sweatshirt of Williams, and head out with the dog.

After about twenty minutes of our usual circuit, we happen upon George and Sally.

"What great timing! Fresh back from therapy, and now we meet up with Abbie!" George says as he gives me a hug.

"Don't get too close, I'm getting over being sick."

"You need some chicken noodle soup to get you better,"

Sally says.

I push my hands out as if I'm full. "Thanks but no thanks. Plenty enough of that on this stupid diet of mine. I'm chicken souped out, thank you. In fact I'm avoiding all things edible right now."

"Ack. I can relate. Can't eat a thing!" Sally adds, rubbing her stomach.

George rolls his eyes. "She never eats anything. Afraid she'll gain weight. Meanwhile, she could use some extra meat on her bones, don't you think, Abbie?"

"Now that's a loaded question I'll steer entirely clear of. We all have our issues with food. Speaking of food, I have to get this one back home soon or he'll eat me up for dinner." I point to Cognac.

As I'm walking away, Sally slips me her number on a calling card and motions with her pinky and thumb sticking out at her ear for me to call her. Don't you love that she has a calling card? Guess we're trying to keep this dinner gathering on the down-low to keep George from getting cold feet. Well, I'm determined to get him there one way or another so she has nothing to fear there.

The sidewalks are getting heavy with pedestrians as rush hour thickens. Up ahead, across the street, I see a street vendor with one of those fake airplane things that hover above your head. Before I can even give a secure tug on the leash, Cognac sees it too, and takes off. Weakened from being sick, I can't keep my grip on the leash and he's gone in a flash.

"Cognac!" I scream as he gallops off ahead of me. I try to wend my way through the mass of bodies but I'm no match for an agile dog who already got a head start on me. People are staring at me, wondering why I'm screaming out so desperately for an after-dinner drink at this hour, probably thinking this is par for the course in this crazy city.

I lose sight of him between everyone's coats and briefcases and then I hear a sickening screech of tires up ahead. I push through the crowd, knocking down a couple of people in the process and hearing in the background a good handful of expletives aimed my way. And too soon I see what I feared: the limp and impossibly bent body of my baby, my beloved dog, knocked unconscious and looking for all the world to be dead. A trickle of blood drips from his nose and I lay down to protect him as I scream his name over and over again.

Tears obscure my vision as I lay there, my body wrapped protectively—too late for that—around him, afraid to move him, not knowing if doing so will further damage his already obviously damaged body. A cabby is standing nearby telling everyone who will listen that he didn't do anything, the dog ran in front of him, he didn't even see him till it was too late. A cop shows up and leans down to talk to me. He tells me someone is coming to help with the dog and tries to calm me down but he can't understand, Cognac is my baby. Besides William, he's all I've got. Well, until recently, anyhow. But I've invested all of my love and caring into this dog and, and, and I can't lose him, I just can't. I just can't—

The next thing I know I know nothing. I lose all consciousness, right in the middle of a filthy Manhattan street (even though really, they're much cleaner than they used to be). Or so I'm being told, fifteen minutes later in some anteroom of an emergency veterinarian's office. It seems they have me laid out on a makeshift couch in the head vet's private office.

"Cognac?"

"He's in surgery right now," a vet tech tells me.

"Oh, God. Surgery?" I shoot her a terrified look that asks all of my unasked questions.

The large tech, who looks so cheerful in her pink cotton scrubs with wagging dogs all over it, scrunches her brows. "He's suffered a lot of internal trauma. They're doing whatever they can for him."

"You can't let him die, you just can't. He's all I have—"

She reaches out and strokes my head. "They're doing everything they can for him. Have faith. The police went through your cell phone and pulled up your emergency contact. They've called that number and someone should be here shortly for you. In the meantime, can I get you anything? You should stay laying down for now." She looks at me and must see the terror in my eyes. "It'll be okay, dear."

A few minutes later I hear a familiar voice. "Abbie?"

I look up to see William standing in the doorway. "William?"

"I just talked to one of the vets assisting in the surgery," he says.

"Is he going to be okay?"

William looks grim. "They don't know yet, Abbie. His body suffered a lot of damage. We aren't going to know till they're all done."

I begin to cry all over again. William walks over and sits down next to me, wrapping his arms around me and letting me cry. We don't talk for a lot of minutes, and all I can hear are my muffled sobs and the clock ticking along the minutes of Cognac's surgery. Finally William speaks.

"You want to tell me what happened?"

"It was an accident, I swear it was. I was sick and I hadn't walked him and he had all this pent up energy and we'd been walking for a little while already but then when I headed back toward home he saw something and he ran after it and I couldn't hold onto the leash and I was still feeling so weak from being sick and the next thing you know I heard the screech of tires and then I saw my baby bleeding on the ground. I didn't mean for it to happen—"

"Of course you didn't mean for it to happen, honey. I know that. Look, accidents happen." He scratches the back of my head in a soothing way.

"If something happens to Cognac I'll—"

"Let's not go there. Let's just hope that they can patch him up."

"Patch him up? He was bleeding from his nose! That's not exactly Raggedy Ann material, you know."

"Take a deep breath, Abbie. Let's just wait and see what we hear. No sense in jumping to conclusions, right?"

Except that is one thing I'm really good at. I come from the "we're all gonna die!" school of thought. Why think things will turn out right when I can imagine all of the horrible alternatives to that sunny scenario?

For the next two hours we just sit there, me weeping intermittently, and William leafing through very old issues of Cat Fancy Magazine. You know things are dire when a middle-aged man is fixated on reading about the mating habits of Maine coon and Javanese cats (and here I thought Javanese described a coffee bean).

"Did you know the Korat is an ancient Siamese breed?" he asks me.

"Huh?" I must've drifted off to sleep after a heavy bout of sobbing.

"Considered a good-luck cat. Given to brides on their wedding day."

I wish I had a korat cat right now in that case. I need some good luck.

"Mr. and Mrs. Jennings?" my very large, jovial-looking tech suddenly calls for us. "Follow me." We tail her as close as possible without being considered stalkers, hoping to get quickly to see our dog. She shows us to a room and the vet, a Dr. Dawgley—no joke—comes in.

"First things first," he says, after introducing himself. "I think Cognac is going to be fine."

We heave a collaborative sigh of relief.

"He lost a lot of blood. Perforated his liver, and has a broken leg. You're really lucky that car wasn't going faster—HBCs don't usually have much of a chance. He's lucky it was rush hour and traffic wasn't moving as fast."

"HBC's?"

"Hit By Car. I think the combination of Cognac being big enough to take the hit and in excellent cardiovascular health really helped him weather the worst of it."

"You mean all that walking I've done has done him good?"

"The dog's in great shape. Well, discounting the injuries he's suffered from this accident. He's going to have a very slow road to recovery. He'll have to stay here for a while, to make sure he's stabilized."

"But we'll be able to bring him home once he's all better?"

"I think he'll be fine."

"Can we see him now?" I ask.

The vet nods. "Now you'll probably be disturbed at the sight of him. He's still pinned down and has IV's running in him. Patches of his fur are shaved off. He's still under sedation."

William takes my hand and we enter the recovery area and see our baby looking so weak and vulnerable. With bald patches where he normally has that wonderful teddy bear fur I love to run my fingers through.

I lean over and kiss his head, scratching his ears like he loves so much. Even though he's still asleep I swear his tail wags a little bit.

"Sweet dog, I'm so sorry I let this happen to you," I whisper into his ear. "I don't know how I let go of you but I'm so grateful your life was spared. I don't know what I'd do if I lost you like this."

I try to wrap my arms around him but with the fluid attached to him and tubes all over the place I'm afraid I'm going to disconnect something vital.

I lean over and bury my face in William's neck and cry.

"Hey, why ya crying? He's going to be fine, sweetie. Only happy tears now, okay?"

William reaches out to wipe my tears away with his thumb.

We sit with Cognac for a good long while as he comes out of the fog of anesthesia. He's weak and not very responsive but he does know we're here and I can tell he wants to move to greet us but his body won't let him.

The vet techs tell us we need to let him rest, so finally, with great reluctance, we leave the room. We're given information about his stay at the vet clinic, and hours during which we might be able to visit him, and warned that he's got a long road to recovery ahead of him. I feel horrible about it all and can't help but beat myself up over the what-if's, even though I know it's not particularly productive.

As we're walking out of the clinic, William leans over to give me a simple kiss on the lips. "You'll call me if you hear anything on him?"

"You're not coming back home?" I'd just assumed he would, what with this crisis and all.

He shakes his head. "Not yet, Abbie. I'll let you know when I'm ready."

With that he turns and begins to walk the opposite direction that we were going, never once looking back, as I stand, empty-handed. No dog, no husband, no nothing. If I thought things felt empty before, that was nothing compared to this.

OATMEAL CHOCOLATE CHIP COOKIES

Preheat oven to 350°.

1 c. (2 sticks) butter softened

1 c. Brown sugar

1/2 c. sugar

2 eggs

1 tsp. vanilla

1-1/4 c. flour (I used Wondra flour which is pre-sifted—I also use this for my pies, but it's not always easy to find it)

1 tsp. baking soda

1/2 tsp. salt

3 c. oats (use old-fashioned and not the quick oats)

2 c. chocolate chips

Cream butter and sugars till creamy.

Add eggs and vanilla; beat well.

Add combined flour, baking soda & salt, mix well.

Stir in oats and chocolate chips.

Drop by rounded tablespoonfuls onto ungreased cookie sheet. Bake 10-12 minutes or until golden brown. Cool 1 minute on cookie sheet and transfer to wire rack.

Yields about 4 dozen cookies

(Can also spread out on ungreased 13" X 9" metal baking pan and baked for 30-35 minutes, then cut into bars)

Ginger and Spice and All That's Nice

Seize the moment. Remember all those women on the Titanic who waved off the dessert cart.

–Erma Bombeck

COPING. I'm all about coping right now. And part of coping for me means pretending that my dog is not recovering from near-death without me by his side while also pretending that my husband is just away on business and not on an extended hiatus away from me. Hell, I wonder if this was what Sally went through when George disappeared. I don't suppose there's much chance that William is lounging on a park bench anywhere in town, though. He likes his creature comforts too much for that.

Oh, God, what if his creature comforts involve large breasts and an hourglass figure? I mean maybe that Vespa girl wasn't the one, but maybe there is a one. Maybe even if there isn't one this very second, maybe there'll be one in an hour.

He might meet her at the bus stop today. Even though he doesn't ever ride a bus. Well, maybe he'll be pressed up against her on the subway. What greater way to achieve instant intimacy with a gorgeous blond—and they're always blond—than to be flesh-to-flesh in a rush hour subway car, when there's no way to move, or if there is, it's minimal. Only enough to get a little more intimate.

Maybe she'll have just stopped off for a mojito for happy hours, the crushed mint still lingering on her breath. And there they'll be, jostling with the jiggling motion of the train, back and forth, side to side, over and under. Wait, no over and under.

And maybe William will really notice another woman, for the first time in all these years. A tall, blond, well-endowed woman. A thin one, with no food obsessions whatsoever. In fact, she probably eschews eating in favor of herbal tea and colonic cleanses. They're all the rage, you know. Maybe he's already taken her back to his little pied-a-terre. Not that he has one—I mean as far as I know he doesn't. But where is he, anyhow? And it seems like this would be just the right time to have a pied-a-terre and use it accordingly.

You might be thinking that I am losing it and you might well be right about that. But how can I not be under the circumstances? My whole life has gone topsy turvy on me and I feel like one of those enormous sea turtles that got flipped over on my back on the sand when the tide went out, flapping my flippers helplessly, completely unable to right myself without outside intervention.

Only I don't think there is any outside intervention—no one waiting to swoop in and save me this time. I guess it's up to me to figure that out.

A week has passed since the accident and I've thrown myself into not being all about myself. Gym, work, gym, work. I've written enough columns to get me through a couple of months at this rate. And at the gym, I got weighed and found out I've lost another fifteen pounds: it seems that the tragedy diet does me well. Nothing like losing all that's important to you to take away your appetite I suppose. The only way to lose is to lose. Hell, I can't even muster up enough desire to eat the usual stress-eating standbys. It's all very weird.

Speaking of weird, I got a call today from Ling Chung, he of the recent phone conversation I heard with Barry. Seems Ling wanted to let me know that Barry had been up to no good with me, too. He had received my photograph way back when, before I was outed. I asked him whether Barry was trying to extort money out of him in order to get a good review, and he finally 'fessed up. Seems he was worried he'd ruin everything if he admitted that, what with Barry's strong-arm tactics.

Surprise, surprise. Luckily I've concocted a little surprise of my own for Barry, with the help of a new-found sister of mine.

It's midnight and I'm lurking behind the trash dumpster in

the grim alleyway behind Happy Chung, with Jane, of all people. After hearing all about Barry while we did the weight circuit the other day, she begged to join me to witness his comeuppance. I've toted along a camera I borrowed from one of the photographers at work. The only reason I didn't call in a photographer from the Post to do the honors is I'd like to spare my paper any public humiliation and I hope that Mortie will deal with this discreetly. Though part of me would love the joy of having Barry's weasel-face splattered across the pages of the paper in my stead. I can see the headline: GOTCHA UNDER GLASSE. Revenge would be delicious. Of course it would probably only resurrect my shame, so who needs that?

"You think he'll really buy into this?" Jane whispers to me.

I hold my finger up to my lips to indicate silence. I hear a man getting out of a cab just down the way, slamming the door, then whistling the tune "Whistle While You Work" as he strolls along the alley. I peer around the side of the dumpster and see it's Barry. Thank goodness he's so entirely predictable! What a fool.

He approaches the unmarked entrance to the restaurant and taps out the first six beats to "Billie Jean" against the metal door—honestly, the man is such a drama queen. Ling Chung opens the door and steps out into the alley, the two of them brightly illuminated by a streetlamp directly overhead, Ling in a heavily-stained apron, with a cleaver in his hand, Barry in a slick long black leather duster coat and dark shades, evidently channeling The Matrix.

"You have what I came for?" Barry asks.

Ling nods and glances around in search of us. Jane has the camcorder rolling now. "You wanted it in all fifties, right?"

"You've got a hundred of 'em?"

"Count it out if you want."

"Ling old boy, I trust you. Now I got my money, you'll get your review."

Ling hands Barry the envelope. In the shadows I'm snapping away, the loud exhaust fan from the kitchen just barely blocking the sound of the motorized film advance.

A rat skitters across the ground near their feet in perfect timing. Jane—recording it all for posterity on a camcorder—and I step out of the shadows.

"And now it seems you'll get yours, Barry, old boy," I say.

He gasps, staring at me, then Jane, then me again. "Abbie! What are you doing here? And who's your little friend? What's this all about?"

"Why don't you tell me what it's all about Barr?" I say, pointing to Jane's camcorder. "Don't you have something to say to the camera?"

Barry starts to lunge at us but Ling is a quick little guy and inserts himself, cleaver and all, between us and Barry.

"I think this is what we call in the food biz your 'just desserts,' isn't it Barry? You screw me, I screw you. You didn't think you'd get away with this, did you?"

"Wh-wh-what do you mean, Abbie? I'm not doing anything." He's inching away.

"Besides, I'm back in shape, now, Barry. Your gig was only a temporary one. It's all over for you."

"You call yourself in shape?" he says, scoffing at me. Ouch. Low blow. Of course he knows my Achilles heel and would say that to me even if I were as thin as one of Ling Chung's famous sambal pepper five-spice noodles.

"Sticks and stones may break my bones," I say, sticking my tongue out at him. Jane cracks up. Barry tries to lurch toward the camera again but Ling lifts the cleaver, at the ready. You ever see a Chinese chef with a cleaver? Barry knows not to mess with the dude.

Jane holds the camcorder up and points it right in his face, zooming the lens for a tight shot. She starts talking to him like you would to a child you're videotaping trying out a bike without training wheels. "Wave to the camera, Barry! Why don't you tell us all about how you've ratcheted up the expense accounts? Oh, and about the money you've been extorting from restauranteurs? Now it's time to wave bye-bye to your sweet little job, because you are so out of one, as of now."

Barry tries to run but he trips over a recycling bin and

sprawls on the ground.

"Hey, come on now, Abbie, friend. You gotta tell me what's going on here?"

"Just about the most perfect time I've had at a restaurant in ages, that's what, Barr, old boy. I can't thank you enough for such a lovely evening."

With that I grab Jane's hand and with the added security of Ling's protective cleaver, we back toward the door into the restaurant.

"Gee, Barry, it's been real. Hope you enjoy being on the other side of this job, because that's precisely where you're gonna be. Bon appétit!"

With that I wave with my fingers and we escape into the restaurant, high-fiving each other on a perfectly-executed operation.

Mortie's late-night email contains the incriminating video footage—uploaded to Youtube, conveniently—and the photographs, as well as an attached letter attesting to the events of the evening from Ling Chung himself. I prefer to not even deal with Mortie directly and instead just want Barry to fade off into the sunset. Which seems to be precisely what happens, as Barry simply doesn't show up at work, from what we hear.

By dawn, Mortie's leaving me message after message, wanting to talk turkey. As if I have any interest in talking turkey, trout, even water buffalo with the guy. I've got too many other things I need to deal with in my life right now; somehow the whole Sentinel and my former job just seem entirely irrelevant, when viewed in light of my missing husband and wounded poochie.

The next day my doorbell rings. What I would give to have Cognac barking needlessly at the door right now. I can't bear the silence of his absence. Not to mention the silence of William's void. I peer through the peephole to see Sally, aqua Lilly headband in place, oversized Gucci sunglasses dwarfing her skinny-lady cheekbones. Today she's in her off-to-play-mahjong outfit: bright aqua velour Juicy Couture sweatpants and coordinating hoodie.

"Sally!" I greet her warmly. That I'm welcoming near-strangers with the warmth reserved for long-lost friends is a sure sign that I'm lonely.

She marches in like she owns the place and plops herself down on a kitchen barstool.

"Nice," she says, nodding and pointing around my near-commercial kitchen.

"Thanks."

"You like to cook?"

"You think I'd have a set-up like this if I didn't?"

She dangles her sunglasses from her teeth and stares at me like I'm nuts. "Doesn't everybody?"

I'd forgotten she hails from the school of thought that more is better and that goes for everything in your living space, even if you don't know how to use it. I just shrug and continue on.

"To what do I owe this visit?" I daren't say pleasure, as that would be stretching things a bit.

"I came to show you the guest list before I share everything with Gretl."

"You need to show her your guest list?"

"She stays up on the gossip so she always wants to know if anyone she's seen in Page Six will be there."

I roll my eyes. Household help of the rich and famous.

Sally whips out a guest list that could be for a State dinner it's so long.

"I thought this was an intimate affair with just family?"

"It is an intimate affair with mostly family," she says. "I had to throw in a few extras—I mean everyone's going to want to see George, you know. But I kept the extras to only our closest friends."

Oh, Lord, I worry that George is going to turn tail and run for cover if he shows up to a whole horde of people.

"You're sure about this?"

"I insist," she says. "I know my George. There's not a name on here that wouldn't be glaringly missing if I omitted it."

I throw my hands up. "You're the boss. I'm just in charge

of getting him there."

"And you've got everything set for that?"

"Not exactly, but it's all under control."

"Not exactly? Abbie, I would be the laughingstock of Pound Ridge if we did all of this and George didn't show."

"We couldn't have Pound Ridge laughing at you. Not to worry, he'll show. Trust me." The things I get myself into sometimes.

"And you've got the menu all set?"

"That's Gretl's problem. I trust her to keep the menu dignified and in keeping with the importance of the occasion." I hesitate to speculate on what would constitute an undignified menu—a phallic-shaped pound cake for dessert?

She whips out a folder with detailed information on getting to the house.

"And when you get to the gate, tell Junior you're a friend of the family's."

The gate? Junior? "Won't he recognize George?"

"Last time he saw George he didn't look quite so, uh, urban as he does now. I have a feeling no one's going to recognize the man." She rolls her eyes at the thought of him appearing so vagrant-like.

Well, it'll be my surprise, then, to gussie him up for the event.

Sally and I talk a little bit longer and then I show her to the door.

"Don't worry, this will work like a charm!" I assure her.

She waves with her sunglasses before hiding her face behind them and she's gone.

A few hours later I receive a flower delivery. I quickly sign for the flowers, one of those spectacular arrangements you'd see in the lobby of The Pierre or something. Surely these are my much-anticipated truce flowers from William.

I race to open the card, but am instantly deflated.

Dear Abbie,
I'm not exactly sure how to make things right with

you. I know that I betrayed you and I know that you're disappointed that I used you to help me with Dex. It was wrong and it wasn't the type of thing a good friend does. I hope you'll find a way to forgive me for my selfishness. If not, I might just jump off the Brooklyn Bridge in despair. Ha ha. Just joking! I miss you, Abbie. Call and tell me we can be friends again.

Love,

Jess

Sheesh, how's a girl to stay mad when she gets a letter of apology like that? Plus this arrangement has the most divine aroma, the exotic scent of an Asian market almost.

I guess I'd better reach out to Jess. I just have to figure out how and when. In the meantime, I've got to put the finishing touches on my column and send it over to my boss.

Being Jiggly in My Piggly Wiggly
By Abbie Jennings

I was standing in line at the grocery store the other day and it brought to mind that my favorite shirt in the world is from the Piggly Wiggly, a grocery store chain popular in the South. Only never would I wear this shirt in front of a soul. I don't dare wear it for anything but a nightshirt. Because I fear that I am setting myself up for public ridicule if anyone but for my all-forgiving husband sees me wearing this thing. Ah, the irony, they'd say, the piggly wiggly wearing a Piggly Wiggly shirt. Designer fatso. I'm left to wrestle with this all-important dilemma: Do I dare be jiggly in my Piggly Wiggly?

Of course, if you're like me, sometimes you lose perspective on exactly how bad—or good—you look. You go along ignoring the reality of your appearance for awhile, but then you see someone who you suspect looks much like you and you wince. "Oh, no. Do I look that bad?" you think.

I used to always ask my husband that question. I'd point

out some stranger at a party, or walking down the street, and I'd say, "Okay, do I look that bad?" Early in our relationship he was foolish (or in love!) enough to obligingly respond. Eventually he knew that no matter what he answered (he: "honey, you're not that fat." Me: "Well, what do you mean by that fat? Are you saying I'm fat?"), he was in trouble, so he gave up attempting to placate me.

Since then I've been left to my own devices to gauge my size against other women of comparable girth. A while back, I saw a woman at the gym wearing the exactly same bathing suit I own but haven't tugged onto my body in five years, it was so tight the last time I tried. When I saw her, packed in like a bratwurst in the thing, the first thought that came to mind was this: "I really have to do the South Beach diet and not cheat this time." She looked that bad. And so, evidently, must I.

So a few days later, I was at a dinner at a high-end restaurant. Amongst those at the table were: two slim and gloating South Beachers; one over-exerciser, who has the body of a goddess; one Neanderthin (in which you must eat like a caveman, although I'm pretty sure cavemen didn't pound Jack Daniels, as did he); one who stays-slim-courtesy-of-her-antidepressant; one who claims to be perpetually on Atkins all the while guzzling wine (an Atkins no-no) and eating more than her share of carbs; two diet-at-dawn-turned-dessert-at-duskers (we can assume that I fall into this category); and one who just couldn't give a damn, as he happily drank his dinner: a bottomless tumbler full of Ketel One on the rocks with a twist.

The courtesy bread found its way down to our end of the table by its rejection at the other end (they acted as if it was radioactive as they hurled it toward us). Which was fine by me: made me happy, tasted delicious. As did the complementary crostini goat cheese bruschetta appetizer we ate (and our end of the table gladly consumed the other ends' allotment). Obviously as the meal progressed, I'd forgotten all about my twin from the gym who hardly shone in her Land's End blivet-wear.

Admittedly, I was self-conscious in my too-tight dress that night. I gazed enviably upon my good friends who looked so thin and so damned happy that they were thin. I am assured that coursing through their minds weren't feelings of remorse over the umpteen million moments of caved willpower they'd suffered through during the past six months. But I also was kind of left to wonder why people who don't actually eat go out to dinner. It seems a practice in futility. Although I will grant you, they can drink hard liquor to their heart's content on these carb-free existences. If that could be considered any healthier than binging on crostini.

I don't know. After all of the back and forth, to eat, to starve, to live a balanced life—and is that even a possibility when your metabolism doesn't allow for that?—I'm still wrestling with what would truly make me happy when it comes to my body size. The older I get, the more I am inclined to just say "to hell with it, life really is too short to waste time and effort worrying about these things." But those notions of body image ingrained in our minds from an early age are hard to exorcise.

Which brings me back to the grocery store, to my morning's dilemma (while not wearing my Piggly Wiggly t-shirt). Standing in the check-out line, I couldn't help but notice out the myriad magazines on display. The grocery store is one of those places of irony where the entire time you're stuffing your cart, you're fantasizing about what to make (and then stuff your face) when you get home with all the new fun foods you're about to buy, but then you get in line and are guilted into at least pondering every diet known to mankind on the cover of twenty some magazines featuring impossibly-thin-bordering-on-anorexic celebrities. All this while checking out with a basketful of ingredients intended for use in that Amaretto torte with drizzled marzipan icing and crumbled toasted almonds that sounded so damned good only minutes earlier.

And so I'm left to wonder: do I really care? Or would I rather wear my Piggly Wiggly, done that lumpy bathing suit, shame myself perpetually in public, because I'm fighting a losing battle anyhow? Or can I really go out to dinner and never again eat a carbohydrate again? Do I have to decide that now? I think I'll just mull it over while I sleep tonight, in my soft, comfie

Piggly Wiggly t-shirt. I'll let you know in the morning.

Two hours later the door bell rings yet again. Honestly, it's a man bearing flowers. Now these must be from William. I tip the deliveryman and slam the door, setting the beautiful arrangement down and grabbing the card.

> *To my Muffin,*
>
> *I just want you to know how much I appreciate your coming to visit. Janie told me all about your subterfuge and I'm glad you collared that creep and got your job back. They're lucky to have you. I thought this was the perfect bouquet to send someone like you.*
>
> *Love,*
>
> *Dad*

I look closely at the arrangement and see that it's made up of herbs and spices and everything you can re-use in the kitchen. How very thoughtful. I wish I could feel more enthusiastic about my beautiful arrangements but neither of them is from the one I'd hoped would send me something. That certain someone who's starting to seem like he's on permanent hiatus.

Stir in Two Cups Kindness

Part of the secret of success in life is to eat what you like and let the food fight it out inside.

–Mark Twain

I'M having yet another bad dream about Cognac's accident, turning over and over in my sleep, like a free-range chicken over a spit. No, wait, more like one of those horrid-looking unidentified doner kebobs (what is in those things, anyhow?). Correction: I toss all night like a salad. With a tiny splash of oil and fig vinegar. Much more dietetic of me.

Suddenly the blare of the phone jars me awake. I glance at the clock to see that it's barely seven in the morning.

In my sleep fog I can't find the phone anywhere. By the time I do, my number has been re-called three different times. Someone must really want to talk with me. God, I hope it's not an emergency to do with William or Cognac.

"This is Abbie," I answer on about the fortieth ring.

"Abbie—it's Sally. We have a crisis on our hands!" The woman is panting into the phone like she's having a panic attack. She probably broke a fingernail or something: crises of the rich and famous.

"Calm down. It can't be anything we can't deal with."

"Oh yeah? Well, how about this? Gretl refuses to cook," she says, as if she's thwacking me with a leather glove and saying "take that!"

"Isn't she your employee?"

"Been with us for twenty five years."

"And isn't she in your employ to cook for you?"

"Uh huh."

"Then why won't she cook for you? Surely she's anxious to see George and ply him with her weiner schnitzel or whatever her specialite de la maison is."

"It's you." Sally let's that drop like a thud.

"Me? I'm the house special?"

I can practically hear Sally rolling her eyes at that one. "No! You're the reason she won't cook! She knows you'll be there."

"How'd she find that out?"

"She saw your name on the guest list."

"Yeah but how'd she know I was anybody?"

"She saw your picture in the paper. Read about your little exposé back in the springtime. Never forgets a name or a face. Abbie—you're notorious!"

God, even the hired help knows about my humiliation? Besides, I'm not notorious! That would imply something bad about me. And I can't think of a bad thing about me. Although perhaps my reputation is a bit tarnished, what with my being demoted and all.

"Just what we need. A housemaid with performance anxiety. Can't she at least take some pity on me?"

"Heavens no! She won't dare serve you food. She thinks you'll be feeling vindictive after the incident and give her cooking a bad review."

"Oh, come off it. Vindictive? Me? I wouldn't hurt a flea!" I can't seem to get a break these days, can I? "Besides which, what food critic gives reviews to home cooking?"

But Sally is too busy verbally wringing her hands. "What are we to do? This dinner is only days away—who can I get to help?"

"What about all of your friends' chefs. Don't they moonlight for extra cash?"

"Tried that. Couldn't even get Bittsy Malone's cook, and she'll do just about anything for enough money," she moans. "What am I going to do?"

"She'll do anything? Sounds like deep in the jungles of your version of suburbia instead of Desperate Housewives you have Desperate Housemaids."

"This is no laughing matter."

"Of course not. So let's think. Who can we get to prepare an elegant dinner for a slew of people on short notice?"

Sally's silent for a moment before yelling out loudly into my ear as if she's got BINGO. "You! My God, Abbie, why didn't I think of this earlier? You are the perfect person to prepare this meal. There's no way that George could bag out on this if you're at the helm in the kitchen. He loves your cooking too much. Plus you have that kitchen! You cook! Oh, this is absolutely perfect. Wait'll I tell Bittsy. The food critic for the Sentinel being my personal chef!"

"You can't boast all around town about something like that! I'm not anyone's personal chef! Not that there's anything wrong with that. It's just not what I do! Besides, you have that kitchen too! Why don't you roll up your sleeves and give this little thing called manual labor a whirl?"

How do I get myself involved with this stuff? Here I was trying to do a little Good Samaritan deed and next thing you know I've been impressed into servitude?

"Oh, Abbie, I'll pay you handsomely, of course. You just send me the bill and I'll pay you on the spot for everything. It'll be just divine. Tell me, what are you going to prepare?"

Well, if there's one thing I'm not, it's a quitter. And I'll be darned if this thing will lose momentum over lack of kitchen staff. How hard can it be to do this? I've been cooking my whole life. This is what I've been preparing for, forever. Sure, I'll need a sous chef, but I've got just the slave labor in mind: Jess owes me one. I'll rope her into helping me and we'll call it even with the Dex affair. Literally.

"I can't believe these words are about to pour forth from my mouth, but…I'll do it," I say, sounding more enthusiastic than I'd have expected myself to sound. I must be losing my marbles. "But you really can't be bragging to your pals about this. You need to keep this on the down-low. You got it?"

"I could hug you! I knew you had a heart of gold. I can't thank you enough for doing this for me. This is going to be a night to remember, I just know it."

Let's hope it's not a night destined to be notorious, that's all I have to say.

It seems to be the trend of late to destroy my well-intended sleep with phone calls. This one is well past bedtime. A glance at the caller-ID shows that it's Jess calling. I hesitate to pick up, but then I reconsider, since I'm trying to just take the chill approach to life now. No sense in having a million axes to grind. I'm all about good ju-ju and holding a grudge against Jess isn't going to benefit me one iota. Plus I need a huge favor from the woman.

"Jess?"

"Hey, Abbie. How's it going?"

"It's going, all right," I say, figuring it's going to be a long conversation if I get into my whole gloomy saga at this very minute. "You?"

"Oh, same ol' same ol'," she says. "Did you get my truce offering?"

"Yes, I did, and they're gorgeous. Thank you for the gesture and the sentiments behind them."

"Look, I just wanted to call to apologize again for how things happened. I didn't want to stick you in the middle of things. It was wrong of me and I really am sorry about that."

I'm quiet for a minute, digesting this.

"Uh, you could say that again, just so we're clear on the matter? As much as I can appreciate your situation, I just don't want to be any part of it, and you made me a part of it. It was just so awkward, Jess. Obviously, your private business is your business, but please, please don't make it mine, ever again. Friends?"

"Friends. I really am sorry, you know."

"I know you are. Otherwise I'd have told you what to do with your apology. But with my acceptance of your apology comes a slight penance."

"Penance?"

"I need your help. I've been corralled into fixing dinner for an important family gathering—"

"Uh, Abbie, you don't exactly have a family, last time I checked."

"Not my family. But actually I do. So much has gone on, I have to catch you up. But before that, here's what I need from you."

I tell her about George's reunion dinner and Jess is so charmed with the notion of helping out the wealthy homeless man that she immediately accepts the challenge.

"As long as I can also go along to Pound Ridge. I love Pound Ridge!"

"Actually, that would be good. Maybe we can get your husband's driver to take us out there? I hadn't quite figured out how I was getting to their house."

"Not a problem."

Jess and I talk longer, I fill her in on the unfortunately turns of events around here, she's duly empathetic, and then we say our goodbyes.

One important project I'm left to do in planning this sweeping dramatic reunion is to clean George up. I mean who wants to embrace someone who smells like a candidate for a body odor transplant? And this is my project du jour.

It's cold out today so I throw on my leather jacket—noticing it's gotten rather loose on me, and take a walk, minus Cognac, who I'll visit later today, in search of George. I need to get all of my plans in place.

I find him at my third stop of his regular haunts.

"George!" Normally I'd hug someone I haven't seen in a while but I am partial to cleanliness and instead wave. Is that bigoted of me? I hate to be scent-biased. I guess I'm just partial to lovely aromas, kitchen ones.

"Abbie, my dear, where have you been hiding? And don't you look skinny? It appears those peanut M&Ms are doing you well!"

Me? Skinny? And the man doesn't even want anything out of me. He's just saying it because, well, just because.

"Why thank you, George! And I suspect my sweet tooth has little to do with it and it has more to do with other things." I'm trying to take a compliment at face value, no small task for a girl used to being invisible to men.

"Things? Like what kind of things?" I update George on Cognac, what happened since the time I saw him and Sally. I fight back the tears as I talk about it because I can tell George is squeamish around waterworks.

"Enough about me. Today is going to be about you. Today it's time for George."

"Time?"

"Prep time, George. Prep time."

He raises his eyebrow, curious.

"For the dinner. It's time to polish you up a bit. Turn that lump of coal into a diamond."

"I'm a lump of coal then?"

"Course not! But we need to unearth the former George just a little bit."

"But I like who I am!"

I tut-tut him. "We're not changing anything about who you are—only changing how you look."

"What's wrong with the way I look?"

"Sometimes we all just need a little overhaul. And I'd like to be truthful here—to put it delicately, um, George, you could use a good scrubbing. You could use a good overhaul, for that matter. I'm all for putting a spit shine on you if that's fine by you."

I think George must feel badly about my misfortune because he holds up his wrists as if allowing me to cuff them. "I'm all yours," he says. I'm touched that he's willing to do this. I've never given someone a makeover before. This should be fun.

First we go to Metro, a chic little man-spa in Soho that Jess suggested. I don't dare tell George that the full name of the place is Metro(sexual). Even I would be put off by that. I think the well-groomed receptionist is a bit repulsed by George's appearance and ushers him quickly back to the facilities.

"Don't forget to shower first, George! And scrub yourself really well!" I tell him, speaking the obvious.

I have him slated for the works: a cut and a shave, a mani-pedi, facial, massage, even back-waxing. By the time he's done in here he won't ever want to look back on his days of wandering the streets. Although that waxing might be enough to send him back there regardless. While he's in the oven, so to speak, I grab a cab and head uptown to visit my pup at the animal rehab center.

"Cognac! Baby! Come tell mama how you're feeling!" I talk in sickening baby talk to him as he limps his way over to me. He's wearing an enormous radar dish on his head to keep him from chewing on his bandages, and he looks as if that alone is worse than all his injuries put together.

"Oh, fella, you are a sight for sore eyes!" I scratch behind his ears and shower him with kisses and I can't believe he's right here, all warm and furry and clean-smelling. My perfect doggie. He tries to lick me but that radar dish keeps bumping into me so I stick my head right up to his head inside the dish so he can lick me all over my face. I'm tempted to lick his own face right back, I miss him so much, but that might be a little weird. I brought him cookies and feed him too many so he knows who loves him the most and finally have to let him go back to rest for a while. At least this place isn't as dreary as where my father is a permanent resident. "Dad and I will be back to pick you up in just a few days, I promise," I tell him before giving him one last kiss. Of course I don't know if William will be with me to pick him up, but I can't foresee him missing such an auspicious occasion. He's mad at me, not the dog.

When I return to retrieve George, he's wearing the pair of loose-fitting jeans of William's that I lent him, along with a black t-shirt and too-large sneakers. George looks so normal, albeit it in an ill-fitting manner.

"You sure do clean up well," I tell him. "Who'd have known your skin was so pale! I didn't realize you were Caucasian!" I lightly brush my fingers across his newly-shorn face.

He looks worried.

"Joking! But you are a few shades lighter. Doesn't it feel good to be so clean?"

He nods his head. "I have to admit I forgot what being

pampered feels like. It's not so bad after all. I could get used to it. Minus that part where they ripped off a layer of flesh from my back."

"Oh, that? I didn't think you'd notice. But Sally will, trust me." I wink at him. He shakes his head at me. "Next on the list is clothing. Can't have you showing up in William's baggy clothes."

This time we hop a cab to mid-town, where I take him to a haberdashery William favors and get him suited up with a few outfits. By the time I'm done with George, he's truly a new man.

"You sure you want to go back to the park tonight, George? You know I'm gonna make you clean up at my brownstone before the party on Saturday, don't you?"

"I need to say goodbye to some of the guys," he says.

"Fine, but I'm taking all of your new things for safekeeping at my place—deal?"

"Deal."

"And you promise to show up at my place Saturday by nine? Gives us time to get you all spiffed up, right?" I write down the address and tuck it into his hands.

When I get back, I decide to email in my column this week, as I just haven't drummed up the interest in dealing with the office fallout of Barry's demise. Happy it happened, sure, but not quite sure ultimately at this point that I give a care about my old job. Amazing, I know. But I owe it to my readers to keep up the dialogue, as word has it I've garnered a bit of a fan base. Now if I ever get really skinny I wonder if I'll lose them, if I stop talking about weighty matters. Because it is interesting how people receive you once you've lost an obvious amount of yourself…

Warm Up Reluctant Spouse, Sprinkle with Sugar

Food, glorious food! We're anxious to try it. Three banquets a day — Our favorite diet!

–The chorus, Oliver

I'VE decided to launch my day early and energized, with a trip to the gym. Rumor has it Thor has something in store for me this morning. I'm sure it's nothing edible. When I arrive there, well before dawn, I see Thor in his usual spot. He's drumming the calipers against his thigh this time.

"Please say you aren't going to use those on me," I say, my eyes squinting in fear.

"Do you remember what I said about when we use calipers, Abbie?" he asks.

"Uh, to measure globs of body fat?" Not to be gross, but still.

"And when we see noticeable changes in body size." He looks me up and down and gives me the thumbs up. "You, dudette, are kicking weight-loss ass and it's time to prove it."

I can't believe I am voluntarily offering myself up for the calipers. But here I am. As I stick out my arms like Christ on the cross, I can't believe what all has happened since I stood here so many months ago. So many changes in my life. Not all for the better, but changes nonetheless. I suppose change is better than stagnant. Unless you're a swamp-dweller.

I squeeze my eyes tightly, hating to watch the process.

"You should see this, Abbie," Thor says. "I can barely grab your skin in some places compared to the first time."

By the time Thor finishes I have a small audience of ooer's and ahh'ers. Everyone is patting me on the back for the inches I've lost.

"And more importantly, Abbie, look at these guns!" He squeezes my biceps. "You are a lean, mean fighting machine!"

"Sheesh, I don't know if I'm exactly lean, but I'm trying," I say. "And I have to give you a lot of credit for believing in me. I couldn't have done it without you."

Thor taps me on my head. "Wrong. You couldn't have done it without you."

I guess he's right. It did take me to be involved in the process. Me and a whole lot of circumstances, I guess.

After thirty minutes on the treadmill, I have to rush out of my workout to get back to my enormous amount of work facing me.

Spending any amount of time in an empty brownstone is like cooking for one: without that communality, that sense of sharing, it's just lonely. It doesn't help that Cognac's not even here to create at least some noise. The place is like a mausoleum. Throw in all those flower arrangements and it's like a damned funeral home too.

Welcome to my new reality—cooking solo. But even if I plunged way off the deep end and decided to cook for the dog, for lack of anyone else for whom to cook—I could make some doggy biscuits (though really, who's got time to make beef stock for dog food?)—it lacks the conviviality of sharing with William. I miss him, and I wish he were here so I could talk through what I'm supposed to do with this crazy meal I've obligated myself into but cannot complete without help, what with all of the miscellaneous family Sally's thrown onto the guest list. I'm sure

William would have a great solution to my problem. Though knowing him at this point it would involve my birthing a baby.

I walk into the kitchen to make myself a cup of tea, hoping that will take the edge off of things. I fill the kettle with cold water and set it on the stove, turning the flame to high. I pull up a bar stool and plunk myself down, staring at the teapot, willing the water to boil, for lack of anything better to do. Not so long ago I'd not step foot in the kitchen without an armload of groceries and a clear plan of what I was going to cook—and subsequently eat. Now I don't even have the stomach for a cup of black tea. Although the chamomile hibiscus oolong tea I bought a few weeks ago at Tea for Two might be nice and soothing, so I rifle through the food pantry to find it.

I pull down a china cup from a tea set that William got me for my birthday last year. I didn't even know he realized I'd coveted the set that I'd noticed when we were buying a wedding gift for a colleague at Bloomingdale's. And he went back to the store and bought it for me, hefty price tag and all. My mind drifts to too many happy times that William and I have shared over the years—countless times that he's been so considerate like that. What the hell have I been doing, diddling around with his head? He's made it abundantly clear to me that he's tired of our static existence, that he's ready for new things. Yet I've dug in, entrenched in what's been comfortable, in the known, so afraid of what might be if we changed. If I changed. And now what do I have? Me. Just me. Who's finally working on that concept of change, after all this time, but too late because William got sick of waiting for me.

I stir just a dash of honey into the tea and watch the water swirl around. What would the old Abbie do? Maybe bake a pie. Throw in a batch of snickerdoodles perhaps. Better yet, probably whip up some comfortable chicken pot pie, food that fits you like a pair of sweat pants. Stretchy ones. Anything to plug the hole. But I'm trying hard to get away from old Abbie. So what should the new Abbie do? Fight for what she wants and not just let events wash over her, that's what. No longer be a passive participant, that's what.

Resolved, I pick up the phone and punch in William's speed dial number: number one. I'm not just going to let my number one go without a fight.

After far too many rings, I get his voice mail. My voice trembling, I leave a message:

"Baby, it's me. Abbie. Your wife. Of course, you know that." I pause to take a sip of tea, slurping it in the process. "Sorry, didn't mean to show such bad table manners. Well, not that it matters. You aren't exactly Emily Post, are you? Oh, never mind my table manners. Look, William, I have so much to say. I hoped I'd get you and not a recording, but I better talk now before I lose the courage. So I know you've been exasperated with me. No, exasperated might be too weak a word at this point. Furious. Yes, furious. I know you're furious with me. And I can understand. I haven't exactly been much of a partner in this marriage, have I? I've been stubborn and selfish and I haven't really thought about what's most important to you because I was too busy thinking about my own needs. At least what I thought I needed. And I know that's not a recipe for a happy marriage. And trust me, if there's one thing I know about, it's recipes." BEEP

Oh, crap. I hate those things when they cut you off. I dial back again, and hear his voice and now I'm starting to choke up. Great: stammering and crying on a time clock. The beeper goes off: "Sorry, got cut off on my little joke there. Okay, I guess I have to talk fast. I know I've been a jerk. I'm sorry. Really, I'm sorry. But more important than that, I've learned some important things. I promise. Cross my heart and hope to die. Well, I don't really hope to die, because I've got so much I want to live for. You see, I've learned that I don't want to—no, wait, I can't—lose what's most important to me. When Cognac was laying there with his little doggie IV in his arm and all that blood matting his fur and I stared at his bony little x-rays, God, it killed me to imagine losing him. Besides you, he's about the most important thing to me. All right, maybe there's something crazy about a dog being the second most important person in my life. Well, not that he's a person, but you know what I mean. But what it made me realize is that the first most important person is someone I can't afford to ever lose. Ever. And that's you. I can lose the cupcakes and the foie gras and the decadent dinners and all of the material things, even my stupid job. But life without you isn't worth a hill of beans. Ack, there I go talking food again. I mean I don't want my life to be missing the most important ingredient in it. Life without you is like" BEEP

Dammit. Technology is such a bitch sometimes. I dial back again.

"I wish they had a special voice mail option for apologies, one that let you talk on and on. If you would like to amend this message, press 8, if you would like to record an extended apology, press 9. And shame on you, for whatever you've done! I don't even know why I'm spending all this time talking to a voice mail. Especially when I've got to figure out how I am going to prepare a six-course dinner for forty people for tomorrow without anyone's help. But that's okay because you're more important than anything as trivial as that. Look, what I started to say is life without you is like banana cream pie without the bananas—it just makes no sense. It's missing the flavor, the texture, the main ingredient. You're my main ingredient, William. I want you to know that. And I hope someday you'll forgive me for being such a putz. And maybe you can realize that sure, I'm a putz, but I'm a putz in progress. And hopefully I'll work my way toward being a mensch and I'll prove to you I'm better than what I've shown you to date. I love you, William. I really do love you. And I'm growing up finally. And I'm ready to take responsibility in our marriage. I just hope you can find it in your heart to forgive me." BEEP.

I return the phone to the cradle and survey my kitchen, mentally mapping out my plan of attack for preparing for the big dinner. My eyes are streaming tears as if I've been cutting raw onions. Of which I will be cutting plenty for George and Sally's dinner party, so at least if I can't turn off the waterworks, I can blame it on something other than my being a heartbroken dumpee (is that what you're called when your husband drops you?).

I've got much to do before the courier service arrives to deliver the food supplies after I get everything as prepared as I can for the dinner. Then it'll be my job to rally George, re-clean him up and ferry him to Pound Ridge for some quiet time with Sally while I coordinate this dinner party for a platoon without any help. How I got myself into this one…Me and my brilliant ideas.

I don my banana split slippers, change into a pair of spiffy new yoga pants and matching workout top that doesn't make me look too ridiculously lumpy, tie on my apron that reads My Cooking: Love It or Heave It then set to work chopping onions, mushrooms and thyme and bringing to boil so many bottles of cabernet and port wine for my reduction sauce that I think I'll be drunk on the fumes before the stuff has a chance to heat up on the stove. The sheer volume of what I need to cook for this will strain even my extensive stash of kitchen supplies, no doubt. I sure wish I had some kitchen elves to help keep up with the dirty dishes.

After I have the onions, mushrooms and thyme simmering in butter I peel ten pounds of jumbo shrimp for the appetizers. To think hundreds of shrimp died for this dinner—probably an entire undersea neighborhood of little shrimplets. It's like shrimp genocide. I can't even contemplate the cow carnage involved with this meal.

Do you know how tedious it is to peel and devein that many shrimp? This is where I need to stop being so fastidious and instead buy the already peeled version—I could have saved plenty of time had I not been so exacting. Nevertheless, Tartare's happy about it, and meows repeatedly at my feet, demanding a share of the seafood tidings. Finally a little noise around this place. God, this is my future. Abbie Jennings, alone in the kitchen with her cat and a mountain of crustacean carcasses. A cat lady! I don't want to be a cat lady. Not that there's anything wrong with that, mind you. It's just not for me.

I refer to my detailed list of to-do's, which I've carefully counted to the minute backward from the moment of serving. Sometimes it's overwhelming the amount of detail needed to bring a perfect meal from idea to table. But I find I really enjoy the challenge of it, and the creativity is very rewarding. Plus it seems the more I cook, especially in large volume (and for someone else) the less I want to eat it myself. The food loses its charm en masse.

I begin to chop clove after clove of garlic, smashing each clove to remove the stubborn papery skin and then rendering them into a fine dice with the gentle rocking motion of my cook's knife. As I cut, my eyes blur with tears, and this time I can't blame the onions, which are cooking down to a lovely caramel color, fragrant with the sugar that slow cooking brings out, married with the perfume of thyme, the mushrooms lending an earthiness to them. Soon tears are dripping into the pile of garlic that's accumulating on my cutting board. All this garlic reminds me of the time that William and I challenged each other to a garlic-eating contest when we were in Rome. Granted it was roasted garlic, spread over thin crostini, so it wasn't quite as powerful. We lost count after about forty cloves. The two of us reeked for a week afterward.

I can't taint the garlic with tears—if nothing else that seems like bad luck when I'm trying to help George get back together with his family. Serving tear-stained garlic mashed potatoes seems like bad ju-ju. I turn on the radio and as luck would have it the song is a perfect blend of mournful and suicidal. I collapse at the high counter and slump into a barstool, burying my head in my arms, my face plastered against the stark reality of the cold granite. The tears are accompanied by sobs now, with howling probably nipping at their heels. If Cognac was with me listening to that noise, he'd join in the chorus. God, I don't know how I'm going to accomplish my immediate goal. It's as if I have to translate a language for a foreign dignitary after having only studied it for a few months. Sure, I might get this done, but it's going to be rough and regrettable. But in the bigger picture, I don't know how I'm going to embrace life without William in it. There's simply nothing about it that sounds joyful.

"Somebody call for a special delivery?"

I gasp instantly because no one's supposed to be here but

me, and reflexively I swing my arm around, making contact with William's nose.

"Oh my god! I'm so sorry! William! What—"

He runs to the counter and grabs a dishtowel to press to his nostril, which is beginning to stream blood. He's wearing a chef's toque.

"Oh, honey, I'm so glad I didn't have my knife in my hand—just think what I'd have done! You can't scare a girl like that! What are you doing here?" He talks muffled through the towel. "I heard your message. You sounded so low when you called. I thought you could use the help. Never thought you'd get me with a left hook though."

"Let me take a look at that." I throw some ice in a zipper-bag and remove the towel and oh, wow, noses sure do bleed, don't they. We squeeze the towel back over his nose and I tip his head back and eventually the bleeding stops.

"I feel like such a jerk," I say.

"For the nose?"

I look down at the floor before looking up at him. "Amongst other things."

I put my hands in my pockets only to realize I have no pockets, so I sort of fumble around with nowhere to fumble around, just making nervous. Instead I twiddle the strings of my apron.

"Why'd you come?"

William looks at me and holds my gaze firm. "Because you needed me, Abbie. You're my wife, I'll always be there when you need me, honey."

Well if the onions evoked tears and the garlic yielded even more, you can imagine how much that simple sentence could force out of me, even though by now my tear ducts should be depleted of all supplies.

"Really?"

William reaches out and pulls me into his comforting domain. "Would I lie to you?"

I shake my head no.

"I know things have been tense with us and I know we

haven't seen eye-to-eye on our needs and wants. I haven't been sensitive enough to what your job loss has meant to you—"

"And I haven't been sensitive enough to how much you yearn to get away and start a new phase in our lives," I chime in. I steer the two of us closer to the cooktop to give the caramelizing mixture a stir before it burns. "Sorry, can't risk having to do a do-over after chopping ten pounds of onions."

William smiles. "So like you, Abbie. Always mixing business with pleasure."

I move the towel away and it looks like the coast is clear as far as bleeding goes, even though he's going to have a nice bruise on the side of his nose.

"That's the other thing, William. I'm going to stop doing that."

"Doing what?"

"Mixing business with pleasure. I've gotten so confused over the years about what is business and what is pleasure. And somewhere along the line I lost you in the equation. It wasn't fair to you, and I'm so sorry I've been so ignorant of your needs."

"Maybe we both have. Let's say we just back off of all our worries and go with the flow. Things have a way of working out, and I think things will with all of this too." He spreads his arms out to indicate the workload ahead of us.

"You're really gonna help me?"

"I brought my hat, didn't I?"

"Where'd you get that thing, anyhow?"

"I stopped at a hotel on my way over here, went to the catering department and asked if they could scrounge one up for me. I even offered to pay but they gave it to me for free when I told them who it was for."

"You told them it was for me?"

"Of course I did. And you know what they said? They missed your reviews in the paper and wish you'd come back."

How nice to know I'm not totally forgotten, I guess.

"Where were you all this time?" I finally muster up the courage to ask.

"I camped out at Matt's loft in Soho."

"Matt? You mean you weren't with some blond bombshell?"

William laughs. "Well, Matt is somewhat blond—with a touch of gray around the temples. But I don't think his partner would appreciate me hitting up on him."

"Matt's gay?"

"You feel better now, knowing that?"

It's my turn to laugh. And here I was worried that my husband was in the throes of a torrid affair with some fantasy woman. Instead he was sleeping on a spare mattress and clearly not the object of anyone's deep desires.

"Much better," I say, taking a taste of the caramelized onions and licking the spoon clean.

For the rest of the day William and I work as a team in the kitchen, prepping, chopping, sautéing, steaming. It seems to re-define our relationship of late, the happy but silent give and take that comes with a couple so in tune with one another. Again, finally.

The last thing I make before calling it a night is my grandma Gigi's rice croquettes, a recipe that was handed down to her grandmother and then to her and then to me. Maybe someday I'll have a little girl I can pass this recipe on to, to keep up the tradition. There's something reassuring about something so lasting that can transcend generations and changes in tastes and still have appeal. I've never shared this with anyone; maybe it's a sign that I'm becoming less covetous where food is concerned.

GRANDMA GIGI'S RICE CROQUETTES

1 quart (4 cups) milk
3 tbl. sugar
1 tsp. vanilla extract (not vanilla flavoring)
1 tsp. kosher salt
4 sticks cinnamon
3/4 c. raw rice (long-grain)
Kellogg's Corn Flake Crumbs (about 3-4 cups)
Peanut oil (2-3 bottle of Planter's brand)
Red currant jelly

In double boiler on high, with water in bottom pan just shy of touching the bottom of insert pan, bring to scald one quart (four cups) whole milk. You will know it is scalded when a thin skin forms on surface of the milk. Then add 3 tbl. Sugar, 1 tsp. vanilla, 1 tsp. salt, 4 sticks cinnamon, and 3/4 c. raw rice. Stir well.

Cook on low to medium temperature for several hours, stirring occasionally, and checking to be sure water doesn't boil away from bottom pan (add more when necessary), until mixture is so thick you can barely stir it with a wooden spoon.

Let cool (can refrigerate overnight if need be).

Shape into 1" balls, roll in egg and then in corn flake crumbs to coat.

Deep-fry in peanut oil at 375° or in wok on medium high. Can be refrigerated and reheated in 350° oven for about 12-15 minutes.

Serve warm with currant jelly.

Two Parts Good Cheer Served Over Easy

It's amazing how pervasive food is. Every second commercial is for food. Every second TV episode takes place around a meal. In the city, you can't go ten feet without seeing or smelling a restaurant. There are twenty foot high hamburgers up on billboards. I am acutely aware of food, and its omnipresence is astounding.

–Adam Scott, The Monkey Chow Diaries, June 2006

BY the time I make it to bed, William is sound asleep. So much for that long-awaited reunion. Guess that'll have to wait. For now it's enough to settle into bed and wrap my arms around him, drifting off to sleep knowing he's home for good.

The delivery truck arrives early in the morning to collect all of the food that's going to Sally's. It seems half the dishes in my kitchen are headed that way. George arrives as the truck pulls away.

"You're early! I thought we said nine!"

"You did, but I'm an early riser. Street-sweeping machines start going in the city, you know."

The things you don't consider about roughing it in a city, I guess.

I hand George a towel and all the accoutrements one needs to clean up and direct him to the guest bedroom, while William and I shower and get ready ourselves. Within the hour we're all dressed and ready to go.

When George appears in the foyer, I gasp slightly.

"Oh, George, you look just perfect," I say, giving a tug on his suit jacket to straighten it out. "Are you ready for this?"

"I guess I'm as ready as I'll ever be. And I can't wait to eat whatever it is you're fixing."

We all laugh, considering dinner is all about food. Though in truth this one's about far more than merely that.

"Sally's got everyone lined up, it's going to be quite the gathering."

I look over at George who still looks quite anxious.

"You okay?"

"Yeah, though I'm not sure about this whole shindig."

"Shindig? Are you from this century?"

"Matter of fact, no, I'm from the last century, and proud of it."

"You want to hear my sage advice to you?" I ask him.

"So far you haven't steered me wrong. Fire away."

"Life is all about changes, all about moving forward, keeping things from getting too stale. Nothing static can last, nor would you want it to. So maybe there was a time when it was right for you to spread your wings, get out of your rut, even if it meant committing something pretty off-the-beaten-path as far as mid-life crises go. But now you're ready to take those experiences, apply them to your life, your marriage and your family, and go off in a new direction. It's time, George. And everyone's waiting for you."

"You trying to reduce me to tears? Bad enough you had me going to some metrosexual spa."

William laughs. "And you listened to her?"

"Abbie didn't give me a choice, really."

William looks at me. "She rarely does." Then he smiles. "So what time is our ride getting here?"

"Our ride! Jess! The driver!" Oh, crap. Yeah. Transportation. One little detail I neglected. "That was Jess' thing. I forgot all about it. She was going to send her husband's driver. I guess she forgot. And I forgot. And we need to get there. I've got loads to do and not enough time as it is. We don't have time to fetch a car service at this point."

William looks at me, that light bulb illuminating in his eyes. "But we do have a way to get us there." He crooks his finger for us to follow him, down the narrow steps to the basement, and points at his motorcycle and sidecar.

"That's fine for two of us. But what about the third?" I ask him. And then I look in the corner and see it, in all its hot pink glory. The Vespa, which has been waiting all this time for the perfect moment, which, like it or not, has finally arrived.

William nods first at me, then at it.

"Maybe I do have time to call for a driver," I say. "I bet I can find a cabbie who wants the fare."

But William shakes his head. "It's now or never Abbie. Use it or lose it. It's why I bought it for you. Don't be afraid, babe. I'll be riding right behind you, making sure nothing goes wrong."

If only I was afraid about something going wrong. Oy, that's the least of my worries. I'm more worried about nothing going. As in it not going. Due to overload. And I can only imagine the hind view of me on this thing: like family of five sitting on one of those bikes with a banana seat.

I look at William, my eyebrows furrowed. I glance at George, who appears giddy at the notion of riding in a sidecar—even if it does currently have a bit of dog hair strewn about it.

"We need to get the mini-vac and clean that up for our guest," I say, pointing at the mess.

William retrieves it and does a serviceable job of de-furring it. I want to collect up of Cognac's fur and pocket it as a good-luck talisman. Then he takes my hand and walks me over to my scooter.

"Your carriage awaits you, my dear." He holds his hand at my fingertips and kisses the top of it, as if I'm royalty.

Ever so carefully, even more delicately than when I've stepped onto the scale lately, I approach the beast, lifting my leg over the seat, straddling it, on my tiptoes, fearful of the big ka-boom I know must be about to come. I inch my behind down, an elephant stepping on a mouse, and finally settle onto the thing. I squint my eyes, awaiting the noise. After a few minutes of only hearing my heart beating in my ears I open my eyes and to my surprise, I'm sitting on top of my Vespa, looking as sporty as I can in my Johnny Cash-wear (all black—you know me). Of course black and pink go great together, so there you have it.

Maybe if I keep losing weight I can try this in the black and pink Victoria's Secret boy shorts some day. Just joking.

"I'll run upstairs and grab the keys—you need anything else?" William asks, his smile splitting his face, obviously pleased with himself at performing a small miracle and managing to get me onto this thing.

"My purse." Though I haven't the slightest idea where that's going to go for the ride. "Don't forget my coat—the black one! Oh, and grab the directions in a folder on the kitchen counter!"

He's back in a minute, opening up the extra-wide basement door that leads out to the alley behind our place so we can waddle the bikes out the door. William reads over the directions, and George assures him he can help him find the place.

We talk over our plan of attack to get out of the city then William bends down and gives me a long, heartfelt kiss. "You've got a good heart, Abbie Jennings, doing all this for George. Now let's go enjoy this ride." He lets out a whoop and puts my helmet on, helping to secure it in place. So much for my hairdo. Poor George is stuck with our spare (and extra-lame) helmet and only needs a horn jutting out of the top and he'd be taken for a modern-day Kaiser Wilhelm. Except that he's got my purse in his lap, bless his heart. As we weave between the lighter Saturday morning traffic, I glance in my mirror to see him just laughing and laughing, clearly enjoying the ride. And it's actually not such a bad ride; it's all coming back to me. Just like riding a bike.

Once we're on the West Side Highway I've got the hang of the thing and start to remember how much I loved riding our scooter, back in my salad days—as if I had salad days. And by the time we get to the Saw Mill, well, I'm hooked. What kind of idiot was I refusing to ride this thing for vanity's sake? I love it. And I love that William thought so much about me to ever buy it in the first place.

The leaves are changing and the diversity of colors is spectacular—it's a feast for the eyes. Now that's my kind of feast, these days, one that isn't at all fattening, but is delightful nonetheless. Being on the Vespa makes me feel so much more a part of the experience than I would in a car with a roof overhead. Instead it's me, surrounded by stunning foliage. I really ought to get out more often.

By the time we arrive in Pound Ridge I am exhilarated and ready to take on my task at hand. I find the hidden driveway that leads up to George's house and clear my name at the gate, sort of bummed I won't miss the reunion between George and Junior. Ahead of me, rows of Italian cypress-like trees hug the mile-long drive (although I'm sure those trees can't withstand the bitter Westchester winters, though I suspect Sally would pay to heat the ground just to keep the things alive if it meant that much to her). I finally arrive in a clearing to see a palatial estate before me. I knew George had money, but damn, George has money. The home looks more like a grand Italianate palazzo or some last vestige of the Holy Roman Empire than someone's humble home. I dismount the Vespa near one of several apparent parking areas, after seeing where George has directed William to park. We stand in awe for a few minutes, until Sally comes squealing out, several dogs in tow, and stops abruptly in front of her husband.

She whistles low and long. "Well, well, well. Would ya look at that." Her eyes trail him from top to bottom, looking somewhat dumbstruck.

George sticks his arms out and does a slow twirl, just to emphasize the transition. "You like?"

I think Sally's speechless. She just keeps staring at him.

"Well? What do you think?" I ask her. I can't wait to hear what she thinks.

"Abbie, you're a miracle-worker. I mean look at him—" she reaches out and grabs him by the shoulder and gives him a little shake like he's on display. "In a million years—"

"Uh, I am an actual living, breathing, creature," he says to her. "You don't have to talk about me as if I'm an inanimate object!"

At that Sally reaches out for him and gives him an enormous hug, one so hard it's lucky she's a size zero or she'd squeeze the life out of him.

“I didn’t think you’d ever come home,” she whispers in his ear.

“I didn’t think you ever really wanted me home,” he whispers back.

After a few minutes of them talking quietly and William and I staring in awe at our surroundings, Sally ushers us inside. Of course the inside is even more stunning than the outside, with one-of-a-kind paintings gracing the walls of the enormous open foyer, with a split staircase spiraling up either side to the next level, complete with a domed, frescoed ceiling.

William leans over and whispers in my ear, “You mean to tell me your buddy gave up all this to live on a park bench?”

“I know, it seems crazy, doesn’t it?” I say, rubbing my hand along his chin. “But look what I was blindly giving up. Sometimes you need someone to shine a light on whatever’s under that rock, eh?”

We hold hands as Sally tours us around, first to the receiving room, where appetizers will be served. Then the dining room, which is almost clichéd with one long gleaming mahogany table, polished so much it’s like looking at glass. Three chandeliers suspend at intervals from the towering ceiling, their Swarovski crystal prisms scattering sunlight like confetti throughout the room. Even the light is celebrating today. The staff has obviously already been in here, as the table is brimming with crystal and china and silver and only the finest of everything. Tall floral arrangements are interspersed with candelabra, all elevated so as to not obscure the view of others a table.

Nothing prepares me for the splendor of Sally’s kitchen. It is the Cinderella’s castle of all kitchens, it’s that fabulous. I might just become a squatter here. They’d never know. Though I’d have to bring along William and Cognac, and I can’t forget Tartare. It might get crowded in this ballroom of a kitchen with so many of us taking up residence here.

Sally excuses her and George and asks a butler to show us where all of our supplies are. And then all of the lifestyles of the uber rich and famous fantasies evaporate and William and I have to hunker down to serious work. Sorting the tenderloins, all of which are marinating in Ziploc bags (who could figure out where to find enough roasting pans in which to marinate them all?), finding pans for the sauces, serving dishes and utensils for the various courses, chafing dishes for the appetizers. By late afternoon the meat is coming to room temperature on the countertop, in preparation for roasting. Ovens are pre-heated, soup and sauces are simmering, appetizers have been laid out on silver trays and guests begin to arrive. As much as I'd love to witness each of the guests greeting George, I can't leave the kitchen for even a moment until the main course is served. But in the distance I can hear the din of laughter and squeals of joy as one after another, family and friends welcome their wayward member back into the fold.

At last, once meals have been plated and are ready to go out, William and I prepare to join the dinner party, already in progress, having left strict instructions to the Gretl-less kitchen help on everything left to be done. Between the helmet and the heat of the kitchen my hair has fallen limp like the fine coat on an Irish setter, nearly obscuring my view of things. William pulls me aside for a moment before we leave the butler's pantry.

"Hey, Mrs. Jennings," he says, cupping my face in his hands, wiping a few beads of sweat from my forehead and straggling hair from my eyes.

"Hey back, Mr. Jennings," I say, smiling at him.

"You did good here, you know."

"Thank you. Though let's hold out final judgment until we get a sense of what's happening out there on the Western Front. You never know with this lot—things could be going to hell in a handbasket for all we know."

"Well, I want you to know how proud I am of you, babe. You've done something really special here, reuniting George with his family."

He takes my hand and we step out into the dining room and join the group, who are clearly enjoying themselves, if I can judge that from the number of empty bottles of wine, beer and liquor I saw piling up in the recycling bin.

Sally has saved seats for us close to the immediate family and we are introduced to George's kids and grandchildren. As luck would have it, I'm nearest five-year old Katie, who is as poised and sophisticated as a sixteen-year old and decides to help me navigate the array of utensils at my place. Clearly she never got the memo on my food critic past. She and I talk about her school and about boys and she tells me that she has no patience for dolls and would rather play with her dog more than anything in the world.

"That's funny, me too," I tell her. Turns out Katie has a Saint Bernard, so she knows big dogs when she sees them. I tell her how Cognac is being patched back together as we speak, and she tells me she'll say a prayer for him at bedtime tonight and how could I not be charmed by such a delightful little girl.

Funny thing is I've never given much thought to children in a practical sense. The idea of children to me has always been featured as this daunting project—some nebulous goal that is so grandiose it's hard to imagine taking it on voluntarily. Which is perhaps why I've shuddered repeatedly at the notion and run for cover each time William has introduced the concept to me. But in practicality it seems that children have all sorts of features of them that can be downright desirable: cute and charming and adorable and, well, tempting. Little Katie, sitting there with her silky blond hair pulled back in a ponytail, her green and blue plaid dress with the smocking on it, her white tights and navy blue Mary Janes. What's not to like about such a creature? I'm starting to realize that children are far more than little creatures set upon this earth to be victimized by the vagaries of selfish parents. They can be living, breathing little souls, their own thoughts and deeds, their own wants and needs.

Come to think of it, they can be little girls, cooking away to fend off the dark, hiding behind a warm batch of cookies, seeking solace in a loaf of freshly-baked bread. And there's nothing wrong with that kind of little girl, either. It's just not how I'd want my little girl to do it. No, I'd want my little girl (or boy) to take pleasure in wrestling in the yard with the family dog, with chasing a butterfly, with sitting in grandpa's lap reading a story. And maybe, just maybe, these things are possible.

I'm jarred away from my thoughts as George stands, dinging his crystal champagne flute, preparing to speak. His sons are both smoking cigars now, relaxed, sprawled back in their seats, their girlfriends chattering amongst themselves. His daughter Jenna is holding hands with her husband, and his daughter Tamara is smiling and whispering into the ear of a man next to her who is rumored to be her estranged husband, back for the grand re-introduction of her father.

As George stands, everyone begins to clap, but he motions with his hands to stop with the praise. "I can't thank you all enough for joining Sally and I tonight for this remarkable occasion. I'm sure plenty of you never thought you'd see me back here for our thirty-fifth anniversary. Not the least of whom was me!" Everyone laughs at him and Sally rolls her eyes skyward. "I hate to admit it but there's a damned good chance I'd have never made it back tonight, in all honesty. To that I owe a great deal to an unexpected friend I met along the way."

George tips his glass my way and I instinctually shrink at the suggestion of eyes focusing on me. Once an attention-shunning critic, always, I guess. "Abbie Jennings happened upon me one cold night in January. When I say cold, I know that everyone here will never understand exactly what I mean. We're all so used to a reliable furnace that circulates warmth throughout the winter and an air conditioner that ensures we never have to break a sweat in the summertime. Even up here, where we rarely need it. But when you are relying upon yourself, out in the elements, cold becomes a very different thing altogether. And sometimes it's quantified not in temperature but in warmth. Human warmth." He chuckles for a moment, reflecting on something we'll know not of.

"But there I was, freezing my ass off, really. I'd found a grate, but damn, those things blow up at you and sometimes they get too hot. Not to mention smelly. But it was that or turn into a lump of ice on the sidewalk, so you take what you can get. It was late, and I was trying my best not to rely upon everything I knew I could have relied upon had I really needed to. Yeah, I was avoiding checking in for just one night at the Plaza, as tempting as it was. I wanted to make it on my own, just me against the elements. Prove to myself that I could do it. That I didn't need anyone. I was tired of being so damned needed by everyone else and I just wanted to walk away from it all. But there it was, nearing midnight probably. And this woman came up to me and handed me a bag with a couple of meals worth of food in it. Didn't say much, just slipped it into my lap, told me to take care of myself, and walked on."

Everyone's staring at me and I am feeling awfully embarrassed. God, I hate to be the feature presentation. At least I'm not sucking on baklava, that's all I have to say.

"The next time Abbie happened upon me, we talked for a few minutes. She asked if I was okay, asked if I needed anything. I thanked her for her kindness. And soon she started seeking me out. A couple of times a week. If it weren't for a few strange chance encounters, it might have remained just two strangers who make a little connection. But Abbie is a special person, and the next thing I knew, she'd taken it upon herself to help reunite me with all of you."

Everyone starts to clap again and he shushes them. "Please, please, don't clap for me. I didn't do anything. I ran away from home. I wasn't much more than a tough-talking little kid escaping from his parents. It's Abbie you need to applaud, because Abbie's motivations were entirely selfless, completely caring, and without a hidden agenda. Abbie Jennings showed me that family really can be so much more than those whose blood you share; rather family extends to those you care about, one way or another."

He raises his glass. "I know I was a royal pain in Sally's ass for a good long while. I know my kids thought I was half-cocked when I disappeared like I did. But we all learned some lessons from this experience. And instead of my running away being all about just a bad thing, we've come full circle now, thanks to Abbie giving me a shove in the right direction, and I'm thrilled to be back home, right where I belong." With that he tips his glass in my direction and everyone raises their glasses and toasts.

The delicate tinkling of so many crystal glasses is almost as musical as the voice of sweet little Katie.

Everyone is looking at me, suggesting that I say something but Oh, God, I am not one to ever—make that ever—say something about myself. But then William pushes me up to standing and I'm here with eighty eyeballs on me and little Katie thinks I will have some words of wisdom so nothing like being on the spot.

I clear my voice. "Well, George might like to think I've taught him something about family, but the crazy thing is he's taught me more about family than a whole lifetime of experiences has." Everyone starts to murmur a little bit.

"Yeah, I know, it's crazy to think that some nut job homeless guy—" I tip my flute toward him and we all laugh, "—could provide any insight for me, but he has. I guess in some bizarre way we've tutored each other without even knowing it. I've been taking my lessons as they come. But I can't look around this room without realizing how much family matters. Whether they come to you late in life, or have stuck with you through your insanity." I tip my head to Sally at that comment.

"Family can be ugly. Family can be messy. Family can be beautiful. Family can be insufferable. But you know what? I've had my share of meals over the years—you might be able to tell—" I rub my stomach and people chuckle a little nervously.

"So I know from a good meal. Sometimes you have a meal that looks so beautiful it's almost untouchable. Yet it doesn't end up tasting that great. And then sometimes you have a meal that is slopped together in chipped bowls and passed from person to person, but how it looks is irrelevant because what matters is how it tastes. I'm starting to realize I had this vision of family that was supposed to be a perfect meal, plated just right, no sauce spilled on the side, appearances perfect. I didn't understand that it's okay to have a messy family, one that might look pretty bad from the outside, but once you slap it all together, it's not so bad. I lost sight of the truth of it. I've had my family alongside me all this time—" I point to William, whose damp eyes reflect the candlelight. "I've had the family, and the ability to create and sustain a family. I was just so afraid I couldn't create that perfect meal, but I'm coming to realize I don't have to. I just didn't get it. Until now. And I have to thank all of you for bringing home that simple truth to me." Out of words, I raise my glass. "Salut," I say, and we all toast again.

I sit down and William wraps his arm around me, and finally, like rainwater navigating a leaky roof, the pressure of a wealth of unspent tears are seeking the path of least resistance, coursing their way toward my vulnerable eyes. I fight the temptation—the last thing I want to do is cry in front of everyone—but what the hell, it's family right?

The rest of the dinner flies by, a whirl of conversation and many more toasts and meeting everyone at the party and I have to say I'm really glad I don't have to wash the dishes. When Sally said this would be a night to remember, she was so very right.

Steep in Bliss and Savor

Food is our common ground, a universal experience.

–James Beard

"MORE prosecco, babe?" William pulls the bottle from wine cooler and begins to refill our glasses.

I hold my hand over his. "I know the doctor told us a little champagne won't hurt the baby, but my half glass was plenty, thanks."

I pat my burgeoning belly for emphasis. For once an expanding waistline is a portent for good in my life and I'm nothing but elated about it.

Despite the slight autumn chill in the air, I feel warm all over, gazing out to the sapphire waters of the Tyrrhenian Sea spread out before us like a willing mistress offering herself up to her lover. My stomach is full, having just shared a Caprese salad, grilled swordfish for a secondi, and biscotti di mandorle with my cappuccino. And getting fuller, with our much-anticipated added ingredient cooking inside of me right now.

Life is good. Better than good. Life is darn near perfect. I know my poochie and my kittie are safe at home, cared for by my sister Jane, who's enjoying a stint at our place while caring for our four-legged children. When we return from our extended tour of Italy, we're planning to decamp for a while to the countryside. We're renting out the brownstone and will live in a cottage not far from George and Sally, in fact. Sally's hooked me up with a bunch of catering jobs which will keep me busy until I will be ready to be off my feet when the baby comes along.

Mortie begged and begged for me to return to the *Sentinel*, but I realized I just didn't need it. Instead I'm keeping my column, and it's a little less about dieting and more about food and traveling, called *Life in the Slow Lane*. And I'm thinking of writing a diet book. I'll call it the *Goombah Diet: Shut Your Mouth*. Surely there's a market for it. And believe me, I know from diets.

I'm glad I've lost a decent amount of weight along the way. I suppose I can thank Mortie, peripherally, for that. I hate that it ultimately took nearly losing my dog and my husband for it to really happen. But at least it finally did. I'll never be rail thin, but at least I'm back in the low double-digits, size-wise. Not too shabby.

It's all a little scary, departing from what I have known so intimately, but it's also reassuring. Forever fluent in food, it's been the language of my life. In fact I'm practically a food linguist. So I'm learning all over again, trying on other languages that might be equally pleasurable, and maybe a little less physically taxing. Which brings us back to Italy, where the language of love is omnipresent, and this is a language with which I've become reacquainted, at last.

Thank you for reading!

Dear Reader,

I hope you enjoyed ***Slim to None***. It's been a while since I re-visited this novel, which I wrote a few years back. Believe it or not, I tend to forget much about my books once I'm done writing them, so I had to do a little refresher course when I got ready to re-issue ***Slim to None*** once I got my rights back from the publisher. And I'm always happy when I re-read one of my books and I have fun reading it. I thoroughly enjoyed joining Abbie and her mis-adventures in dieting ;-). (and, um, er, should take a page from her ultimate success and get myself back to the gym!).

If you'd like to download a printable booklet of the recipes, many that have been very popular with readers, you can find it on my website:

http://www.jennygardiner.net/wp-content/uploads/2016/01/Slim-to-None-recipes-1.pdf

I had been writing a lot of women's fiction and chick lit type novels, but turned my attention to writing a series of contemporary romantic comedies titled ***It's Reigning Men*** last year. It's still my voice--which you might have noticed is a little snarky and veering toward laugh out loud when I succeed at it—only now it's a story set in a modern-day fictional European royal principality. Because hey, I like royal things and figured there must be others like me too. I admit it, I've awoken in the middle of the night to watch those British royal weddings. And I even got to photograph Prince Charles (back when he was still supposedly happily married to Diana) so I feel like I had enough of a connection to give it a go. The fifth book in the series, ***Shame of Thrones***, will be released in December http://bit.ly/iBooksSoT, and I hope you'll give it a try.

Turn the page for a sample of the first book in the series, ***Something in the Heir***.

I love to hear from readers, so please, tell me what you liked, what you loved and even what you hated. You can keep up with the latest news of releases and even get added tidbits and fun extras (including a downloadable recipe booklet from Abbie's recipes) if you sign up for my newsletter here: http://eepurl.com/baaewn. You can write to me at jenny@jennygardiner.net, and visit me on the web at www.jennygardiner.net. And of course I'm on Facebook (maybe when I should be writing…)

https://www.facebook.com/jennygardinerbooks.

And if can ask a huge favor of you, if you are so inclined, I'd be so grateful for your review of any or all of my books you've read at retail sites and Goodreads—I really appreciate your feedback, and it also helps other readers when they're looking for books to read. Reviews are really hard to come by, which is totally understandable because we're all pressed for time and crazy busy. But please know that your review helps authors tremendously and I for one am incredibly appreciative of anyone who is able to take the time to review my books and share them with others. You, the reader, have the power to make or break a book! You can find links to all of my books on my website.

Thank you again for your ongoing support!

Jenny Gardiner

SOMETHING IN THE HEIR

Chapter One

EMMA Davison had a date with a prince. Well, not really a date, but yes, really a prince. Calling it a date would be a bit of a stretch, considering she would only be within breathing distance of the man by dint of her professional skills. Emma had been hired to photograph His Royal Highness Crown Prince Adrian William Philip Nicholas Winchester-Westleigh, future King of Monaforte, in a series of grip-and-grins with wealthy donors at a Washington, DC charitable event. For Emma, this was a perfect night out with a man: one for which she'd get paid, and only for her skills. Professionally-speaking, that is. It was about as much of a pseudo date with a guy as she'd expected for the foreseeable future, since she'd sworn off men for a while after a series of dud relationships.

And while it was hard not to fleetingly fantasize about being swept off your feet by royalty, the fact was, those types of princes only came in fairy tales, and Emma wasn't a big subscriber to that sort of fiction. Having already tossed back into the swamp more than her share of warty toads over the years, she knew that at the end of the day, even a prince was just a man. And in her world, men hadn't exactly panned out. Besides, she'd seen the tabloids: this pretty boy was a player, a new woman on his arm in every city, rumor had it. As far as she was concerned, they could keep him. *Prince-schmince.* She sure wasn't looking for another love 'em and leave 'em type in her life. She was here to do a job, and the sooner she did it, the sooner she could go home and take a nice hot bath with a good book and a glass of red wine.

As she awaited the arrival of the guest of honor while hovering just inside the cordoned-off velvet rope section in the palatial Great Hall of the Library of Congress, Emma mentally ticked off the essentials she needed to keep in mind for the shoot. She'd thoroughly reviewed the protocol handbook with the palace's press secretary earlier in the week. All forty-six pages of it. She'd been told a curtsey would be a nice gesture, and warned not to shake the man's hand, which sort of seemed annoying, as if her own wasn't good enough or something. No vulgar language in his presence, which made her laugh, since under other circumstances she'd maybe have to show a bit of restraint in that area, but she figured she could refrain from an f-bomb for an hour or two.

Emma had actually practiced how to address the prince for a good while in advance of the event so that she wouldn't come across like a complete country bumpkin in his presence, repeating in front of the mirror, "*Pleased to meet you, sir*" till she could say it no more. She was ready. She'd even straightened her shoulder-length chestnut curls for the occasion, thinking straighter hair lent her a bit of gravitas. Yeah, she kept telling herself, she didn't care one bit about impressing even a prince.

She'd brought along her assistant and best friend Caroline McKenzie, whom she knew wouldn't screw up—though it was a crap shoot whether she'd hit on the man herself. Caroline, a green-eyed redhead with a penchant for serial flirtation, was known for her ability to pick up pretty much any guy she wanted without batting an eye. But Emma knew even she had her limits and would, with any luck, respect royal protocol, in deference to her friend's career.

Tonight Emma would remain on the VIP side of the velvet rope as she set up to shoot the prince alongside all sorts of deep-pocketed D.C. dignitaries, with the President of the United States thrown in for good measure. Lately she'd found it hard to remain too starstruck in her line of work, shooting famous people as regularly as she did. But a prince *and* a president? As much as she wanted to play it cool, even she had to admit that was none too shabby.

Caro, standing just behind Emma, squealed in surprise when the prince's arrival was announced with blasts from those long royal trumpets draped with crimson flags bearing the Monaforte royal crest. It was straight out of a Disney movie when Prince Charming's arrival was heralded to the guests at the ball. As soon as the trumpets fell silent, a deep blue velvet curtain parted and the prince, followed by his right-hand man, stepped forward to the thunderous applause of the audience.

Emma was close enough to see that he had mesmerizing bright blue eyes. She was a sucker for blue eyes.

Just then a quartet struck up a tune and the music shattered her momentary reverie. She knew she had all of about two minutes to greet the prince and then get started with the host of images she needed to capture. There were titans of industry, political bigwigs and a collection of pandering celebrities already queued up, desperate for their own eight-by-ten glossy with famous royalty that they could mount on their wall like some taxidermied bear head. She had no time for gawking.

The prince walked slowly down the line, greeting one by one the organizers of the charitable event and members of the Monafortian embassy staff, all standing in the VIP zone near Emma. Everyone seemed to do a perfectly fine job with his or her allotted three seconds of undivided royal attention, making casual chitchat with the prince. Until it came to Emma. Because as soon as the man approached her, she felt as if her tongue had become a sandbag weighted down in her mouth. And while a curtsey wasn't mandatory, it was what she'd planned on, until that very moment when her eyes made contact with his deep, sapphire ones, and she knew for certain she'd face-plant on his expensive royal bespoke Italian shoes if she dared try any tricky maneuvers.

Emma tried to give him a discreet once-over, but it felt awkward, like gawking at a stranger's tattoo, or trying to read the T-shirt message on the chest of a person walking by. She definitely wanted to avoid coming across like a sad-sack groupie, and had planned to play it cool. But then she found herself focused on his thick, wavy black hair, which led to a fleeting fantasy that involved burying her fingers in it while he was busily…*Oh, stop!* She tamped down that betraying though, dismissing it as some stupid latent celebrity crush, all the while recognizing that her darned body was selling her out and swooning over the guy despite her strong inner protestations.

So when Prince Adrian stopped before her, bent his head down but raised his gaze and continued to fix it on Emma's eyes only, reaching both hands out for hers — totally defying that whole handbook of royal protocol — she simply stammered. And when he pressed his lips to the top of her hand, she could only gulp as she tried to clear what felt like a giant hairball lodged in her throat.

"Peas to greet you, slur," she said, failing miserably to just mouth correctly those five simple words, turning about fifty shades of red in the process. She felt certain she was going to be fired on the spot.

But instead of calling for his royal bodyguards to toss her out into the cold December night on the grounds of complete idiocy, he clasped her hand in both of his for a moment longer, his eyes continuing to hold hers, and smiled broadly. Emma could feel her heart beating in her throat, and she wondered for a minute if he was only holding onto her hands until someone else could grab them and haul her away. In handcuffs maybe.

"The pleasure is all mine. And please, call me Adrian," he said in what seemed barely a whisper, adding with a wink, "Oh, and by the way, I'm most peased to greet you as well."

Emma was so glad she wasn't prone to throwing up because if she were, that would've been the unfortunate outcome of her moment in the spotlight with her "date." Instead she let him cling to her hand a second longer while she trembled just a bit and hoped to God her palms weren't sweating too badly.

The spell was broken when Caroline elbowed her, blurting out, and not in her inside voice, "Oh, my God. His accent is orgasmic. And did you get a look at that friend of his?"

Adrian and Emma's heads followed her friend's pointing finger, which led right to the tall, handsome brown-eyed blond man standing beside the prince.

"Who? Darcy?" Adrian said, waving his hand dismissively. "He's hardly anything to write home about!" He laughed as he gave him a friendly smack on the back.

"Don't listen to a word he says," Darcy said. "He's just jealous that women always choose me over him."

Which meant those women must have been certifiably insane, if they didn't want Adrian to keep for all eternity. Emma wondered if she could stuff him in her camera bag and no one would notice. And then she could have him all to herself. To join her in that bubble bath even. Which was an insane thought, considering she'd just met the man minutes ago. But he was obviously so good at charming the pants off of a girl, how could she not maybe at least ponder having her own pants charmed off, at least for a second or two?

By the time Emma snapped out of that delusional fantasy, the prince had finished greeting the receiving line and was engaged in conversation with some member of Congress. That was her cue to get to work, so she raised her camera up to her eye, her other hand turning the zoom on the lens to frame the shot, and started making pictures.

A short while later, a syrupy-drawled senator approached and glad-handed the prince with a too-firm grip and slap on the back. So much for diplomatic decorum.

"You gonna tap that one?" he said to Adrian, his booming voice resonating. He nodded in Emma's direction, rubbing his paunchy belly like he'd had a satisfying meal, as she snapped the two of them in conversation. He might as well have been licking his chops like a starving dog. It wasn't the first time she'd been exposed to obnoxious good-old-boy comments from an old fogey politician. Such crassness seemed to be elevated to an art form in this town.

"You mean our lovely photographer?" the prince said, playing along. "Actually, she's the woman I'm going to marry." He gave her a wink, assuming she'd be complicit in his joke.

Instead Emma blanched, mortified that they were discussing her as if she was a slab of meat they were choosing off a hot grill, all for their boys-will-be-boys amusement.

"Yeah, in your dreams, buddy," she said in too loud of a voice as she continued to snap pictures, handily obscuring her face and thus her emotions. Her royal subject squinted his eyes at her and pouted, as if she'd hurt his feelings, and she immediately regretted her words. It made no sense to be annoyed with the prince; he was simply defusing the obnoxious comment made by the senator. But it was too late. Within a minute he had his arm draped around the sexy trophy wife of a well-known lobbyist, and so Emma did what she always did to hide from the world and resumed snapping pictures.

"I'm so ready to get out of here," Caroline said as they sipped sparkling water while taking a five-minute break. "These old geezers around here with those gold-digging bimbos on their arms are giving me hives. Maybe I can kidnap blondie over there and make a run for it. Think his friend would notice?" Once again she pointed toward Darcy, who was dominating the conversation in a circle of women nearby.

They'd been notified by the event coordinator that the president would be arriving shortly, so Emma was taking advantage of a momentary break to run to the bathroom and double check that her equipment was ready for the big moment. Despite an encroaching sense of ennui about her job that had settled in recently, she was feeling anxious about shooting the president and wanted to be sure she got off all the shots she needed.

When she returned to Caroline's side, they worked their way back toward the front of the crowd to get in position for the president's arrival. She noticed how Caroline's gaze rarely left Darcy.

"Forget about him," Emma said, nodding toward the prince's assistant. "This place is crawling with Secret Service, at least until the president's gone. If you try to bag that one, you'd be hauled off for interrogation by Homeland Security, never to be heard from again."

Her friend shrugged. "You know, some of those Secret Service guys are pretty hot."

"You do know you've got a one-track mind, don't you?"

Caro shook her head in dismay at her friend. "At least there's something going down my track. Ever since that last derailment with Richard what's-his-name, yours has been a whole lot of nothing. No train ever stops at your station."

"Please," Emma said, annoyance flickering in her hazel eyes. "I do not need to be reminded of that regrettable relationship. The jerk still owes me five hundred dollars I lent him. Not to mention my dignity, which he took off with along with that stripper from his buddy's bachelor party."

"Pretend I didn't even mention him," Caroline said, holding her hands up in defeat. "I totally forgot I promised I'd no longer resurrect your litany of painful break-up stories. At least not while at work. Although, you gotta admit," she said, wrinkling her nose as she held back her laughter, "it was sort of funny to watch him on YouTube jamming fifties in her g-string. Just think how romantic it is that one day they'll be able to show their grandchildren the video of the very moment they met."

Emma made a grumbling sound. "At least I figured out where my money went."

"And it was money well spent, darlin', if it meant finding out the truth about that one. Way cheaper than alimony."

"Which I'd have had to pay since he couldn't keep a job for more than six months." Sometimes Emma wished there was a punching bag nearby, just to get out her aggression toward the loser.

Their conversation was interrupted by the unmistakable sound of drums and bugles that precede "Hail to the Chief." Emma snapped one wide shot of an audience's worth of hands raised in the air, smart phones at the ready for their very own money shot with the president.

The president parted the velvet curtains, waved to the crowd, then greeted the prince and his entourage while Emma clicked away on her camera. After a brief, five-minute address, he was whisked away by a coterie of security guards, *tout de suite.*

Once the headliner was gone, the crowd began to dissipate quickly. Emma managed to pop off a handful of shots with other guests and the prince, and finally the embassy press secretary thanked Emma for her service and dismissed her.

She scoured the room in search of Caroline, who'd taken another bathroom break, just to let her know she was off the hook and could leave. She found her friend chatting up a cute bartender.

Emma tapped her on the shoulder, trying to draw her attention away from tall, dark and hottie, who seemed intent on slinging mixed drinks to impress, shaking cocktails atop his head like he was go-go dancer from the sixties

"I'd tell you that you can leave but it looks like you don't want to have a reason to slip out quite yet," she said.

Caroline startled and gasped. "You scared the crap out of me!"

"Just wanted you to know you're technically off-duty in exactly T minus ten seconds," Emma told her, pointing at the time on her cell phone. "Obviously you can feel free to stick around and latch onto some useless guy, but if I were you, considering the caliber of this crowd, at least I'd aim a little higher."

"Thanks for the sage advice, relationship expert that you are." She laughed at Emma. "But seriously, you know I'm not looking for the guy with the deepest pockets," Caroline said. "I'll take the hot bartender with the smooth moves anyday," she said, pointing over to the guy pouring her drink, "— over some snooty, rich country club-type who wouldn't abide my less-than-uppity ways." She lifted the tip of her nose with her pointer finger as she said that, her long, straight red hair falling into her face.

Emma laughed and mussed her friend's hair. "Whatever. Have fun, and don't do anything I wouldn't do…"

"That leaves my options wide open," she said, holding her thumb and pointer finger up in an "L" shape to her chest. "How about just to prove you're not a complete loser, why don't you see if you can snare that cute prince and get your wild on?" Not that there was a chance of that anyhow, as the prince and his entourage had already taken their leave.

Emma fake-glared at her. "Thanks, but I'll take a pass on the Cinderella fantasy. Though he was pretty easy on the eyes. I'm surprised you didn't already commandeer that friend of his."

"Sadly, once I got finished wiping the drool from my chin, he'd disappeared."

"Leave it to you to not miss out on the eye candy, whether he's your basic bartender or a royal footman," Emma said, pausing to contemplate the thought. "Is that what you call them? Footmen? Do they do something with their feet, or have a creepy foot fetish? Sort of weird name, isn't it?"

"Probably more like henchman is my guess. Back in the day his footman would've cut off the enemy's head. Am I right? Ah, well, clearly we weren't born into that world, so I'm not gonna bother even fantasizing about it, not to mention decipher the terminology."

"Yep. Besides, imagine how high maintenance a prince would be. Sheesh!" Emma stuck out her pinky finger while pretending to pick up a delicate china teacup. "Spot of tea, Mummy? Oh, royal knave, fetch me my slippers!" she said with an exaggerated accent.

The two women practically fell over laughing, until Caroline's mixologist cleared his throat at an elevated volume, trying to rein in his audience.

"Okay, then. Looks like Bartender Ben over there wants your undivided attention," she said, aiming her thumb over her shoulder at the guy. "I've got no shoots scheduled for the next week, which means I won't be requiring your assistance, so have fun mixing it up with this one."

Caroline's eyes grew wide and she mouthed "Shut up!" to Emma, then turned back to her man of the moment.

Emma took a final quick glance around the room as she packed up her camera bag. After working more hours than she cared to count with her feet wedged into a torturous pair of black stilettos, she wanted nothing more than to peel off her floor-length, black satin sheath, lose the strapless bra that was cutting off the circulation in her mid-section, and tug on her favorite oversized sweatshirt and yoga pants. Then she'd finally pour that very full glass of Chianti she'd been craving, and return to her natural slothdom.

The party was still going strong, but since she was only contracted to do grip-and-grins of Prince Charming, there wasn't truly a reason to stick around much longer. Hell, she'd likely get pressed into service with the wait staff if she wasn't careful. Not like she had anyone she could hang around and chat with anyhow, with Caroline being preoccupied. That was the thing about her work world: being a worker bee at the ball wasn't really much fun, even if the top-tier champagne was flowing freely and the passed canapès probably bore a per-piece price tag that exceeded her daily meal budget.

For Emma, being an outsider at an insider's party was losing its luster; she was getting old enough to appreciate that it wasn't what it was cracked up to be. Sure, she got to share proximity with some of the world's elites, but since she wasn't a member of that rarified universe, it didn't rank a whole lot higher than being the one polishing the silver at the palace. It wasn't as if she could chat up the guests, comparing notes on their winter holidays in Aspen, shared vacations on Necker Island with Sir Richard Branson, or summering on Nantucket. The closest Emma got to summering (and when did that become a verb?) —

not counting Caroline's annual skee-ball smackdown on the boardwalk in Ocean City, Maryland, which didn't quite elevate vacationing to the next level — was escaping to her parents' beach house in North Carolina every August.

Okay, she had to clarify this a bit: her job sure beat working in a windowless cubicle. And tonight's venue, The Great Hall, on a scale from one to wow, was no doubt a wow. Picture every little girl's fantasy of taking that Cinderella descent down a grand marble staircase, garbed in a luscious tulle ball gown twinkling with crystal beads, with the man of your dreams (like maybe that Adrian guy) waiting at the bottom to clasp your outstretched hand and pull you into an intimate dance. Throw in that two-story tall Christmas tree, which would put the famed Rockefeller Center version to shame on grandeur alone, and, well, this was where that dream would come to life. That is, if that was the kind of fairy tale you could somehow work out for yourself. Good luck there. Nevertheless, she attended interesting events, met fascinating subjects, and did so in some pretty spectacular venues. But for some reason this wasn't thrilling her the way it used to.

As Emma was working her way toward the coat check, she spied the obnoxious senator pawing at what looked to be a Capitol Hill intern, judging by the badge dangling from her neck. Emma quickly opened up her camera bag, pulled out her camera, and began snapping pictures of the senator in a clinch with the girl, his hand squeezing the young woman's butt.

"Hey, Senator," she shouted over the din of the crowd. "Wonder what your constituents would think about you tapping that."

She moved the camera away from her face and gave him a big thumbs-up as he quickly detached himself from the girl, who had to be fifty years his junior.

Gotcha.

With that, camera still slung over her shoulder, she grabbed her coat from the coat checker, handed the girl a buck, and slipped out a side door, never to be missed by those inside. Now to get back to the car, cross the bridge into Virginia, and be home in twenty-five minutes, tops.

Chapter Two

HIS Royal Highness Crown Prince Adrian was one very ticked-off man. He paced the floor of the private office-slash-holding room in which he was holed up as if he had somewhere to go. Only he didn't, since somehow his driver had yet to arrive to usher him back to the embassy. Although he might, soon enough, right on down the aisle, what with his mother force-feeding him a heaping helping of Lady Serena Elisabeth Montague, Duchess of Montague, like a fat spoonful of that disgusting, overpriced caviar that girl seemed to be on a steady diet of.

Despite Adrian's repeated entreaty to the contrary, his mother the queen had deemed Serena to be "ideal marrying material," via yet another text message to her son, and palace efforts were now under way to ensure the fulfillment of her wishes, regardless that they were in direct conflict with her son's own desires. Certainly it hadn't helped that Serena's mother, Lady Sarah, a close consort of the queen, had been touting the glories of her daughter to his mother for years now.

"*Serena Montague.*" He said, growling her name, swatting away his equerry and trusted confidante, Lord Darcy Squires-Thornton. "Despicable would be too generous a word to describe that manipulative witch. I'd no sooner wed that scheming, conniving—"

"Adrian," his aide said, stopping him with a hand against his chest and a stern look in his eyes. "The walls have ears."

Adrian glanced around the room, remembering that there were indeed others nearby whose discretion wasn't guaranteed. It wasn't easy always having to worry that what you said could be broadcast publicly and not in a good way. Ridiculous, really. He was starting to feel almost imprisoned in his life of privilege, what with the extreme limitations on his privacy, his freedom, and, point in fact, his choice of life partner. He never chose to be an heir to a dynasty; rather, it was thrust upon him thanks to that outdated primogeniture nonsense. Who was to say he was any more deserving of the throne than his siblings, or even Darcy, for that matter? It all might have made sense a few centuries ago, but now?

He was beginning to wonder if being a relic of days gone by wasn't more of a strange curiosity that ought to be relegated to sideshow status or somehow set up as a tourist attraction to sustain the royal needs, of which there were plenty.

"Besides which, she's a complete drunk!" he whispered in his friend's ear.

"True, but you have to admit it was kind of hilarious when she took that spill down the grand staircase at your father's birthday party last month. Without that you'd have been left to listen to a string quartet as your only entertainment."

Adrian laughed. "Would have been preferable. And here I thought seeing her tumble head over heels down a flight of steps would have been enough for my mother to finally realize the woman's a total lush. Instead she bought into the whole excuse about Serena's blood sugar dropping so quickly, and Mother swoops into care for her. *Bah!* Maybe if she'd eat a meal once in a while, she wouldn't be so embarrassingly smashed every time I see her."

"Obviously, she's head over heels for you," Darcy said, smiling. "What better way to prove it to you than quite literally showing you?"

Adrian moved into a smaller office within the confines of the larger one in which he was pacing, seeking a moment's solace from onlookers. He pulled Darcy close to him.

"Darc, I can trust you, no matter what, right?" he asked, his brow knit in concern.

"We're mates, Ade," Darcy said. "But you already know that!"

"And you don't want to see me stuck with Serena for the rest of my life, do you?"

"Are you kidding me? I'd practically marry her myself just to spare you," his friend said. "Although, honestly, I couldn't be that devoid of self-respect, so sorry, she's all yours." He chucked him in the arm, a sign of friendship he could only display amongst their closest of friends lest the "hired help" look like more. That whole propping up the royal stature thing really bugged Adrian, but Darcy didn't mind at all.

"I need some space, Darcy," Adrian said. "I need time to think. And maybe to give my mother reason to care more about me as a person rather than a mere branch of the family tree that needs to be spliced together with what she deems to be an appropriate mate. I'm more than a glorified version of one of my mum's beloved horses, set out to stud to sire racehorse-quality offspring.

"I can't even stomach the *concept* of spending the rest of my life with Serena, let alone the reality of it. I'd give up my royal status and take a job waiting tables in a dingy bar before I submit to my mother's demands on this one."

"Good luck with that. You know your mother always gets what she wants. She's the queen, for God's sake."

"Maybe the queen needs to realize her once-little boy is a man now, capable of acting on his own behalf. And I'm going to start that right now."

"By?"

"By slipping away from here, unannounced. Getting out. Going somewhere. Doing something. For once not being led around with a bit in my mouth and a crop at my flanks. I need to get away, Darcy. And I need it now. I can't hide in Monaforte. But I can easily get lost in America. Think about it — it's a brilliant idea. Disappear for a while, see what it's like to actually live a bit."

"So you're running away from home then?"

"Don't make it sound so childish. It's nothing of the sort."

Darcy stood back and stared hard at his friend, his hands in his pockets, his shoulders back, his closely-cropped blond hair in direct contrast with the shiny black waves Adrian sported. He leaned forward and fixed his brown eyes to Adrian's blue ones.

"You're really serious about this, aren't you?"

"I think it's the first decision I've been serious about my whole life. I'm tired of living the life everyone expects of me. I need to see what it's like to just be *me* out there, Darcy. I really need you to help me escape. You can hold everyone at bay when they start asking questions. I know I'm asking a lot of you, but I swear to you I'll be safe and I will return, soon. But not before I discover who the hell I really am."

His friend thought for a few minutes, rubbing his chin with his thumb and forefinger, staring off into space. Finally he looked back at Adrian.

"You really think this is what you should do?"

Adrian nodded his head. "Look, not to slight you, but I don't think you can totally appreciate where I'm coming from. You're a marquess. If you decided to quit me, you could go back and lord over your father's estate and manage the family business. You aren't stuck as an appendage to the institution of the palace. You aren't carrying the weight of a country on your shoulders."

"You know one day I'll have no choice in that matter," Darcy said. "Once my father's gone." He looked down, hating that idea, since he adored his father.

Adrian waved his hands, dismissing that concern. "Your father's healthy as a horse. It'll be years till it's your problem to deal with."

"We can only hope," his friend said. "Though yes, you're right, I don't have to partake in the dog and pony show of being the heir to the throne that you're stuck with. I get that. And you know I'm only here for you because it's you. We've been best friends since we met on the train on the way to boarding school when we were five. Hard to turn down a bloke I've known since his voice squeaked like a mouse."

"At least mine deepened into a man's voice," Adrian said, chiding him.

"Oh yeah? You think I still sound like a little girl?" Darcy said, making his voice go as high as possible.

The men laughed.

Darcy shook his head. "This goes against my better judgment. The queen would about kill me if she knew I was going to do this. Make that she would *actually* kill me. With her bare hands. But your wishes take precedence over hers for me," Darcy said. "If for no other reason than to spare you a lifetime of high-maintenance, low return-on-investment Serena, I'll do it."

Adrian looked puzzled, like he'd just been awarded a huge prize. "Seriously? You'll actually go along with this? You're not going to try to talk me out of it?"

"Christ, Ade. You and I practically finish each other's sentences. I've seen what your life is like. I know a lot of it is fun and games, beautiful women, fawning attention, but I also know how much pressure rests on you to always be perfect, to never fail your family, your adoring public, and your family."

He put air quotes around that "adoring" part.

"Yes, well, I do have a lot of adoring fans," Adrian said, mocking himself. "What with all those little old grannies who give me crocheted booties, begging me to produce a royal heir."

"Good lord, the last thing you need right now is a royal heir, particularly minus a royal bride. And I can promise you, Serena is *not* going to fill that void on my watch."

Adrian grabbed his friend by the shoulders. "You think we can make this work?"

Darcy buffed his nails on his chest as if showing off his prowess. "Are you kidding? With me as the brains behind this operation?"

"Perfect. Then how are we going to pull this off?"

"We? I thought this was your plan!"

"I don't have a plan, simply a need. I hadn't thought through how to implement the thing," he said. "How about we just work our way out of this holding room and I sneak out some back door, unnoticed. How hard could that be? There must be another way to slip out — maybe an employee entrance?"

Darcy chewed on this idea. He looked over to see a computer on a nearby desk. "Hmmm, let's see here," he said, walking over to the computer to see what he could find.

He typed in a bunch of keywords, trying a variety of searchable words until he finally found what he was looking for — a map of the building indicating various exits and detailing all rooms and spaces within.

"So much for national security. You can find pretty much anything on the Internet these days," Darcy said, shaking his head. "Looks like you can work your way down this back staircase. Along this long corridor there appear to be a series of rooms. One would think there should be an unlocked room or two along there you could pop into to remain undetected, in case a security guard comes down that hallway. If nothing else there's always the loo." He pointed to the men's room sign.

He reached into the breast pocket of his cashmere overcoat.

"Here, take this," he said. It was his wallet, containing plenty of cash and credit cards.

"These are what you call dollars in America," he said with wink as he opened it wide to reveal a thick wad of bills.

"Ha-ha. Very funny. I'm not stupid, you know."

"So you like to tell me. But it's not like you've been out painting the town red on your own before."

"I'm not planning to paint anything red, or blue, or purple for that matter. That would draw a bit of attention, don't you think? Besides which, I'm not Zander."

Sometimes he wished he could be his brother Alexander, famously known as Zander, last year caught by paparazzi while cavorting naked in a Las Vegas swimming pool with a bevy of equally unclad, very young and very hot women. Seems you could get away with just about anything if weren't the heir to the throne, and the worst that happened to you was a little tongue-lashing from Mother, once the tabloids had their fill of splashing the overexposing pictures across their front pages. And Zander could hardly have cared less.

Darcy shook his head.

"Just having at it with you, boss. Listen, I'm giving you my credit cards. The cash is from the palace anyhow — it's what I use as mad money when you need it. I don't want to give you the palace credit cards as they'd find you immediately if you used them."

He fumbled around in another pocket.

"Oh, and you'll want this." Darcy handed Adrian's passport to him. "I know you wouldn't be daft enough to leave the country, but it's always a good idea to have this on you just in case of an emergency. That way if you have to prove you are the future heir to the throne, maybe they'd actually believe you.

"Right now, I'm going to provide some pass interference for you. I'll tell the bodyguards that there's a woman involved and the two of you need some privacy, just to keep them at bay. I'll escort you to a lavatory and give you a chance to be out of the line of vision for enough time.

At that point, you need to follow this path, and get out fast. Once you're out, hail a taxi — you do know how to do that, right?"

"I think I can figure it out." Adrian rolled his eyes.

"Once you're in a taxi, you need to figure out a way out of town. You've got two phones on you: your official palace one, and your own private one that I lined up for you. You'd better hand over the palace version or else they'll find you in no time."

""You're so organized, you'll make a great mum some day." Adrian grinned.

"Please. I've got my hands full enough being your de facto governess. And that's why you're paying me the big bucks." He raised his eyebrows and pointed to his friend. "This is the most important thing: stay in touch with me. I am ultimately responsible for your well-being, so you owe it to me to keep the lines of communication open. You can call, you can text. Whatever you do, keep me apprised of where you are going and whom you are with. And most importantly, be wise about who you fraternize with."

"Fraternize? I'm going to find myself, not find a hook-up. Trust me, I sure as hell don't need to complicate things even more by adding a woman to the mix. Particularly an American one who lives thousands of miles away from me and hasn't a drop of royal blood in her. Wouldn't my mother just love that?"

"Might be better if she at least has less liquor in her blood than Serena. Oh, I nearly forgot the most important thing. Just in case." He reached into yet another pocket. "Whatever you do, take these. The palace can't afford to have unwanted princelings popping up in the States nine months from now." He tucked a wad of condoms into Adrian's palm.

Adrian rolled his eyes. "Unnecessary optimist. Besides, I'm pretty sure I can keep my pants on for a few days."

"Well, I wouldn't be much of a friend if I didn't wish for you to get laid, now would I? Now, go, before I change my mind about this completely ill-conceived escape plan."

About Jenny

Jenny Gardiner is the author of #1 Kindle Bestseller ***Slim to None*** and the award-winning novel ***Sleeping with Ward Cleaver***. Her latest works are the ***It's Reigning Men*** series, featuring ***Something in the Heir***, ***Heir Today Gone Tomorrow***; ***Bad to the Throne; Love is in the Heir***, ***Shame of Thrones***; and the upcoming ***Throne for a Loop***. She also published the memoir ***Winging It: A Memoir of Caring for a Vengeful Parrot Who's Determined to Kill Me,*** now re-titled ***Bite Me: a Parrot, a Family and a Whole Lot of Flesh Wounds***; the novels ***Anywhere but Here***; ***Where the Heart Is***; the essay collection ***Naked Man on Main Street***, and ***Accidentally on Purpose*** and ***Compromising Positions*** (writing as Erin Delany); and is a contributor to the humorous dog anthology ***I'm Not the Biggest Bitch in This Relationship***.

Her work has been found in Ladies Home Journal, the Washington Post, Marie-Claire.com, and on NPR's Day to Day. She was also a columnist for Charlottesville's Daily Progress for over a decade, and is the Volunteer Coordinator for the Virginia Film Festival.

She has worked as a professional photographer, an orthodontic assistant (learning quite readily that she was not cut out for a career in polyester), a waitress (probably her highest-paying job), a TV reporter, a pre-obituary writer, as well as a publicist to a United States Senator (where she first learned to write fiction). She's photographed Prince Charles (and her assistant husband got him to chuckle!), Elizabeth Taylor, and the president of Uganda. She and her family and menagerie of pets now live a less exotic life in Virginia.

Visit Jenny at her website and sign up for her newsletter: http://www.jennygardiner.net/index.html, her blog, http://jennygardiner.net/blog/ , or find her on Facebook https://www.facebook.com/jennygardinerbooks and Twitter https://twitter.com/jennygardiner

21596655R00157

Printed in Great Britain
by Amazon